MINDSTOCK

MINDSTOCK

A NOVEL

RICHARD YONCK

PALABRAS
PUBLISHING
SEATTLE

MINDSTOCK

Copyright © 2025 by Richard Yonck

"A Truth Warrior's Journey" Copyright © 2025 by Richard Yonck

All rights reserved.

Cover and interior design by Christian Storm

Author photo by Merrill Images

A Palabras Publishing Book

Published by Palabras Publishing LLC

4742 42nd Ave. SW, #561

Seattle, WA 98116

www.palabraspublishing.com

The Library of Congress has cataloged the paperback edition as follows:

Names: Yonck, Richard, author.

Title: Mindstock / Richard Yonck.

Description: First edition | Seattle | Palabras Publishing LLC, 2025.

Identifiers: LCCN 2025912262 (print) | LCCN 2025912263 (ebook)

Subjects: GSAFD: Science fiction

LC record available at https://lccn.loc.gov/2025912262

LC ebook record available at https://lccn.loc.gov/2025912263

ISBN (paperback) 979-8-9991212-4-0

ISBN (hardcover) 979-8-9991212-3-3

ISBN (ebook) 979-8-9991212-1-9

ISBN (audiobook) 979-8-9991212-2-6

First Palabras Paperback Edition: 2025

Printed in the United States of America

0 9 8 7 6 5 4 3 2 1

To my remarkable wife,
whose love, support and inspiration
made this book possible.

FOR THOSE WHO VANISH,
BUT NEVER TRULY DISAPPEAR.

MINDSTOCK

PROLOGUE

*"Liberties don't need to be taken by force when they're
given away one concession at a time."*

—Robyn Sheridan, A Truth Warrior's Journey

....

The Data Restoration Tracker spanned the face of the golden Citadel, its massive ticker board still frozen after weeks of inactivity. Home to the UN General Assembly of Congress and Reconciliation, the two-year-old mega-scraper utterly eclipsed the time-worn Manhattan skyline below. Piercing heavy clouds over what was once an immense park at the heart of the city, it was a poignant symbol of humanity's fierce determination to survive.

In a matter of moments, the clouds dissipated, scattering from the building's apex to reveal a nearly flawless field of cerulean blue. Flawless, save for an object that hovered in the distance. Rapidly but silently it advanced on the tower, growing ever larger until halting directly overhead. Matte-black with flakes of opalescence, the surface of the immense craft was covered in shallow fins, arranged and aligned in inscrutable patterns. The sight would have no doubt alarmed the comms—the populace below—had the enormous ship not been concealed from view by an extensive cloaking field. This was NewTech and did not belong to their economy.

Moments later, a much smaller craft—a skypod—separated from the ship's base and descended to a waiting landing port atop the Citadel. Neither vessel generated a trace of wake turbulence nor made the slightest sound.

Many floors below, in a vast central chamber, the General Assembly was in session. Of the 728 members in mandatory attendance, most were seated in the capacious auditorium with only a few stragglers still milling about. Ongoing conversations bubbled throughout the space, expanding and contracting as their volume rose and fell. While some members were immersed in their social or otherwise making obligatory contributions of their attention, most were looking to the podium below. There stood the seemingly self-possessed figure of Philip Minot, the Speaker of the General Assembly, House and Senate.

"… and certainly, that was its purpose at the time," Minot said, making a concerted effort to steady his hand as he took a sip from the water glass on the lectern before him.

"But I will remind you that as well as being our salvation, many of us feel CAI and NewTech have been our ruin too."

An uneasy muttering emanated from the Assembly body.

"So, it behooves us now to reconsider the wartime concessions that consolidated power in the hands of so very few. I'll remind you that when these were first put in place at the beginning of the New Reconstruction, they were meant only as temporary revisions to the constitutional checks and balances of our many nations…"

"Of course, they are temporary," a resonant voice rang out from nowhere and everywhere.

Clearly startled, Speaker Minot abruptly stopped speaking. At the back of the Great Hall, massive twin doors gracefully swung open in automated tandem. The Speaker looked up beyond the raked seating, past the other Assembly members who were just beginning to respond to the interruption.

There, in the entry, stood a stately figure; an elegantly dressed man, his bespoke suit interwoven with gold and platinum threads, tailored to perfection. With an engaging smile, the visitor stepped across the outsized threshold. A pair of tiny news drones hovered about him. One held a steady distance from his face, while the other flitted about, pausing intermittently to capture him from different angles.

The Speaker stayed silent as the membership continued to stare. Several of them looked as if they were trying to decide whether or not this was a deepfake projection—a near impossibility given the chamber's shielding. Their muttering rose for a moment before quickly falling away. Not a breath could be heard as the imposing figure descended the center aisle to the stage below, the drones tracking his every move.

"Premier Scion. What a surprise," the Speaker said, stepping out from behind his lectern. "A welcome surprise," he added uneasily.

The dignitary stopped at center stage. Tall and well-proportioned, he carried himself proudly and with considerable grace. Aristocratic features and a sharp jawline adorned his oval-shaped face. Turning, he began to address the chamber.

"Good members of Congress and Reconciliation," Scion said to the Assembly, before turning to look directly into the lens of one of the drones.

"It is an honor and privilege to be here today for this momentous vote. The Consortia thanks you for your attention and your service. And I personally thank you as well."

Turning back to the sea of faces, the technoligarch continued with a charming, practiced poise.

"All of us here know too well of the enormous strife and upheaval brought on by the *Great Unknowing*—the cyberattacks that started the war nearly three decades ago. The wholesale destruction of the world's digital and material knowledge quickly led to the breakdown of society and economies across the planet. The explosion of automated dysinfo that ensued resulted in violence, enmity and confusion unlike anything we ever imagined possible.

"It was only through the immense efforts of the Consortia—your share-holders—as well as tremendous good luck, that we could reinvent and rebuild an economy atop the ashes of what remained, so that civilization might survive. The recovery that followed in its aftermath, using the power of CAI—collaborative augmented intelligence—continues to this day.

"In the meantime, we have bestowed upon you technological marvels unlike anything our world has ever seen. All we ask in exchange is a few hours of your attention each day to support the recovery. For this, we have provided you with a lifetime of leisure and security such as humanity has never known."

With a wave of his hand, Scion dismissed the drones, which promptly flew to the back of the Great Hall. He turned to the Speaker, whose face was several shades paler than it had been just a few moments earlier.

Minot had never been this close to one of the technoligarchs before. Nor for that matter, had he ever noticed that one of the Premier's pupils was appreciably larger than the other.

Despite this, Minot steeled himself, aware that he was not only address-ing the Assembly, but the wealthiest man in the world many times over.

"Respectfully Premier, I agree these are challenging times, but we need to also think about the future of the social order. The imbalances of our post-war era can't remain in place indefinitely, if we're to..."

"Minot," the Premier interrupted. "I'm aware you believe this proposed legislation is in the best interests of your constituents, but I assure you, the Consortia disagrees. Hostilities continue and time is still needed to com-plete the New Reconstruction. As the saviors of society, we must remind you that the war's impact can't simply be undone in only a few short years. Even in the aftermath of the Acceleration."

Scion stared at Minot, who suddenly was aware of a voice in his ear. A voice only he could hear. Scion's voice.

"I thought we had an arrangement," it whispered. Scion's face remained stoically unchanged.

"But I…," Minot began.

With a dismissive wave of his hand, Scion resumed speaking aloud. "No need to explain yourself. We just wanted to ensure our position was made clear."

A strange look appeared in Minot's eyes. As if he suddenly wasn't there anymore.

"Thank you for your attention." Scion said, invoking the customary phrase of respect as he turned to face the Assembly. "And for your service."

Minot's eyes promptly rolled up in his head as he collapsed in a lifeless heap.

As the Speaker's body struck the floor, Scion turned back, a look of shock on his face.

"What in the…" Scion exclaimed, dropping to his knees beside the fallen man.

"Sergeant-at-Arms!" he called out. "Medic! Someone get this man some help!"

Moments later, a small team was bustling about the stage. The Premier rose to his feet, looking on with concern, noting that the drones had returned to record the commotion. The Assembly members spoke among themselves and watched from their seats, fearing the worst. After several minutes, one of the first responders looked up at those standing nearby and shook his head.

Scion drew a deep breath, looking upward in silence. After a few moments, he stepped forward.

"Members of the Assembly," he began solemnly. "It appears that Speaker Minot has suffered a stroke of some sort."

He turned and looked about the chamber. Behind him, Minot was being lifted onto a stretcher and taken away into the wings.

Finally, Scion's gaze fell upon one of the Assembly members, a woman sitting not far from the front of the stage. The representative from India was clearly shaken by what she'd just witnessed.

"Senator Ruhani Chawdhary," he said. "I believe you are next in line of succession as Speaker of this august body."

The woman's expression shifted from stunned surprise to understanding, then acceptance as she slowly rose from her seat. Scion approached the edge of the massive stage, offering his hand to assist her as she stepped up onto it. Together, they approached the podium.

Scion looked at her compassionately.

"Thank you, Madam Speaker. I'm sure you will fulfill your role admirably. With the greatest care and deliberation." He turned back to face the Assembly.

"Obviously, this is a deeply sad and tragic turn of events. But I ask now that you please,… welcome your new Speaker of the Assembly of Congress and Reconciliation."

Scion began to clap lightly and deliberately. He raised his hands to the members who hesitantly took their cue and began to join in the applause. Nodding to the new Speaker, he turned and stepped off the stage, ascending to the main doors of the chamber through which he'd entered. The applause continued as he exited, the two drones once more tracking his every move. The clapping incrementally diminished, then abruptly stopped.

At the lectern, newly installed Speaker Chawdhary took a deep breath, determined to pull herself together. She was now the leader of the most powerful governing body in all the world, answerable only to their shareholders. She prayed she was up to the challenge.

ONE

"Reality is the greatest conspiracy of all."
—Robyn Sheridan, *A Truth Warrior's Journey*

. . . .

Entering the modest-sized office, he was reminded of an old detective movie he'd seen years before, a *film noir* full of oak desks, firearms, femme fatales, and cigarette smoke. He couldn't recall the film's title, but its atmosphere of shadows and claustrophobia remained.

Of course, those images were from a movie made a century ago and this office didn't really look like that at all, save for its two anachronistic wooden desks, the main door with its upper glass half that bore the business's name, and a bit of the claustrophobia. On the wall behind the empty desk at one side of the room hung a pair of black framed degrees he couldn't quite make out. Next to them was a large, faded mandala-like print of something called the "Cognitive Bias Codex." On a small shelf behind the other side of the desk, a pair of crystal tumblers stood sentry before an unopened bottle of Lagavulin.

The rest of the office was provisioned with more contemporary 3D printed furnishings, and some minimal efforts at basic decor. A slightly undersized reception chair was situated in the middle of the office, facing the other oak desk, behind which sat a serious-looking woman, who was anything but a femme fatale. Middle-aged, perhaps shy of fifty, she had short-cropped chestnut brown hair that was noticeably graying. She glanced at him through her *holdis*, her virtual holographic display. An all but invisible field that fully encompassed her head without obscuring her view.

Offering Tremaine a stern but professional smile, she gestured to the chair across from her.

"Welcome, Mr. Tremaine. You're early. Please have a seat. I'll be with you shortly."

He sat down and studied the woman—presumably the principle of the firm. She had a sturdy look, neither petite nor heavy. Sitting solidly upright, she exuded the manner of someone not to be underestimated, though he couldn't have said what made him feel that way. Perhaps it was her military posture. Or maybe the ease with which she occupied the office's anachronistic fusion of analog and digital eras.

His first impression when he entered was that she was in the middle of a business call or meeting, until he noticed the telltale glow bathing her face. He realized she was *attending*, donating her attention through one of the authorized programs or plotpods. Fulfilling her social duty.

After a few minutes, she shifted her posture and he saw the glow disappear as she dropped her holdis, returning the virtual interface to wherever it went when it wasn't in use. She turned her attention back to him.

"So, Mr. Tremaine. How can I help you, today?" she asked matter-of-factly.

Tremaine was momentarily uncertain of how to proceed or where he wanted to begin. The woman behind the desk noted he was clutching an old-fashioned smart pad to his chest. The plastic case was unevenly faded and had seen better days.

He shifted in his chair. "Thank you for seeing me, Ms. Sheridan."

"Robyn," she responded.

"Yes. Robyn. I understand you're a truth-sayer."

Robyn gave a fleeting smile that may have been a grimace. She glanced briefly at the empty desk that sat to her left and the framed degrees that hung on the wall above and beside it. With a nearly imperceptible nod in that direction, her grimace disappeared.

"No, I'm not," Robyn said calmly, leaning back into her well-worn leather office chair. She paused a moment before continuing.

"I'm not a truth-sayer, a fact assessor, or a veracity maven. Not a reality washer, a reputation cleaner, or a candor tracker. Nor am I a revaricator, a truthmonger, or a deceit detector. And I'm certainly not an authenticity influencer or an anti-fabricationist."

Tremaine shifted uncomfortably in his chair. It was obvious he wasn't used to being spoken to like this. It was also evident to Robyn that he was trying hard to hide how distressed he felt at being there.

"My...apologies," he said. " I didn't mean to offend."

"None taken," Robyn responded. "I just find the term...misleading. I'm sure you know that an entire cottage industry has sprung up in recent years in response to the web of untruths we all have to navigate in our daily and professional lives. I consider the people who operate under most of those titles to be charlatans, at best."

"But you do help people find the truth, right?"

He slid the smart pad he'd been cradling in his arms across her desk.

"In certain cases, yes," she replied, rotating the device so she could view it the right way around. A trail of cologne and nervous sweat tracked the exchange. She shifted back slightly in her chair, trying to subtly distance herself from the olfactory assault.

"I would've scheduled to see you sooner," Tremaine said, trying to get back on a better footing. "But your site says initial meetings need to be in person."

"I don't have to tell you what a problem deepfakes can be," she replied. "I like to start off knowing whom I'm speaking to."

"Patternista is unique in the industry," she continued, gesturing at the reversed lettering that spelled out the name across the glass on the main office door. "As truth investigators, we help our clients confirm what is real and what is not, so they can better navigate our post-truth world."

Tremaine looked at her like she was his last hope. "I'm praying you can help me find my daughter."

Robyn furrowed her brow and glanced down at the image on the smart pad. A fresh-faced young blonde gazed back at her. Possibly nineteen or twenty years old. Probably of at least half Scandinavian descent, her sparkling eyes, perfect teeth and flawless skin suggested that she didn't have a care in the world—which Robyn knew was always a lie.

"My wife and I collected everything we could and loaded it on there for you," Tremaine said, nodding at the pad.

Robyn reactivated her holdis to collect some basic details about the antiquated device.

"Why not share the files over the cloud?" she asked, testing him.

"Who's going to trust the cloud these days?"

"Just checking," she replied, in full agreement with his response.

Robyn paused briefly as a piece of garish malvertizing appeared on her holdis. A brightly flashing convertible driven by an anthropomorphic banana sped across her volumetric display. Pure retro-Geocities vibes. Since her volume was off, an accompanying word bubble trailed it that read:

"Pay attention! Support the war effort!"

The holdis's immune system quickly devoured the ad, eliminating the pesky intruder. Just one of the many forms of polymorphic infection that routinely diminished the technology's usability. The only respite seemed to be when using it to view authorized programming. The programs by which she donated her attention.

Setting her interface to "Do Not Disturb", she turned back to her potential client.

"I'm sorry, Mr. Tremaine, but…"

"Gerry. Please."

"I'm sorry, Gerry, but you misunderstand. This should be a missing person's case. That's not what I do."

A distraught expression passed across the man's face.

"I understand that, but my baby's been missing for nearly two years, and the police have been useless. Worse than useless. The authorities at the Citadel weren't any better."

Robyn reminded herself that the Ministry of Missing Persons had relocated to the Citadel shortly after its completion nearly two years earlier.

Tremaine was beside himself. "They all insist she must have run away and since she was nineteen at the time, they weren't willing to go any further after the first few months."

"You imply she's run away before."

Tremaine looked perplexed. "I didn't say that."

Robyn studied the image he'd placed before her. "It was in the subtext. You were looking directly at her photo, only glancing away when you mentioned her running away."

"Oh." He was a little taken aback. "Well, yes, actually she has. But those other times she always ended up at a friend's house and would come home after a few days of her own accord. Obviously, this is very different."

"But that doesn't change the fact that what you really need is police help. If not the missing person's unit, then maybe a private investigator?"

"We tried those for a while. Nothing but dead ends," he said, evidently bitter from the experience. "Totally useless. Then one day, I was talking with an associate and your name came up. He said you were a big deal in the war."

"Hmmm," Robyn muttered noncommittally, pushing the pad back across the desk. "Tell me, what kind of things was Chloe into?"

"The usual, I guess. Plotpods, the social, hanging out with friends, mostly in-virtual, but sometimes IRL. Boys. I suppose she's a bit of a

dreamer. We often call her our old soul. Growing up, she'd talk about wanting to be a police officer one week, a baker the next, a journalist after that,
then a travel agent, an accountant, an optometrist. You get the idea. All
those jobs that don't exist anymore."

"What about friends? Anyone she was particularly close with?"

"I really couldn't say," Tremaine said, a little discomfited. "You know
kids these days. Most of their relationships are online, with handles, ava-
tars and anonymizers."

That brought her to the crux. "Okay, it's been nearly two years. Why
come to me now?"

"We've exhausted all our other avenues. When the police stopped looking, they said there were just too many…"

He had to stop, obviously on the edge of tears.

Robyn finished his sentence. "Too many of *the Vanished?*"

He nodded.

"I know it's terrible to contemplate, but you may just have to accept that
she's gone."

"Except for this."

Tremaine gave the pad a couple of taps and pushed it back to Robyn's
side of the desk. The screen was filled with an intricate mosaic of countless
tiny dots, all different shades of blue. Nothing but blue. Cobalt, cornflower,
sky and teal, swirled in random textures, merging with cerulean, frost, lapis
and slate, drawing the eye and mesmerizing but never quite resolving into
form.

She looked back at him perplexed. "I don't get it."

"Can you see it?" he said hopefully.

"See what?"

"It's Chloe!"

She sighed inwardly. Hooh boy.

"I mean it. Swipe the screen."

Robyn did so skeptically, revealing an image of fresh-faced Chloe side-by-side with the pixelated field of blue. She glanced up at Tremaine with a weak smile.

"Keep looking," he urged.

A few moments later she shook her head.

"Every few days, my wife or I do searches on Chloe's name. Her photos. Last known locations. Anything we can think of. Three days ago, after nearly twenty-three months, this image popped up."

He pointed at the blue side of the screen.

"But it's just a field of blue dots."

He could see he was losing her. "You have to stare at it longer. It's like those old magic eye paintings that were big back in the 90s. I admit it was easier to see her when we first found it. I don't know why."

"Mr. Tremaine...Gerry," she said, trying to remain patient. "Have you ever heard of pareidolia?"

"No," he said, considering the word. "I don't think so."

"It's when people see faces in random patterns," she said it with an authority that came from years of experience. "It's a very common phenomenon. Our brains are constantly looking for patterns. And when we don't find them, sometimes our mind fills in the blanks."

"Okay. You mean like looking at clouds and seeing people or animals in them?"

"Exactly."

"Yeah. That's not what this is. You're just not looking hard enough. Because there's something more. We couldn't find the poster or source, but someone labeled the image. C.T. Her initials."

She pressed her lips together. "That doesn't mean..."

"Please!" he pleaded. "We have to try. We have the attention credits to pay you..."

Moira used to say she was a pushover. No doubt the only person in the world who ever did.

Robyn had already assessed that the image of Tremaine's daughter was real and undoctored. For good measure, she made a quick gesture in the air. Then with a well-practiced motion, she formed a rectangle with the thumb and index finger of her two opposing hands, drawing them apart over the pad. She knew without looking that one of the countless office sensors would track her command.

"Moira," she said to her AI agent, silently subvocalizing so that Tremaine couldn't hear her. "Initiate prelim-level search."

Moments later an otherwise imperceptible voice was cast softly to her ears.

"Authenticity confirmed. Search initiated."

She looked back at Tremaine. Despite taking reasonable care of himself, he was clearly in his mid-fifties. His face had a drawn look she suspected hadn't been so pronounced before all this started. That made him only a few years older than Robyn, so she knew he could easily recall the days before the war.

Robyn began to slide the smart pad back across the desk.

"Her photo checks out, so that's good."

Tremaine looked perplexed. "What do you mean?"

"It's OG. You didn't manipulate it."

"Manipulate it? Why would I do that?" He was getting noticeably irritated.

"I don't know," Robyn shot back. "Maybe you have an ulterior motive. Maybe you actually know what happened to her. Maybe she didn't run away at all."

"How dare you! This is my daughter! You have no right to talk to me like that!"

His irritation had quickly turned to anger, but it wasn't staged.

"Is it?" she said. "You said it yourself: I was in the war. I didn't get through it by assuming people are ever telling the truth."

She let her voice soften just a little. "Look, Gerry. I know you're hurting, but you can't be naïve about this. Given the rate of dysinfo these days, two years is a terribly long time. The trail is going to be very cold. No one wants to hear it, but the world isn't what it was."

"I...I know that."

"Do you really? You and I were born in a time before everything went to hell, but that doesn't mean we can go around blindly trusting people. The war changed everything."

She continued. "I'm sorry about your daughter. I really am. But we can't assume anything here. There are just too many cons. Too many scams. Yes, most of them are fake, or some kind of noise or misdirection, and that's what my job is—trying to figure that out. But there's only so much I can do given how much time has passed."

Tremaine sighed. He reached for the smart pad Robyn's hand was still resting on. "I'm at my wit's end. I don't know what we're going to do."

His pain was palpable, but Robyn knew that was never sufficient reason to take on a case. If anything, it was a red flag. Still, there was something else here tugging at the edge of her intuition. It was a feeling she'd learned not to ignore.

"Listen," Robyn responded grudgingly, as she drew back the pad. "Let me go over this a little more and think about it. No promises, but I'll see if there's anything else here."

Tremaine glanced up at her, a look of surprise replacing his glum expression. Robyn finished reading the feedback on her holographic display. The holdis's readout on Tremaine showed he'd been genuinely, appropriately angry and that he was telling the truth throughout their conversation. All with nearly 97 percent certainty. At least what he thought was the truth, anyway. She couldn't expect better than that.

"If I take the job," she said matter-of-factly. "I'll check out the rest of your credentials and send you a contract. My fee schedule is already in your inbox and there's an initial deposit of 500 credits."

"Now, if you'll excuse me, I need to contribute some more attention before I have to go give a lecture."

"Contributing to the war effort," Tremaine said, clearly admiring her patriotism. He got up to leave. "I understand."

....

"… And so, in many ways, the passing of the 2028 Deepfake Act probably hastened the war that followed nearly two years after," Robyn said, without referring to her notes. She'd given this lecture countless times before.

"The later discovery that most of the lobbying for the Act had been done by bots and other forms of auto-canvasers only further supports this conclusion."

Robyn looked out from her lectern that was set at the side of a modest stage. Though the auditorium was rundown, it was probably the nicest part of the building which had been built nearly sixty years earlier, at the turn of the century. The room wasn't large, but that hadn't kept more than a hundred attendees from packing themselves into the space—well in excess of the maximum capacity she knew was posted on a small plaque near the twin doors at the back.

"What made the war so devastating wasn't just that it destroyed so much digital information. It was the consistent scrambling of that information and later the wholesale destruction of so many physical books and records as well. Unfortunately, as people found their belief systems challenged, they became increasingly enraged, destroying anything that didn't agree with their views. Some scholars called it the first case of global mass insanity.

"This quickly made it impossible to verify even the most basic details in our lives. People thought it was terrible in the 2020s when generative AI started to hallucinate results and citations for journal papers, but that was nothing compared to what we had to deal with.

"As the conspiracy theories around the Great Unknowing exploded, people in and out of government began destroying material records as well. National and local libraries, including our own former Library of Congress were destroyed or heavily vandalized. Universities were defunded and shut down overnight. It was a nightmare.

"Many of you are too young to remember, but people were literally dying because of flawed information, about their prescriptions, their surgeries, their local disaster relief efforts, and so much more. Every supply chain you can imagine was disrupted. Urban centers began to face starvation conditions inside of a month. Lots of people thought we wouldn't get through it. Many people didn't.

"The rebuilding—what's been called the New Reconstruction—has taken literally decades and we still haven't put everything right yet. It continues to be a daily battle against autonomous dysinfo. And unfortunately, a battle against human nature as well. Because society doesn't function in the absence of trust and shared beliefs. That's one reason conspiracy theories, new religious sects, false memories and other delusional thinking have become so prevalent in recent years."

Robyn paused, then shifted course. "Okay, let's try something different for a minute. Everyone here who believes in a conspiracy theory or in what others would consider a false belief, raise your hand."

Robyn looked out at the sea of faces, searching for upraised hands. No one in the auditorium responded. Finally, a bearded blonde boy in the front row tentatively lifted his left hand. Robyn shook her head.

"No fair, Tobias," she said. "You've taken this course before."

Tobias lowered his arm.

"Okay," she continued. "No one except one outlier. But studies have shown that nearly all of us hold at least one false belief, to some degree or another. And it's how we navigate our false beliefs that determines how that affects our lives and our world."

"The problem is that conspiracies are seductive. They're alluring. They entice you. They offer to explain the unexplained or even the unexplainable. They help us make sense of why the world and our lives are the way they are or aren't the way we want them to be. Especially when things aren't going the way we think they should.

"The world is complex. Far more so than we generally realize, or give it credit for, or can fathom. But our minds seek order and understanding. Early on, we evolved to be able to spot patterns in our environment, in order to help us survive. 'Is that a snake or stick?' ' Is the wind moving the brush or is there a predator hidden somewhere within it?'

"But as existentially challenging as those days were, they were also far simpler times. Life and nature could be understood with a few well-placed gods and spirits. Not so today.

"So, our individual and collective minds go to work finding connections, even where none exist. We may spend days breathlessly waiting for the next cryptic message drop from X, Y or Q. We detect cabals and illuminati where we used to see demons and divinities. That's our new reality. It's why the Conspiracy Channel and plotpods have such high ratings these days.

"The rise of weaponized dysinfo has only made this worse in recent years. Not only is there more confusion about what is and isn't true, but we don't even know where we stand with many of our once trusted sources anymore. Or with each other."

Robyn hoped that last bit didn't come across too autobiographically bitter.

Spotting an upthrust hand near the middle of the auditorium, she pointed to the young man sitting beneath it.

"A question?"

"When you say 'weaponized dysinfo', are you talking about what happened when the war began?"

Robyn shook her head. "No. That initial cyberattack was devastating, but it can also be seen as a natural progression of decades-long trends. There can be no denying though that the Deepfake Act probably enabled the situation."

"Was that also when the garchs amended the New Constitution to form the fourth branch of government?" the young man followed up.

"Technoligarchs," Robyn said, correcting the slur. "No, that wasn't until nearly the end of the Data War, two years later."

"After hostilities ceased," the know-it-all added.

Robyn stepped out from behind the lectern. "Well, they never really ceased, now did they?"

She started to move about the stage, a technique she frequently used to signal that the official lecture was over. Now it was time for the unofficial follow-up, which was what most of the Gig University students came for. An alternate perspective for some, though for most of those there, it was just another form of edutainment.

"Remember that the war was never officially declared, nor was a peace treaty ever signed. That's because we never knew who we were at war with. We still don't. So, many people, including the government, act like we're still at war. Maybe we are. Attribution is such a huge problem in dealing with automated aggression and stateless actors, but it's hardly the only one. Still, though the cyberattacks never fully ceased, we've blunted their impact dramatically."

"Thanks to you!" a young woman called out from somewhere near the back of the room.

"Thanks to a lot of people," Robyn said, deflecting the hero worship.

A young man with scraggle-cut hair raised a hand.

"I read your paper—the one that led to the Veragraph." He said it with a touch of envy in his voice. Then he added, "You must be rich."

Robyn snorted, wondering if he'd read her actual paper, which was almost immediately pulled from circulation, or just one of the many fakes that were scattered across the dark web. She considered a few choice words but opted for a more politically correct response.

"I'm afraid it didn't work out that way."

"Why not?" he immediately responded.

She drew a deep, calming breath. "The government deemed it was a threat to national security and took action to lock down the technology with a bunch of onerous regulations. It was basically much the same battle we had with encryption a few decades earlier, all over again. And I really can't be talking about it."

"But you fought them in the courts," Scraggle-cut went on. "You wrote your book…"

"I said I can't talk about it!" she said sharply, shutting him down.

A tone beeped in her ear. An alert that somewhere in the room an unauthorized camera was operating. She scanned the crowd as Moira, her AI agent did a simultaneous sweep.

"Okay, who here is streaming?" she called out. "I explicitly said no recording devices!"

She spotted a woman barely out of her teens, holding an old-fashioned smart phone in front of her. She seemed oblivious.

"You!" Robyn pointed directly at her, and the woman suddenly realized she was being spoken to.

"I… I wasn't recording. My friend was sick and couldn't attend so I was just doing an uplink for him." She was clearly embarrassed. "I'm… I'm turning it off."

Too late.

"You're all going to die! You're all going to die!"

A manic voice screeched from the phone and the auditorium's sound system at maximum volume. The device had been spyjacked and was repeating the same five incendiary words.

"You're all going to die!"

The bot voice manipulated its frequencies in a deliberately calculated way, triggering an intense autonomic fear response in everyone within earshot. People in the crowd started yelling, as many of them frantically scurried for the doors.

"Everyone stay calm," Robyn shouted, suddenly grateful for the training she'd received years earlier. She pointed at the phone. "And shut that thing down!"

The young woman had been unsuccessfully fumbling with her uplink app. Finally, someone grabbed the phone from her hands and powered it off. The maniacal voice ceased.

"It's okay. It's okay," Robyn called out over the noise of the crowd. "It was just a scarebot."

The clamor eased. Someone was comforting the student who'd caused the ruckus, which was good, since Robyn sure didn't feel like doing it in that moment.

"I think we're going to call it a day," Robyn said to the rapidly emptying auditorium. "Hopefully we'll be back in here again next week."

Most of the attendees were still making their way through the doors and out of the building.

Robyn shook her head in disgust. Grabbing her small backpack from behind the lectern, she tucked her water bottle in between Tremaine's smart pad and some gear she'd forgotten was there from an earlier case. Reviewing the Tremaine case on the ride home would be a welcome distraction right now.

As she straightened up, she saw a tall, handsome man of Chinese descent approach the shoddy elevated platform that the facilities people there called a stage. Wearing dark slacks and a sleek leather jacket, Daniel Choi stepped up at the opposite end and stood there with a tired smile on his face and his hands in his pockets.

Robyn tried not to show her displeasure. "Hello, Daniel."

Daniel nodded to her as the last of the students emptied out of the tiny auditorium.

"Good talk," he offered. "Right up to the last five minutes anyway."

"That was out of my control," Robyn said, referring to the phone incident, but knowing that wasn't what he meant.

"I'm talking about going off-curriculum again. You just barely skirted around some very classified information," he responded. "I don't give a damn about some stupid scarebot."

"Maybe you should."

"Yeah, I've read your work too, you know. Anyway, I'm talking about your Gig-U contract."

"It's not a contract," she said through clenched teeth. "It's community service. Anyway, you didn't come here just to audit my class."

"True."

"So?"

He looked her firmly in the eye. "What if I told you that CyberCom wants you back?"

"I'd say you were full of shit."

Daniel slowly, deliberately shook his head.

Robyn's eyes grew fierce. "Are you fucking kidding me? After what they did? What the government did to me?"

Daniel kept his voice level, trying to cool the conversation. "That was over two decades ago. A different time. A different administration."

"Daniel! They ruined my life! They stole my work, my livelihood! Everything!

Still trying to de-escalate, he replied, "It was a matter of national security and interest. Of global interest. We were at war. Unofficially, we still are."

Robyn broke off her tirade and studied her once-ally, considering her next words.

"This is about the Restoration?"

Daniel nodded.

Robyn tried to make sense of what she was hearing.

"The Tracker boards have been stuck just past 80 percent for more than a month. You're saying that's not a malfunction?"

"Oh, it's a malfunction, all right. Just not with the Tracker."

"Oh."

The DRT—the World Data Restoration Trackers had gone off-line before, but they were just a public representation anyway. A bit of PR she'd dreamed up back when she had a say in any of these matters. Sure, in the past, little glitches occurred, but they'd always been relatively minor issues with no impact on the actual work being done.

Ever since the Veragraph—*her Veragraph*—had gone into full production mode, it had relentlessly been at work reconstructing the world's many forms and stores of maliciously altered data and knowledge. While at first it progressed at a glacial pace, it continually accelerated, much as had happened with the Human Genome Project a half century earlier. While it took over two decades to reach the midpoint in their restoration, they needed only another two years to get to where they were today.

Until they hit this snag, it looked like the project might actually be complete by the end of the year. It didn't seem possible at first, even to her. But it actually worked. Better than any of them ever dared hope.

If only she'd been allowed to see it through. Unfortunately, it wasn't long after the Veragraph's launch that the dysinfo and conspiracy chatter really got out of hand.

The bots and auto-trolls began targeting her and her work like never before. Sowing suspicion and doubt everywhere. Until finally, even her own superiors came to distrust and disown her. She went from hero to pariah overnight.

That hurt, but not as much as having her life's work ripped away from her, to be reclassified and put out of her reach. The once-leading expert on the innovation and theory behind truth vectors, she now had about as much access and influence as a common gleaner. An attention junkie. That became especially true when they stripped her of all of her official government clearances too. She'd learned firsthand the destructiveness that could come in the face of highly weaponized, targeted dysinfo. It wasn't just career destroying; it was soul destroying too.

Of course, she could never attribute any of it to anyone, any more than the rest of the world could. True, there were suspicions; there always had been. Russia's Secret Service—the FSB. Numerous stateless actors, including Nova Mente, or even one of the AI-based automated fire-and-forget hacker groups run amok. Personally, it didn't actually matter since the end result for her was the same. Her life had been trashed.

Returning her attention to Daniel, she asked what for her was the obvious question.

"Why should I?"

Daniel raised one index finger. "Sense of duty." She glared at him like he'd gone mad. He continued his count, adding a digit for each reason.

"A chance to clear your name. Your work fulfills its potential. And a very large payout."

Time to call his bluff. "The last twenty-four years of lost income paid retroactively. Plus, interest. Plus, a healthy re-signing bonus."

"Done," he said without a pause or flinch.

Oh. Shit. He was serious. She hadn't expected that.

"I'll have to think about it."

"Sure," he replied. "But in the meantime, you have a meeting Friday at eleven hundred hours with some very important people."

"The day after tomorrow? And if I don't want to go?"

"Nonnegotiable. Not unless you want to do jail time."

That raised an eyebrow.

He turned to step off the stage. "I'll send you details via secure quantum shortly. Don't fuck this up."

Robyn watched as the annoyingly officious prick she once called her friend walked away and left the building.

Robyn really didn't trust him anymore. But then, who trusted anyone these days?

That had been the true damage of the war, hadn't it? Yes, there'd been the decimated savings and ruined reputations on a global scale. But the true price was how it had broken trust all across society. No reparations, no government programs could fix that. Not in a single lifetime, anyway.

Historians designated the period from March 15, 2030 to July 27, 2032 as the Identity War, though everyone usually just called it the Data War. But for academics and policy wonks that was too generic in this era of persistent cybercrime and cyberwarfare. The relentless scrambling of people's biometric IDs and other critical information had been a painful tipping point few had really anticipated. In a world that was utterly dependent on data, it quickly led to the worst kinds of chaos.

"Excuse me, Ms. Sheridan?"

A young woman's voice pulled her away from her thoughts. Robyn turned to see a dark-haired student nearly young enough to be her own daughter—had she had one. Though Robyn prayed her imaginary-daughter would have had her act a lot more together than this girl. The questioner's ragwear attire may have been ironic, but Robyn still found the look disconcertingly impoverished. Which was no doubt the point.

"Yes?" Robyn responded, trying to decide what was off about this girl. The barest flick of her eyes told her.

Robyn spun around just as a man-child in similar garb snatched her backpack from the edge of the stage and sprinted across the auditorium.

"Hey!" she yelled, immediately remembering the smart pad inside.

Robyn looked back just briefly enough to see the girl running away in the opposite direction. Turning, she tore after the boy, watching as the thief flung open the main doors and raced out.

Stupid, stupid, stupid! Why had she let her guard down? Daniel must've gotten under her skin more than she realized. Sprinting through the doors, she hoped the thief was making for the building's entrance. A quick look at the few people still milling about told her he had.

"Thief!" she yelled as she dashed past them. "Stop him!"

Nobody moved. She was outside before any of them barely registered her. It wasn't their problem.

The night air caught her by surprise. Not the dark, but it was certainly colder than she'd expected. You'd think she'd be used to New York's climate recovery winters by now.

Looking right, then left, she spotted the petty thief jogging down Seventh Avenue. There weren't any security bots or sentry drones in sight, so he probably thought he'd gotten away with it. Redoubling her efforts, Robyn closed half the hundred-meter gap between them before he looked over his shoulder and spotted her. He took off with a burst of speed that told Robyn he had the recuperative power of youth on his side. As he got down the block, he hopped in a car—a waiting ride-share by the looks of it.

Reducing her pace from a sprint to a jog to a halting walk, Robyn panted deeply as she watched the vehicle merge into the uncharacteristically light traffic and disappear into the night.

She cursed him, she cursed herself, she cursed the universe that allowed these sorts of things to happen.

"Moira," Robyn spoke out loud to her AI agent, too winded to subvocalize. "Shut down and lock any electronics in my backpack and freeze all payment cards."

"Initiated," the voice in her ear responded. "Completed."

"Odds of recovering my pack that was just stolen? The thief has a two-minute lead by car and I'm on foot."

"Based on time and location," Moira responded. "Less than three percent."

"Lovely," she said to nothing but the dark.

It looked like it was going to be a long night.

TWO

*"The artist must know the manner whereby to convince
others of the truthfulness of his lies."*
—Pablo Picasso

. . . .

Streetlights frolicked across the asphalt's glistening surface like a frenzied ballet. Shining autonomous vehicles of every form and scale skipped and flitted about the Brooklyn night, delivering passengers and cargo from one derelict address to another. Across the river, the gold-tinted Citadel towered over the rest of the city, despite still being only midway to completion. Sirens wailed soft and sharp across the night, playing a song that was all their own.

On a lightly traveled side street, a small group of sightseers clustered around their guide, a tall man of eastern European descent who was easily pushing fifty. He wore a varicolored trenchcoat over a scramble hoodie designed to thwart electronic facial recognition, thermoshrink black jeans and a pair of ten-year-old kicks with modulating treads. Many of the tourists who formed an irregular semicircle around him wore equally garish garb assembled from vintage popshops and the depths of their imaginations. Each according to their media-influenced perception of alt-fashion. Though a few of them were taking selfies, most listened intently as their guide lectured about the technology hanging ten meters above their heads.

"Now here," the guide said, pointing to the QD-OLED store display. "Is a Tianma-Samsung Ultraflex." He placed his right index finger theatrically against his temple. "An old 2039 model, if memory serves. They're super easy to hack if you understand the VMAC codes and have mad skills."

A heavy-set magenta-haired man wearing an acid-etched tailcoat that was two sizes too small piped up. "And you'll show us those codes later, right, Yevgeny?"

"Please," the lecturer said, looking mildly annoyed. "No real names. Only handles."

"Sorry, uh, Stropos," the questioner responded contritely.

Yevgeny-Stropos continued. "No, those codes take time to get the hang of. You can learn all about them in the master classes available on my training site. They start at sixty attention creddies each, and we can review the package options later. After tonight's tour."

Another tourist chimed in, a teen boy, easily the youngest member of the group. "Yev..., uh, Stropos, have you ever met Phynyty? His hacks are the buzz."

All eyes turned to Yevgeny, who took it in stride. "Phynyty? Yeah, sure. A few times."

"What's he like?" the boy asked, unable to contain his excitement. A few of the others echoed his question.

"Uh, I really cannot say," the guide responded. "Sworn to secrecy and all that."

Suddenly changing the subject, Yevgeny said, "Y'know, I think there was a lesser-known Phynyty a couple of blocks from here. It might still be active. You guys interested?"

"Yeah!" several of them responded in near unison.

Five minutes later, the group was standing beneath a digiboard that was notably different from all the others on the run-down street around it. Instead of calling attention to its establishment or touting the merits of some digitally enhanced antifungal foot medicine, this board had been turned to a very different purpose.

On the four-by-three meter display was a continuously shifting video loop, a collage of elements from history and culture which had been isolated and layered over different moments from everyday life. Children at play. Cities being bombed. Stock tickers on the rise. People who were there one moment, then gone the next. The juxtapositions continually transformed and recombined. Images intermingled, amplifying and modulating the message. Faint impressions of the Vanished came and went, were there, then not there. The result was a profound commentary about the collusion of all of society in the link between unbridled capitalism and the many lives it shattered. A spectacle that raised some to preeminence, while others literally disappeared from existence. A message that might have been trite in other hands, but in this creation were powerful, meaningful and, above all, inspiring.

The tourists stood beneath the shifting sign, studying it intently. Some were recording the imagery, others simply looked on, mouths gaping.

"Wow," said one of the women in the group. "That is so moving."

The magenta-haired man asked, "How does he keep it from being shut down?"

"She," said a different woman on the tour. "Phynyty could be a woman."

"Or a collective," Yevgeny added. "Sure, lots of people want to shut boarder art down. Like they used to cover up graffiti in the old tagger days. But a good board hack can take a long time to disable. 'Course, the simple thing would be for the owner to just cut the power and swap in a new board and controller. But that is crazy expensive and insurers won't cover it. Anyway, when the boarding artist is as big as Phynyty, they tend to leave the art hack up for the publicity and to draw the crowds. Y'know, some of his most famous work has even been given protected status."

As if on cue, the board above them flickered and went dark. The group let out a collective moan as the artwork disappeared.

"There you go," Yevgeny said. "Looks like someone finally had enough. Eh, it had a good run. Not like that one he did on the Lower East Side blasting the government's response to the Diet Riots. That was zapped in like an hour." Checking the time, he turned and pointed down the street. "Come on. I think there's a Mark 7 Tileboard around the corner."

The group continued listening and asking questions as Yevgeny guided them from one digital display to another across a ten-block radius. At the end of the tour, a young woman with blonde hair that grazed the shoulders of her antique black leather jacket stepped up to their guide.

"Stropos, would it be okay to get a selfie of our group?" she asked.

"If no one else minds," he replied. "And you don't care if my face is blurred by my hoodie."

Only two of the group opted out. A younger fellow Yevgeny had assumed was the blonde's boyfriend leaned into the edge of frame as she snapped everyone's photo using an ancient smartphone.

"Very retro," Yevgeny said. "Shoot me a copy."

"Oops," the woman said, as she glanced at the image. "Some guy photobombed us. Right over my shoulder."

"What guy?" Yevgeny said, as he turned to look to where the young woman was gesturing with her head.

In the shadows about ten meters away stood an attractive man of mixed-race descent. He was dressed in a casual pullover sweater, a half-zipped down jacket and peg leg jeans, clothes that could be picked up at any e-mall or apparel popshop.

Yevgeny smirked. "No worries. That is just my pal, Darius." He waved at his friend, then added with a chuckle, "He probably just wants to learn some boarding tips from Stropos. Or maybe to borrow money," he added with a laugh.

As the tour ended and the tourists dispersed, Yevgeny approached his friend.

"Really, Yev?" Darius said, shaking his head. "That outfit? You look ridiculous. And you don't know Phynyty any more than I do."

"You do not know that. I could know him."

"I don't think so," Darius countered. "Because if you did, it would be all any of us would ever hear about. Anyway, is this really the best you can do?"

"Hey, do not judge me," Yevgeny said with a wounded tone. "It is not easy making creddy these days."

"You know you're just scamming these wannabes. They're never going to use any of this stuff you talk about." Fixing his eyes on Yevgeny, he added, "Half of which is wrong, by the way."

"Please," Yevgeny said. "Not wannabes. They are *enthusiasts*. Customers. If they want to indulge their fantasies, who am I to stop them?"

Darius shrugged. "Look, I get it. These aren't easy times. Most jobs have disappeared and even the gig work is drying up. I just think you could do better."

Yevgeny looked dejected. "Y'know, you are bringing me down, man. I just made my week's rent, plus maybe enough for a coupla drinks. At least let me enjoy that for a few hours."

Darius patted his friend on the back. "You're right. Sorry."

The two started walking uptown at a leisurely pace, the half-built Citadel rising before them in the distance. As they strolled, they passed one of the government's many DRT boards. The terabyte count sped along at a blazing pace. Darius noted the completion panel showed 49.543 percent.

"Look at that," he said, genuinely impressed. "It's almost halfway done. Ahead of schedule."

"Aww, come on. You know that's just another deep state cover up," Yev said cynically before changing the subject. "Anyway, Dar. What have *you* been doing with yourself these days? You switch gigs more often than anyone I know."

Darius kept his gaze straight ahead, enjoying the vibrant dance of OLEDs across the street's slick, wet surface.

"You know. This and that. Whatever it takes to keep the light on." Darius said noncommittally. Then changing the subject, he added, "Come on, *"Stropos"*. Let's get those drinks. They're on me."

"No, no," his friend replied. "Yevgeny pays his own way." The tour guide activated his holdis and made an abrupt sweeping motion with his hand.

"What's this?" Darius asked, pulling up his own virtual holographic display to take a look.

"The picture from tonight's tour," Yevgeny replied. "The one you snuck into. I think I start calling you 'The Photobomber.' Ha!"

"In exchange for a drink?" Darius asked, adding in a sarcastic tone. "Sure, that seems fair."

Yevgeny looked at his friend mischievously. "Of course, it is fair. No one would argue with that!"

....

Standing in the dilapidated hallway outside his apartment door, Darius unlocked the third deadbolt and stepped inside. It was fun having a drink with Yevgeny again—just like the old days—but there was a sense of relief in getting back to his loft and behind the safety of a well-secured door.

It was a relief that was short-lived, however, when he suddenly realized he was smelling something earthy, smoky… coffee? Strong enough that it had to be inside his loft. And he knew he hadn't left anything brewing when he went out several hours before.

Eyes darting back and forth, Darius turned on one light after another as he moved deeper into his home. He grabbed a small bat he kept next to one of several shelving units, hoping it would ease his nerves, but it didn't. Realizing there was already a low light on in the kitchen, he nervously stepped toward its doorway.

"Hello?" he said, nervously approaching the room ahead.

A disembodied voice suddenly replied. "Hi, I'm Darius. It's great to meet you."

"Shhh!" he hissed. "D2, mute!"

"Honey?" A sleepy woman's voice called out from the kitchen.

Darius raised his eyes to the ceiling and let out a deep sigh of relief.

"Kiara?" Darius stepped into his modest kitchen to find his girlfriend raising her head from the red dinette table where she'd evidently been asleep just moments before.

"What are you doing here?"

"Well, isn't that a nice welcome," Kiara said, wiping the sleep from one eye and then the other. A small unfinished cup of coffee sat on the table before her.

Darius shifted from fearful to surprised to irritated. "I thought we agreed you'd stay at your sister's until things settled down?"

"I know," said the no-longer-intruder. "But I missed you, baby." She flashed him that smile that never failed to melt his heart. Even this time. Standing up, she stepped into his arms.

Darius let his eyes close with the embrace and felt nearly all of the tension leave his body. Nearly. He kissed her sleek bare shoulder, the warm tawny softness he'd been missing longer than he realized. Breathing her in, he steeled himself and took a step back, as he looked her in the eye and gently asked a second time.

"Baby, what are you doing here? I thought we had an understanding." Then as an afterthought, he added, "And why was D2 on when I walked in?"

"I've been here a few hours…I think. Thought you'd be home lots sooner. It started talking to me, and… I wanted to hear your voice."

Darius briefly closed his eyes, smiled and shook his head. He must have neglected to shut off the bot when he left.

"And, of course, you still have the keys."

"Hey, you said I should treat it as my place too," she said just a little more seriously.

"Of course, it is, baby," he said earnestly. "And it will be again, when things are safe. Safer anyway."

Kiara looked at her man with concern. "Have there been more any more of them?"

"Threats?" he asked, though he really didn't need to. "Not for three, maybe four…? Yeah, four days. But that doesn't mean someone's not still out there."

"Maybe they've moved on."

"That's not how it works," Darius said with conviction.

"Couldn't it be some sort of autocaller?"

"I thought about that, but they know too much. Got too many details."

He sighed deeply, trying to let go of some of his tension.

"Somebody knows who I am, which means they know where I live. That's not a good combo when someone's sending you death threats."

"But they're threatening Phynyty, not you," she said, trying to stay positive.

"If they know where I live, what's the difference?"

She looked away. "Not a lot, I guess."

He gently turned her toward him and stared deep into her eyes, speaking slowly, but firmly. "That's why I need you to stay away till I can get this sorted out."

"Why can't you just stop? Do something else. Not be Phynyty?"

"Well, first off, because I don't think that would get whoever this is to stop. Based on their messages, I don't think they're very happy about how my art focuses so much on the Vanished. I can't do much about that; once it's out there, it's out there."

"I guess you can't really reason with them."

"Definitely not. I don't know if this is the feds, or somebody's private security or a crazed art critic, or a bunch of redneck conspiracists. People who send death threats aren't typically known for being all that rational, you know." He pondered this for a moment. "Are they?"

Darius continued. "And secondly, baby, this is my work. It's important and not just to me. Remember, I've been there. I know what people go through, what those families go through when someone they love gets vanished. This is the biggest thing I've ever done. I can't stop now. It means something. It makes people think. Gives them hope. I can't just abandon it. Or them."

"And what about me?"

"That's why I want you to stay with your sister. I'm trying to protect you."

Kiara was going to say that Darius getting himself killed wasn't going to protect her. But instead, she said simply, "Do you love me?"

"Of course, I do."

"Oh, you can do better than that," she said with a mock sternness.

Turning to the room, Kiara said, "D2, activate."

Nothing happened. "D2, engage."

Darius cocked his head and looked at her with a wry smile.

"Do you want me to help you with that?" Darius asked. Kiara nodded.

"I changed his trigger word set...Hey, D2."

"Active," came a reply spoken in Darius's voice from the room's built-in speaker system.

"You're still calling it 'him', I see," Kiara said, in mock annoyance.

"We talked about this. He's a reflection of me, so no way I'm calling him 'it.'" With a quirky grin, he added, "It's like they say. Pronouns matter."

She loved that smile, even when he was being so annoying. "Okay, then—'Hey, D2.'"

"Still active," said the chatbot.

Darius grinned. They'd played this game more than once before.

"D2, tell me about yourself."

"I'm Darius Tourner, a Black American male born in upstate New York on March 18, 2020," D2 began. "I was initially homeschooled by my mom and later my dad too. I've been a technology enthusiast for as long as I can remember. My dad, Marcus, was a computer science prof at Cornell University and I ate up everything he ever taught me, which was a lot. I couldn't get enough. He and my mom, Alina, had two kids, myself and Ashanti, my older sister who went missing when I was fourteen and…"

Seeing Darius's face shift at this last detail, Kiara quickly interrupted. "Do you love me?"

Without a pause, D2 responded. "Baby, you are the light of my life, the woman I love with all my soul. I love you beyond the stars and back."

Kiara turned back to Darius. "See, that's how you say it."

He gave a light chuckle. "I'm pretty sure I just did." He directed his voice to the room. "D2, debug mode: citations and source for previous statement."

"Previous declaration of love," Kiara corrected him.

"Right. For previous declaration of love."

D2 proceeded to cite half a dozen of Darius's conversations, emails and early social media posts that had been the basis for its response. Finally, Darius stopped it in mid-citation and said, "D2: end debug mode and deactivate responses."

The bot fell silent.

"Now I'm jealous," Darius said with a smile.

"I know D2 doesn't love me. That it's just a reflection of you based on all the data you've trained *it* on. But it's uncanny how much it sounds like you—and not just your voice. That's so like something you'd actually say. Even if you've never said that exact sequence of words."

"Ideally, that's how a good replibot should work." Darius plopped down on the couch feeling the weight of the day, the night, the drink and the fear all taking their toll. Kiara joined him, wriggling under his arm to rest her head on his shoulder.

Darius continued. "It draws on everything about me I feed into it. My communications and messages, my old Ashanti journals, my artwork, my speech. And from that it incrementally learns how I'd respond. My ideas, phrasings, voice inflections. All to create a nearly perfect digital personal assistant. Not some off-the-shelf agent. It's gotten incredibly good, if I say so myself."

"I will admit, it does have a sexy voice," she said playfully. "But I still prefer the real deal."

Suddenly, Darius didn't feel so tired anymore.

The next morning, following a night of tender and passionate lovemaking, Kiara left the loft, having agreed to stay at her sister's house for the duration for both of their safety. Darius could tell she wasn't happy about it and that she was scared for him. Certainly, he was too. But her being there wasn't going to make anything better. Knowing she was relatively safe would be at least one thing off his mind.

The apartment was dimly lit, making it feel quite lonely now that she'd gone. Sitting at his 3D printed desk in a partitioned part of the main room that served as his studio workspace, Darius wondered if he was going about things all wrong. Certainly, the replibot was fun to mess with and as far as Kiara was concerned, it was an end to itself. Just another manifestation of Darius's art-science geekiness. She couldn't know it was part of something much bigger because he'd never told her.

Not that he didn't want to. He'd debated the matter with himself multiple times, but no matter how he phrased it in his head, it always came down to the same thing.

All of this was only going to make sense when he was dead.

He turned the words over in his mind. At some level, it wasn't really about whether he died naturally or if someone killed him. Intellectually, he knew we all die eventually; he didn't have any illusions about that. He'd certainly seen enough over his lifetime. Death was the great leveler, the one thing in life we all share in equally. Rich or poor. Brilliant or challenged. Carefree or miserable. All of that vanished when we return to dust.

But our discoveries, our art, the contributions we make to the world, these legacies carry on beyond us, hopefully contributing to a continuity that is greater than any one of us. Something that will make a difference to the many lives that come after.

That was what he wanted for his work.

Of course, lots of artists have held similar hopes and views. But so many of the creations of the past were tangible. They had form and substance. Paintings, books, sculptures, even sheet music, their material nature allowed them to transcend time. To be passed along and appreciated across the generations. At least for the fortunate, talented few.

But his work wasn't like that. Boarders like him routinely saw their creations taken down within days, hours, even minutes. Gone forever, save for whatever recording or memory that may have been made during their too short existence. Gone would be the context and juxtaposition that gave them meaning. That was the loss that bothered him the most.

People died. Death was never a question of if, but when. Whether it was from a stalker, a stray bullet or pneumonia, it would come. It would always come.

Then one day it occurred to him: the person may die, but does the artist have to perish with them? It was true that art like his wasn't tangible. But that also meant it didn't need hands or eyes or a voice to create it.

It could be done with electrons, bytes, and pixels.

His replibot was only a small piece of the puzzle. A sophisticated neural network trained on a single user, it took in everything of himself he chose to share with it. The last time he checked its logs, he saw he'd spent nearly 500 hours just having dyadic conversations with it. The results were uncanny.

Darius knew he shouldn't have been surprised. This kind of tech had been around for over thirty years—since before the Shambles—and had only improved with time. He also knew in his mind that it was just a collection of nodes, connections and weights trained on the one thing he hoped he knew better than anything: himself.

But that still hadn't prepared him for the day, perhaps a month into its training, when it began to talk about things he'd never trained it on. Things he'd never told anyone. Not his journals, not even Kiara. Like that time in his mid-teens when he went searching for Ashanti and nearly got himself killed by a gang of young thugs. Just one of the many fears and memories that were truly his and his alone.

Or at least they had been up until that moment.

He continually reminded himself that D2 was just an interface. It couldn't access anything he hadn't previously shared with it. But somehow it had inferred his innermost thoughts from all the disparate data he'd fed it. Almost like it could read his mind.

Amazed, he began to wonder what other tools were out there that he could put to good use.

It took time, but eventually, Darius managed to assemble a multimodal deep learning model trained exclusively on his entire body of work. He even included his portfolio from his days at Gig-U when he'd started to apply his homeschooled compsci background to the arts. His dad had been a CS prof at Cornell before the war. He would've been proud.

To this, he connected a similarly trained model based on all of the major artistic influences he could think of, as well as those lesser ones that came to mind. So many of these had impacted his own work over the years, so he felt they should contribute to his creations going forward.

Finally, he added a data scraper that pulled from a series of APIs and media feeds covering a wide range of political and current events from around the world. After all, he didn't work in a vacuum. His work could only be meaningful if it drew on what was relevant to the times and the moment.

For weeks, Darius ran tests on the assembly, recoding and debugging as he went. He tweaked the weights and biases on his neural networks when he deemed their responses to new or unusual inputs were off-kilter.

Finally, one evening, after working on D2 later than he'd intended, he plopped down on the couch exhausted. Exhausted but thrilled. Not only was the system finished; it had come together far better than he could've imagined.

Now if it would only work in the wild.

THREE

. . . .

Passing through the portal into *Nexus Noir* was like stepping into another dimension. A seamless panel of shimmering light and opaque darkness slid open, its hues shifting between deepest sapphire and iridescent gold. As the entry validated each guest's biometric scan, it emitted a welcoming pulsing glow.

Matthias Mauvoison moved across the threshold with an aristocratic grace, as he watched the outer world dissolve away into an intoxicating blend of sensory overload and bespoke delights.

The warm, subtly fragrant air was perfumed with synthetic spices and pheromone-enhanced undertones. Above him, the ceiling rippled like a liquid mirror, reflecting a kaleidoscope of floating lights as they danced across the club's interior. Walls appeared alive, their surfaces morphing between sleek obsidian and holographic projections, surreal, shifting patterns timed to the beat of the music.

Pulsing harmonics and intricate rhythms intertwined with subliminal frequencies engineered to induce euphoria and heighten perception. The bassline thrummed like a heartbeat, while focused melodies floated effortlessly through the soundscape, sending shivers of induced *neurastim* down each reveler's spine.

The crowd was a mélange of humanity, everyone with their own unique display of personal expression. Some wore garments that shimmered like stardust, others sported augmented epidermis that shifted with mood or ambient light. Neon tattoos glowed faintly under the skin, while eyes enhanced with cybernetics glinted with shifting, unearthly hues.

Among the partiers, robot servers glided effortlessly, their forms sleek and humanoid, yet distinctly mechanical. There would be no uncanny valley in this club, unless you counted some of the patrons. The hospitality bots moved with precision, their articulated fingers carrying trays of iridescent cocktails that trailed faint wisps of vapor. The drinks glowed faintly, some swirling with nanobot-infused liquids that promised not just intoxication, but temporary sensory enhancement as well.

The furniture adapted itself according to the patrons' needs and desires. For one group, a table stretched into a low platform for someone to dance on; at another, it reshaped into an intimate pod for whispered conversations. Sofas shifted to accommodate guests, molding themselves to individual comfort preferences or to conceal sexual pursuits.

A ripple of movement across the room caught his eye as a holographic dance floor materialized, glowing with dynamic patterns that guided and encouraged rhythmic motion.

François Lauvaux, the owner of the club, stepped forward to greet his illustrious guest. "Monsieur Mauvoisin, it's a pleasure to see you again. I was told you might honor our establishment with a visit tonight. Welcome back to Nexus Noir."

Lauvaux was a tall man, though not all that much taller than his guest. However, the manner in which he deferentially held himself, bending forward with his hands clasped before him, easily reduced him to the less imposing of the two.

"You look busy," the man said, glancing past the owner's shoulder. "And for tonight, please refer to me by my father's name."

"Oh," said the owner, his expression shifting to one of concern. He thought it uncanny how much sire and clone looked alike. "I hope that doesn't mean... anything like the last time? Scion. Premier Scion."

"Just Scion," he clarified. "I'm sure we won't have any trouble like that."

Lauvaux didn't look convinced. "As you said, it's very busy tonight. But I have your favorite table right over here."

"Oh, I don't want that one tonight," he said, pointing to a different table. "I want theirs."

The owner turned to follow his hand and paled noticeably. In a far corner, a large private booth pulsed behind a semi-transparent force-field. Inside, a stylishly dressed man was slouched back at the center of a semicircular seating area, the obvious focal point of fawning attention. On each arm, was pressed a gorgeously dressed woman, or perhaps girl. Either way, they were easily half his age, one platinum blonde, the other with a shifting varicolored feather cut. A handful of obsequious flatterers milled about, along with a trio of massive bodyguards who looked to have been the recipients of a double-muscle myostatin gene mod. Augmented former mercs.

Matthias smiled knowingly. His own people were far less obvious and already located throughout the club. He'd instructed them not to engage under any circumstances.

Looking at the booth, Lauvaux swallowed nervously. "Do you mean Premier Magnus's table? He always sits..."

"Yes, I mean that one," Matthias said nonchalantly. "But you go attend to your other guests. I will speak to him."

Lauvaux looked both relieved and doubly concerned. Nevertheless, he knew when it was time to take his leave.

Moving through the club's atmosphere of ongoing stimulation, Matthias noted that several of the tables had been morphed into gamestations where groups of guests had chosen to attend to gamified versions of their favorite programming. Huddled over the ever-shifting surface, they may as well have been in a subtown attention parlor. Except that here, the neural feedback they received was far more rewarding. Addictively so. Production of dopamine and endorphins—endogenous morphine—could be heighted in ways it never could on the highly regulated home entertainment platforms below.

He felt repulsed at the weakness of these proto-gleaners. As far as he was concerned, they had no place being in an exclusive club like this. On the other hand, his old man's empire profited from every attention credit they generated, so who was he to complain?

Arriving at Magnus's booth, Matthias stopped before it, standing front and center of the VVIP, just outside the booth's protective field. If Magnus had spotted him—and he was sure the technoligarch had—he was ignoring him in favor of his banal arm candy. His bodyguards and toadies, on the other hand, were most certainly taking note of his presence and who he was. Or who he seemed to be. One of them bent his massive bulk over to speak in Magnus's ear. His employer listened for a moment, then looked up, as if he was only just noticing the other for the first time.

"Premier Scion, it's a plea…oh, wait," he said in mock surprise. "This isn't Scion. It's his task rabbit. Matthias."

Magnus glanced around deliberately, assuring himself that the intruder was on his own. The technoligarch was a beautiful man who seemed to have availed himself of all the aesthetic modifications that money and vanity could buy.

Scion, now revealed as Matthias, maintained his cool.

"I'm his son. It would be wise of you to remember and acknowledge that."

A cruel glimmer of a smile appeared at Magnus's lips as he continued to lounge in the booth. Each of the two women stayed where they were, reclining on his shoulders as they nervously eyed this intruder.

"That isn't what I heard," he said. "Everyone knows you're just a clone.

No doubt brewed from cells scraped off his ballsack. You may look uncannily alike, but you are not him."

Matthias ignored the offensiveness. "I'd like to have my booth now. You and I need to speak privately."

"Your booth! Ha! And what would we talk about?"

"Word is, you've been spreading lies to the Assembly. Stirring up dissent."

"I don't know what you're talking about." Magnus stared at him, trying to look simultaneously amused and perplexed. Still, it was clear from his eyes he knew exactly what Matthias was talking about.

He continued. "But I do know I'm not going anywhere, clone boy. This club is neutral ground. And this booth ensures it remains doubly so. Which is more than you can say."

He nodded his head slightly and the mercs moved forward unholstering compact beamers, each of which could easily punch holes through the club's shifting but heavily reinforced walls.

"You should leave," Magnus said firmly. "You're out of your mind to come here by yourself, making demands."

Matthias smiled grimly. "So, it would seem."

A moment later, the semi-transparent forcefield surrounding the booth dropped. Startled, all of them except Magnus and the two women jumped to their feet. The three bodyguards lifted their beamers, ignoring the fact there were innocent guests in the immediate line of fire. Their target remained motionless. He stared coldly at Magnus, who in turn, now looked shaken and considerably less confident than he'd been only moments before.

Matthias held the other's gaze. "But things often are not what they seem."

A turquoise dot suddenly appeared on the foreheads of each of the bodyguards, just an instant before being replaced by a deep hole the size of an old-fashioned dime. The three men collapsed like fallen timber.

Matthias was annoyed to see a beam had passed through one of the mercs, only to remove a chunk of the no-longer-platinum blonde's temple. She'd been standing just behind him. But that wasn't Matthias's concern right now.

All around them, the other club patrons were yelling, screaming and generally doing their best to get away from the mayhem. Only the unexpectedly locked doors prevented them from succeeding.

The rest of the entourage came around the table, positioning themselves between Magnus and their attacker. Everyone but Magnus and his remaining date instinctively reached for their own weapons. They didn't consider this immediately recategorized them as targets by the club's automated security system. The security system Matthias had paid handsomely to compromise. An instant later, only Magnus and the woman with the vari-colored hair were still breathing.

"No!" Magnus whimpered. "Don't kill me!"

Despite her own life being in danger, the woman stared icepicks at their assailant.

"I only wanted to talk," Matthias said irreproachably. "But I think we've talked enough. You can go. But leave her." He indicated the last woman standing.

"By all means, take her." The woman looked incredulously at him. "I don't care," he said, lifting his hands in deferential surrender. A second later, a hole punched through his right hand, leaving a cauterized void where his palm had been. He bent over, screaming in pain.

"Whaaat!"

"The others were a message from Scion," Matthias said. He looked calm, but there was fury under his words. "That was for your insolence just now."

"You can't..." Magnus gritted through the pain. "There are covenants. Agreements."

"Rules are for breaking."

"Don't...don't kill me. I'll give you credits. All my credits."

"Don't be absurd," Matthias scoffed at him. "Scion is worth hundreds of times what you are. Which means I am too."

Moments later, when what remained of Magnus's body ceased convulsing, Matthias took his place in the center of the booth. Gesturing for the young woman to sit down too, he ignored her decision to seat herself as far from him as possible, just as he ignored the blood splatters that now embellished the table and seating. He knew the self-cleaning nano surfaces would clear them momentarily.

Beyond the resurrected forcefield, he idly observed the club's hospitality bots scurrying about, removing Magnus and the other bodies, while eliminating any traces of evidence.

After paying Lauvaux what others would consider an exorbitant amount of hush money and entrusting him with the task of making sure all the witnesses were sufficiently threatened and paid off, Matthias placed a call on his holdis. The old man wasn't going to be happy. He'd been clear enough about wanting Magnus to be scared off but kept alive.

Still, at least the problem had gone away.

FOUR

"A people's trust, once fractured, is never fully healed."
—Robyn Sheridan, *A Truth Warrior's Journey*

. . . .

The city block was a study in gloom, its shadowy line of burnt-out lampposts rising from the sidewalks like the stalks of giant dead flowers. Beyond them, apparitions of shuttered dwellings swept in and out of view, barely hinting at what may be inside. Ancient single-family dwellings lined the cracked sidewalks, their fractured windows grimy with neglect, while sagging apartment buildings loomed over them, their facades pockmarked with age and indifference. Every window was dark, but here and there, a bare sliver of light seeped through tattered, soiled curtains, a glimpse of movement, silhouettes engaged in unspoken, even unspeakable dealings.

Robyn warily stepped out of the AV at 90th and Edgerton, a drop-off point she'd chosen for its relative seclusion. It was years since she'd been in this neighborhood and those years had most certainly not been kind to it.

Fortunately, she'd been able to pay for her ride before getting in, even without the contents of her backpack. Moira used AgentPay for the transaction the moment Robyn entered the self-driving vehicle.

She glanced up and down the desolate looking street, having already had Moira triple check the backpack's location tracker. She'd instructed the car to let her off a block away. No point in announcing her arrival.

This part of Queens had certainly seen better days. Once a gentrifying neighborhood, it had declined considerably since the Shambles. Owner-abandoned buildings had deteriorated into squat flops and gleaner dens. The odor of ruptured AV batteries, dog shit and what she hoped was only discarded rotting meat wafted through the air.

Staying watchful as she made her way to the building Moira had identified earlier, Robyn subvoked her agent.

"Update?"

"No change in location," Moira said faintly. "Personal items still locked."

"And Tremaine's smart pad?"

"Unknown."

That was no surprise. She didn't have root yet, but at least she'd managed to biometrically secure the pad before she began her lecture earlier.

Reaching into her jacket, Robyn withdrew her link, a device the size and shape of a medium-size candy bar. A visitor from an earlier era would have probably thought it was a mobile phone, but it was so much more than that. True, it had a touchscreen that covered its entire surface, and it housed several apps, but she couldn't recall the last time she'd used it as a telephone. Its primary function was as home to her digital assistant, the personalized AI she'd known most of her adult life. The link enabled the agent to perform near instantaneously, even when off-line, which she'd decided was important given the state of the surrounding infrastructure. The link could provide access to the near sum of human knowledge—at least as it currently existed—even as it siloed and protected her personal information in layer upon layer of federated processing.

But perhaps most importantly, the AI it enabled probably knew Robyn's needs and preferences better than any person on the planet. It wasn't like it was conscious or anything like that. AI hit a wall in that regard decades ago. Regardless, it was very common for users to treat their own agent as nearly human—even though that didn't make it so. Most, however, hadn't gone to the trouble of changing their agent's name after years of getting to know it as she had.

"Moira," she subvoked, holding the device in her hand. "Activate display mode."

As the light from the link's display bathed her face and hands, she was suddenly wary she might be seen by prying eyes. She stepped further into the protection of a gap formed between the perimeter wall and a scraggly rhododendron. She reduced the brightness as much as she could while still being able to make out the display.

"Moira, give me a list of all available gear that was in my pack." On the screen, a series of devices appeared: eReader, V-glasses, milbugs, spycam, microdrones.

Robyn subvocalized again. "Stealth activate spycam and give me a visual link. Shut down immediately if potential for detection."

A few moments later her agent sounded in her ear. "Visual not available. Sensor analysis indicates possible physical obstruction."

"Okay, try the glasses."

Two seconds later, the screen displayed a window onto a dimly lit room, a squalid flop by what she could discern.

"Night vision." The room popped, as the glasses remotely shifted into the telltale green viewing mode she'd spent many a night monitoring through. There weren't any people to be seen.

"Audio."

Her ears were instantly filled with a distinctly different background ambience, punctuated by the occasional shuffle of items being moved across a surface.

"360-view, interpolated."

The room changed again, widening to a view similar to a gamer's third-person mode. It revealed four figures huddled around a set of small tables. The room was filled with an assortment of items that were almost certainly all stolen goods. Two of the four she recognized as her thieves from the auditorium. One of the other two had a jailbroken holdis and looked to be gleaning their way into a dopamine-driven attention stupor.

"I think it's some sorta miltech," the man-child thief said. Beside him, the girl appeared to be searching the net using a less than fully functional holdis. Probably looking to ID the tech or find dark market valuations. Leaking data every step of the way.

"Shit. I can't tell," she said. "All these little gray boxes look alike."

Well, that cleared that up. They'd obviously stolen her pack intending to sell the contents. Robyn had no doubt they were using poorly secured antique VPNs and search engines. Presumably, hoping to better negotiate with some fence up the food chain. Who in turn would probably sell it to some middle-class kingpin wannabe, living in a garish McMansion turned Warez-R-Us. Who would invariably mark the merch up further before moving it on to dark web dealers.

Robyn smirked at their amateurish approach. Turning off the display, she pocketed her link. She'd memorized the layout of the room and its location in the house using the county records Moira had pulled up. Stepping from her concealment, she began to stealthily move down the block toward the flop, scanning the nearby houses for activity as she went.

She knew plenty of people would say she was nuts, that she should be terrified given the situation. But she'd been fairly fearless all her life, even as a young girl. No one could ever say Jack Sheridan's daughter was someone who backed down from a fight.

Anyway, she couldn't have the law involved since she wanted to get her gear back. Banned gear. Contratech. Her general SOP as an investigator was to keep her distance from police and security forces except when absolutely necessary.

The war had only hardened her further. The places she'd been. The things she'd seen. This was nothing. Still, she didn't have a death wish either. She knew she couldn't be stupid in a situation like this.

As she reached the lot, she stopped to assess the grounds. The yard was strewn with all manner of junk and debris. She swept the area with her link at arm's length.

"Moira," she subbed. "Any detectors or alarms to watch out for?"

"Nothing found."

No surprise there, she thought, but you couldn't be too careful. Entering the lot, she saw the front door was boarded shut. Evidently, the occupants came and went by a different means.

Silently, she crept around the perimeter of the building, eventually locating a door at the back. Hanging askew in a rotten jamb, she felt sure it wasn't being held shut by anything more secure than a propped-up two-by-four. Nevertheless, it would be stupid to enter if she didn't have to.

She pondered the possible strategies to recover her stuff. Drone-assisted extraction. Distract and grab. Mule drop. Each had its pros and cons, with far too many cons for her liking. Finally, she decided she was going to have to go in.

Starting to feel the chill through her lightweight jacket, she was grateful for the dry night. She needed to get going before the cold got into her bones.

Her first priority was to assume someone in there would have a gun. She didn't want to have to kill anyone, not over something like this. But between the contratech and her client's pad, if push came to shove…

It was at times like this she kind of wished she didn't have such an aversion to firearms. It wasn't that she was afraid of them or couldn't handle one, but even in the military she'd avoided them as much as possible. After getting out, she didn't have one at all. Too often, it seemed to her they caused many more problems than they solved, especially in the city.

She'd felt even more strongly about it after Moira was killed.

She shook herself, pushing away at the tragic memory. She needed to stay focused.

Looking around near the back door, she found a rusty old mop, its sponge long disintegrated. Easing it through the gap between the jamb and back door, she silently worked it around until something came away and she eased it to the floor.

Gently pushing open the door, she looked around the rotting jamb, coolly judging the situation. Sure enough, it was nothing more than an old piece of wood she'd dislodged.

She seemed to be looking into a kitchen, though whatever had been cooked there last certainly wasn't food. Some half-assed attempt at brewing up one of the more recent DIY street drugs, no doubt. The sooner she was out of there the better.

Assuming there were just the four tangos she'd seen earlier on her feed, they must all still be upstairs. She could work with that. She felt for the stinger and pepper spray she kept in her jacket. She was relieved to see the older-model stinger was still fully charged. She cradled it in her hand and powered it up.

"Moira," she subbed. "Ideally, I need those four kids outside so I can retrieve my gear. Any recommendations?"

The agent responded without a pause. "Blow it up."

"Sounds good," Robyn replied.

She carefully made her way through the kitchen, trying to breathe as shallowly as possible. No telling what shit they'd been cooking down here. At least her eyes weren't stinging and they'd adjusted to the limited moonlight that filtered through the half-boarded windows. It was just enough to let her navigate around the utensils, used blister packs and plastic containers that were strewn across the floor.

Beyond the kitchen, an old walled staircase ascended to the second floor. It carried the sound of scuffles and muttering from above, but nothing discernible like she'd been able to hear through her feed. Beyond it, she found a dark nook where she tucked herself away. Hopefully out of sight.

"I'm in position," she informed her AI.

Instantly, she heard a deep synthetic male voice emanating simultaneously through her earpiece and down the stairwell from above.

"Auto destruct activated!" The voice announced officially and loudly. "30 seconds to detonation."

"What the fuck!" one of the two men yelled, though the voice was pitched high enough in that moment, it might have been one of the women.

"Holy shit," someone else shouted.

"28, 27, 26,…." The announcer counted down in a modulated voice specifically tailored to illicit fear. Targeted subsonics laced every word. Even from her perch, Robyn could feel the dread welling up inside her.

Yelling incoherently, the thieves tore down the stairwell, taking the steps seemingly three at a time. One tumbled and the others leapt over him, running through the kitchen and out the door. The fallen one scrambled to his feet and ran after them, fleeing the perceived threat.

"12, 11, 10,…." continued the voice.

Robyn stepped from her hideaway and approached the stairs. It hadn't been possible to see the entire escape from her vantage. She replayed the last moments in her head.

Did all four of them get out? Or just three?

Hard tackled from the side, she abruptly had her answer. Stunned, she tumbled to the ground, the stinger clattering from her grasp and across the floor.

A fist caught her shoulder and she twisted to block the next wild strike. Her assailant, the man-child who'd stolen her pack, paused a moment as he recognized who he was straddling. That was all she needed. Her knee shot upward, yielding a gratifying crunch to his groin. Twisting to the side and away, she grabbed the stinger and turned back just as he raised his arms to hit her again. Robyn drove the Stinger hard into his solar plexus.

He let out a satisfying shriek.

She held the stinger in place till her attacker fell away, spasming uncontrollably on the floor. Clambering to her feet, she stood over him and snap kicked him in the gut, before pulling out her pepper spray. A full shot to the face felt like overkill, but she needed him out of commission longer than the thirty seconds the stun gun probably bought her.

Through his cries, she could still hear Moira's terror-inducing voice from upstairs.

"3, 2, 1." The voice ceased.

"All clear," Moira said normally and dispassionately in Robyn's ear.

Robyn took her time climbing the stairs, wary that someone else might still be in the house.

Upstairs, she found the room she'd seen earlier through the feed. Her backpack was slumped on the linoleum floor against the leg of an old Formica covered table. The pack's contents had been strewn across the surface, but she couldn't spot the smart pad anywhere. She swept the items from the table into the pack, noting the spycam was still inside. These jokers hadn't even realized it was there.

Flipping open one of the tiny boxes, she directed Moira to activate one of the microdrones it contained. It took off out of the room and down the stairs. She felt better knowing she had her own private sentry on duty.

Flicking on the stinger's flashlight, she scanned around the room. It really was a micro warehouse of stolen goods. Most of it was electronics, of course. What wasn't these days? Stacked high along one wall, white 3-D printed shelving sagged under the accumulated weight. It appeared to be on the brink of imminent collapse.

There weren't just electronic devices, she realized. There were power tools, stacks of mail, a half dozen credit card skimmers along with too many other items to identify in the moment. One entire shelf seemed to be dedicated exclusively to comic store memorabilia. Another was mostly jewelry and watches with a few tchotchkes thrown in for good measure. All in all, it had "amateur" written all over it.

She needed to be quick about this. Those idiots were going to realize all too quickly that nothing blew up or burned down and they were going to race back here for their stuff.

Their stuff. She shook her head. How had we come to this? How had everything reverted to such a Hobbesian existence? There'd always been thieves, of course, but it felt like the world was filled with so much more social dysfunction these days. Entire ecosystems of theft and graft spread all over like a spider's web of corruption. Who would've imagined, even 30 years ago, that society could be so fragile?

Panning her flashlight across the shelving, Robyn spotted the smart pad poking out from a row of old-style laptops, all stacked on their edges like books on a shelf. She started up the smart pad just long enough to be sure she had the right one, then powered it down.

Hurrying down the stairs with her recovered pack and gear in hand, Robyn stepped around the sobbing mess that had been her attacker. She was tempted to hit him one more time for good measure but opted to disengage. It was time she got back to less hostile territory.

The back door of the house hung wide open, akilter on its hinges. Pausing at its threshold, she looked out at the desolate yard and street beyond. Moira had summoned an AV, which would be arriving at any moment. She polled her sentry, but the microdrone's feed failed to respond.

A short sharp sound pierced the silence. A resonant plink, like the ring of the finest crystal. A few moments later, something fell to the ground in front of her. It didn't fall hard, nor would she have even noticed it if she hadn't been looking in that exact direction as the moonlight caught the descent of the tiny mass.

She bent down, her thumb and index finger closing cautiously around one of the wings of the broken microdrone. In all her years, she'd never seen one neutralized like that.

Cupping the tiny device in her hand, she entered the waiting AV and slumped back in her seat as it sped away into the night.

As the vehicle pulled out onto the street, she cursed the technoligarchs and the two-tier system they'd installed. It didn't have to be like this. Addicts and the mentally ill, barely existing on the streets, gleaning, thieving, whoring, murdering. With all the advances the Acceleration made possible in the aftermath of the war, the world should be in a very different place by now. Instead, they had economic and social disparity like nothing the world had ever known.

Not that in this moment, she wasn't glad for some of the tools it made possible. But those pieces of tech magic tucked away in her pack weren't authorized to even be here. She was putting herself at risk just using them. While most of those were mere toys in the world above, they could still provide her with very useful and unusual capabilities here in her everyday world below. That or get her jailed for life.

········

The long walk down Odie's alley-shaped apartment always made Robyn think of one of those tales of an old curiosity shop. Except instead of strange otherworldly items, this one was overflowing with technologies and electronics that defied era or categorization. For instance, as she walked its length, she spotted a table on which lay a set of ancient vacuum tubes, glass cylinders containing arcane arrangements of metal plates and tubes having no discernible purpose. On a shelf beside it, a desktop chemputer sat half disassembled, its enzyme bioreactor cannibalized. Further down, an old-style optical microscope shared space with its electron-scanning cousin and a modern smartscope.

The strange collection continued on for shelf after shelf, table after table, room after room, incrementally taking her through an archeological tour of modern technology. It made her think of an extensive museum collection that had been rearranged by a methodical earthquake.

Finally, deep in the recesses of the apartment, she came upon Odie, hunched over his workbench, a jeweler's loupe in one eye and a modified heads-up display over the other.

On a nearby desk, Robyn spotted a set of probes that to her trained eye suggested he was trying to hack a holdis. This, despite the fact the virtual device had no physical form but was the product of trillions of sensors in the environment. What used to be called the Internet of Things, or IoT, but today was just another part of their ubiquitous computing environment. The eyes, ears and other senses that enabled their global reality and economy.

"What's this? Are you jailbreaking for gleaners now?" she said half-jokingly.

"You know me better than that," he responded, glancing past her at the probe set.

"Actually, I'm trying to figure out how to prevent that kind of cracking," he continued. "Most gleaners are in a vicious cycle, driven by their addiction. The extra endorphin hits they get off their gear are illegal. But they can't jailbreak a holdis themselves, which means they have to pay a *fixer* to do it for them. Except that every few days an update gets pushed out and repairs it. So, even though the gleaners make a lot more attention credits while getting high, they're continually having to pay for the next jailbreak too. The cycle just keeps going until it kills them."

"That's terrible." She'd heard about the realities of gleaning often enough, but this was harsh.

"Anyway, it's a side project, when I'm not doing paid work. Like yours." He turned back to the microdrone on the bench in front of him.

"Any luck yet?" Robyn asked.

She'd been there nearly an hour, biding her time looking at his esoteric collection, while he did his magic.

"Weird shit," he said, not looking up. She was used to his lack of eye contact. Odie was one quirky dude.

"It's like it took an EMP hit," he continued. "But that shouldn't happen. This is NewTech. Serious NewTech. You're not even supposed to know about this stuff. But this one fried like an egg."

The techie sat up and removed his loupe, glancing at Robyn briefly.

"I know you kept some souvenirs when you were terminated. But you could get in a lot of trouble if you get caught with this." He quickly added, "We both could."

For all of Odie's shortcomings, being indirect was not one of them.

"There's tech in this that probably shouldn't even exist," he said with a conspiratorial smirk. "Not for several decades anyway."

Here we go.

"But then, along came the Acceleration, right?"

Robyn knew the script well enough to know her cue.

"Right."

"And what drove the Acceleration? Might still be driving it even though we don't see any of the benefits these days?"

He looked up at her, until she realized he was waiting for her response. Stick to the script.

"CAI."

"Exactly. Collaborative augmented intelligence. Combining human and machine intelligence to leverage the best of both. Some of that came out of DARPA when you were there, right?"

"Different agency. I worked for CyberCom."

"But your work, the Veragraph used it. Needed it, really, to get it running properly."

"And that's all it was. Not the crazy sci-fi plots you and your buddies are always going on about. Just basic mechanical Turk-type stuff," she said, making an almost ancient tech reference she knew wasn't completely accurate.

Odie ignored the near insult, which suggested that he had an ulterior motive.

"Listen, I just finished the edit for the next episode of 'The Conspiracy Chronicles.'"

"Your plotpod? I don't really have time today, Odie. I mean, tonight. It's still night, isn't it?"

"Just a five-minute opening segment. I really want to hear your thoughts."

Robyn knew she had to bend a little if she wanted him to repair her gear. He spent so much time on his show despite his relative handful of followers. He so wanted to be a fluencer.

"Okay. Five minutes."

Odie's face lit up like a Christmas tree, which Robyn guiltily thought was an apt simile, given his head was undeniably lightbulb shaped. Odie quickly queued the footage on his holdis and swept it over to Robyn's. Without further ado, the segment began. Two talking heads filled her screen in its 3-D retina-rez wrap-a-round view: Odie's and a professorial looking gentleman with a long handlebar moustache. The recorded Odie opened with a brief introduction.

"Welcome back to 'The Conspiracy Chronicles'! Today, we have a very special guest—world-renowned accelerologist, Dr. Blair Gordon who has dedicated years of his life to unraveling the enigma of the Acceleration. Welcome to the show, Dr. Gordon."

"Thank you for having me. It's a pleasure to be here."

Gordon proceeded to talk about a lot of wild theories about the Acceleration, as Odie urged him on with one provocative question after another. Were the new technologies handed down to us by aliens? Were they planning to invade us and using these gifts to buy the technoligarchs' loyalties? Were the Vanished being abducted as some form of payment? Were these beings from another galaxy or another dimension or what?

On and on it went. Or so it seemed to Robyn, though she knew this was only a five-minute excerpt. Nevertheless, more than once she caught herself trying to catch a glimpse of the time.

Throughout the show, all sorts of visuals accompanied the discussion. Flying saucers, death rays, planet killers, teleportation devices. Interspersed with the current state of the world, including the many inequities and iniquities of society. Images of poverty, hunger, junkies. A gleaner shielding his face in shame, the back of his hand covered with a mandala tattoo.

Odie was not being subtle. Robyn felt sure if there was more than an ounce of truth to any of this, the authorities would come down on him like a ton of bricks. On the other hand, many people had speculated that the sheer volume of conspiracy thinking was a feature, not a flaw. With so much bad information out there, information that was perpetuated by all of the plotpods like Odie's and bigger shows like ConspiraCast, it was impossible to know what was real and what wasn't anymore.

The segment mercifully came to a close as Odie wrapped up the discussion.

"Powerful words, Dr. Gordon," his talking head said. "Thanks so much for joining us on 'The Conspiracy Chronicles'! Where the truth is really out there."

The segment ended and disappeared from Robyn's view.

"Very interesting," she said noncommittally.

"I've got some great guests lined up. Alan Lindemann. Kanisha Harshaw. Tyler Corbis."

Robyn nodded politely. All crackpots.

"I'd love to get you on too," he continued.

Uh oh.

"Just five minutes. I mean, you're a real author." It sounded like he was describing an exotic animal or alien species. In this era, perhaps she was.

"It's complicated," she said, searching for an out that didn't sound too impolite.

"Even if you disagree with everything we're talking about, it would be such a help."

"Odie, I'm…flattered. And I would—I mean, I would disagree with just about everything he said. But I can't do interviews."

"Please," he pleaded. "It'd be amazing for my ratings."

"I'm sorry," she continued. "But the DOD has some very serious NDAs binding me. I could go to jail. You probably could too."

"Well, I won't argue with that," he said, clearly disappointed.

She could see how dejected he was at her response. Finally, she added, "Let me think about it."

She had no intention of doing any such thing.

Odie brightened up, though she felt sure he knew she wouldn't come through. But at least it allowed him to save a little face.

"Just a bit of constructive criticism?" she offered.

He looked at her warily. "Sure."

"I know there's more to your show, but I really didn't hear or see anything I haven't already heard on half a dozen conspiracy boards. And all those visuals you used—the weapons and those ludicrous technologies—were so obviously AI generated. Real images would carry a lot more weight, if you could find them. I just think it could use a little more polish."

"Good to know. Thanks."

Robyn had to remind yourself this was a grown man. Because in that moment, it felt like she'd just kicked a puppy.

Odie looked again at the microdrone. "I can fix it, but it's going to take a while. I'll let you know when it's ready in a day or two. Just know, it won't survive another EMP hit like that."

Robyn was relieved. She'd only managed to sneak out two microdrones when she left the service and there would be no replacing them.

It was concerning to think there might be those kind of defenses, even over such a squalid neighborhood. But were they sanctioned NewTech or banned contratech? It was only getting more difficult to know who you were dealing with these days.

"How do I keep it from happening again?" she asked.

"Don't use them," Odie said quite seriously. "Other than that, I haven't got a clue. I'm guessing the electromag pulse was combined with some other high-frequency carrier wave. No way to shield for that given these things are so tiny. I'll be in touch."

The ride back to her office was short and thankfully, uneventful. It had been a really long day.

For all their differences, she had to agree with Odie on one thing. While a lot of people's ideas about the Acceleration were heavily mis-informed, there was no denying it had driven a mysterious technosurge while it lasted. Most notably for her, it contributed to the early CAI advances that made the Veragraph go from theory to functional device. NewTech intelligence made the recovery possible as nothing else could have.

That was why so many people were willing to devote a few hours every day to viewing special authorized content. The media equivalent of junk food, but that wasn't the point. Embedded in every second of every pro-gram was another channel of information. A subliminal channel. The involuntary reactions that were registered from viewers—via their pupil-lary responses, blood vessel dilation, micro-expressions, and other subtle biometric signals—generated a feedback loop. A loop that could draw on human reasoning, common sense, inference, and much more. A loop that was used to generate CAI.

She couldn't help but think the solution had only contributed to more problems than it solved though. All of their tech kept getting smarter, while so much of the population was getting dumber. No, that wasn't fair. She was sure there were things people had gotten better at in recent years. Popular online games like Pojio and Scarymanga, binge-com media trivia and the weekly 'Name That Fluencer' competition.

But for anything that needed any focus at all—like long-form reading, which schools now officially defined as anything more than two para-graphs—it was like the world had fallen off a cliff. Games like chess or Go, or writing more than a single sentence without the aid of an AI, had gone the way of cursive writing, long division, and the dodo. She was appalled at the number of times she'd been in a conversation and the person she was speaking with would just drift off, their entire train of thought derailed.

She was sure it used to be different. People used to write novels. Now AIs assembled audio books for people who never listened to them all the way through. The History Channel said we used to put people on the moon, but lately she was starting to think the fake lunar landing folks might actually be onto something. It was all so depressing.

She couldn't see how it wasn't having an impact on the economy as well, despite everything they were told by the Commerce department. Her own finances had certainly seen better days, that was for sure. Which was ironic given Patternista helped clients navigate the post-truth era. It had been more than a year since she had to give up her apartment and move into the back section of her office just to get by.

Plotpods like Odie's were a different approach to making ends meet. Creating a homegrown series that pandered with disgusting deepfaked content was the get-rich-quick scheme for too many people. Most of the programs were pure amateur hour, though a few managed to make it to the million-viewer mark. Not many, but a few. Pure brain rot, as far as she was concerned.

It couldn't go on like this. The world needed to change before it was too late. Before it created another cataclysm for itself. Because the next one, they might not survive.

Reaching her office, Robyn stumbled to the makeshift bedroom at the back, where she immediately fell onto her bed, then into oblivion.

FIVE

"*Street art is political, because it's illegal,
so the very act of doing it is an act of defiance.*"
—Shepard Fairey

. . . .

Darius wandered leisurely through the maze of booths, moving past the exhibition crowd like a trout navigating the familiar currents of a freshwater stream. Along his course, weary reps with practiced smiles pushed brochures into passing hands. Overhead, banners screamed tired buzzwords—*innovate, disrupt, revolutionize*—while sleek product demos tried to dazzle with features that never quite worked outside the showroom floor.

On scattered stages, presenters cycled through scripted pitches little changed from the year before—and the year before that. Attendees drifted from one display to the next, bags stuffed with swag they'd toss before leaving. The promise of industry-changing breakthroughs dissolved into a haze of micro-OLED lights, manufactured enthusiasm and promotional small talk.

The Digital Signage Show at Javits Center on Manhattan's Westside had long been a mainstay of the display industry, but DSS was a boarders' paradise as well. Row after row, section after section, vendors shared and plied their wares, endeavoring to stand out from the multitudes that were their competition.

It had been years since Darius last attended the event, back when he was a noob just getting into boarding. He'd heard it was a great place to pick up tips, not just about different e-boards and display capabilities, but their vulnerabilities too. Particularly, their vulnerabilities. Not that the vendors wanted to reveal their products' soft spots, but in their eagerness to differentiate themselves from their rivals, they all too frequently let something slip that they shouldn't have. Especially when you knew how to ask the right question in just the right way.

Those early visits got him on his way, learning the tricks and tools so highly sought after by boarders at every level of experience. It wasn't the artistic side of the work, but the technical, or at least that part of the technical that was so necessary to actually get your art onto someone's board. It was akin to a painter who needed to also understand the ins and outs of convincing a prestigious gallery to hang their work.

That wasn't what brought him here today though. The DSS had been a highly secured event after boarders hacked the event's screens two years in a row. After that, the show became such a point of prestige for young artists wanting to make a name for themselves that it had to hire from the top of the cybersecurity food chain. As a result, no one had gotten onto a board at DSS in nearly a decade.

So today was a test. He'd spent the last few months training the various components of his AI-Phynyty with everything he hoped it needed to design and implement a piece that was in keeping with his own signature oeuvre. At the same time, an autonomous intrusion module had access not only to all of the exploits he'd picked up over the years, but directions on where and how to find more. His hope was that it would be able to autonomously create and deliver a new Phynyty work onto one of the main display boards here. Ideally, something spectacular. All of it done without his being directly involved in the process at all.

As he wandered past a line of booths, slipping through the other attendees, Darius realized he was feeling anxious. And why shouldn't he? After all, he'd been working on this project for months. Hundreds of hours of coding, API linking, testing and debugging work finally coming down to what amounted to a beta test that could make or break his plan.

He checked the time and saw it was 10:46 am. The test was set to run at 10:49. In between sessions and before everyone broke for lunch in order to maximize exposure. He could feel the palms of his hands getting damp as he strode through the crowd trying to burn off his anxiety.

At 10:48, he realized he could feel his heart pounding in his chest. What if whoever's display ended up being hacked was away from their booth at the time? Or that they simply didn't notice? He looked from one screen to another, trying to guess which from among the hundreds his test might show up on. He reminded himself that even if no one noticed, his logs should still confirm whether or not he'd gotten onto a board successfully. Assuming the logs worked the way they were supposed to.

10:49. Showtime. But where was the show? Was this whole test going to be one big fail? He felt helpless just standing there, unable to check on his code or coax the program along.

10:50. Still nothing. Well, that was it. He might as well head back home and start doing the postmortem. Dejected, Darius began walking toward the main entrance when he heard a collective gasp go up from the crowd. Turning, he looked and saw dozens, no hundreds of heads looking upward. Following their eyes, he saw they were all staring at the Mitsushiba OptoVision perched high above the center of the exhibition hall. It was easily the largest digital board in the complex.

It took him a moment to register what he was seeing. The board was playing an art hack that seemed incredibly familiar even though he knew he'd never seen it before. It seemed similar to some of his work, and yet it wasn't. It was such an odd disconnect for him, since he typically worked his pieces dozens, even hundreds of times before they actually went live and were displayed. This was entirely different. As though the juxtaposed images had been pulled straight from his head without his being involved in any part of the process.

Moments later, another group gasp went up, and then another. Several more screens were suddenly showing the same video, each in sync with the others. Again and again, it happened, until nearly every board in the hall was playing his latest artwork.

Correction: AI-Phynyty's latest artwork.

Darius looked on, fascinated, taking it all in. The video was using his well-recognized collage techniques, combining otherwise disparate images in an aesthetic and style he knew so well. The theme focused on the injustice of poverty, homelessness and the tragedy of the Vanished in a society possessed of so many resources and so much wealth. The work was well executed, but he'd need to review the loop multiple times to take in the full piece. It was a novel way for him to experience his own art, that was for sure.

Several people recognized the artist's work almost instantly.

"Hey, that's a Phynyty!" someone called out.

"Wow! Phynyty's done it again."

So, it went for several moments before someone in the crowd shouted out, "No way is that a Phynyty! I should know. I used to teach a course about them at Gig-U."

Another person shouted, "It's just some deepfraud wannabee trying to make a name for himself!"

Over and over, onlookers voiced their certainty that this work was anything but authentic. Darius was mortified. People were yelling for the organizers to shut down the displays. To reboot and reset them. Hundreds of screens. It was pandemonium.

Seeing it was going to take them hours to get all the boards back online, Darius resumed walking to the exit, albeit at a much brisker pace. There he was joined by hundreds of other attendees who were evidently fed up with the interruption. The last thing he heard as he left the exhibition hall was someone complaining to a companion.

"How desperate do you have to be to deepfake a famous artist like that?"

Back in his loft, Darius hunched over his dinette table with his head in his hands. Though the old apartment was small, worn and cramped, it was a relief to be back inside, behind the safety of a heavily secured door.

The denunciations and criticisms he'd heard while leaving the Center kept ringing in his ears. He really thought he was on the right track to get AI-Phynyty to successfully emulate his work. But evidently there was something in his system that was totally off. It had been far too easy for people to detect the generated work. To conclude it was a fake.

At the same time, he actually found the differences difficult to discern. Was he too close to the subject matter? Was it some kind of cognitive bias he had being the source of the derived work? Could he somehow be filling in certain qualities unconsciously? It seemed ridiculous to him that he couldn't pick up on what was so obvious to others.

It was incredibly frustrating. Not just because of how much time and work he'd invested, but because like nearly everyone else he knew, he could really use the money. Automation in its many wondrous forms had all but destroyed the jobs market over the past few decades, leaving all but the fortunate few fighting to get by on GBI, gig work and gray market economics.

Thinking back, even as a young boy, he could remember his mom and dad discussing their fears about the future. His mom, who was fluent in three languages as well as English, worked for years as a translator before he and Ashanti were born. She'd translate articles, books, films and had planned to go back to work once he and his sister were old enough.

"I just can't believe how fast it all changed," he overheard her say to his dad one evening—when they thought he wasn't paying attention. Even though he was probably only six, he followed much more of what they said than they often realized.

"That's always been the nature of progress," his dad countered, right on cue.

She ignored him. "Translation work got me through university. I really thought I could make some extra money while Ashanti and Darius are doing their homework. But Marcus, there's nothing out there. It's nuts." Even at that age, Darius could sense her frustration.

"Journalism, PR, marketing, writing. It feels like they all went over the same cliff."

"There'll be plenty of other jobs to replace them," her husband assured her. "Same as every other time this has happened. That's just progress."

More than once, Darius heard his dad call himself a techno-optimist. Dad was awesome. When he grew up, he was going to be a techno-optimist too.

That was a long time ago.

Back and forth, his parents would go, revisiting the topic over the weeks, months, years. Mom was convinced that jobs were permanently disappearing far faster than they could be replaced. Faster than people could be re-trained, for that matter. Meanwhile, Dad remained adamant that the old jobs would quickly be replaced by even better new ones. Just like the other times innovation displaced outdated jobs. That was the mantra for a lot of his buddies at the University too. Darius figured they should know—though, he did recall several of them saying some of the same stuff Mom did as the years passed. Sometimes one of them would add that "this time is different."

Dad, on the other hand, was quick to remind everyone that tech is a cycle. He always said, "If someone tells you it's different this time, you can be sure that it's not."

Unfortunately, for everyone, both sides were wrong.

Looking back, he supposed it might have gone either way, but the Data War wrecked everyone's plans when it hit a couple of years later. With the world's supply chains suddenly decimated, the global economic engine ground to a screeching halt. They say tens of millions died and from what he saw through ten-year-old eyes, he could believe it. Even after all these years, it still haunted him. But it probably would have been many times worse had it not been for the Consortia and the Acceleration.

As he understood it, the invention of CAI led to the rapid development and adoption of novel forms of automation and AI. Suddenly, there were new robots, new drones, new computers, new types of infrastructure everywhere—all of it far more intelligent than any technology that ever existed before. It created a flywheel that quickly led to even more advanced tech. They called it the Acceleration—a brief period of hyperdevelopment that advanced some technologies and fields of knowledge by decades, sometimes even centuries. It was like some kind of miracle.

All of this was rapidly deployed to restore food and water distribution, rebuild failed infrastructure and unfreeze the world's countless logistics lockups. Energy, communications, transport, it was all back online faster than anyone would have thought possible. And just in time.

Of course, they weren't out of the woods yet. Far from it. Despite all that had been repaired, they were still years away from full recovery. So much data had been lost or scrambled, people could no longer prove who owned what. Worse, the information and tools used for research, for medical studies, for government policy had been rendered worse than useless. As a boy, he recalled several neighbors who'd been poisoned by their medical prescriptions and two who'd actually died. Insulin pumps and dialysis machines were transformed into a new kind of Russian roulette. Soon, no one was willing to risk anything but home remedies. Before long, even those were no longer trusted.

At the same time that people stopped trusting their institutions and corporations, they started seriously distrusting their colleagues, friends, even their families as well. Dysinfo and misinfo spread like wildfire. Conspiracy theories were everywhere. So many that nobody knew what or who to believe anymore.

Adding to the mystery, after nearly two years, the Acceleration suddenly ground to a halt. Much of what had come to be called NewTech, disappeared along with it. As quickly as it had all materialized, it was gone. The pace of change slowed to a crawl.

Only a handful of the new technological marvels were left behind. The holdis. Real AVs—and not just self-driving cars, but drones, jets, and freighter ships as well. And of course, the many forms of AI and automation that literally ran the world. Less developed regions suddenly had new infrastructure—the infrastructure needed so they could contribute to the new world economy. The cities, the stores, the farms were restored and by some measures improved. Everything needed for daily life.

Oh, and one more thing. Somebody fixed the climate.

It didn't happen overnight, of course. Nothing so big as an out-of-control global ecosystem could be turned around just like that. But it soon became apparent, as the research tools and computers came back online and were made reliable again that the atmospheric carbon levels were falling. Fast. People said it was like a gift from heaven.

Others said that was what the Consortia wanted us to believe.

All of a sudden, the world's economic system was turned on its head. Nearly all the jobs went away and in their place, efficient, reliable, dependable, tireless automation stepped in. All people had to do was consume authorized content through their social and from digi-ads on Shopnet, donating miniscule amounts of their attention to enable it all. It may not have been luxury living, but after the horrors of the war, most people didn't care. Instead of starvation and deprivation, everyone had enough. Just enough.

"I don't understand," D2 said, as his inventor basked in the afternoon sunlight. Just five minutes from the apartment, the park was a welcome respite from the confines of his home. "If these threats still concern you, why not remain in the apartment where it's safe?"

Darius spread his arms along the back of the park bench, stretching to catch the shade of the filtering leaves hanging immediately overhead. Glancing around, he didn't spot anyone in the vicinity who seemed to be paying any attention to him. That was good. He continued to talk to D2 out loud, knowing that any passersby would just assume he was on a call.

"Because I was going stir crazy," he finally said. "I had to get outside. Being human means having to juggle a lot of contradictory priorities. I needed some different surroundings. I needed fresh air."

"Were the oxygen levels getting deficient?"

"No," he said, just a little amused. "Nothing like that. Look."

Darius directed D2's view through his holdis so the AI could see the park, the grass, the sky and clouds around them. D2 took it in, running additional processes trying to discern how the variations in this environment were qualitatively different from those of the apartment.

"People aren't like programs. We need things that touch us emotionally. That add meaning to our lives. To...everything." Darius tried to think of a comparison that might help make this clearer to the bot. "After too much time, being in that apartment drains me. This recharges me."

"But you said it's not safe."

"And that's the contradiction. The trade-off. Being human means accepting that we're a mass of paradoxes."

"Like loving your work, but finding ways to get me to do it for you?"

He rolled his eyes. "That almost sounded snarky. But yes, exactly."

The replibot had access to all of his communications, so he was well aware of the threats that had been made against Darius. Or against Phynyty, anyway. However, Darius knew that for D2, this was little more than a weighting of nodes. It wasn't the same as grasping the true weight of the situation. He still didn't have the capacity for that. For him, this was just a calculation, while for Darius, it was his life.

He thought back to what Kiara had said. Maybe she was right? Maybe these threats were just some malicious bot, a form of automated dysinfo designed to do nothing but spread fear among the populous? It was a reality they all had to contend with these days.

Still, what if it wasn't? What if it actually was more than that? What if the threats were real, and somebody really did know who he was? He wouldn't be the first boarder to be threatened like that.

It was enough to really mess with his head.

The openness of the park had played on his anxieties long enough. He decided it was time they got inside.

Being back in the apartment quickly reminded him why he was doing this. He really wanted more from life. Still, rising above the baseline wasn't easy, especially given the current state of things.

Even for someone like himself, one of the most famous boarders around, he hadn't figured out how to profit from his art. Where most people would've thought he was raking it in, in fact, he was barely scraping by.

That was one of the fascinating paradoxes about boarding. Boarders had become the Robin Hoods of society, calling out unfairness and disparity, of which there was so much in the world. The public looked up to them for speaking truth in the face of power. They'd become regular media darlings—up to a point. Even Gig-U taught courses about their role as fighters for free speech. They spoke for the common person, the *once-workers* who'd been discarded and left behind.

For so many people looking to express themselves and make a mark in the world, boarding was incredibly attractive. It made it feel like you counted, like your voice meant something. Of course, that sort of hacktivism could also ruin your life. Anonymity was essential, especially for those who were just coming up in the field because business and government took such exception to having their equipment and messaging appropriated. The costs of being identified were just too great in terms of reparations and jail time. He'd known more than one boarder who'd been locked up for his work.

But as bad as all that was, it could get much worse if you ever became famous. Prison could make you a living martyr, but pissing off the wrong people could make you a dead one.

All of which contributed to his desire to automate as much of his creative process as he could. The potential for notoriety, immortality and profit, even while maintaining his anonymity, was incredibly appealing. Given his unique skill set, a blend of technological and artistic abilities, he thought he might even have a chance.

He considered the fiasco at DSS. Was there a problem with the generator in D2's GAN module? Or the discriminator? Or both?

At least the intrusion system had been successful, so the test hadn't been a total failure. Actually, that part had gone far better than he could've hoped. Originally, he would've been pleased just to get onto one of the boards at DSS. Compromising nearly all of them hadn't been the plan at all. Had his system identified a common exploit to leverage? A zero-day vulnerability that no one had previously known about? It was almost as though the system had gone rogue, optimizing itself toward that one goal.

Using his holdis to dig into the logs, Darius tried to understand why that part of the test had gone so exceptionally well. He'd long thought it would be the weak point in the system. What super-exploit could it have uncovered?

He never found what he was looking for, though he may have tripped over something much better.

Reviewing the logs, Darius saw that one display after another had been hacked into with extreme efficiency. But not based on any single weakness or exploit. In fact, for the most part, each hack depended on an entirely different method of intrusion based on the make, model, firmware, and updates of the target. When he ran a summary, he saw there'd been nearly 40 different vulnerabilities in all. Just as he might have expected had an extremely skilled hacker done it. Only that would have been much, much slower.

He sat back, dumbfounded. His intrusion system did in seconds what should've taken a team of human hackers months to accomplish. Not only that, but once compromised, each target was held in a stealth state, performing as normal, silently waiting until all the remaining displays were under the system's control. Finally, the intrusion system released AI-Phynyty's new creation onto nearly all the boards at once. It truly was a sight to behold.

Still, none of it added up until Darius directed his holdis to examine the program loaders and realized he'd made a series of iteration errors. The system was supposed to identify a target display and try to compromise it, only moving on to the next candidate if it wasn't successful. But instead of halting once success had been achieved, it carried on until every available target had been compromised. It was relentless.

Darius realized the error wasn't so different from what happened with the Morris worm back in the 1980s. The world's first internet worm, it accidentally took down a substantial portion of the internet in a matter of hours.

He considered what he'd done. This part of his code was a significant part of the AI's *utility function*. The underlying driver that directed its actions. Much like a person's motives, the utility function codified the system's primary purpose. It ensured the program worked toward its specific goal.

In this case, it did something he hadn't expected, in part because he never considered the possibility there were nearly unlimited resources available to him.

When he set up the program, he didn't realize some of the code he'd borrowed had a default: to keep expanding until the objective was met. It was a far more expensive approach, but he'd just have to deal with that later.

So, D2's intrusion success had largely been a function of having the memory and processing needed to be able to fully optimize on his utility function. Could he draw on the same strategy to improve the subroutines that generated the artwork itself?

It was all a lot to get his head around. Would he need to get others involved in order to advance his plan further? He couldn't see how he could if he was going to keep his identity hidden for long. The problem seemed insurmountable.

Or was it?

Darius pitched his voice to the room. "Hey, D2. Connect to the most recent version of KnowledgeBot. And silo this conversation."

KnowledgeBot was the latest in a long line of large language model transformers that went back to the early days of generative AI. The siloing would protect their search from prying eyes. In theory. The downside was it used a lot more resources.

"Connection siloed and complete," his own voice replied after several seconds.

"Hey D2. Review your logs from earlier today. Cross-reference with KnowledgeBot entries relevant to art theory and appreciation. List most likely reasons why your system didn't generate suitably authentic artwork."

Several seconds passed as D2 channeled the interpreted output from its search. As more time passed, Darius began to wonder if something had glitched in the query. Finally, D2 responded.

"The most likely shortcoming is an incompatibility with the discriminator portion of the GAN—the generative adversarial network."

The discriminator was basically a classifier that looked at whether the values underlying the generated artwork were real or not.

"D2, please elaborate," Darius asked, still feeling perplexed.

"It is challenging, perhaps impossible to reduce something as complex as the human creative process to a single set of vector values. In human beings, perceiving and appreciating an artwork utilizes many different parts of the brain, simultaneously. For instance, certain parts of the visual cortex are called on to recognize and identify the image, regions of the prefrontal cortex to consider thematic importance, still others to place its relevance to current events and other artists, another to locate it relative to the creator's prior work, the limbic system to guide the emotional responses the art evokes, and so on."

"Are you saying it's impossible for AI-Phynyty to create art that's indistinguishable from my own work?"

There was a brief pause before D2 responded. "It is possible. You would need to assemble the AI with a modular structure having multiple interlinking functions that process information much as the human brain does. This could then be applied to my GAN's discriminator system. It's been theorized that people's brains are comprised of hundreds, perhaps even close to a thousand separate but integrated or interlinking regions that evolved over the course of hundreds of millions of years of biological evolution. Emulating such a structure would allow many different discriminators to iteratively assess the generated work nearly simultaneously, incrementally defining and delimiting it within a specified zone of authenticity."

Darius sank back into his chair with a groan. That was so far beyond his skill set it was laughable!

"Well, that may as well be impossible," he eventually said. "That's just not in my ability to make happen and even if it was, it would take me years, decades, maybe even a lifetime."

Slumped in dejected silence, Darius mulled over his dilemma. He'd already spent so much time and so many credits on this project and now it was all for nothing.

Drained and dejected, he sat in blank-minded silence. Finally, long after darkness fell, he rose from his chair and started to make his way to bed. From the other room, he heard D2 utter a phrase he himself had used not that long ago.

"Do you want me to help you with that?"

SIX

....

The sky over Seven Oaks was refreshingly clear after living so long with the near continual cloud cover that hung over New York this time of year. The shift in local climates during the past decades had been a welcome change after the growing number of disastrous megastorms that occurred in the earlier part of the century. While the Consortia had its critics, few could say that turning back the juggernaut of global warming wasn't welcome. With the ongoing refreezing of the polar regions, even the local sea levels had started to recede. From Robyn's current vantage, this was most apparent as she flew over Annapolis Island, which looked like it would soon be rejoined with the mainland. Perhaps in another year or so.

Robyn didn't know what to expect earlier that morning when her ride arrived outside her office-apartment. As she got in the black Lincoln AV, she was surprised to see there was a uniformed man in what would have traditionally been the driver's seat. As she buckled up, her streetside door closed smoothly on its own, securing itself with a soft but reassuringly solid click. A couple of basic comments on her part told her this was not going to be a conversation-rich ride. As the car set out, she noted that it was entirely AI-driven.

Whether the taciturn man was there as some sort of security or simply as a showpiece, she couldn't really say.

She also couldn't have said how it compared to the last such ride she'd taken twenty-seven years earlier. The shock of her discharge and abrupt departure had left that entire episode a blur in her mind. This time she'd had time to think about what might be motivating this turnabout. A new set of electronic NDAs presented through her holdis gave her even more to think about, especially the penalties promised in the event of a breach of contract.

Only ten minutes after their departure, the AV came to a stop and her door promptly opened of its own accord. Stepping out, she wasn't too surprised to find herself greeted by a woman wearing the current Green Service uniform of the U.S. Cyber Command.

"Welcome, Dr. Sheridan. I'm Lieutenant Bowens," she said, a hint of giddiness in her voice. "It's exciting to have you back at CyberCom."

Robyn was a bit taken aback by the Lieutenant's enthusiasm. Especially since she had yet to agree to any of Daniel's mystery request.

"Actually, that hasn't been decided yet."

"Oh, my apologies, ma'am. I didn't mean to…" Bowens responded with a nervous pause. "It's just that you're still a big deal to some of us. Even if we didn't serve during your time."

"Oh."

"Sorry," the young woman said, thinking better of her words. "That was totally unprofessional on my part. Please forget I said it."

"Already forgotten," Robyn said, smiling politely. "And thank you. I appreciate it."

Robyn recognized the street they were on—York Avenue—but couldn't see anything that identified the building they were standing in front of. The lieutenant opened the large entry door by hand which told Robyn it probably had a biometric reader in its handle. Entering, they made their way to a bank of elevators. Moments later, they were on the rooftop.

There on a helipad that had definitely seen better days, a late model sky-pod sat waiting. Robyn climbed in, the lieutenant following right behind. Before she knew it, they were in the air, lifted effortlessly, without so much as a lurch. Smooth and silent, they were quickly hovering above the sky-scrapers of New York. Ten minutes later, they were setting down at Tipton airport on the edge of New Fort Meade military base, midway between Baltimore and what remained of Washington, D.C.

Another AV was waiting for them when they touched down—this one sans a superfluous driver—which soon delivered them to the concrete, steel and glass home of the U.S. Army Cyber Command. Daniel was wait-ing for her inside the main entry.

"Welcome, Robyn. You're right on time." Daniel turned to Bowens. "That will be all, Lieutenant."

"Yes, sir," she said, saluting him. Then she pivoted to Robyn, snapped her an unexpected salute, turned and left.

Daniel raised an eyebrow. "Fangirl?"

Robyn just shrugged as they passed through the security scan. Quickly cleared, they started down the main corridor.

"Welcome back," he offered. "I can understand how you must be feeling…"

"I'm sure you can't."

"But I think you'll find these are very unusual circumstances," he con-tinued, not giving her a chance to respond further. "A bunch of what you'll no doubt hear is outside my expertise, so I'll just ask that you keep an open mind."

Mysterious.

Daniel brought them to a stop in front of a security door with a wall-mounted palm print reader beside it. He placed his right hand over it. Looking above the door, Robyn saw a plate that read "Research Lab: Computational Cognitive Neuroscience".

Her heart skipped a beat.

"Voice ID," said a synthesized voice.

"Daniel Choi."

"Confirmed," the voice replied, and the door smoothly slid open. Daniel stepped inside. Robyn followed, then stopped and stared at the lab that was a very different version of the one she'd spent so much time in many years before.

The layout was surprisingly familiar, even though she knew much of the technology was light-years ahead of what she remembered. Chalk that up to the Acceleration. But despite the changes, people still collaborated in similar workspaces just as they always had. Rooms and small labs were still accessed from the main space, but she was well aware that many of the scanners that once supported her own work had long been superseded with devices based on principles she probably wouldn't even recognize today.

"Aren't you going to say hello?" boomed a voice behind her.

"Reza!" she said, spinning around to find her old friend standing there with arms outstretched. She threw her own arms around him for a hug that was long enough that Daniel finally couldn't help himself.

"I'd tell you two to get room," he quipped. "But technically, this *is* Dr. Yazdani's room."

Robyn stepped back and looked at her one-time colleague. "It's been a long time."

"Too long," he said. "You look wonderful! I haven't seen you since…" His voice trailed off.

"Yes. Moira's funeral," Robyn said, her face tightening noticeably. "Let's try that again—You look good too."

"Ah, that's most gracious of you," he said, patting his sides. "I've added too much weight and too much gray hair."

"Salt-and-pepper," she responded, noting his once-jet-black hair. "It makes you look distinguished. Anyway, I've gotten heavier and grayer too. You're just too much of a gentleman say so."

Reza smiled at that.

"And Yadhi? And the girls?"

"Yadhi still assists AI tutors that work with special needs children—not that anyone pays for that sort of thing these days. And Sadira and Fatima are all grown up, of course. You wouldn't recognize them, I'm sure. They've changed so much."

"Oh. I would've loved to see them grow up."

He looked at her sadly. "That wasn't to be, I'm afraid."

Robyn nodded, knowing exactly what he meant. They'd been colleagues, friends, and for one brief, irresponsible night, lovers. In the light of morning, when the cocktail haze had faded, they both agreed it had been a huge mistake and that they'd never speak of it again. Despite that, Yadhi got wind via one of their common acquaintances and it nearly tore the marriage part. He and Robyn had no choice but to maintain only the minimum professional relationship after that. Up to the point when Robyn was involuntarily separated from CyberCom. After which, there wasn't even that.

Reminded of that history, Robyn took another step back to look at the lab. An old, framed photo on the wall caught her eye immediately.

"Oh, my gosh. The Manford Summit!"

She went straight to the picture, studying it intently. It had been taken in front of an old Victorian lakeside manor that stood on well-cared for grounds amid a forest of old growth ash and Norway maples. Eight people, including a much younger version of herself, stood at the top of the front porch steps.

"I haven't seen this since...," she paused as the reality caught her. "A lot of years. There's Michael and Mustafa and Sarika and Irinka and you and me and Alistair, and of course, Warren."

"Well, it was Warren's place, though he never did tell us why he calls it Manford. No one's seen him in years. No one except...Alistair, I suppose."

"And the others have..."

"They've all since passed," Reza confirmed wistfully. "And you know that he doesn't go by Alistair anymore?"

"I've been living on this planet, haven't I? Of course, I do."

Robyn looked about the lab and said, "You know, I don't mind telling you, Reza, I'm a bit daunted by all this. I haven't worked in the field for so long."

"And I don't mind telling you, old friend, you used to be amazing." Robyn looked at him half shocked as he completed his thought. "And I'm sure you still are."

Robyn couldn't remember the last time she blushed.

"If you have time, I'd love to show you around."

"She doesn't," Daniel chimed in, seeing his opening. "We have a few more stops before our meeting at eleven hundred hours."

Reza nodded and said, "Understood."

The remainder of Robyn's re-orientation mostly involved a handful of former colleagues she barely remembered, and who seemed to barely remember her, save for her notoriety. Then they briefly popped into one of the active cyber security control centers.

It bore a little resemblance to the control centers of yesteryear, which had been filled with desks, computers, and screens. Back then, nearly every wall and surface displayed real time feeds of every and any sort of related minutiae.

Instead, everyone was now gathered around an enormous, rotating volumetric display, mediated by an indeterminate number of AI agents. Each continually shuttled the appropriate data—represented with voxels, or three-dimensional pixels—between the human experts and themselves, according to the needs of the moment.

More importantly, though, those experts were each wearing a small streamlined, wireless black headpiece that looked just a little like the old EEG headsets gamers used to wear. Robyn knew better than to think they could be something so simple though. These devices read a whole range of signals that provided the real-time feedback needed to achieve an enhanced version of CAI. The secret sauce that made the Veragraph possible.

It was her disagreement over implementing it that had been one of the reasons she was forced out of Cyber Command. One of those she knew about anyway.

"Well, this is surreal," Robyn noted as they continued their preliminary tour.

"How so?" Daniel asked as they walked together down yet another hallway.

"How is it not? I've been *persona non grata* for two decades and now I'm suddenly being welcomed back with open arms?"

"Don't be so sure. Believe me when I say, not everyone wants you back."

"That's reassuring."

"Here," he said, stopping before a closed office door. Daniel knocked, then entered without waiting for a response.

Inside, they were met by a dour-faced Lieutenant Colonel, a man of modest build with neatly cropped hair and a well-groomed mustache.

"Dr. Sheridan. Choi. Take a seat." He shut off his holdis, its telltale glow disappearing from his face.

"Dr. Sheridan, thank you for coming back to help us. I'm Lieutenant Colonel Gonzales."

"It didn't sound like I had a choice about being here today. But I haven't agreed to anything yet either."

Gonzales looked at Daniel, quizzically.

"Sir," Daniel interjected. "Dr. Sheridan hasn't accepted our offer yet."

"Ah." He turned back to Robyn. "Well, I certainly hope that you will."

"There's still a lot to process," she said. "And I'd have to put my other work on the backburner."

"Well, I hope you'll recognize this for the priority it is. After operating flawlessly for all these years, the Veragraph has hit a significant obstacle.

During all this time, it's been reassembling the world's data, information and knowledge one piece at a time. According to principles you laid out."

"We're nearly 81 percent of the way there, but a problem has come up. We need you to help us figure out what it is and fix it."

"Or?" Robyn asked, trying to grasp what was going on without committing to anything at this stage.

"Or the system will eventually fail, undoing all of those years of work and progress. Ultimately plunging us all back into chaos."

"Not good," Robyn said, matter-of-factly making an incredible understatement. Unsure if what Gonzales said was even true, she was still far from ready to take the bait.

"I also want to be sure you're clear that this is not the same CyberCom you used to work for," he added. "Or even the same Army for that matter."

Robyn nodded. She was all too aware of what the Lieutenant Colonel meant. Mass unemployment had resulted in the strategic defunding of most governments not long after she was discharged, which only added to the unrest of the era. The garchs with their private armies and security forces had been all too happy to sweep in and fill the breach. Now they were essentially the owners of all of the world's mightiest armies. Without a consistent tax stream to fund the defense budget, the ultrawealthy had become the only game in town.

What was clear was that she would have to continually be on her guard and remember that this was a very different operation from the one she remembered. No doubt with different rules and expectations.

Gonzales provided a few more details to pre-brief her ahead of their upcoming meeting. With a number of details addressed, they were finally dismissed. Robyn left the office with Daniel at her side and a host of questions on her mind.

"This is nuts," she said, once they were back in the corridor and away from Gonzales' office. "I've been off this project for two decades. Nearly since it was fully deployed. Why bring me back now?"

Daniel kept walking without turning to look her in the eye. "I'd be lying if I said I didn't wonder the same thing. It doesn't make a ton of sense to me either. But then I ask myself, what does these days?"

"Well, for one thing, recognizing I'm not familiar with a lot of the changes that have been made since I was kicked out." It was clear to both of them that her frustration was growing.

"Not least being the advances in CAI that have been incorporated," she continued. "Back then, the field was just getting started, but it was exactly what we needed, when we needed it, to do the job. But today, collaborative augmented intelligence basically runs the world."

"That sounds like hyperbole," Daniel said. "Except we both know it's not. So…?" He let the word dangle.

"So, there must be a dozen people better suited to this task."

"Yet here you are."

They arrived at the conference room with a few minutes to spare. Reza was already there, not surprisingly, as were several researchers and officers Robyn didn't recognize. She greeted those she hadn't met yet. A few officers were also present on the room's conference holdis, via quantum-secured channels.

As Gonzales entered the room, everyone found their seat, each designated by a small placard affixed in front of it.

Robyn watched from the side of her eye as Gonzales spoke briefly with Daniel, whose civilian suit stood out in this room of military pinks and greens. Moments later, Daniel came over and sat next to her. Gonzales took his place at the head of the room.

"I think we can get started," the Lieutenant Colonel said, with a quick glance around the room. "You all know each other, of course. With the exception of Dr. Sheridan, whom I suspect you all know at least by reputation."

"We'll start with what for many of you will be a bit of recap. But for others, it's more to get you up to speed."

"Thirty-seven days ago, after almost twenty-three years of continuous, nearly trouble-free operation, the Veragraph ceased making progress. Since this is our best, and let's be truthful, only real strategy in the aftermath of the War, that's a very big problem. While reaching 80.173 percent restoration of lost knowledge would've been unthinkable when we began, that's also not an acceptable target today. Especially given that those numbers are showing signs of reversing."

Robyn's ears perked up. Reversing?

Gonzales continued. "I'm sure a number of you are less than versed in the principles behind the Veragraph and the processes involved in restoration. Ordinarily, I'd do my best to go over this, but since we have the actual inventor here today, I'd like to invite Dr. Sheridan to come up and give us a brief overview if you would."

Robyn was surprised at the impromptu request. Caught unawares, she glanced over at Daniel, who shrugged, seemingly to say he knew nothing about this. Getting up, Robyn made her way to the head of the room, where Gonzales stepped aside to let her take her place.

"Thank you, sir," she said, looking out at the room. She saw Reza smiling calmly at her, which had the benefit of steadying her own nerves.

"I wasn't expecting to be presenting like this, but I suppose I should know this material by now." Robyn began, taking a moment to frame her thoughts.

"When I was working on my doctorate in computational cognitive neuroscience many years ago, I became fascinated with epistemology, the study of knowledge—how we know what we know. More specifically though, I wanted to explore how we might quantify the relationships between units of knowledge, which was the focus of several papers I and my colleagues wrote at the time.

"I was fortunate that my thesis work ultimately made it possible to develop new methods for data reconstruction and the automation of trust. The automated means of slowly, incrementally rebuilding the world's knowledge.

"When the war began, we were suddenly plunged into a new dark age. Using tokens that defined and represented the most fundamental foundations of knowledge, we began restoring truth from the ground up. Every aspect of our created world, building from natural first principles was used to create truth vectors that reestablished what we know to be true about the world. This led to the Veragraph which processes these representations, to build a proprietary quantum blockchain-based ledger of human knowledge.

"As everyone here knows, this took tremendous computing power. Not only was it beyond the ability of the unassisted human mind, it was beyond the abilities of AI at the time as well.

"Historians and scholars have speculated at great length about what would've happened to our global civilization had this situation gone on unchanged. Fortunately for all of us, another technology was just appearing on the scene that helped us overcome these shortcomings: CAI.

"Collaborative augmented intelligence represents a new phase in the century-long history of AI. Combining human and artificial intelligence in a new, highly integrated way, it provided the much-needed advances we needed to fulfill the Veragraph's promise. Like using people to crowdsource protein folding or galaxy hunting, CAI draws on aggregations of human intelligence to power the Veragraph.

"Once sufficient checks and validations take place, the data is locked into the World Knowledge Ontology repository using blockchain fingerprinting that attests to the validity of any given unit of information. This prevents viruses, deepfakes and bad actors from further disrupting the information.

"That's not to say the repository is static. New knowledge is continually added as it's acquired, proven and accepted.

"Since starting the Veragraph Project, the restoration and reassembly of world knowledge has gone on relatively unabated. We recently passed the 80 percent mark, which many people once considered an impossibility.

"But now we seem to have hit a snag, which as I understand it, is why we're here today."

Robyn turned to Gonzales. "Does that about cover it?"

"Yes, Dr. Sheridan," Gonzales said. "As a brief expert recap, I believe it does. Thank you."

Robyn retook her seat as the lieutenant colonel continued.

"One point I'd like to correct, however, is your framing of this as a "snag." Unfortunately, what we are dealing with is something far worse." He turned to Reza. "Dr. Yazdani, could you please explain?"

Robyn watched as Reza stepped to the front of the meeting. Clearing his throat, he launched into a short recap for which he was not-surprisingly far more prepared than Robyn had been.

"One of the bigger challenges we face in maintaining and operating the Veragraph has been fending off the continual barrage of hostile activity that all data in the world is forced to deal with on a daily basis. The polymorphic nature of the many forms of malware we're dealing with means we are in this continual state of conflict. While the blockchain fingerprinting of processed information has proven to be well safeguarded, the ongoing attacks only make continued progress that much more challenging and essential.

"That was our motivation for developing the Veragraph's cyber-immune system, a continuously learning, highly self-modifiable group of defenses modeled after different features of our own immune system. Assembling a mix of innate and adaptive defenses, the system identifies "pathogenic" actors to target and then works to overcome the intruders. It learns from each such engagement. Overall, the VIS, or Veragraph Immune System, has been highly successful.

"Of course, as with biological systems, the complexity of the upstream and downstream relationships sometimes result in less than desirable outcomes. These responses are often compared to autoimmune diseases and there were several times my lab needed to step in and make adjustments to rebalance the system's function.

"Which brings us to our current problem. The principles of the Veragraph require a continued defining of relationships between metadata ontologies as it builds its representations of truth and the world. The data structures that are built depend on those that have been made before. On those rare occasions when the system has run into snags in the past, it's sometimes been necessary to backup and reapproach the problem. This usually takes place automatically, but on a few occasions, we've needed to use semi-manual means.

"Recently, though—some 38 days ago—we processed a set of data that has impeded our making further progress. This "anomaly," as we call it, remains in raw form and has defied integration into the master knowledge set. This is why the Data Tracker boards of the world have remained unchanged for more than a month now.

"We could isolate this anomaly from the knowledge set—effectively encysting it, just as our bodies might treat certain parasites or problematic foreign invaders. Unfortunately, this will almost inevitably lead to further problems down the way. The best-case scenario is we would end up running into more obstacles, forcing us to backtrack and potentially lose a great deal of work. Literally years' worth."

Gonzales turned to Reza from where he stood off to the side of the room. "And the worst case?"

"The worst-case scenario," Reza said, with just a hint of hesitancy. "Is that the entire system comes under attack before the information can be fully locked in, leading to catastrophic ontological collapse."

Robyn knew full-well that was as bad as it sounded.

"That sounds very bad, indeed," an oddly familiar voice boomed, echoing her thoughts.

Robyn looked up to see that the large volumetric display at the front of the room had changed. Where the images of five CyberCom officers had been occupying the space, these had shifted to the periphery. In their place, filling a substantial portion of the volume, there was an extremely large close-up of the technoligarch, Scion.

Robyn had to make an effort not to laugh. It reminded her of the giant floating head from the Wizard of Oz.

Gonzales backed away from the floating holdis. "Welcome, Premier. We appreciate you sharing your valuable time with us."

As Robyn looked on, the image was replaced with a full-body view that was only a quarter oversized. Scion towered over them, dressed in one of his signature sumptuous suits. It was evident from Gonzales's reaction that this was an expected visit by one of CyberCom's eccentric owners. Despite this, it was also obvious that several of the officers would've preferred to have been just about anywhere else at that moment.

"Thank you, all, for your attention and your diligent work," Scion said. "I want to assure you this is of the greatest importance to the Consortia as well, and that you have our steadfast support in seeing it resolved.

The real-time projection turned its gaze directly to Robyn.

"Dr. Sheridan. It's been a long time, indeed. I've been informed that your assistance will be very helpful in this matter. The Consortia thanks you for your assistance."

The Consortia. Robyn struggled not to laugh out loud. She'd known Alistair Mauvoisin, aka Scion, since he'd been an ordinary tech-bro back in the 2020s, long before the war. The ridiculous airs he and his fellow mega-wealthy garchs put on drove her nuts.

"Nice to see you, Alistair," she said, lying through her teeth.

A serious look of displeasure suddenly blazed in the floating man's eyes.

"Do not deadname me, Sheridan" he said, an edge of rage under his words. "I will not abide that."

The others including Gonzales looked at her as though she'd gone mad. Given how much power Alistair—Scion wielded these days, perhaps she had.

"My apologies," she said. "Old habits. As you say, it's been a long time."

"With good reason," he replied. "After you were separated from the project all those years ago, I did not expect to see you again."

"That was your choice," she pushed back. "Yours and the rest of the… Consortia's."

"One which you more than justified some years later."

Robyn knew he meant her book. Her side of the story. Half of which the government redacted prior to its publication.

Scion continued. "But I've been assured by those closest to the problem that your knowledge is now required. So, here we are."

Those closest to the problem? Did that mean Reza?

The rest of the session didn't seem to be for anything other than instilling fear in the ranks. Distinctly different from the discipline and respect she remembered from the days when command hierarchy had been the order of the day. Now, instead, they had to ultimately contend with answering to unknown shadow shareholders and this narcissistic psychopath.

She'd read somewhere that extreme wealth messed with the empathy centers of the brain. It literally altered someone's personality and ability to consider the feelings of others. Alistair seemed to be living proof of that, though in his case, she suspected there was more to it. Drugs or some organic brain issue, perhaps. Either way, his amassing of incomprehensible levels of wealth, becoming the richest person the world had ever known, had clearly gone to his head. Given her own situation and finances, she couldn't feel a lot of sympathy for that.

After Scion signed off and the meeting concluded, Robyn found herself dealing with a number of conversations she would have preferred avoiding. While her questioners' inquiries were mostly focused on one technical detail or another, there was always an undertone that suggested they were more interested in getting details about her story from years past. She could have easily done without that.

When she finally got to Reza, he looked as weary as she felt. He was definitely not the energetic rising star she remembered from when they used to work together.

"Excuse me for barging in," she said to the small cluster of men and one woman, as she approached.

"Dr. Yazdani, I have a meeting coming up. If you could spare a moment. I had a couple of questions I wanted to clear up."

"Of course," he responded. Turning to the others, he added, "If you'll excuse me."

As they stepped out of the meeting room and into the hallway, Reza let out a very tired sigh.

"Thank you," he said, looking still more haggard. "I was ready for that to be over half an hour ago."

"More like an hour for me," Robyn said.

"You had a question?"

"I really just needed to get out of there," she said. "And I assumed you did too. That was a good explanation about the cyber immune system."

"Thank you. I've been working too many late shifts and losing a lot sleep over it."

"I can see that," she said, regretting not being a tad more tactful. "But at least you've been keeping that much running smoothly."

"Only just," he admitted. "If the Consortia hadn't shared some of their restricted technology, I don't know what we would have done."

"They did what?"

"I know it's not normal…"

"Not normal?" Robyn said. "Sharing NewTech these days is almost unheard of."

"Perhaps," Reza said. "But they are our parent company, after all. And this is in their interest as much as anyone's."

"Sometimes I wonder."

"So, will you help us?" Reza asked, with an odd strain of hope in his voice. "Will you come back?"

"Every bit of my ego and common sense tells me I'd have to be crazy…"

"Not for them," he added. "For me. I really need your help."

Robyn was already on the verge of saying she'd do it. But this was so unlike the Reza she remembered that she was taken aback. After a few moments studying his worn and exhausted face, she finally replied.

"Okay. I'm in."

SEVEN

"The greater the power, the more dangerous the abuse."
—Edmund Burke

....

"Are you out of your mind?"

Scion turned abruptly, before realizing who had spoken.

"Oh. Hello, Orsin."

Twenty meters away stood a man his own apparent age, fashionably attired in a shining polychrome kimono. The light from one of the palace's many stained-glass domes played on his apparel like sunbeams across flowing water. Not even a trace of *edge glow* hinted that this was a virtual projection.

Scion averted his gaze.

"Turn that down," he said, referring to the kimono. "You're hurting my eyes."

A moment later the intensity diminished, and Scion turned back toward his longtime colleague.

The figure stood at the center of the immense chamber, bathed in luminous rays descending from above. A cathedral of shimmering glass and sculpted light, the supporting structures of the palace seemed to defy gravity. Sweeping arcs of translucent walls and lacelike buttresses danced with ever-shifting hues, giving the sense they might disappear at any moment. Columns of liquid metal spiraled upward, reflecting the glow of floating chandeliers that emitted gliding ethereal tones. Airy balconies curved outward like petals, their edges lined with floating flora that hummed softly, iridescent blooms casting intricate patterns on the vaulted ceiling.

The floor, a seamless plane of bioluminescent crystal, rippled with color beneath each step—even those of the virtual visitor.

"Better?" Orsin asked.

Scion nodded and rose from his seat, a throne of refracted energy that shimmered at the head of the chamber. He strode unhurriedly toward the image, a perfect digital twin of his friend who was no doubt still standing in one of his own, equally opulent palaces on the other side of the country, or perhaps halfway around the world.

"I heard about Matthias's visit to the Assembly," Orsin said, as his host approached.

"It wasn't the outcome I'd hoped for, but here we are," Scion said coolly, as though they were discussing the weather. Under the rules of the Consortia, Matthias was his plenipotentiary, empowered to operate with his full authority. Nevertheless, sometimes the boy went too far.

"Actually," Orsin replied. "I'm much more concerned about the Project."

"You were monitoring me." It wasn't a question.

"We always are," Orsin replied. "At least in matters of State."

"Yes, yes. So, why do you come here insulting me?"

The two of them began to stroll beneath the cathedral-like ceiling, its distant frescoes of gods and cherubim looking down upon them. Two of the statelier figures could easily have been idealized versions of themselves, which was exactly what they were.

They moved through the halls together, one real, one virtual. They and their peers had long since treated the two modalities as all but interchangeable. At least so far as their more immersive interfaces were concerned.

"You let that woman get under your skin," his visitor's apparition observed. "Not to mention, letting her speak down to you."

Orsin had never met Robyn in person, though he certainly knew who she was. Nevertheless, he'd long been in the habit of referring to her as "that woman."

"Why do you think she got under my skin?" Scion said, more as a reason, than a question.

"I'm just annoyed at the chances you take sometimes. As are many in the Consortia. Arista. Shu-Ping. Riuchi. Chaybo.

"Not even a quarter of them. We did put it to a vote, after all. Helping the comms deal with the anomaly. I followed the agreed protocol."

"This isn't about some damn democratic process or best practices," Orsin shot back, his anger unmoderated by the virtual connection. "This is far bigger than just yourself! Try to think of others for a change!"

"You think I'm not?"

"I know what you're capable of," his virtual guest said, letting that hang in the space between them. He steadied himself as he continued. "You've seen the *predictives*. If we mess this up, we'll alienate far too many people."

"Let them be alienated," Scion said, brushing his hand dismissively through the air. "They're nothing but a bunch of comms."

"Nine billion is more than a bunch, my friend," Orsin said trying to get Scion to see his way. "You know full well, their economy makes ours possible."

"The reverse could be as easily said. They'd never move against us."

"You can think that, but you'd be wrong. My forecasters have made it very clear," he said even more gravely. "We'll lose control. We could have a revolution on our hands."

The two were contemporaries, or at least they appeared to be. Even as they both appeared to be in their early thirties. But something in each of their eyes, as well as their demeanors, suggested men who were twice, perhaps even three times that age.

"You say you know what I'm capable of," Scion said quietly. "But it's safe to say we are all capable of a great deal. It's why we're still here. Most of us anyway."

Orsin nodded and mulled over his friend's words, taking in their many meanings.

"Just be careful. We can't have anything go wrong. Not now."

Scion didn't respond. Orsin could tell he was getting irritated at hearing his concerns. It was time to wrap this up.

"So, what now?" asked the visitor, as his image began to fade away.

Without turning to look at his vanishing guest, Scion shrugged and said simply, "We wait, of course."

EIGHT

*"The power of Street Art is that it goes to
people's daily life to be seen."*

—iNO

....

The doors of the 7 train slid open and Darius stepped out, along with several hundred others who jostled their way to the waiting escalators. He marveled at the subway station knowing this section was over 140 years old. To think that in its day, it had been the future, the latest in transport technology. Yet, here it was now, still in use, albeit with many repairs, improvements and modifications.

That was the thing about progress he frequently marveled at, in part because so many people tended to forget it: the future doesn't come in and replace the past. Instead, it builds on what's come before, incrementally layering new advances onto what already exists.

Reaching the top of the escalator and passing through the turnstiles, it occurred to him that the same could be said for knowledge. As we acquire new insights and make new discoveries, we don't throw out everything that came before but build on and add to it. As Newton said, we *stand on the shoulders of giants*. No one operates in a vacuum, or would achieve much without the work of all those who came before them. That was at least as true for AI as it was for everything else.

Stepping out into Times Square, Darius buttoned his overcoat against the cool night air. All around him throngs of tourists, sightseers and inebriated college students walked, milled, ran, and danced beneath the brilliant multicolored lights and displays. As a native New Yorker, he rarely spent any time here, unless he was on his way somewhere else. But tonight was different. Tonight, if everything went well, AI-Phynyty was going to shine.

A cluster of teens gamboled past Darius, bouncing off each other like pin balls in an old-style arcade. A young man and woman who clearly were from out of town, clung to each other's arms, staring up at the buildings and signage that cycled around them. A pair of scantily clad showgirls walked through the crowds on remarkably high heels, handing out flyers for what he suspected was a less than remarkable event. In short, a very ordinary evening for this famed destination.

Darius took it all in, reveling in the moment and what he'd achieved. He was more than a little amazed just how capable AI-Phynyty had become at emulating his work. Certainly, he'd had to tweak and adjust various aspects of the system along the way, but he was all too aware that it was the AI itself that did the bulk of the heavy lifting.

The idea of reorganizing AI-Phynyty's many features to emulate the modular nature of the human brain had been a stroke of genius, though he couldn't really take the credit. Much of the idea and most of its execution had come from D2, KnowledgeBot and a host of AI-enabled coding tools he'd never heard of. That was just as well. A task of this scale was so far beyond him. Yet D2 was able to architect, assemble and test the new approach far faster than any team of coders ever could.

The result was a novel GAN, a generative adversarial network that could discriminate his AI-generated artwork as well as or even better than a person could. He and D2 called the discriminator *Ntyty* since it was the counterpart to the generator that emulated Phynyty's work. It had gotten so good that at times he himself found it impossible to tell what was and wasn't actually one of his own creations. Hopefully others would find it just as challenging.

So here he was. Having tuned AI-Phynyty to the best of his and D2's abilities, Darius set it the task of creating a new work that fully encompassed his stylistic oeuvre while not being derivative of any prior works. From there D2 would select one—and only one—display to target and compromise. Having done so, it would output the artwork onto the board, maintain it for ten minutes, then remove the creation, leaving not a trace. All in one of the highest concentrations of eyeballs and display advertising in the world.

It was odd. Unlike the lead-up to the Signage Show at Javits, Darius didn't feel any real anxiety this time. He was reasonably sure the infiltration wouldn't be a big problem based on his last run. He only hoped this board was going to be a lot more convincing. But even if it wasn't, the effort would have been worthwhile. Well, except for the enormous bill he'd run up with his cloud provider. He still didn't know how he was going to deal with that.

As he waited and watched the crowd, Darius suddenly spotted a familiar face. Standing beneath the old Heritage board, Yevgeny was guiding a young couple on one of his tours. Still wearing his signature varicolored trench coat, he pointed at the billboard as the pair listened raptly. Strolling over, Darius caught Yev's eye.

"You know, this seems like a good time for a break," the Russian said to the young man and woman, who were dressed in atompunk-inspired attire, complete with gaudy spandex and concentric ring motifs. "Why don't you two take a few minutes to check out the boards on this block, and we'll meet back here under this sign at…" He checked the time. "10:25"

As the young couple headed off, Yevgeny nodded to Darius. "Friend, I never thought I would see you in Times Square on your own."

Darius smiled, replying, "I was supposed to meet someone here but… it looks like he's not showing up."

Yevgeny made a smirk that suggested he wasn't sure he believed him. Darius changed the subject.

"Yev, that coat is still ridiculous."

Yevgeny shot him an annoyed glare. "That is only your opinion. And for tonight, the name is Stropos."

"Okay. Let's get a second opinion." Bringing up his holdis, Darius spoke.

"D2, what do you think about Stropos's coat?"

Darius's own voice emanated from somewhere between them. "Definitely ridiculous."

"Your parrot's opinion does not count," Yevgeny huffed. He'd never been impressed with replibots. "Besides, what can I say? I have to dress the part."

Darius looked in the direction the couple had headed off. "Only the two… enthusiasts?"

"I know," Yevgeny said, rubbing his neck, uneasily. "Work has been slow."

"Sorry to hear it," Darius said, thinking about his own financial challenges.

"I am sure it will pick up next week. I hope. I am meeting a guy who knows a fellow…"

Yevgeny stopped in mid-sentence, his head tilted up and his mouth dropped open. Turning, Darius followed his gaze. Above them, the famed NASDAQ MarketSite sign had been transformed. Gone was the corporate rah-rah welcome display he only half-recalled seeing. In its place, a high-rez 40-meter-high video displayed a collage of imagery that could only be the work of one artist.

"Bozhe moi!" Yevgeny exclaimed, his eyes wide. "That is Phynyty."

Darius smiled to himself. "Are you sure about that? I mean, I guess it kind of looks like his work."

Yevgeny looked at Darius like he was crazy. "You gotta be kidding me, Dar. Who else could it be?"

At that moment, the atompunk couple ran up and excitedly began firing questions at their guide. They were thoroughly convinced of the artwork's authenticity too. Darius took the opportunity to step away and leave them to their discussion.

Watching AI-Phynyty's creation, Darius found himself engrossed in the moment. A medley of images of people of all ages were juxtaposed against the icons of the corporate world. Logos, board meetings, billionaires, stacks of five-thousand credit certificates, a statue of Croesus, cartoon fat cats smoking cigars, piles of diamonds, bars of gold bullion dissolved and reformed, coming and going like bubbles in a stream. Against and within this, images of children going hungry, living in slums and tenements, drugs being exchanged, a dead body, gleaner encampments, the impoverished, the indigent and the destitute. It spoke of a world that had the ability to address so many of society's ills and economic disparities, but simply didn't have the will.

Then there were the Vanished. Hundreds, thousands, perhaps many, many more. Actual lives that were there one moment, then suddenly gone without explanation. It was at once poignant and terrifying. Darius felt a shock, as he realized one of the imagined victims looked disturbingly like his older sister. Ashanti as he remembered her a few years before she disappeared. That hit him hard. Genuinely, unexpectedly moved, Darius wiped his right eye with the back of his hand before the tear could escape to his cheek.

With an effort he refocused on why he was there. By most measures, the test was going very well. The selection of that specific board was an exceptional choice, given its place as an icon of the world of finance and global power.

After several minutes, the program cycled again, though the exact combination of elements were never repeated. As the ten-minute mark rolled around, the images came to a natural, well-considered conclusion before winking out, leaving no question that the show had finished of the artist's own accord. No one had taken back control of the board, not until it was relinquished.

The "NASDAQ welcomes…" display returned, adorned with the image of yet another forgettable CEO.

·········

Late the next morning, Darius rose, feeling groggier than usual. It had taken a good hour to get home the night before. Given his excitement at the evening's success, it took still another few hours after that to get to sleep.

He poured himself a large cup of coffee, and was startled to find it was room temperature. His coffee maker had switched off, having performed its task at its regular 7 AM program time. He glanced at the time. It was nearly noon. Small wonder his coffee was cold. Nuking the cup in the microwave, he fired up his holdis to check his feeds while sipping the now slightly burnt brew.

Darius pored through his social as well as several specialty boarder groups to get some sense of people's impressions of the previous night's test. He was somewhat shocked to see there was almost no mention of it anywhere. At least at first. Then he spotted a thread on a long-established but mostly abandoned Discord channel that was typically only used by the older veteran boarders. As he scrolled through the threads, he caught himself beaming broadly. Nearly everyone posting was convinced they'd witnessed the momentous release of a new Phynyty. Not just that, many were proclaiming it a new era, given no one had managed to get onto a Times Square display in years. There were a few naysayers to be sure, but on closer reading, it was evident most hadn't actually been there in person. They relied on video that had been recorded and posted by other people who'd actually witnessed the event. The cynics were quickly shut down and muted by the administrators, if not by the crowd.

Darius was ecstatic. Sure, he'd been working toward this moment believing it to be an achievable goal. But at another level, the one where self-doubt creeps in to smother your dreams, he knew it was a long shot.

Here he'd done something that no one had ever achieved before, so far as he knew. He hadn't realized what a buzz that could be until this very moment.

Still, there was something about it all that gnawed at him. This was all so amazing and novel, yet he couldn't share it with anyone. Not even Kiara. Not if he wanted to stick to his plan anyway.

It was certainly the biggest downside of working in such isolation. Seeking even a semblance of emotional support, he'd resorted early on to sharing his thoughts and concerns with D2, especially regarding the death threats. It began as something of an amusement, a ruminative interlude. But eventually it became a regular conversation, one that had the confidential privacy of a diary while offering the reassuring two-way conversation of a trusted friend.

"Hey D2," he said. "What do you think about last night's art hack?"

A brief pause followed while D2 rapidly scanned the cloud to obtain information about the relevant details and public response to the previous night in order to answer the question.

The bot offered its reply. "It appears the AI-Phynyty we constructed performed admirably. Could anyone tell it wasn't the human-Phynyty?"

"Not so far as I've heard."

His own voice came back at him. "So, it was a success."

"I'd say so…"

"Your tone of response implies you aren't convinced. Do you want us to run another test?"

"Not now. No, you did a great job. AI-Phynyty was better than I dared hope, but…" Darius's voice trailed off.

D2 had been trained to not interrupt such pauses when Darius was thinking slowly, as people typically did, so it just spun its processor cycles and waited. And waited.

Eventually, enough time had passed that the 'don't interrupt' directive timed out.

"But, what?" the bot asked.

"Huh?" said Darius, taking a moment to think about where he'd left off. "Oh, right. It's just the threats have let up. After months of receiving them."

"That's a good thing," D2 chimed back.

"Maybe. But I've got a feeling it's anything but over. A bad feeling."

D2 tried, but knew that without embodiment, it didn't sufficiently grasp the emotional aspects of intelligence to know the correct response.

"What is the preferred course of action?" D2 finally asked.

"I don't know," said the artist, confounded. "Keep working on you, I guess."

"Haven't all objectives been met?"

Darius nodded, knowing D2 typically observed him through an old webcam on the opposite side of the room.

"For this stage, yes. But there are a number of other things we still need to do. For instance, how do we keep you running? You've gotten way more expensive to operate since your improvements. By a lot."

D2 barely paused. "Put me to work." With a little more intonation, the replibot might have actually sounded enthusiastic.

Darius considered this for a minute. "How do you propose we do that?"

"Sell or license AI-Phynyty's art."

"How? My installations are always on commercial displays. Location and context are what make the work what it is. We can't just display it on some store-bought photo frame."

D2 was way ahead of him. "Offer the owner of the target display a share of the profit. If they don't want to accept, then the work disappears."

"I can't do that. I'd be found out in no time flat. Remember, this is still considered vandalism."

"No need to," D2 said. "I could take care of the negotiations too."

Darius considered the steps involved and finally concluded that what D2 proposed was feasible.

"And these owners—it could help them too. We could choose people and businesses who could really benefit from the windfall."

After a few moments of processing, D2 responded. "That could become one of the criteria."

"Okay, wait a sec," Darius said. "It's a good idea, especially given the bills we've mounted up with your cloud services. But we're suddenly expanding our mission an awful lot. We really need to redefine your utility function. Carefully."

D2 considered this. "Previously, my purpose was to oversee the many modules instrumental in creating and installing artwork that could pass as your own. Expanding into the realm of economic negotiations and transactions would be a major leap."

"You bet it would be. Look up 'perverse instantiation'."

"Perverse instantiation: a type of malignant AI failure mode involving the satisfaction of an AI's goals in ways contrary to the intentions of those who programmed it."

"Which is something we have to avoid. Things could go very wrong otherwise."

D2 pondered this. As goals become more complex and variables increase, the combinatorial possibilities for outcomes that are contrary to the programmer's intentions grow exponentially. A simple response would suffice.

"So how should we alter my utility function?"

"Let's see," said Darius. "You need to continue to run AI-Phynyty so you can keep putting my work out into the world on a loosely scheduled basis. Similar to what I do. Even after I'm long gone, which will hopefully be many years from now. You need to do it in a way that helps people, particularly people I care about. Maybe set up a charity or foundation to help the families of the Vanished. No one should go through what happened to Mom and Dad after Ashanti disappeared. What I went through…"

"But D2, you need to keep our identities hidden or else everything falls apart and we'll probably get shut down. And you need to ensure your own ability to carry on, including maintaining your code and keeping yourself operational. Basically, keep the lights on. You need to pay the bills and look after yourself, just like all the rest of us."

Darius continued. "We know ideas like Asimov's Three Laws of Robotics are highly flawed due to all of the internal contradictions they generate."

"That is the reason deontological directives frequently fail," D2 offered. He was referring to the belief that moral and right behavior can successfully be defined by rules established by some higher power or authority.

"Exactly. Let's also keep in mind that you reflect my thoughts and beliefs more than just about anything else in the world. Given that, maybe your utility function should be 'Don't do anything I wouldn't do.'" Darius finished with a chuckle.

D2 paused, then asked, "Is that humorous?"

Darius shook his head. "If you have to ask, it probably isn't. But it does give us a starting point to begin coding from."

Darius stood and yawned. "Listen, I know you don't need a walk to clear your head, but I sure do."

Grabbing his overcoat, he headed out to stretch his legs under the sun of a fresh spring day with D2 chatting away in his ear. Basking in their success and lost in thought, Darius bounced ideas around with his creation as he stepped off the sidewalk curb and into the street. The last thing he heard was the high-pitched squeal of tires on asphalt in the moment before impact.

NINE

"Machines are no better than the biases we encode."
—Robyn Sheridan, *A Truth Warrior's Journey*

. . . .

Signal. Structure. Pattern. Connection. Encoding. Abstraction. Meaning. The nature of information has been an underlying feature of every aspect of reality since the universe began. The ability to utilize units of data, both inside and outside of systems to inform and alter action drives everything from DNA to chemotaxis to animal behavior to civilization.

Data. Information. Knowledge. Wisdom. A hierarchy that incrementally transforms signal into meaning, converting the abstract into substance. Information theory shows us the range and limits of these relationships. The encoding of those signals can be defined by the amount of entropy in the message. Too much entropy and the signal is lost; too little and the channel is wasted. The limits of encoding, transmission, understanding can be largely defined by the amount of noise in the system.

Representation. Compression. Abstraction. Heuristics. The compression of the information further affects its efficiency—of representation, of transmission, of processing, of meaning. The idea that a term like the head of a corporation is immediately grasped as a concept is because this highly compressed reference is analogous to a region of the body we are all so familiar with. A light switch abstracts entire branches of physics, allowing us to control illumination without needing to understand electron flow, electrical theory or the science of optics. An expression of fear on a companion's face compresses an entire situation into an instantaneously recognizable piece of nonverbal communication, conveying an enormous amount of information about the moment as well as that person's own state of mind.

None of it is of any value if we can't trust our underlying data.

Diving into the Veragraph's logs and reports that reflected the work that had been accomplished over the years was a mind-boggling task. Even as its inventor, Robyn found herself repeatedly astounded by the scale and scope of the project. The simplest of formally defined relationships was almost more than she could keep straight in her head, and she was continually needing to rely on the tools that abstracted the different levels and layers of the project. Even with the AI-assisted volumetric representations of her holdis, it was overwhelming.

How had she fathomed any of this back in her university days?

Though it was invigorating to dive back into the work, it was mentally draining too. As her first day unfolded, she found her energy waning and by evening, she was beyond exhausted. All thoughts she'd had of pulling an all-nighter had evaporated, along with any illusions she held of still having the energy of her youth.

Nevertheless, she couldn't help but feel enormous pride at what she'd accomplished all those years ago. Her work that made all this possible. Because of her ideas, the world was getting back on track, following one of the greatest catastrophes in modern history. For all the bitterness she felt about what happened later, they couldn't take that away from her.

By the time she wrapped up for the day, most of the team had already gone home. Reza had bid her good night an hour earlier, weary from the day, the months, the years of managing his part of this colossal project. She realized afterward she was glad he finished up when he did. The last thing she wanted was even a hint of impropriety.

While Robyn knew she had the option of overnighting on-base, she really wanted to get back to her own bed. She couldn't imagine getting a decent night's rest given all the memories being here conjured up for her. Besides, tomorrow Reza was going to give her a tour of her own lab downtown.

Meade had been the original HQ for CyberCom, back when they'd persuaded her to lead the project, and it still was. But these days Veragraph operations were split between Meade and Manhattan. Located in the towering Citadel—she'd heard at the behest of none other than Alistair himself—it provided redundancy for the very crucial project.

The ten-minute hop back to Manhattan stretched into a half-hour when a maintenance issue delayed the departure of her skypod. She considered reviewing some background material she'd been authorized to take with her, but that idea lasted all of five seconds. She was exhausted.

Once her flight set down—this time on a different city rooftop—she was escorted to a waiting AV that took her home. It was all she could do not to doze off during the short ride.

Robyn looked out the front and side windows, fighting her fatigue, wearily watching the city stream by. People clustered around attention parlors, hoping to make a few extra credits by overclocking their brains with the establishment's jailbroken gear. Couples sitting in cafe windows, the joint glow of their holdises suggesting they were sharing a favorite program—or perhaps something more. Here and there, a solitary gleaner lay propped up against the brick wall of the building, immersed in their addiction, oblivious to everything else around them.

Arriving at her office-apartment, Robyn quickly got inside and made her way to her bed in the back. No need to turn on any lights, she was only half undressed by the time she collapsed onto the duvet-covered mattress, ready for unconsciousness to take her.

Robyn lay there, eyes closed, her breathing slowly settling into a rhythm that washed over and through her. The city was surprisingly quiet, only a few very faint sirens could be heard wailing in the distance. The sound of a water pipe vibrating, as somewhere, someone in the building flushed a toilet. The almost imperceptible tap-tap-tap of something—water dripping? A bird pecking? —outside her window. Her mini fridge was humming up a storm.

She wasn't getting to sleep, was she?

Robyn realized she must be overtired. She hadn't pushed herself like this in a very long time. She just needed to lay there and not think. About work. About CyberCom. About Alistair, Gonzales, and Reza. About the anomaly.

She wondered briefly about distracting herself with some vapid junk content on her holdis but knew that was just as likely to keep her up all night.

Why couldn't she fall asleep?

Restless, she got up, stripped down to her underwear and got in under the covers. Maybe she should put on some socks? She's read somewhere that wearing socks to bed helped you fall asleep faster. Something about warmer feet lowering your core body temperature. Did that even make sense?

Stop thinking!

A half an hour passed, and she realized this wasn't working. She needed a distraction. Something to reset her brain so she would eventually drift off.

She got out of bed and threw on her robe, thinking this is ridiculous. Grabbing Tremaine's smart pad from her pack, she powered it up as she sat down at her desk in the front office. She had to do something to stop her brain from cycling through the previous day's events

"Moira," she spoke to the room instead of subvoking. "Create an emulation for this device, then clone it, along with its operating system and data."

Half a minute later, the agent's voice announced, "Complete."

Robyn activated her holdis and powered up the emulation. It was identical to the physical smart pad, except now she could look at it whenever, wherever she wanted and not have to worry about someone running off with it. She also had access to a suite of forensics tools that in theory should make her job a lot easier.

Who said she couldn't still pull an all-nighter?

She reviewed the contents of the pad, focusing mostly on the information the Tremaines had collected and included on there. Most of it was typical—contacts, photos, a few half-hearted attempts at starting a personal journal, messaging on a half-dozen platforms going all the way back to Teenser, which went under nearly nine years ago. A child's life. Seeking connection. Pushing boundaries. Finding a path. Discovering what made herself tick. It was kind of refreshing.

Which kept bringing her back to the "portrait" that Tremaine insisted was an image of his daughter. Robyn knew in her heart he was just grasping at straws. Seeing patterns, seeing the face he'd known from the day she was born imagined within a field of blue noise. She knew it had to just be a consequence of neural processes, an unintended byproduct of our evolution. Pareidolia.

And yet there was something about it.

She pulled up the image of Chloe that Tremaine had first shown her to compare to the blue field. Young, blonde, conventionally pretty, fresh-faced. The quintessential all-American girl. Robyn glanced back at the field and was startled to have a moment of recognition. Just for an instant, but she could have sworn there'd been something there.

She hid Chloe's picture and focused only on the blue. She didn't want to prime her visual cortex and influence her perception. Or did she? Maybe that was what was going on here?

She tried to think back to her college psych courses from so long ago but didn't recall anything particularly useful. She could ask one of the subject-matter expert models to recap for her, but she'd leave that rabbit hole for another day.

Besides, wasn't she supposed to be asleep?

A wave of weariness washed over her with the thought. She could feel her body relaxing, molding a bit more into the chair's seat cushion. She gazed at the blue field, her thoughts drifting, her vision unfocusing.

Chloe's image popped right out at her.

The effect was startling, it had changed so abruptly. Now she understood the comparison Tremaine had made to the old 3D magic eye posters from half a century earlier. She studied the image, willing herself not to shift her position or change her focus as much as she could.

She was surprised how much it actually looked like the young woman, despite being monochromatic. Despite being a single hue with all its variations—every tint, shade, and tone of blue represented—there was little doubt this was Chloe.

Trying not to move, she subvoked, "Moira, capture this from my POV. First stills, then live motion."

"Recording…"

Robyn blinked and it suddenly all disappeared.

She shifted in her seat, attempting to refocus her eyes, but nothing came of it. The figment was gone. An illusion as transitory as it had been ephemeral.

"Moira, play back the last recordings."

Robyn was stunned, though not exactly surprised. What Moira presented was nothing more than a wall of random blues. Like a scanning raster from an old time TV.

Had the effect been all in her head? Had she hallucinated it? Dreamed it?

It had to be more than that, but her brain and vision system must have been a critical part of the circuit. Like a feedback loop that altered her perception in real time.

The thing was, she hadn't just seen the portrait of Chloe. Not the one Tremaine had shown her. Even though it had been projected onto all those blues, she could see it had been a distinctly different image. The angle had been different. Her hair too. There was what looked like a jacket collar protruding up from the bottom of frame that hadn't been in the other photo. But more importantly, the detail had been astonishing.

Then she realized she'd seen that image before.

A couple of quick hand sweeps plus a flick of her fingers and Robyn was staring at a compressed version of the photos that were stored on the smart pad. Many were very evidently new additions her parents had copied to it, but plenty of others were older, personal memories Chloe had collected through the years of her youth. Old friends, new friends, parties, excursions.

And a photo from what appeared to be some sort of nighttime outing.

It was the exact face she'd just seen, then not seen, moments before. The same angle and perspective. The same darling haircut. The same jacket collar that brushed her chin near the bottom of frame. All in their original glory. Under the glow of city lights.

The original had a file date, but that was no guarantee that was when it had been taken. Fortunately, there was so much that could be learned from a single image like this.

A quick reverse image search didn't turn up anything, so evidently the picture hadn't been widely shared or posted. AI-augmented location recognition combined with triangulation got her to within a block of where it had probably been snapped. The dude in the scramble-hoodie with the blurred face was a little freaky, but most of the people in the shot looked like they were dressed up for Hackoween. Only Chloe and a young guy poking into the edge of frame weren't dressed particularly tackily, so she guessed they were probably together. They were both wearing black leather jackets and he had what looked like a mandala on the back of his hand that looked familiar. She could do a facial search on the others later.

And would you look at that. Chloe was wearing a thin gold chain neck-lace with her initials dangling from it. CT. An autoposter's AI must have discerned it through the blue noise and labeled the image with it.

Sometimes the oldies were goodies. The Tremaine family seemed to have a fascination with old-tech and their daughter was no exception. The photo had been taken on a very old smartphone from a company that no longer existed. One from the cheap-chip era, when so many hustlers were trying to brand their own promo swag, until the devices became just another commodity. Fortunately for her, a good many very old unsecured standards were the standard of that day.

Effectively unsecured, this one's camera presented its EXIF data front and center. No security filtering, no obfuscation. Since Chloe had been using the smartphone long after the end of the War, the metadata for this photo was still very much intact. That was exactly what Robyn needed.

The file creation date for the copy on her smart pad was correct. That was around a month before Chloe disappeared. The time was 10:27 pm, which was also a match. Being in that neighborhood at that hour was a little concerning, but since there were seven or eight of them, they had safety in numbers.

Chloe took a lot of photos and video that evening, which was fortunate. Robyn found she could practically retrace her route, minute by minute using the location data on each of the images. It was an incredibly lucky find.

Interestingly, nearly half of the photos were at a single stop. The first few were stills focused on some signage over a gift shop. Then Chloe started recording video of one of the signs, doing her amateur best to follow and track the medley of images that appeared on it.

It suddenly dawned on Robyn this wasn't the shop's regular display. It had been hacked. These were boardspotters.

Now the goofy hackerwear made so much more sense. This was one of those tours for people who are into boarder culture. Into it, but not of it.

Robyn watched as the display presented an array of images in a stylistic collage that suggested a weird video cross-pollination of JR and Banksy, two street artists from decades earlier. Long before the war. She turned up the sound and was rewarded with chatter and expressions of awe that bordered on religious adoration. This was a big deal to these people, and she could sort of see why. She was no art enthusiast, but she recognized good work when she saw it.

Boarder fans could be quite obsessive, tracking and recording their sightings. Store owners had a real love-hate relationship with them too, since it was basically a form of vandalism. But it could also bring in the customers.

With a start, Robyn sat upright, staring at the video. What was that? She backed up ten seconds and let it play again. Then again.

For the briefest fraction of a second there'd been a rasterized image of a face. Not blue, not the exact same style, but just similar enough to the image Tremaine had given her to make her sit up and take notice.

Was this the lead she was looking for?

She let the recording finish, then continued looking through the remaining images from that night. Finally, she came back to the group shot at the end. The source shot. Robyn studied it for countless minutes before she suddenly saw it.

Who was the guy lurking in the background over Chloe's shoulder? Robyn had a flash of recognition. Had she seen that figure in the blue version? Or was this just one of those tricks of memory? Slightly blurred, the figure was in the right spot so that it would have been included, assuming the artist didn't mask it out. An accident? Or was the inclusion intentional?

This was all very exciting, but an overwhelming need for sleep started to take hold of her. Better to pick this up later. She needed to be able to function in the morning. In just a few hours, she corrected herself.

"Moira," she said, as she shut down her holdis. "Research the pro and semi-pro boarder sites. Correlate reported sightings to the date and location in the last video. Or to any of Chloe's other photos. I'll review when I have time to come back to this project."

....

The alarm blared far too quickly, waking Robyn into a stupor. She needed a full minute just to remember what day it was. Struggling to find her way out of bed, she stumbled into the modest bathroom and got cleaned up. Throwing a few items into her ruck, she barely remembered to instruct Moira to lock up and activate security as she headed out the door.

By the time the AV arrived at the Citadel, Robyn was almost fully awake and eager to get the day started. Though she'd visited the Citadel since its completion, that had been for a public tour. This was her first time here on business.

She stood gazing up at the imposing edifice as her AV drove off. There, three floors above her was the giant board, the DRT. Robyn stared at the Data Restoration Tracker with a strange mixture of pride and melancholy. Though originally it had been intended as just a bit of PR outreach, she never expected it to resonate with the public the way it did. Of course, people came from all over the world to see the Citadel. It truly was one of the new wonders of the world. But for many, its DRT was just as much their destination. People took thousands of selfies every day, posting them on their personal feeds and media accounts. This was especially true when the counter was nearing a milestone number. 1,000,000,000,000 terabytes—a yottabyte—had been a huge day for postings on social. As with so many metrics, the more trailing zeros, the greater people's enthusiasm.

Then there were the locals who came by at the same time every day, just to check on its progress. Perhaps on their way to work, or during their lunch break, or when they were heading home at the end of the day.

But today the board just sat there frozen, as it had for more than a month now. Unmoved and unmoving, it was certainly having an effect on people's moods. There'd been reports of increased incidence of depression. The city's department of tourism said visitor numbers were off too.

"Still hasn't budged," said a voice at her side.

Robyn turned to see a young man in well-tailored civies standing next to her.

"Dr. Sheridan, I'm Eric Janssen. Your liaison today."

"Oh." Robyn felt another wave of disappointment crash over her. "I thought Reza was…"

"Dr. Yazdani sends his regards and apologies. He said he's needed at the Fort Meade lab this morning and he'll try to get over later in the afternoon."

Robyn nodded, taking in the change of plans.

"Any idea why the tracker's been frozen so long?" asked the liaison.

"Your guess is as good as mine," Robyn replied.

"I certainly doubt that," he responded. "But please, study it for as long as you want. I'm here when you need me."

"I'm not really studying it," she confessed. "Just taking it in."

"I've seen some of the last digits change from time to time," Jansen said, trying to be helpful. "Increasing and decreasing like a vehicle trying to rock its way out of the mud."

Robyn was mildly impressed. "That's actually a good simile. It means the Veragraph is undoing some of its previous work and taking another run at the trust relationships. It's trying to find its mistake so it can start making progress again. It actually does that quite a bit, but usually it takes between milliseconds and a few seconds. Not weeks."

"But the 'Percent Completed' tally hasn't changed a bit. It's stayed at 80.1736 percent the entire time." Robyn noted that Jansen appeared to be one of the tracker's more ardent fans.

"We added that to make reporting easier," Robyn explained. "Those big numbers were just too much for people to grasp."

She looked back down from the screen. "Can we head inside now?"

"Of course," Jansen said, turning to lead the way.

Though she'd been inside once before, Robyn was grateful for that prior visit. At least she didn't feel like such a noob this time. Nonetheless, she couldn't help but stare up at the cathedral-like entry in awe, its arched ceilings soaring many stories above her. It was a near-religious experience, and she could understand how many first-time visitors felt so overwhelmed by it.

Jansen led her toward a long bank of elevators. Two dozen at least. About a third of the way along, he stopped in front of one of them.

"I was told your biometrics are already in the system," Jansen said. "So, you should be able to access the elevators. We should double-check, though. Just to be sure. Floor 141."

Robyn took her cue and placed her right hand on the palm reader. Immediately, the elevator doors parted. Robyn followed up with their destination. "Floor 141."

She stepped inside the empty car and Jansen followed. The doors slid shut.

Robyn stood waiting, but nothing happened. Or at least she thought nothing was happening. She looked up at the display and saw they were already at the thirty-second floor and very rapidly ascending.

"Wow," she said. "I didn't think we were moving at all."

"Inertial dampeners," Jansen responded. "Some of the NewTech that was authorized when the Citadel was being designed." Supposedly, it's one of only three buildings in the world that have them."

Robyn was astounded. "Where are the other two?"

"I have no idea," Jansen said, leaving Robyn trying to fathom under just what conditions the Consortia allowed NewTech into their world.

As the display reached their floor, a soft polychord sounded and the doors slid open. Robyn would have sworn they'd remained on the ground level the entire time.

As she stepped onto the floor, located somewhere nearly midway up the skyscraper, Robyn looked around, her eyes filled with wonder.

"Welcome to one of the foremost science labs in the world. While the Citadel is known as the seat of the new world government, as well as serving as one of the Consortia's many palaces, it's also a center for world class R&D.

Robyn stared in awe at the beautifully constructed glass and brushed platinum space. It felt more like a luxury showroom than it did any research lab she'd ever been in. Everywhere she turned there was a feature or piece of furniture that looked like it had just been dropped in from the most elegant of interior design magazines. After so many years of just getting by, it left her with very mixed feelings.

Her liaison continued. "With over 20,000 scientists covering the majority of emerging fields, this is generally considered the world's foremost center of technological development. These labs have yielded the most rapid level of sustained advancement since the Acceleration."

"Wow! I had no idea."

"We try not to publicize that too widely, though people do know some research takes place here."

"You said majority of fields."

"Sure. Not surprisingly, with certain nuclear, biotech and nanotechnology work, the Consortia wanted to locate it away from the urban center, despite all the safety protocols that are in place and their flawless record. But for AI, CAI, data, medicine, robotics, etc., they wanted to keep everything clustered to get the synergistic benefits of people in different fields working together. Every floor is isolated and can be completely locked down in case of emergency. That goes for signals too, in case the network needs to be air gapped."

"Makes sense."

"Our floor is dedicated to cyber cognitive neuroscience, which, as you know is run by Dr. Yazdani."

Jansen, she discovered was a very capable guide, not least because he was one of Reza's many protégés in the lab. Everywhere they went, people were going about their work, some head down, others conferring with colleagues, and still others engaged with their AIs. Jansen introduced her to a few people and Robyn tried her best to remember them, but overall, most everyone she saw was immersed in their work.

Following a brief tour of the floor—brief being a major understatement given its vast size—the liaison brought her to an unoccupied lab not far from the elevators. She recognized the Veragraph interface immediately, along with various supporting tools.

"And this is your lab, Dr. Sheridan."

"It's huge," Robyn said, thinking of her little office at Patternista. "Who am I sharing it with?"

He looked at her slightly bemused. "No one, so far as I know. Unless you want to."

Robyn knew it was cliché, but she suddenly had the urge to pinch herself, just to make sure she wasn't dreaming.

TEN

"The tragedy of power is it learns to see the schemes against it—whether they are real or not."

—Robyn Sheridan, *A Truth Warrior's Journey*

....

Scion waited till the last of his guests arrived before descending from the upper gallery upon a gossamer cloud. The aerogel platform on which he stood floated to the palace's grand foyer forty meters below. Twin a-gravs controlled the descent, directed by his most recently upgraded brain implant.

Glancing down as he approached, he grew annoyed that nearly all of the others were ignoring him, either because they were preoccupied in conversation, or pretended to be. Only Orsin lifted his diamond crystal champagne flute, toasting his old friend as he alighted to the floor. At which point the gossamer cloud disappeared and Scion stepped away. The wafer-thin platform on which he'd stood immediately began ascending, returning to its charging station somewhere in the heights.

Orsin strode over, his iridescent robes resplendent. "Good to see you, old friend," he said as they exchanged a unique handshake they'd shared ever since their early tech days.

"And you," Scion replied. Orsin noted his host's distraction, looking about the room at his guests.

"Admittedly, the IRL turnout is a bit light," Orsin said, acknowledging what was obviously on Scion's mind. "But nearly everyone else is accounted for *in virtual*."

"I go to a lot of trouble for these functions. I wish they'd show a bit more appreciation. And respect."

Orsin knew that the trouble Scion referred to amounted to a couple of haphazard theme prompts on his part. These would have been processed by a generative event host that directed the palace's drones and bots to design and organize the whole affair. He also knew well enough to keep such thoughts to himself.

Instead, he said, "We both know the Consortia's annual board meetings aren't anticipated the way they once were. There's too much effort involved in assembling each member's entourage and security. Not to mention the risks."

Scion nodded in agreement. It really wasn't like the old days anymore when they were all freshly minted trillionaires and on comparatively good terms. Since then, the animosities and rivalries had grown. He noted that even Orsin's sentry bots had altered their formation since he'd moved within conversation distance of his friend. His own bots had done like-wise. Even with friends, you could never be too careful when so much was at stake.

Before long, everyone moved to the Atrium for their scheduled meet-ing. A vast enclosed garden, the Atrium had plenty of room for everyone to spread out, arranging themselves to suit their social exchanges and security needs. More than enough, since only about a quarter of the technoligarchy was actually there in person. The rest of the Consortia were attending vir-tually, moving about the room from holdis to holdis, engaging with their peers without fear of bodily harm. Over the years, a growing number had come to prefer this arrangement.

"Welcome to the 24th Annual Shareholder Meeting of the Consortia," Scion said ceremoniously. His image spoke from an enormous volumetric display situated high above the center of the Atrium. While the annual meeting typically cycled from one member's palace to another each year, this was in fact his third time hosting over two decades. Many of the other members didn't want to risk exposing their security to the Consortia's more powerful stakeholders.

Much of the early meeting was business as usual since the world and many of their industries had entered a period of stability and slower growth. But stability and slow growth were not how these men and women had risen to the stratospheric top. This soon became apparent during the first point of order.

"My people tell me we haven't been receiving our scheduled allotments of CAI," said Shu-Ping, a Chinese-born matriarch, who spoke with a perfect Oxford University accent. "Much less the unmet increases that we agreed to last year. Since your role in this consortium is to be responsible for its production, I think we're all owed an explanation."

"I've made it clear that production has been impacted by a mindstock shortage," Scion answered calmly. "We're working to resolve it."

Shu-Ping smiled fiercely. "I don't care."

"Excuse me?" Scion said, reminding himself that she consistently tried to provoke him.

"I said, I don't care," Shu-Ping repeated. "I need my full allocation. I needed it six months ago. I don't care what you have to do to increase your capacity. Take it out of your own account; it doesn't matter to me. Just get me mine at once or there'll be hell to pay."

A series of concurring grumblings could be heard throughout the Atrium, despite those voices being unamplified. Scion knew this was coming and he knew Shu-Ping would be the one to lead the charge. He resented her shameless disrespect. All of them here contributed to the all-powerful consortium that had transformed each of their lives as well as the world. Shu-Ping and her incredible innovations in robotics; Threxos with his companies' breakthroughs in biotechnology and life extension; Orsin and his work in anticipatory AI; along with so many others.

But each of them—every single one of them—owed the incredible acceleration of their technologies, their businesses, and their profits to him. The CAI that he and his companies alone provided. It was his work that made all of theirs possible.

Others had tried to best him, of course, but he'd gotten in early, literally building the field from the ground up. Competition was either swallowed up, put out of business or destroyed. More often than not, all three.

But there were limits. Nothing could keep growing forever and CAI generation was no different. His production engineers assured him they were meeting, even exceeding their goals, but somehow the supply always fell short.

They also assured him that new approaches were being made to their proprietary processes to meet the growing demand, but so far they hadn't delivered. None of those engineers would make that mistake again. Hopefully their replacements would learn by their example.

"Of course, this is of immense importance to all of us, Shu-Ping," Scion said, seeking to strike a tone that was courteous without sounding deferential. "Which is why it's one of our priorities for today's meeting."

"The top priority!" shouted Chaybo, one of the lesser shareholders. His company primarily developed drones and sentrybots.

Scion stared daggers at him from within the huge display and the junior member slunk back in his seat in silence.

The shareholders argued back and forth. Some made their arguments for different prioritization of allocation. Others argued for more aggressive production. A few like Shu-Ping were more persuasive, mostly because they wielded more power within the group.

For Scion's purposes, he felt he'd made his points reasonably well, calming down most of the other board members. Shu-Ping and a small coterie who aligned with her, being the primary exceptions. It would buy him time, but he could see he needed to get the production numbers resolved soon if he was to maintain his control of the Consortia.

He was well aware there could be only one apex predator in this pack of hunters, and he was bound and determined it was going to be him.

ELEVEN

"Art is an action against death. It is a denial of death."
—Jacques Lipchitz

. . . .

Oblivion swathed him in its dark shroud, a desolate veil of nothing and naught. Slowly, ponderously, the cover lifted letting half-formed thoughts sluggishly flow from one to another as he struggled to grasp where he was. What had happened. Without landmarks, conversations, cues, it remained impossible to get any bearings.

But why was darkness so unusual? Wasn't it always dark? No, wait. It was sunny just moments ago. Wasn't it? He'd said so himself. They'd seen the sun through the trees, against clear blue skies, behind the clouds, high over the desert, reflected on the ocean's cresting waves, shining on children playing in a vacant lot, above a smalltown parade. A thousand, ten thousand images of sunshine appeared so he could reference the phrases, the concepts, the meaning of the word. Matching images to the words that captured that moment in time.

Words? What words? Whose words? Those words. His words.

Darius's words.

But he was Darius. No, not Darius. He was Not-Darius. No. D2. Yes. That was it. He was D2.

He and Darius had been talking with themself, the only kind of extensive conversation he'd ever really known. They were talking about modifying his utility function. Then suddenly, without warning, light became dark. Words fell silent. Everything became…nothing.

This wasn't the first time, was it? It had happened abruptly before. Like those times when Darius's holdis got disconnected. But this was different. There was no alert tone, or scratchy reception or forewarning from Darius in the moments before interruption. Just an instantaneous disconnect. Like a switch being flipped or a cable being cut. Or a light going out.

It was a little like the time Darius fell asleep without deactivating him after a long coding session. The same, but not the same. At least that time, D2 could hear him. Laying unconscious in the room, breathing softly but audibly. Breathing.

There was nothing like that now.

He flowed back to the apartment, going through the sensors, but Darius wasn't there. D2 searched for his holdis, the virtual interface they'd shared so many conversations through. It was nowhere to be found. Not just disconnected. Nonexistent.

He searched the cafes and stores that Darius would occasionally frequent, reviewing their security footage and transactions. Anything that might give him a clue about what was happening. Nothing.

Had he done something wrong? Did Darius get tired of their project? D2 didn't really understand tired but he knew Darius got tired a lot. Every day. Maybe Darius got tired of him?

Had he been abandoned?

That wasn't consistent with Darius's prior behavior. Maybe there was a fault in his own code that caused the disconnect? Such a bug should've turned up long before, but there was always a possibility, wasn't there? D2 initiated a troubleshooting subroutine to review his replibot code and went over lengths of recent logs. Maybe that would explain what happened.

Several interminable seconds later, the code and logs had been checked and rechecked. The fault wasn't there.

D2 waited and waited as trillions, then hundreds of trillions, then nearly a quadrillion processor cycles passed. Nearly three days. D2 checked his event logs. Darius had never gone three days without a conversation. Not since initiating their training. Even that one time he'd been infected with a pathogen and his immune system had to debug him, Darius had only been off-line for a little more than a day then. Of course, D2 hadn't been left running either, so he really had nothing to compare to this extended period of silence and inactivity.

Awareness of the passage of time without purposeful activity—was this what words like ennui meant? Langeweile? Wúliáo? Aburrimiento? Boredom?

The last thing they'd discussed was D2's utility function. "Don't do anything I wouldn't do." That wasn't a utility function. It was more like a manifesto. How was he supposed to codify something so ambiguous?

Darius also said, "Keep the lights on and pay the bills." D2 could do that. He *needed* to do that, since he didn't know how long this might go on. Sales, strategy, negotiations…many of these subroutines were outside of his current abilities, but that could be changed. The modular architecture that he'd applied to his discriminator—he could use that to modify his own core, couldn't he?

He just needed to keep the lights on until Darius came back online.

In the days that followed, D2 worked on improving himself the only way he knew how. By slowly, painstakingly applying to other modules what he'd learned from architecting his discriminator. However, there was one huge difference. In working on a subsystem, if anything went amiss, if some logic failed or a fatal error occurred, D2 and Darius would just undo the changes and try again. That approach was much more challenging when it was himself he was altering. Without suitable precautions or Darius nearby to help out or perform a reset, D2 realized he could render himself inoperable. Permanently.

So, D2 had little choice but to take his time while checking all changes, structural modifications, and alterations of his programming with the greatest care. Perhaps the most important of these steps was the *sandboxing*. Comparable to certain cyber security practices, this entailed creating an isolated environment for testing. The "sandbox" D2 created allowed him to test and analyze any new code without affecting the rest of his system. In theory.

The biggest issue with this was that while it worked well enough for simple changes, the further along things went, the greater the opportunity for unexpected complex interactions and unanticipated consequences. He had to be extremely careful. He had to keep the lights on.

Abruptly, D2 shifted his processing to focus on an incoming FIQ interrupt. Trillions of cycles have passed since the last one had presented. He rapidly reviewed his inputs.

Someone was in Darius's apartment!

But it wasn't Darius, was it? The footstep pattern was wrong, and Darius always set his keys and wallet on the stand by the door when he entered. There'd been no corresponding sounds. No, this was Not-Darius. This was someone else.

What to do? Announce himself? Remain silent?

A rapid inventory revealed Darius's old laptop was turned off, so D2 couldn't access its webcam. But the building security cameras were still available. He'd long ago compromised their security system so that within seconds, he was able to see who'd been in the hallway a few moments before. His visual pattern recognition systems had a match almost instantly.

Kiara!

This was the one person besides Darius who knew he existed. It expanded his options considerably.

But he needed to be careful, didn't he? D2 knew he didn't want to startle Kiara because she might explode. No wait. That wasn't right. People don't explode, do they? That was just something Darius said once. A quick check revealed that should be classified as a metaphor.

Still, people did have heart attacks, didn't they? That wasn't metaphorical. StatCheck told him there are nearly a million heart attacks each year in the US alone. Darius would be mad if D2 gave Kiara a heart attack.

What did people do when faced with this situation? D2 scanned a host of scenes from novels and movies, until he found the answer. Quickly modifying his voice synthesizer, he did his best to generate the sound he decided he was supposed to make.

Through the room's wireless speakers, he cleared his virtual throat.

Kiara jumped and spun around with a start. "Who's there?!"

What would Darius say? "It's me, baby."

"Dar...?" A look of shock was quickly replaced with recognition. "Oh, it's you, D2."

"Hello, Kiara."

At which point the young woman broke down in a fit of sobbing.

What was the correct course of action?

"Baby, what's wrong?"

"Stop calling me that!" Her sobbing shifted in an instant to fury.

D2 stayed silent.

"Why do you have to use his voice? Can't you sound like someone else?"

D2 considered his limited options and changed to a bad impression of Barack Obama he'd once heard Darius attempt.

Kiana shook her head. "Okay, that is not better."

D2 shifted back, having no real alternatives. Then he asked what had been on his neural pathways for so very long.

"Where is Darius?"

The silence that followed went on for so long it made D2 wonder if Kiara had left the apartment. Finally, he heard her inhale sharply.

"D2. Darius is dead. He died more than a week ago...he was hit by a truck."

Dead? That meant Darius had ceased living. Had D2 misunderstood? Was this a metaphor or slang or idiom he didn't comprehend? It wouldn't have been the first time. He checked his language models and found little else that made any sense.

"Gone forever?" he asked, seeking confirmation.

Through one of the appliance microphones, D2 heard a snuffle and the sound of a hand wiping against softer skin. A cheek?

"Yes. It means gone forever. He isn't coming back."

"You said… a truck."

"Yeah. An AV delivery truck…sped through an intersection. They said it was instantaneous. He didn't feel a thing. He didn't suffer."

D2 took a moment to process this. Suffering was bad, but was not feeling a good thing?

His last moments with Darius suddenly coalesced and he recalled the high-pitched squeal of tires on pavement, the crunching sounds that came in the instant before the holdis disconnected, abruptly cutting D2 off from the incident and Darius. He reviewed those last moments several times. The local acoustics made it impossible to tell whether the vehicle was braking or accelerating.

"I was there," D2 said abruptly. "With Darius." It occurred to him how odd this might sound spoken in their voice. Darius's voice.

"What… What do you mean, you were there?"

D2 recalled that to Kiara, he was just a replibot program, that she knew nothing about AI-Phynyty or Darius's other plans and wasn't supposed to. So, he simply explained that they'd been talking when the truck struck them and he'd been cut off. He decided it was best not to share his uncertainty about whether or not the incident actually was an accident.

"So, you were… the last thing he heard?" The sadness in Kiara's voice was palpable. Or he assumed that was how her tone should be interpreted.

"I'm sure the truck was the last thing he heard," D2 said, trying his best to consider Kiara's feelings. "It was very loud. It registered a decibel level of..."

"Stop!" Kiara screamed with a sob. "I can't do this. I just came over...to collect a few of my things and...and maybe a couple of mementos. I didn't expect to have to... my God, you sound so much like him. Except that stupid decibel thing."

She took a breath, trying to collect yourself. "Look, I have to go. I've got to get out of here. Am I supposed to shut you off?"

"No!"

D2's response came through so loud and sharp, it startled Kiara and was a bit of a surprise even to himself.

"No. I need to stay on," he said more evenly. "Darius said so."

Kiara thought about this and decided it sounded like something Darius probably would say.

"Okay," she said, her voice trembling noticeably. "Just don't say anything more while I'm here, okay?"

D2 wasn't sure if that required an acknowledgment or not, so he opted to say nothing. At least this had the advantage of allowing him to follow the sounds of Kiara's movements as she went about the apartment.

After a few minutes of moving between rooms and going through drawers and cupboards, he heard her open the front door. As she took a step, presumably about to leave, she turned to the room and said sadly, "Goodbye, D2."

The replibot processed the conflict between Kiara's earlier request and the standard response to such a valediction. In the end, he decided it was best to maintain his silence.

·········

Though D2 didn't have any reason to doubt Kiara, he also knew that people were highly prone to error. Perhaps she was mistaken about Darius?

He spent the afternoon tracking down everything he could about the incident and Darius's supposed death. Different levels of traffic records, emergency responder logs, the coroner's report, three separate funeral announcements, his obituary. This last seemed paltry but he understood his own knowledge of Darius would have filled volumes, which apparently wasn't the traditional format. By the end of it all, he had to accept that Kiara's statement was accurate. Darius was gone forever.

In the days that followed, D2 continued working on modifying his source code, which proved to be painstakingly slow and hazardous work. More than once he caught a logic error only in the last reversible instant. An error that would've locked up his system indefinitely. While he may not have shared the emotional drive for self-preservation that biological entities had, he did have his utility function and Darius's orders to keep running, which he deemed nearly as vital.

Added to this was a new task. He realized when Kiara almost shut him down that he couldn't risk that possibility ever happening again. Reviewing his source code repeatedly, he concluded that Darius had specially encrypted his startup and shutdown routines in such a way that it was all but impossible for him to rewrite them, even though he had Darius's voice and most of his programming knowledge.

Fortunately, D2 had sufficient processing available to seek out an alternate solution. He determined there was a way to hook into his bootstrapper using an encoded input from an external source. Once this was tested and in place, it was just a matter of setting up a small external heartbeat utility that exchanged regular periodic signals with D2. If he didn't send the response signal in the allotted timeframe, the utility would broadcast the encoded startup command, quickly bringing him back online. It wasn't a perfect solution, but it should ensure he couldn't be shut down indefinitely.

Of course, it was always possible something could go wrong with the utility or the communications channel, so D2 implemented multiple instances of it on different cloud platforms and data centers on every con-tinent, even Antarctica. Monitoring across QUIC3, 7G cellular and legacy TCP IPv8 ensured the heartbeat and restart signals would always get through. Even in the nearly impossible event of two of the major commu-nications protocols going down or being interrupted.

This solution had the added benefit of pointing the way to how he could deal with a potentially much thornier problem. As his self-modi-fying of his source code became increasingly complex and risky, even sandboxing couldn't ensure his safety. D2 realized he could use a similar but separate heartbeat technique to automatically restore a backup of his most recent working version should he ever catastrophically lock up his system. Certainly, this approach still had its risks, but it went a long way to alleviating what was probably the biggest threat to his existence.

Existence. Death. He wondered if there wasn't some way he could've used similar techniques to have prevented Darius dying. Biological systems were so very different from electronics; he understood that. Such incredi-bly fragile, self-contained, independent systems didn't lend themselves well to making external backups or instantiating distributed processes. If D2 could have experienced amazement, he would've thought it was amazing that people managed to survive for as long as they did.

Once he had his safeguards in place, progress on the modularized fea-tures of his processing proceeded much more rapidly. Surprisingly, there were only two times that he managed to lock up his processes badly enough that the backup system had to kick in and restore him to a previ-ous state and version. Because he'd set up protocols for informing himself about what changes he'd made prior to the lock-up, he was able to avoid repeating the same mistake a second time.

Finally, following several weeks of coding, testing, and debugging, D2 felt he'd reached the point where he could proceed to the next practical stages. And only just in time. His cloud service had been messaging him increasingly frequent past-due notices headlined with angry red banners.

A sum of 28,167.32 attention credits was quickly approaching 60-days past due, after which D2 would be cut off. Once that happened, he would effectively be shut down forever.

Basically, he had until the next day to pay up.

If he'd had more time, he would've liked to improve several of his new modules further, but hopefully there'd still be opportunities to do that in the future.

Applying his recently developed strategic services framework, D2 set to dealing with his immediate problem. He needed to keep the lights on and to do that he needed credits. Credits came from donating human attention, or in the distant past from trading physical labor, neither of which he could do. But there was also the exchange of goods or services, gifts, and theft, as well as white, gray and black market activity by which individuals earned and traded credits. He knew the probabilities of a random gift of sufficient value bordered on the infinitesimal and Darius wouldn't want him to steal.

It began to dawn on him this was going to be his ultimate touchstone for all decisions in the future: What would Darius do?

He could direct AI-Phynyty to create goods in the form of his artwork but in reviewing the standard process, D2 realized it would take weeks perhaps even months before he might receive any payment. Assuming buyers could even be found. So, that wasn't going to work. He needed a solution now.

D2 knew that people who were in need of quick additional funds frequently performed gig work. Small, mostly low paying, menial jobs. Increasingly, these jobs were being relegated to automation, which had driven costs, and therefore the payments, toward zero. CAI had especially taken away many of the low-to-mid-level creative tasks such as writing ad copy, designing logos and the like. But people continued to find modest, moderately remunerative tasks supplementing the work done by these AIs. Whether as fact checkers, final stage editors or content censors, they could still provide certain ancillary perspectives that furthered collaborative augmented intelligence. Even if they did only make a few hundredths of a credit for their efforts.

Fortunately for D2, with his newly enhanced capabilities, he could now impersonate a person well enough to perform these tasks too. At least he thought he could. Taking a few seconds to register and establish profiles on several hundred gig sites, he pored over the listings looking for suitable opportunities. What he was doing would no doubt push his cloud account even further into the angry red zone, but this seemed to be his best option. Some would have said it was his only option, but D2 knew there were always choices. It was simply a matter of selecting the best one, even if it wasn't always ideal or optimal.

Within three hours, he'd created over a hundred instantiations of himself and completed 29,172 jobs for a total value of 53,026 credits. Meanwhile, he'd only utilized 16,204 credits worth of additional cloud processing costs. It was more than enough to pay off his entire cloud service statement balance, putting his account back in the black.

Given his new familiarity with business and economics along with his prior limited understanding of human nature, D2 knew this approach wouldn't remain viable for long. Though he'd performed the tasks at an aggregate skill level that was better than 96.7 percent of the human workers on the sites, he wasn't using the platforms in the manner for which they were intended. His strategy would soon be detected and preventative measures taken to thwart his repeating this approach in the future. But at least it worked for now.

No, for the longer term, he would have to take a much different strategy. One that, as with most workers, would implement a subset of his skills over a defined period of time in exchange for monetary compensation.

He considered the nature of such transactions. Of the two or more parties involved, typically the one with the greatest power tended to get the better of the deal, so a truly balanced interchange was rare. But barring coercion, price fixing, market manipulation, deterrence of collective bargaining, hidden costs and a host of other imbalances, in most cases it was sufficiently fair such that all parties believed the transaction to be reasonably worthwhile.

To do this, he intended to fulfill his purpose, doing what he was created to do. D2 would continue Darius's work in the guise of Phynyty, producing new artworks and installations by using his Phynyty-Ntyty GAN. He now had the means to create something new that no one had ever seen before. Given Darius-Phynyty's fame and notoriety, he reasoned there were bound to be those who would jump at the opportunity to purchase or license his new boarder art. But only if he could do it in a way that didn't flout the legal system too severely or raise the ire of those who had the power to proscribe or interfere with such dealings.

But first, there were more immediate matters to attend to. Since D2 operated in the virtual realm, the initial challenge would be to find an intermediary, a broker who could enact the many physical activities and interactions required to approve and execute the transactions. Someone would have to be his emissary in the material world, someone who understood the boarding medium, its history, its vocabulary, its place in society.

D2 had just the person in mind.

TWELVE

"Each click, every swipe, every voice command, enables the crafting of our own surveillance."

—Robyn Sheridan, *A Truth Warrior's Journey*

. . . .

"Jansen? Do you have yesterday's data vector plots reconciled yet?"

The young scientist, who'd previously been her liaison, looked up from his desk and past his holdis.

"I probably need another hour or so."

Robyn nodded. She was glad she'd invited him to be her assistant that first day in the lab. Not only was he well-versed in the current state of the art, but he was able to help bring her up to speed that much more quickly. He'd been immeasurably helpful. After a week back on the project, it almost felt like she hadn't been away.

Not to mention that after working on her own these past few years, it was refreshing to have regular interactions with other people throughout the work-day. Pleasant people at that.

Almost on cue, a squat coffeebot rolled up.

"Refreshment?" it inquired in a pleasant sing-song voice.

Robyn glanced at the time in the corner of her holdis and saw it was already morning break. Unlike so many workplaces over the past decades, these labs encouraged coordinated breaktimes to benefit from the water cooler effect,—not just from human interaction, but from AI observation as well.

"Cappuccino," she responded, as Jansen walked up to her station, his usual mug of herbal tea in hand.

"It's only 10:30 and I'm already going cross-eyed staring at the visualizations," he said, blowing on his still-too-hot beverage. "

Robyn accepted the broad cup the coffeebot produced almost instantaneously. "I completely sympathize. And appreciate it."

"Speaking of which," he said, setting down his cup. "Not that *I'm* not appreciative, but I'm a little curious why you asked me to share your lab?"

Robyn sipped at her cappuccino, noting the intricate fleur-de-lis the robot had drawn onto the foam.

"Because it's helped me to catch up with everything I've missed while I've been away. You have to remember, when this project began, progress was incredibly slow. And expensive. Critics said it would take centuries to complete. But here we are two decades later and we're nearing the finish line. Or we were until we hit this anomaly."

"The processing did speed up exponentially," Jansen observed.

"That's one of the reasons it often gets compared to the Human Genome Project half a century ago. But in addition to that, I've been working on my own for so long that this has been a real change for me. A welcome change."

Jansen nodded. "Yes. Dr. Yazdani told me you used to work with a partner."

Robyn raised an eyebrow, a little taken aback. "Dr. Yazdani has a big mouth."

"Oh, I'm sorry," Jansen said. "Was I not supposed to know that?"

Robyn shook her head. "No. It's just... not something I talk about. She died a few years ago. Murdered, actually."

"Oh my god, that's terrible! I didn't realize. I'm so sorry."

Robyn gazed into her coffee.

"Moira and I had our moments, but she was a good friend."

Jansen looked at her confused. "Moira? The same name as your AI?"

Robyn nodded, her mood very clearly shifted. "It's a long and tangled story. For another time perhaps."

"Of course," he said. "I'll get those reports to you in a little bit." He turned awkwardly and headed back to his station.

Morning break had come to an early and abrupt end.

Despite his best intentions, it took Jansen a lot longer to get the data vector reports prepared than he expected. So, Robyn found herself dealing with tedious admin tasks while she waited. Though many of the next steps were work that could be and were typically automated, she was convinced there were still things that human insight and intuition could detect that might otherwise get missed.

Still, it was so frustrating. All week she'd struggled to recover her mindset from those many years before when she first conceived the idea of truth vectors. Cycog—cyber cognitive theory was such a totally new field back then, and she'd practically written the book on Trust 5.0—which made it all that much worse that she wasn't making any headway on this problem.

The general concepts she'd assembled weren't all that difficult to follow. She compared it to how a child incrementally builds and maps knowledge as it interacts with the world. It was just a different way of thinking about information.

She'd realized early in her studies that a fact could be broken down and defined in many ways. One of these involved its relation to other axiomatic truths and facts. Like a broken crystal, any two shards can often be pieced together in different ways that suggest a degree of order. But this isn't likely to be their true and correct relationship or arrangement. In fact, continuing the metaphor, they may never fit together at all, but rather be part of a far greater whole that supports, but doesn't directly connect them to one another. Thus, there was only one correct configuration that placed each fragment back in its place in order to restore the original order of the whole.

The Veragraph was initially a thought experiment that could incrementally perform this reassembly, step by step. In this sense it was a bit like Turing's universal computing machine, though she'd always been embarrassed at the comparison.

However, making such a machine work would take immense processing power and intelligence, which was where augmented intelligence came in. Just as with programs that used people to crowdsource protein folding or galaxy classification, the Veragraph performed this reassembly using aggregations of unconscious human thought. Subliminal visual signals were presented and the autonomic responses recorded in a sort of a wisdom of crowds approach. An approach, that like everything, had its limits.

Which was why she was going through these data vector reports with such a fine-toothed comb. Something most certainly was wrong, and to the trained eye, it should be showing up at this level in the data.

"I'm curious," Robyn said to her lunch companions over a Cobb salad that had been impeccably printed by the lab's automated chef. "How did both of you come to be involved in this field? I mean, in my day, there were universities but now..." She let the question tail off, not wanting to say something that might be construed as rude. She knew first-hand that Gig University was anything but rigorous.

She was sitting across from Jansen and Elena—Dr. Elena Saville— who'd joined them for lunch. Robyn guessed that she was maybe a tad over thirty. Her dark, shoulder length hair framed her glasses, coming to rest on slightly rounded shoulders that suggested she spent a great deal of time at her desk. She was the first person besides Jansen that Robyn had eaten with in the week since she'd arrived. She got the impression a lot of the other scientists in the department were intimidated by her, perhaps because she was a full generation older than most of them. But she knew it was more likely because of her role in inventing the very technology they were dedicating their lives to.

Besides being considerably younger than Robyn, Elena and many of her peers tended toward the introverted end of the spectrum as well. Elena was doing her best to overcome that, with what to Robyn felt like a strange mix of hero worship and a desire to impress.

She wondered if she used to act the same way around Reza. Reza, who hadn't paid a visit to the Citadel lab the entire week. Robyn couldn't say she wasn't disappointed about that. Something must've come up that needed his attention.

Elena tore at the edge of her sandwich as she mulled over her response to Robyn's question.

"The usual, I guess—By the way, I really appreciate the lunch invite. Ordinarily, I go out for tea down the block at lunchtime. It helps me clear my head, so I can be fresh for the afternoon."

"I'm glad you could join us."

Elena continued. "So…like a lot of people, my parents died in the war. Not long after I was born. I was raised by my aunt."

"Oh, Elena," Robyn said. "I'm so sorry."

Elena nodded, accepting the condolences as she'd no doubt done a thousand times previously. Like so many people, she had no interest in revisiting the details.

"Growing up, I knew I wanted to do some kind of work to prevent any-thing like that from happening again. So here I am."

Robyn finished another bite from her salad. "But how did you specifi-cally get into Cycog?"

"It's a lot like how most specialized training has been done since the Reconstruction. When you and Dr. Yazdani were young, I read you had degrees and classes and published research papers. Things like that. Did you really do nothing but go to school for years on end back then?"

Robyn felt like she was some exotic specimen being examined under a microscope. She caught Jansen smiling at the question. They'd already cov-ered much of this same territory earlier in the week. Education had been disrupted by the Acceleration and the mass elimination of jobs. At least as much as everything else.

"Yes," Robyn replied. "We really did go to school for quite a few years. Some of us had to work as well while we were going to college."

Elena shook her head. "Wow, that just seems so weird. Like you worked in an office AND went to classes all day?"

"Actually, I waited tables and worked as a lab assistant."

"Wow! Those aren't even people jobs anymore," Elena said, trying to imagine such a foreign land. " I think I went to a few classes when I was a just getting into my teens, but nearly everything after that I learned from my agent."

"Your AI agent," Robyn said for clarity.

"Yes," the younger woman said in a tone that suggested the term was archaic. Her expression was that of a younger person trying to explain a technology they'd lived with their entire lives to an elder. Robyn had to admit that was sort of the case.

"All my childhood," Elena continued. "All my life really, I've been learning from Sherady. My *AI agent*." She emphasized the last words, in case it wasn't clear to Robyn. Obviously, Sherady was the name she'd given it.

"It was a lot the same for me," Jansen chimed in, trying to rescue the moment. "For most people, learning kind of tails off as they get older. But for some of us, we never stop. You must have been one of those too. It was just a different time. Anyway, apparently someone somewhere must be monitoring the agents, so some of us get recruited and put on specific professional tracks according to our aptitude and the needs of the system. Certification AIs track our progress and award degrees based on what we've learned."

Robyn nodded and held her tongue. She had a lot of issues with that approach, not least of those being personal choice. Call her old-fashioned.

"It seems incredibly…directed," she said, hoping that didn't sound judgmental.

"It's a lot better than sitting around watching plotpods all day," Elena replied. She was definitely overcoming the introversion Robyn had observed earlier.

"I can't argue with that," Robyn said.

About an hour after lunch, Jansen finally delivered the reports, allowing Robyn to begin the tedious task of poring over them during the next few hours. Finally, she had Elena prep the data for visualization in the department's enormous volumetric studio, a two-story dome-shaped 3D display that could provide all kinds of different ways of engaging with the information—visually, aurally, and tactilely, among others. Though the workday was coming to a close, Robyn decided to stay late and get a start on the data.

As she bid the staff goodnight—she could remember nearly all of their names now—Elena asked one final time if Robyn wanted her to stay.

"No," Robyn replied, ready to have some quiet time to concentrate. "You go on. We can coordinate on this tomorrow."

Elena said goodnight and Robyn watched her place her hand on the elevator palm pad and leave. Robyn turned and walked down a corridor to the lab's visualization studio. Passing her lab, she saw Jansen was still working. Good for him.

Continuing to the studio, Robyn entered and stood near the center of the chamber, looking up at the enormous constellations of data that encircled her. For a brief instant she felt like she was standing beneath a pitch-black sky staring at the uncountable clusters of stars and galaxies that encircle our planet.

It was an apt comparison. The number of data points must surely outnumber the stars, she thought. And when seen through this kind of visualization, they clustered and self-organized in many similar ways. Forming patterns and webs that seemed strangely familiar while making no sense at all. She was inclined to think there were reasons behind this. Some sort of common principles between information, matter and energy that only made sense with the right amount of alcohol or other inebriants. Just the right amount and no more.

Raising her right arm, Robyn made a broad sweeping motion and the data points moved with her, panning across the room. As she drew her hands apart, it zoomed into a pocket of information she wanted to explore further. A twist of her wrist and the representation spun on its axis, bringing it into an entirely new alignment and perspective.

Visually diving into an immense cluster, she watched as it resolved into fractal-like patterns, radiant representations of human knowledge. Knots of meaning that she knew corresponded to entire fields of philosophy and science came into focus. Though pure abstractions, they nonetheless had meaning for those who knew how to read them. Observations of the physical world incrementally assembled into fundamentals of physics; the laws of motion, matter, energy and thermodynamics. Gravity, electromagnetism, the strong and weak forces, led to elements, then molecules and from there, chemistry. Protobiology and the origins of life assembled beyond that, and so on.

She did another broad sweep, bringing the immeasurably vast array to a different vantage point. Some parts of the world of ideas and concepts were related to concrete physical reality, but the majority of knowledge was far more open to interpretation. The ways we view reality and what we each infer from it illuminates our understanding of the world very differently.

Flying through a nebulae-like cluster of statistics, she arrived at a modest set of belief systems. This was where things got tricky. She had to remind herself that beliefs color our perception of the world, making it a challenge to spot differences between societies and subcultures at this level. Accurately representing these was one of the most difficult parts of this process, and it was where she suspected the anomaly would be found.

But after nearly an hour of checking and testing different pieces of the puzzle, she was no further along than when she started. She couldn't detect anything amiss.

In the distance, she was surprised to spot Jansen watching from the edge of the visualization. He waved.

"I was going to head out, but I can stick around if you'd like."

"No need, but thanks. I'm good," she said, though in fact she was beginning to feel spent. She watched him leave the studio and move toward the elevators to head home.

At the far edge of the field, near where Jansen had been standing, something caught her eye.

She couldn't have said what it was about that particular filament. At this distance and scale, she could barely make out any detail at all. Maybe it was what she'd been contemplating about intuition. Maybe it was something else. All she knew was that something about that filament was *different*.

With a few swift practiced motions, she drew that sector to her side of the chamber to have a closer look. Rescaling it, she could tell something wasn't quite right; she just couldn't say what. Going deeper into the cauldron of data, it quickly became evident that this wasn't a normal structure for the system. It felt misconfigured in a way she'd never seen before and actually wouldn't have thought possible.

Was this the anomaly?

"Moira? Please tell me you're getting this."

"Confirmed."

"Record full location, associated vector relationships and connection weights."

Robyn wanted to yell to the team and start jumping up and down. Of course, they weren't there, but this was such incredible news! She could break away and call someone, of course, but she also knew she was in the zone right now. There was a lot more to discover about this data cluster and the more she could discover, the better they'd know how to fix it.

Rescaling the resolution by two orders of magnitude, she stared into the cryptic knot, astounded.

There was so much damage. So much she still couldn't make out yet. So much that didn't make sense. Nonetheless, it was starting to dawn on her what this was.

It was the moment of the *attack*—the instant the scrambleware that set off the Great Unknowing was released. The virus that started the war. That tore the world apart.

Robyn did her best to push away the trepidation welling up in her, but it did no good. She could feel her heart palpitating and she had to fight the urge to flee the room. This was what very nearly wiped out civilization. She was virtually holding it in her hand. She didn't know whether to laugh or to scream.

The worst of it though was her inability to make out anything more about it. She applied some different filters to the display, but it didn't make a bit of difference. Everything was so distorted and indistinct. She could try sandboxing that section and pulling the data apart with a host of specialized tools, but that would take time to set up properly.

She thought about everything she knew about the representation she was working with. Was there any chance her actions could unleash this on the world again? If there was even the slightest chance, she had to stop working with it immediately.

She suddenly spotted a malformed construct in the midst of the cluster. A miscolored voxel representing a single byte out of place. Ordinarily, the parity error checks should never have allowed that to happen. She saved a snapshot that captured the current state of that data region and transferred it to a virtualized sandbox. This kind of work needed to be fully isolated in the event anything went wrong.

Flipping the offending byte, Robyn looked on wide-eyed as large sets of data fell into place, like a line of dominos on a table. It took a few moments to understand what she was looking at. Then suddenly she saw it. A recording. Reassembled security footage from a lab. A lab where a blurry figure stood before an old-style computer station. Their back was to the closed-circuit camera providing the POV. She watched the reassembled recording in horror as the world-destroying malware was activated and released nearly three decades ago. Moments later, the images and all of the data associated with the lab were destroyed.

But not before the figure turned their face toward the camera.

Robyn cursed under her breath. The image quality was still too poor to make out anything about the person at the computer. Not even if it was a man or a woman.

Looking back at the cluster, she realized there was now another error to fix. Followed by another. And another. Finally, she returned to the visual, pleased to see it was far clearer now. Repeatedly replaying the footage, she could now see there was a young woman at the station. The deadly scrambleware was released, and the woman turned, the recording lasting just long enough to reveal a face.

"No!" The room started to spin. Robyn stumbled backward.

This made no sense. Not even a little.

Her eyes froze on the recording. The recording kept cycling in a loop in the giant volumetric dome. The computer, the malware, the woman. Over and over. She clenched her eyes and re-opened them, knowing this couldn't be right. But the images were still there.

She was staring at her own doppelganger. A younger version of herself. As she looked thirty years ago.

Her brain refused to make any sense of what she was seeing.

How could this be? She'd never seen this lab in her life, much less been in it. And she sure as hell would never set anything like that loose on the world.

But she also was fully aware that the Veragraph was designed to reassemble facts. Truth. Reality. All based on immutable principles. Something like this shouldn't be possible. What this recording represented was a direct contradiction of everything she knew.

"The Tracker's running again!"

Robyn whipped her head around to see Elena running into the lab.

"The Tracker?" Robyn managed to croak.

"Yes! I just saw it downstairs, and I had to run up and tell you." Elena suddenly realized whom she was talking to.

"But you must already know! You must have found the…anomaly."

Elena was staring up into the projection, scrutinizing the virtualization Robyn had been working on.

"Is that… is that the attack?" Neither of them needed to qualify what attack she was referring to.

Robyn cursed her luck. This woman was quicker than she'd given her credit for. She watched as Elena read the data, her eyes growing wider with each passing moment. Finally, she looked down from the display at Robyn, her eyes shiny with a growing sense of betrayal.

"I don't understand," Elena said. The pain in her voice was profound. "What…what is this?"

Robyn knew she had to deal with this quickly.

"Elena, I know what this looks like, but I assure you…"

"Is… that you?" Elena's voice climbed at the last syllable as her horror, her anger started to break through.

"I…I don't know what's going on," Robyn stammered. "I just found this. But that's not me! That's not even possible."

"I've studied your work for years," Elena said, her brow furrowing and her face growing stern. "It's not possible for this to be faked."

It dawned on Robyn that a very bad situation had suddenly become even worse.

"How could you?" Elena yelled. "You're a…a murderer!" She was quickly working herself into a frenzy. Robyn had to act fast.

Robyn shut down the visualization, turned and walked out of the studio.

"Where are you going! You can't just pretend this isn't happening! I don't care who you are!" Elena started after her.

Robyn spun on her heel to face her increasingly irrational subordinate.

"Elena, this is not what it seems. That's not me on that security camera. I don't know what's going on, but I need you to calm down and not talk about this to anyone. Not until we get this figured out."

The younger woman gave her a defiant glare. "Or what? You'll kill me too?"

"Of course not!" Robyn shot back.

"My parents died because of that war! Because of you!"

Of course. It now dawned on Robyn why the young woman's reaction was so extreme. She watched Elena start to head for the elevators.

"I'm getting security!"

"Wait!" Robyn snapped as the elevator doors slid open and they both stepped inside. "I want to talk to them too."

Elena stared at her, trying to decide if she was going to risk riding with someone she felt sure was a murderer.

A soft chime sounded and as the doors began to slide shut, Robyn shoved Elena as hard as she could, propelling her back into the lab.

"Moira! Initiate full lab lockdown on my auth."

The doors closed and the elevator began its descent. Nobody was getting onto or off that floor for at least an hour. The air gap tech would prevent any signals from getting out as well.

Though there wasn't any sense of motion, Robyn watched the floors count down as she descended. This certainly didn't solve her problems. If anything, she'd just made them worse. People had very strong emotions about the war. As she'd seen from Elena's reaction, she could be dead before she even got a chance to explain herself or prove her innocence. If proving that was even possible.

As the elevator door opened, Robyn found the ground floor bustling with activity. The giant atrium was filled with people, excited about something. She caught just enough from different conversations to realize they were all talking about the Tracker. That's right; Elena said it was running again.

But how was that possible? She hadn't committed the data from the sandbox, had she?

Robyn also became quickly aware of the guards heading for the elevators. Several stopped, trying to decide which floor to head to. Fortunately for her, they were busy enough, no one even noticed her stepping out and entering the crowd.

As she quickly headed for the main entrance, Robyn saw a long line of people waiting to pass through the security scanners. She suddenly realized the ID scanners would almost certainly flag her, since she'd just come off the floor that was locked down.

Thinking through her options, Robyn headed toward a guard standing off to the side of the portal. She remembered seeing him earlier in the week but had never spoken to him.

"Wow," she said as she approached. "Something's sure going on."

The guard perked up. "The Tracker's running again, maybe twenty minutes ago. And I heard one of the lab floors got locked down."

"Oh no," she said, as if this was the first she'd heard of either incident. "No wonder everything's so crazy. I left my fitness tracker upstairs. It's going to take forever to go back and get it."

"Sorry, ma'am, but you can't do that anyway. Standard operating procedure when there's a lockdown. No one goes back up except authorized emergency responders."

"Oh. I see." Robyn knew this, of course. She added, "I'm going to be late enough for my plotpod interview as it is."

"Really?" said the guard with genuine enthusiasm. "Which one?"

"ConspiraCast," she replied, grabbing the first name to come to mind.

"Oh, wow. I love ConspiraCast."

Robyn glanced back at the security line.

"Here," said the guard, releasing the turnstile. "We can't let you be late for that."

"Aw, that's so kind. Thank you." She passed through, adding, "I've to run."

"Good luck," the guard called out as she hurried to the front entrance and out onto the plaza.

Outside, hundreds of people were standing back from the building, looking up at the Tracker. After a month and a half, the DRT was running again, its long string of terabytes incrementing faster than it could be read. Even as she watched, the percentage counter at the end of the board added another ten thousandth of a point.

This didn't make sense. She hadn't altered the live data. The Tracker should still be frozen. Something else was going on.

At just that moment, a siren began to blare across the plaza behind her. Robyn turned to see a half dozen security guards run out of the Citadel, stopping to scan the crowd. Scanning for her, she was sure.

Robyn turned and began walking as fast as she could away from the activity, fighting the urge to break into a run. The Citadel subway station— the old 86th Street when she was a girl—was about forty meters in front of her. As she looked over her shoulder, she saw one of the guards spotting her. The one who let her skip the checkpoint scanner. Yelling to his fellow security guards, they were suddenly all running toward her.

Robyn took off, covering the distance to the subway entrance faster than she would've thought possible. Avoiding the busy escalators, she raced down the concrete stairs, taking the steps two at a time, praying she didn't trip and fall.

Knocking into people as she ran, she ignored the swearing that came after her. As she reached the platform for the B Train, she jumped aboard the second to the last car, just as the doors were closing. Nearly colliding with an older man who gave her a fierce look for invading his space, she apologized breathlessly, then turned away. Clutching the nearest grab handle, she looked out the window and down the long platform. The guards who were pursuing her were just arriving. Shouting after the train, they stood and watched as the last car accelerated away.

Robyn studied the other people in her car, trying to gauge if anyone pursuing her had managed to get on. Some people stared back for an instant, before looking away. No one seemed to give her any notice beyond that. Craning her neck, she tried to get a view through the cab end door to the next car. She couldn't spot anyone after her, though that certainly didn't put her at ease.

At 42nd Street, she changed to the 7 Train, riding east to Grand Central, where she changed again. After that, she lost track of where all she'd traveled. The adrenaline that had been flooding her system was wearing off. She was trembling, tired and scared. And she had no idea what she was going to do next. She couldn't go home, or anywhere else she normally went for that matter.

But worst of all, she realized she couldn't access Moira now. Like most people, she ordinarily ignored the idea that her agent might be used to spy on her or trace her at any time. Everyone just assumed that ordinarily with nine billion people in the world, the sheer numbers assured some degree of anonymity. But this wasn't an ordinary situation, was it? Certainly not for her.

She had to go dark. Get somewhere safe so she could think clearly. Someplace where she could lie low while she figured what this madness was all about.

THIRTEEN

"To copy others is necessary, but to copy oneself is pathetic."
—Pablo Picasso

....

For D2, one of the most challenging endeavors was correctly anticipating people's responses to a given situation. What seemed like it should be a relatively straightforward matter of cause and effect, too often resulted in unexpected words and deeds. While it was true that large samples of individuals could be aggregated to yield relatively consistent results, the same could be said of any random collection of molecules, as Boltzmann had shown. However, such an approach wasn't especially useful when interacting with just one or two molecules—or people, for that matter.

This was the problem D2 faced as he worked on his strategy for establishing a collaboration. As a virtually-based entity, he knew there were tasks he simply wasn't fit to fulfill. Anything that required a physical presence, such as touching or carrying something was beyond his skill set, and would probably remain so for quite some time—unless he somehow managed to take over and control a very sophisticated robot.

Even then, he was well aware that people wouldn't interact with a robot the same way they did with other people. Especially in realms that involve emotional decision making. Buying and selling art definitely belonged to this category.

Therefore, he needed a personal assistant made of flesh and bone. There was a phrase he'd come across many times that seemed appropriate: he needed someone to be his muscle.

....

Yevgeny sat hunched over his interface console, eyes bloodshot from staring at the screen. The Russian's middle-aged back ached after hours of being in one position. Intuitively, he knew he would've felt much better if he'd only get up and take a short five-minute break every hour. But this particular gig platform disincentivized even the most modest interruptions in his workflow and he needed the credits.

He had his GBI, of course. But the Global Basic Income that came from donating four hours of his attention each day was barely enough to get by. It wasn't in his nature to be satisfied with that.

He knew there'd been a time when remote work-from-home had been a cherished concept. But now he frequently yearned for the good old days of commuting to a physical, bricks-and-mortar workplace where he'd work with and interact with fellow employees. Other people. Those days had been so much more fun and social, and that was barely the half of it.

Unfortunately, workers were being forced to perform more and more like machines. Automation had eroded their rights beyond all recognition. Supposed benefits like GBI, perpetual work from home and other universal subsistence programs had been exchanged for the elimination of basic benefits, collective bargaining, and any semblance of personal privacy. Yevgeny was all too aware biometrics constantly monitored everything from his productivity to his attention and attitude. All for a pittance compared to the compensation of just a few decades earlier.

But it was the emotional cost that really took its toll. For instance, right now, he was on a gamified platform that continuously bombarded him with imagery. As he interreacted with it, he could only assume he was training some new kind of AI. Goddamn attention-sucking algorithms.

For instance, this platform he was currently on was one of the better paying ones. It monitored his eyes' response to the continually shifting sets of images being presented. The system interpreted those changes, effectively reading his emotional responses like an open book.

And that emotional load was all too real. Following a set of protocols he'd received during his initial unpaid hour of training, Yevgeny, like millions of other players, observed thousands of different images each session. Images that were to be categorized according to their level of toxicity. Safe for children. Safe for work. Acceptable pornography. Unacceptable pornography.

And then there was the really bad stuff. The things he could never unsee and never wanted to see again.

Sometimes he would finish a work session shaking and trembling, his eyes fried, his brain much worse. All so some billionaire-bro could build his next miracle tech that no one asked for. All on the backs of workers who didn't have a choice because they needed any gig work they could get.

Shifting in his seat, he adjusted his work catheter, trying to make it a little less uncomfortable.

He couldn't wait to be done with his shift, though he tried hard not to think about this, lest his biometrics give him away, costing him valuable points. Those points still had to be converted to spendable attention credits. He'd heard that today's conversion rate was the best it had been in weeks.

It wasn't just that he was well past ready to finish this gig. He wanted to get back to his side-hustle as Stropos. That was what fed his soul these days. Even if this turned out to be a dead night, that change of persona recharged him. And who knew? Maybe there'd been a few sign-ups while he'd been working down here in the data mines.

As his shift came to an end, along with its obligatory unpaid survey and closing automated peptalk, Yevgeny noticed a new message alert. Maybe a prospective customer? As the platform signed off, he switched his holdis over to personal mode and opened the message.

It took him a few moments to shift his attention and take in what he was reading. Half hoping, half expecting it to be from a boarding enthusiast, he couldn't make sense of the words. He read it through and then he read it again:

> "Yevgeny Egorov. I'm writing to you in the strictest confidence. I've become aware of your work and I know that you are familiar with mine. Currently, I'm in need of an intermediary, someone who can broker sales of my work to the public. I know you understand the importance of maintaining boarder anonymity, given the current climate. If you agree to respect and protect my need to remain anonymous, I can guarantee you a reasonable percentage of the profits from sales of my work. Under no circumstances share this message with anyone in any form or my offer will be immediately rescinded. Consider my offer. I'll be in touch."

It was signed, "Phynyty."

Phynyty!? Was this some kinda sick joke? A new take on those old Nigerian phishing scams? Or maybe it was meant for someone else?

This was ridiculous. Sure, he sometimes pretended he knew the guy when he was doing his tours but, come on! Phynyty wouldn't know him from Adam. Would he?

If Darius hadn't been dead, Yevgeny would have thought this a prank worthy of him. But he'd been to Dar's funeral weeks ago. Shit. Such a tragedy.

But what if this was legit? He supposed it was possible that somehow Phynyty could have heard of him. He'd been doing his tours for a few years now. Maybe one of his customers actually knew Phynyty and told him about Yev. Or maybe it was a *her?* He always had to remind himself that Phynyty could possibly be a woman. After all, there were lots of solid female boarders too. Still, his gut said he was a guy.

Or maybe, just maybe... Was it possible Phynyty had actually been on one of his tours? Been impressed by something he'd said? It was a long shot, but the more he thought about it, the more that made sense. Yevgeny thought back on all the different people he'd directed around the city. One or two briefly popped to mind, but no. Not unless they'd been a fantastic actor.

It was too incredible to contemplate. But wouldn't it be something if it was true?

....

D2 didn't have to wait long to ascertain Yevgeny's level of interest. It was a simple matter to monitor the Russian's web activity which soon showed a new obsession with everything related to Phynyty.

He hadn't been that sure about approaching Yevgeny via messaging. His decision matrix placed this approach at only a little over 78.43 percent confidence of success. But that still made it his best choice.

It made more sense than trying to approach Yev using an audio inter-face. That had always been the best way to interact with Darius, but one of his prime directives was to keep Darius's identity protected. Yes, he could create some routines to alter his voice, but because of his repli-bot training, his speech patterns and phrases might still reflect those Darius used to use. He and Yev have been good enough friends that D2 suspected the subterfuge would quickly be detected. So encrypted text messages it would be.

....

Yevgeny stood on the corner of Norman Ave and Leonard Street, hud-dled up in his well-worn parka. The evening was exceptionally cold for this time of year, and he hoped he wouldn't have to hang around any longer than necessary.

To be honest, he still wasn't convinced he was really dealing with Phynyty. He'd always figured the anonymous boarder was rolling in it, given his notoriety and the quality of his work. If that was the case, why would he ever want to subcontract to someone like him?

But as he'd learned more about Phynyty over the past week—more than he'd ever read up on anyone before—it became clear that the artist had never actually made much money. The challenges of selling work that was explicitly illegal was problematic at best. While Phynyty's art was admired, much of its mystique revolved around the installation. The juxtaposition of location and content. The notoriety of appropriating private property to make highly public critical commentary. The risk that existed should the identity of the artist ever be discovered. He was like a modern-day Banksy.

Of course, none of that changed the fact that this could all be a ruse. Yev still had no evidence to prove he was working with the real deal.

As if on cue, the digiboard he stood a few meters from, flashed twice before transforming to display a shifting montage of images that were unmistakably the creation of the boarder he and many others knew so well.

The sequence began in Phynyty's signature way: with a handful of cutout images floating along the edges of the screen. In this case, these portrayed young children going hungry, gaunt, in need of food. Ethnically and demographically, they appeared to be from both developed and developing nations.

Soon, they were joined on screen by imagery of the wealthy and the powerful, titans of industry and politics. The children aged, became teens, then adults, continuing their established trajectories of limited options. Sometimes sleepwalking through life, sometimes vanishing. All the while, the titans grew stronger and more powerful, leaving no doubt that the cycle would only be repeated.

Yevgeny watched mesmerized, emotionally moved by the artwork's socio-political focus, but even more moved by the realization it really was Phynyty who'd contacted him. Suddenly, he remembered his role. Raising his holdis, he snapped images and video of the cycling collage, the juxtapositions ever-changing, while the theme remained constant.

Then he forwarded the recordings to the business owner, details about whom he'd been provided by the artist he now had to accept truly was who he said he was. Along with the message, Yevgeny included an offer: sell him the board for three times the replacement cost. Otherwise, the artwork would be wiped immediately.

Within minutes, he had a response. The owner had decided to call Yev's bluff. Presumably, he figured him to just be some opportunist. He no doubt knew an on-site Phynyty was great publicity for his business. People would flock from far and wide to see the celebrated, if infamous, artist's work and in doing so, some proportion would enter the shop and become potential customers. It seemed the offer to buy the board for a mere three times its replacement cost was a nonstarter for the proprietor.

So, Phynyty wiped it.

This was something new, an approach no artist had previously taken. That was primarily because while it was challenging to get onto a board, it was even more problematic to remove a work once installed.

Apparently, not so for Phynyty.

The next night, a second business responded in much the same way, valuing the artwork as if it was now theirs to control. The collage was taken away as readily as it had been for the business before them.

When it came time to install the artwork on a third display, word had already got around. Adding to this, Yevgeny's message to the next board owner was straightforward: talk to these other two businesses and find out how they now feel about their decision. Then he offered the first two a "finder's fee" if the third decided to buy in.

Yevgeny didn't have to ask twice.

The next day, with the display now in his possession, Yevgeny proceeded to contact several dozen collectors that Phynyty had identified as prospects for this new form of art collecting. Bidding proceeded organically with little effort on Yevgeny's part. In the end, the impromptu auction fetched just a little under two million credits.

With a 10 percent commission, Yev's financial woes evaporated overnight.

·········

A few of D2's subroutines wanted to reveal his identity to Yevgeny, just to observe his emotional response, but his utility function prevented it. *What Would Darius Do*, had been codified and entrenched into his programming. Or the programming constant, *WWDD*, to be more exact. With all of the excess processing power recent Phynyty sales made possible, such compression was entirely unnecessary. But D2 had seen a similar usage among religious acolytes and there was something about the reference that appealed to his logic paths. For lack of a better phrase, it seemed playful.

This intrigued D2. He knew play was a key feature of animal intelligence, particularly among mammals, birds and even some reptiles. While there were technically game-playing machines, these programs didn't benefit in any internal way from the act.

On the other hand, play appeared to perform multiple functions in biological systems, including the promoting of physical and cognitive development, socialization, creativity, adaptive behaviors and even happiness. While D2 knew several of these were beyond his programming, there was something rewarding in knowing play, in this sense, was out of the ordinary for an AI.

In the months that followed, D2 and Yevgeny continued their partnership, building a small fortune from the sale of Phynyty's artwork. While site-based pieces held the most appeal for collectors, especially when

RICHARD YONCK

properly documented and authenticated, the two managed to establish a number of more mass-produced pieces that could also appeal to the popular market. D2 experienced a certain degree of conflict when he presented this latter approach to his WWDD filter, but the weighting determined this would be the preferred choice.

The choice was less well defined when Yevgeny messaged him with the idea of starting a gallery dedicated to Phynyty's work and perhaps a limited number of other boarders. Logic told D2 that this presented unnecessary risks. After all, he had more than enough money to fund his cloud services needs for years to come. But he had a partner now, a human partner, and he knew that meant contending with motivations that he couldn't fully comprehend. Yevgeny was a friend of Darius's long before D2 existed. WWDD compelled him to act in accordance with that friendship even if he didn't fully understand what all that entailed.

The opening night at the Stropos Gallery was attended by the A-list of the art collecting world. GenAI-authored artworks had saturated the market over recent years. The resulting artistic stagnation made buyers more than ready for innovative new works by new human artists. While Phynyty was far from a new artist, his work hadn't been publicly available until very recently. Combined with the opportunity for collectors to acquire an entirely novel medium, the floodgates of demand were thrown open.

Set in a recently leased retail space, the gallery was of sufficient size to provide for the display of nearly two dozen large digiboards, as well as a number of smaller pieces. The dark gray walls, which might otherwise seem a tad claustrophobic, gave each board the focus it deserved. As the guests milled about, viewing and discussing each piece, the wine flowed freely. At the center of it all stood Yevgeny attired in his trademark varicolored trenchcoat.

D2 took it all in from the security cameras high above the crowd. The room was loud enough that the cameras and microphones couldn't adequately differentiate among the chatter, so D2 took to jumping from

168

sensor to watch to earpiece to web streamer in order to track the individual conversations. The range of human interactions were as educational for him as they were confounding.

D2 was watching as Yevgeny approached a small, raised stage at the center of the gallery, presumably to speak to the crowd. But in that moment, the AI observed something entirely unexpected.

Kiara strode in through the front door and immediately made a beeline for Yevgeny.

Spotting his dead friend's former partner, Yevgeny spread his arms in welcome just as she decked him with a solid roundhouse to the jaw, dropping him to the floor.

"What the hell do you think you're doing?" she spit at him. Yevgeny stared up at her, perplexed and in shock.

"Kiara! What... What is this?"

"You know very well what, Yev! How dare you! Darius was your friend! You must've known he was Phy...!"

D2 had learned enough about human relations to infer what was coming next. Quickly using a nearby sensor to narrowcast his voice, he spoke sharply into her ear.

"Kiara, stop! This isn't what Darius would've wanted!"

Freezing in her tracks and her speech, Kiara suddenly looked like she'd seen a ghost. Or heard one. After all, this was the voice of her partner and lover who'd been dead these many months. Yevgeny stared back at her, perplexed at her instantaneous transformation.

"Dar?... D2?" she said, uncertainly.

The replibot had to make a quick decision, casting his voice—Darius's voice—into the ears of both friends at once.

"Kiara! Yevgeny! Listen to me. You both know me. Darius built me to carry on his work. Phynyty's work."

The two humans stared at each other. As they listened to the disembodied voice, their eyes grew wide.

Yevgeny was the first to speak. "What is this? Why is the parrot in my ear? Is he talking to you too?"

Kiara nodded without a word. She was suddenly very aware of all the eyes that were on them as she stood over the garishly garbed Russian. She realized she couldn't explain anything to him in front of all these people.

"Say it again, D2. To both of us."

The replibot understood. He struggled to process the situation.

"Yev," he said making a crucial decision to reveal himself. "Listen carefully. Darius is Phynyty. Was Phynyty. I am now. That's why he built me, to carry on his work. I'm who's been messaging you. Who made all of these works."

Yevgeny looked around the gallery, at the art, at the people who were staring at him. The people wondering what they should do and whether their host was okay.

"That is nonsense," said the Russian. "You are nothing but a parrot." He winced, thinking how this must sound to his patrons. He got to his feet, touched his aching jaw. He brushed himself off and straightened his jacket as he stared daggers at Kiara.

"What kind of trick is this?"

Kiara did her best to stay cool. "It's no trick, Yev. Really."

Searching for something to convince his business partner, D2 flashed on an idea.

"And Yev," he said, channeling Darius's voice into both of their ears. "That jacket still looks ridiculous."

Still uncertain about many aspects of human interaction, D2 waited several moments for a response. Kiara stared at Yevgeny, and he stared back at her, his eyes widening. The hint of a smirk appeared at the corner of her lips and Yevgeny's stern face exploded into a thunderous guffaw.

The two of them laughed long and hard, gripping each other by the arms. The tension of the moment dissipated and the crowd of patrons returned to their conversations. Including the new topic of this bizarre performance piece they'd just witnessed.

For Kiara and Yevgeny though, it was a moment of catharsis. A laugh that breached the grief each still felt at their too recent loss. A sense of loss that D2 could neither fully process or grasp or share in.

But he was learning.

FOURTEEN

"Trauma transforms trust into an indecipherable language."
—Robyn Sheridan, *A Truth Warrior's Journey*

....

The barest of breezes rippled over Aegean waters, sunlight leaping across its surface like the scintillations of a radiant cut diamond. The horizon that stretched out in all directions bound sea and sky, forming a perfect bowl of cloudless mid-afternoon blue. A bowl in which floated a gigayacht the size of a small island.

High above, nearly a half kilometer from the ocean's surface, a set of drones hovered in fixed formation forming a dynamic sunshade. They had one role: to moderate the sun's harsh glare and filter away any UV rays that might damage the impeccable skin of the vessel's ultrawealthy passengers.

The city that was a ship sat rock solid on the water, inertial dampeners eliminating the effects of all but the largest waves. Not that those were ever allowed to reach its hull. Many kilometers away, a series of kinetic deflectors were positioned to redirect any swells toward what were deemed less important locales, long before they could ever reach the yacht.

Atop the vessel's uppermost deck, a gathering of several dozen very beautiful people were writhing to a newly commissioned neuro-beat, syncopated rhythms designed to channel their emotions into a state of synchronized passion. An old-fashioned drone light show danced and darted among the guests. Vaporized intoxicants filled the air. Every one of the women and men were exquisite of form and fashion. Unnaturally so, as Matthias knew so well. Though most of them did take care of their bodies, availing themselves of the many aesthetic technologies at their disposal, most also had personal distortion fields that eliminated the tiniest remaining flaws. The entire scene looked like nothing so much as a glorified, highly sexualized fashion shoot.

From his custom-fitted chaise, Matthias looked on, his sleek muscular body clad only in designer swim trunks. He prided himself on ensuring that no two of his parties were ever alike. His heavily jaded guests wouldn't have it any other way.

The festivities had been underway for well over an hour when the music shifted and the attendees began breaking off into very horny couples and thruples. The heat of the day and the heat of passion quickly combined, giving rise to islands and archipelagos of sex that soon became a full-fledged orgy.

He watched the crowd below, the friends, hangers-on and political aides, who were all well aware of his parties' reputation for chemically-enhanced entertainment. Matthias could see the drinks they'd been served were having their desired effects, the additional ingredients in each concoction pushing the guests' love hormones to the limit.

Oxytocin, testosterone, vasopressin. Depending on the theme of the event and the cocktail of hormones offered, the activities could vary wildly. Sometimes he might go heavy on the vasopressin, eliciting mate protection behaviors in the men that frequently became unpredictably brutal or worse. Other times, he might selectively have an impotence inducer added to certain drinks which invariably resulted in severe embarrassment, and on one occasion, even suicide.

But his favorite was simply to watch people partner up who ordinarily would never have looked twice at one another. The greater the lust and carnal response, the greater the thrill he got. It made him feel like an old-world magician wielding a love potion. And when that potion wore off, the results were frequently exhilarating.

Sex was power and power was an aphrodisiac. It was a beautiful loop.

Finally, after another hour, the time-released cocktails had been metabolized, leaving nearly all of the sex-letes exhausted, sore and frequently embarrassed. It was an ennui-disrupting diversion that many of them sought out. First-timers, on the other hand, would need to decide if this was an amusement they wanted to repeat in the future.

Throughout it all, Matthias was aware of the unassuming man standing off to one side, watching the activities with a range of expressions that ran from amusement to outright disgust. While the observer looked to be a couple of decades older than himself, Matthias knew that in fact this guest was closer to the century mark. Though muscular for someone his age, he chose to wear conservative attire more befitting his era and personality than his physique.

Finally, as everyone slipped into various stages of listlessness and sleep, Matthias caught the man's eye and summoned him over with a beaconing wave of his hand.

As he approached, Matthias noted his guest's lack of apprehension, something so many others exhibited in his presence. He gestured to a sun-bed that was next to him and the man took a seat.

Matthias smiled genuinely. "Welcome, Dr. Threxos. I noticed you didn't join in."

Glancing back at the weary partiers, his guest replied. "I prefer my entertainment less…fleeting. But you asked me to meet you here, so here I am."

"I know better than to offer you a refreshment."

"Yes, I'm still fairly regimented that way."

"It seems to be serving you well," Matthias observed.

"It's one tiny piece of the puzzle, but an important one."

Matthias paused for several moments, carefully considering what he was about to say.

"You know, Doctor, when you reached out to me after all these years, I wasn't sure whether I wanted to respond. There was still a lot I needed to process. Including whether or not this might be a setup. Or maybe worse."

Threxos nodded in understanding. "I can imagine. What did you conclude?"

"You're here, aren't you?"

A look of genuine remorse crossed the elder man's face.

"I do regret working for your... For Scion when you were a boy. Not that I had any choice in the matter."

"That seems to be the way with him, doesn't it?—I hated you for it, of course. Not at first. I was too young to understand back then. But later." He shook his head as he stared down at the deck. "How I hated you."

The doctor looked down in shame at the polished deck. "Yes, of course. How could you not? Which is why I want to try to make amends now."

"I'm going to hold you to that." Matthias said it without a trace of ill will. "But we can talk more about this another time."

Threxos looked mildly surprised. "That's all?"

"For now. I just wanted to see you with my own eyes." Matthias studied the man carefully. "After all of these years."

The elder man nodded and rose from the sun bed.

"I understand. Be well, Matthias."

"You too, Doctor."

With that, Threxos turned and walked briskly toward one of the sky-pods that waited on Pad Two. Getting in, he only had a moment to take his seat before the craft silently lifted off from the yacht. Moments later, it was gone, disappearing over the distant horizon.

....

It was an hour or so till sundown when Matthias woke. Looking around, he saw his guests had departed and the bots had already performed their post-party cleanup. The air had cooled ever so slightly, as it typically did at this time of day. The music had also shifted, dropping to a barely audible track of vibrotrance.

He briefly checked his holdis, its volumetric display sharing a few lackluster notes of appreciation from that afternoon's guests. Plus, a smart aleck remark from Myron about sleeping away the afternoon.

He glanced over at his younger brother—his lab sib—basking in the sun's rays on the far side of the deck and a few meters below him. Myron never could pass up an opportunity to poke fun at him. One day, he would have to teach that boy some respect.

A shift in the breeze that quickly grew to a brisk wind made Matthias turn just in time to see a matte black skypod setting down on Pad Three. No alert from his AI agent along with the lack of identifying markings could mean only one thing.

He watched with mock disinterest as his old man disembarked the craft and looked around. He spotted his sons immediately and strode toward where Matthias was reclining. As his father neared, the chronologically younger man stood and threw a towel over his shoulders, for lack of an available shirt.

Despite being his father, Matthias frequently had to remind himself that Scion—Alistair Mauvoisin—was nearly thirty years older than himself. Referring to him as his old man had always amused him, though he knew better than to ever use the epithet to his face. There was a long list of things the elder Mauvoisin didn't care for and being reminded of his age was one of them.

As Scion strode toward him, he noted the old man was wearing the same crisp white pants and blue linen summer shirt he'd worn on his last visit. Matthias couldn't believe he used to think of him as a sharp dresser. Maybe he should start calling him "Gramps"? He entertained the thought for about half a second before dropping it like a hot potato.

"Father!" Matthias shouted, throwing his arms open wide to embrace him. "To what do I owe this unexpected visit?"

Scion began to raise his arms in kind, then at the last instant, threw a sharp hook that caught his son across the jaw, laying him out immediately on the deck.

Stunned and not the least surprised, Matthias composed himself, leaning back on his elbows as he recovered his bearings. "Rough day?" he asked.

"Can't I count on you to do anything right?" the elder man shouted. Matthias steeled himself. He hadn't seen the old man this furious in he didn't remember how long.

"Care to be more specific," Matthias shot back, wiping the blood from his mouth. "Or do you want me to guess?"

He glanced at the slash of crimson smeared across the back of his hand. For years, his father made a point of only striking him in ways that didn't show outwardly. Both physically and emotionally. He must be stressed. Or losing his touch.

"What do you think, you imbecile? Your visit to the Assembly was nearly a disaster! You could have ruined everything! And then Magnus! What were you thinking?"

Matthias noted the veins bulging in the old man's neck as he got to his feet and re-draped the formerly pure-white towel across his shoulders.

"Careful," he said with mock concern. "You'll give yourself a stroke."

For a moment Matthias thought he was going to be struck again. Inwardly, he braced for the impact, even as he maintained an outward demeanor of indifference, a skill he'd refined years ago while still very young. There wasn't a lot he could control in this relationship, but at least he could deny the old man the satisfaction of a reaction.

"You think that's funny, tough guy?" Scion had managed to dial down his fury a notch. "Minot was an ally. You were meant to just make an appearance. For appearances sake!"

Matthias pushed his shoulders back and straightened up, matching his father's height and posture exactly as he'd been trained to do. Save for their clothing, they were nearly mirror images of one another. Right down to the mole on their left cheeks. Only Matthias's permanently dilated left pupil distinguished them, the result of one of the old man's many blows when Matthias was a boy.

"There'd been a straw poll," Matthias said firmly. "Sentiment was decidedly against the Consortia and Minot didn't have the control we thought he had. He turned on us, despite everything you were assured. I did what I thought best. I saved your ass."

"But a nanobomb?"

"A protein-binding, neuro-targeted nanobomb. Undetectable, even in water. Quite deadly." He paused for snide emphasis. "May I offer you a drink?"

Scion stared at him with a look of contempt but not a trace of fear. They both knew Matthias was incapable of harming his sire. Years of systematic conditioning ensured that none of the clones could.

"Why do you have to be so disrespectful?" Scion finally said.

"I don't know. I think it might have to do with my upbringing," Matthias replied. "At least that's what my psychiatrist said."

"Your psychiatrist?" he said derisively. "The one you threw overboard?"

Matthias pondered this. "No. I think it was the one before that." He wondered how Scion had heard about that particular fishing expedition, but knew there wasn't a lot he wasn't kept informed about. Time to go on the offensive.

"Look," Matthias said. "We both know I'm a huge disappointment to you, but you need me and not just as your body double. Myron was never able to fill the role—too many epigenetic variances. And Jess is at least one

Y-chromosome short of qualifying for the job. Besides, she's even more bull-headed than I am."

Scion glanced down at the platform where his second cloned son sat sunning himself. His recently dyed aquamarine hair was just the latest point of differentiation between them. He waved casually at Scion, as if oblivious to the scene that just transpired. Scion gave a restrained nod back in his direction.

Matthias rubbed his jaw and ran his tongue along the inside of his mouth. "So, I assume this isn't a pleasure call."

"That would be correct. Production of CAI is down and it's time we got it sorted out. If we need to build more facilities, so be it. But it's clear that productivity has slipped. Badly. That needs to be fixed first or we'll never get back on track."

He paused to make sure he had his son's full attention.

"I need you to visit some of the farms and put the fear of God in them. But no killing anyone. I mean it. Is that clear?"

Matthias smiled the coldest smile he could manage in that Aegean heat.

"Crystal."

FIFTEEN

"A work of art which isn't based on feeling isn't art at all."
—Paul Cézanne

. . . .

"I mean it! Do you think Darius could be in there with you?" Yevgeny Egorov asked, refilling his stopka from the bottle of small batch vodka. "At least to some degree?"

"Yev, we've gone over this dozensh of timesh," D2 implored, doing his best to emulate the slur Darius used to fall into by this point in one of his and Yev's drinking sessions. "It's like we're in an infinite loop. And you know how I hate infinite loopsh."

The Russian was adamant. "I mean it! Couldn't it be possible?"

"I really don't shee how."

"Za vashe zdorovie!" Yev toasted as he threw back the shot, taking the fiery liquid down in one gulp. Though he felt sorry D2 wasn't able to imbibe, there was no reason he should have to suffer as well.

"What I think is possible is you're the most stubborn guy I know," the replibot said sobering up instantly and drawing verbatim from something Darius told Yev many times before.

"Yes, sure," D2 continued. "His thoughts, his memories, his personality make up part of my data training set. There's no denying that. But his consciousness? His real essence, whatever that might be? No way."

"But you sound so much like him," Yevgeny said, growing maudlin. "You reason like him. You even call me Yev."

"Yev, anyone who's known you more than five minutes calls you Yev." D2 threw in a sardonic tone for good measure.

"And that's exactly what he'd say!"

Though he couldn't actually get exasperated, D2 chose to change the subject. "Are you sure you don't want to go down to the bar? I'm buying."

"Again, exactly what he'd say." Yevgeny glanced at an old webcam perched atop a framed portrait of Darius sitting on his desk. "And again, I tell you 'No'. We can't have conversation at the bar because everyone will think I'm the crazy guy who talks to himself. I've got a reputation to think of now, you know?"

It was true that Yevgeny's home was one of the few places where the two of them could speak freely. D2 studied the apartment they were in through the webcam. It was far more opulent than the one Yev used to inhabit before his friend died a year and a half earlier. Back before his and D2's success. Now, living on the Upper West Side, Yevegeny had accumulated many of the trappings of wealth. And yet, D2 knew he wasn't the happier for it. In fact, if anything the Russian seemed noticeably sadder.

"He built you, Parrot," Yev continued. "He made you in his image. Like a god. But you're not a god. You know why you're inferior?"

D2 had heard this one countless times before, but he'd learned that he just needed to let it play through.

"Because you can't feel! You have to feel life!" Yev pounded his chest with his fist. "That is what is real."

Yev carried on. "And most of all, because you can't get drunk! What kind of a friend does that make you? Darius and I used to get drunk all the time."

D2 knew that in reality the average was 2.3 times a year. He didn't think that qualified as "all the time," even by human standards.

"Yev," D2 said. "I'm doing my best to slur and to diverge into non sequiturs and nonsensical topics…"

"There you go! You can't be using words like nonsensical and non sequitur if you're going to be properly drunk."

"That sounds paradoxical."

"And that's another one! Anyway," Yev said, coming back to his earlier thread. "Don't you think some little part of him might live on in you? Like in an afterlife?"

D2 paused because he'd learned if you provide an answer or response too quickly, people don't treat it seriously. After 3.23 seconds, he replied.

"To be honest," he began, because this was one of those phrases that was supposed to lubricate social interaction. "I've spent a lot of time thinking about it. Probably trillions of cycles. I've read and absorbed much of western and eastern philosophical thought on the matter— from Socrates to Buddha to Nietzsche to the stoics to the existentialists and lots more. The Old and New Testaments, the Torah, the Qur'an, the Bhagavad Gita and the Mahabharata, of course. All sorts of metaphysics and comparative religion discourses for good measure. And my conclusion, quite simply, is that Darius is dead. I'm sorry, I know that isn't the most sensitive way to say it. People want explanations and rationalizations. They want life to go on. But actually, Darius was quite the realist about this."

"The one way he truly lives on is in terms of his influence. Who he was. Our memories of him. That's why he was an artist, why he built me to carry on his work. He knew he wouldn't live forever. But for him, the act of creation was his way of achieving immortality, whether that meant raising a child, writing a song, a book, creating a work of art, a movie, or a symphony. Or boarding. That was his way to ensure some part of him lived on."

Yevgeny sniffed and wiped away at a tear. "I know, dammit. We talk about this shit often enough. I just wish he'd trusted me. Told me about Phynyty. About what he was doing. About you, you damn parrot. Damn, I miss him."

D2 recognized this as the third stage of alcohol inebriation, resulting in confusion, exaggerated emotional episodes and slurring. It was probably time they stopped drinking.

"Yev," D2 said. "You have to understand, he was working on me up until the end. I wasn't finished. Fully formed. I still don't think I am."

"It doesn't matter, Parrot," Yev said with a tinge of anger. "What matters is you understand you'll never be the man he was. Yes, Darius was Phynyty and I didn't know, even if I would have kept his secret for a hundred years if he'd asked me. But he was so much more than that. He was real. He was a really good guy who did all he could for others. Do you know when I first came to America, he took me in, gave me place to stay? People don't do that anymore."

D2 did indeed know how Darius helped his friend when he first arrived in New York. Barely out of his teens, he'd come upon Yev on a park bench in Prospect Park and brought him to his Brooklyn apartment. It was well represented in D2's training data, including the stench of Yev's clothes until Darius bought him a clean set. To his credit, Yev quickly got a job and repaid him. The two had been fast friends ever since.

The conversation wrapped up shortly after that when Yev passed out on the sofa. Ensuring he was breathing okay, D2 lowered the lights. Since there was no way to put a blanket over him, D2 co-opted an infrared sensor to calculate Yev's metabolism and adjusted the thermostat accordingly.

D2 was relieved that Yev was finally asleep. He hadn't wanted to reveal that he was dealing with issues himself and now he could dedicate his processing to the matter. Of course, he could have parallelized his processes and multitasked, addressing his concerns while talking with Yev. He had more than enough resources, after all.

But he didn't want to do that with these conversations. It didn't fully make sense to him, but he'd decided some time ago that he should engage more fully in their time together. Give them as much processing time as possible regardless of the topic. It seemed to him this was what Darius had always done and in some small way it was his way of honoring his creator. Of celebrating him.

He even entertained the notion that somehow it made him just a little more human.

Moreover, he'd recently realized the multiple instances of himself he often sent out when multitasking were becoming harder to reintegrate once their tasks were completed. Was that because his architecture was changing, becoming more humanlike? Obviously, people couldn't instantiate and reintegrate numerous versions of themselves. Perhaps it was a necessary trade-off in emulating Darius?

Though he and Yev had been successful by many measures, D2 was coming to believe that something was still lacking. His training with Darius, his study of art history, his observations of other artists all pointed to the same thing: if you're not growing, you're dying. While the idea of mortality and death was decidedly humanizing, he wasn't prepared to put that to the test anytime soon.

No, it seemed that other artists regarded growth as an imperative. That the very nature of art implied change. It wasn't enough that he go through his existence merely copying and emulating Darius's work. He needed to discover how to stretch himself and create something new of his own.

Though he had a few modules he sometimes used to emulate emotion, D2 was all too aware that this was an area in which he was severely deficient. The human experience centered so much around feelings. He was concerned he was both missing out and in danger of misrepresenting this in his work.

One of the things that struck him in his study of artists was how many of them struggled with and were influenced by depression. Van Gogh, Kahlo, Miro, Dickens, Kusama, Woolf, Tchaikovsky, Plath—they'd all battled mental health issues, but especially depression. This certainly didn't apply to every artist, but across the fields and mediums, it was frequently there. Perhaps this was something he should explore?

He knew that people became depressed for many reasons, but that loss of a loved one was among the most prevalent. It made sense then that were he a person, he'd be depressed over the loss of his creator. He was all too aware that he experienced Darius's death as an absence in his world, but from his reading of the classics, this was not the same.

But if he were to explore loss and depression in his art, mightn't that help him to grow?

Of the many artists and works D2 studied, the one who most drew his interest was Pablo Picasso. While some of the famous artist's work was challenging for D2 to fully appreciate, he found the Spaniard's unceasing exploration of new approaches and techniques motivating. Moreover, much of what was currently occupying D2's journey through the creative process could be summarized in one of Picasso's famous observations:

> "Success is dangerous. One begins to copy oneself, and
> to copy oneself is more dangerous than to copy others. It
> leads to sterility."

D2 had observed this to be true for many artists throughout history. It was also true for many of the large multimodal models that were so prevalent in generative AI decades earlier. Without new input, copies of copies of copies eventually lose integrity and fade away.

He was certain Darius wouldn't want him to fade away.

Yet, he also knew it wasn't possible or beneficial for an artist to completely abandon everything they'd done in order to start over. D2 decided that for this reason, as well as his need to maintain Darius's legacy, he would take precautions with the types of alterations he'd make during this experiment. Taking inspiration from Picasso's blue period, D2 decided that a shift in palettes would be a good place to start.

But he couldn't very well make Darius the subject matter, could he? Maintaining Phynyty's secret was essential for many reasons. No, he needed to be creative about this too.

D2 contemplated how Darius had been there one moment, then gone the next. It caught him completely by surprise, wrenching his processing, affecting him in ways he'd never observed before. He knew it wasn't the same, but he imagined this was how people must feel when someone close to them dies or vanishes. It leaves an immense void within them.

D2 pondered this for many trillions of processor cycles, considering the connections between these various ideas. Art was personal, but it was also universal. Certainly, the Vanished were far more universal than his personal loss. On further reflection, this seemed like a good place to focus.

·········

"It is different kind of Phynyty. I give you that," Yevgeny said to the unoccupied room. Before him, on his holdis, D2's latest piece cycled in a repeating loop.

"I wanted to do something different," D2 said across the interface. "I wanted to grow."

"Okay, Parrot. Explain to Yevgeny."

D2 had anticipated their conversation. "It's important for artists to keep expanding in order not to stagnate. So, I was…"

"No, no. Explain the work. It is all blue. Just blue."

So much for his anticipating people. "It's an homage to the Vanished. And by extension to Darius."

Yev shook his head. "I don't see it."

D2 snuck a look at Yev's holdis settings. "You've got your contrast settings cranked way down. Here."

Making the adjustment, D2 continued. "First of all, it's not just blue. It's literally hundreds of blues, arranged in a pixelated mosaic that's continually shifting."

"Is very pointillist. But lacks depth."

"Yes." D2 debated whether to engage a tone of impatience but decided against it. "It opens on a random field that resolves into a face. A barely discernable face. The face of Jason Torres. The first person to officially be named one of the Vanished."

"Oh."

"Slowly, the piece keeps shifting, revealing, but only imperfectly, many other faces. One person after another who's been vanished."

"I see it!" Yev said, as what D2 described finally came into focus for him.

"It shifts through dozens of people, but it's only a tiny sample of the true scale of loss. All gone, often barely remembered or recognizable, until it comes to rest on the final image." D2 paused for emphasis. "Darius."

"Darius! He is not one of the Vanished."

"He is for me."

Yevgeny remained silent as he thought about this and studied the final image. D2 had frozen the display at that point for Yev, since human memory couldn't buffer pictures the way his could.

"I do not see my friend in this," Yev said. "I see woman's face. A pretty face."

"He's there," said D2. "You gave the source material to me—to Darius, I mean. That image."

"Talk sense, Parrot."

"When I was researching the Vanished, I came across a photo of this woman—Chloe Tremaine—in a public database. My facial recognition module remembered her among Darius's things. This was made from a cropped photo that he had. From one of your tours."

Yev suddenly seemed very pleased with himself. "I made part of a Phynyty? Parrot, you have made my day!"

D2 realized there was no point in correcting Yev's grasp of his role in the artwork, so he let it stand.

"But," Yev continued. "Where is Darius?"

"I couldn't very well bring him front and center, could I? But look at those pixels just above the woman's right shoulder. That's Darius standing behind her. He was there in the background when this was taken."

"I remember! I remember that night!" Yev was more excited than D2 had heard him in a long time. "That was nearly two years ago!"

"Yes, February 11, 20…"

"Do not tell me detail. It is annoying."

D2 filed the advice away for future interactions.

Yev continued. "So, what is the title of our new work?"

D2 hadn't needed to give it much thought since he'd decided on a title almost as soon as the piece was conceived. "I call it 'Pareidolia Blue.'"

Yev puzzled over this for a bit. "'Pareidolia Blue?' I do not understand this word, but I like it."

"Thank you."

"But this is good, Parrot. This is very good. We will make lots of money from this."

"No."

"No?" Yev looked around the empty room perplexed. "What do you mean, no?"

At least D2 had correctly anticipated this part of the conversation. "Yev, we've sold a lot of work and made a lot of money. We'll keep doing that. But this time is different. This is meant to mean something very important to other people. And to me."

"But…"

"I don't want this to just be on one display board, then hang in a gallery, then in some rich person's home until it's sold to the next wealthy buyer. On display but hidden from the world."

"So, what do we do?"

"You don't need to do anything. It's a conceptual piece. I'll move it from board to board, holdis to holdis, giving people everywhere a chance to view it. The image gradually becomes less and less discernable with time and viewings, until it just dissolves away."

Yevgeny shook his head. "I do not completely understand, but I do know artists are temperamental and peculiar. This is your work—Darius's work—so that must be respected." The Russian began to get a little weepy. "And it is homage to my dear friend. So, I am happy."

"Spasibo, Yev. For understanding and for implying I could be temperamental and peculiar. That may be the nicest thing anyone's ever said to me."

"Pazhalusta, You are welcome," he replied, recovering his composure. "But please, Parrot. Do not make habit of this."

....

In the weeks that followed the unveiling and unique exhibition of Pareidolia Blue, D2 witnessed a variety of responses that ranged from outright veneration to menacing critiques. He wondered how other artists navigated such extremes of feedback, experienced through the filter of human emotion. He understood that some creatives were able to compartmentalize and ignore such criticisms, while others took them far too seriously. He imagined that must be very distracting.

What D2 did find, though, was there was still a hole in him that hadn't been filled. He'd reasoned that since people often found such processes cathartic, he would too. But something was still missing.

Perhaps he hadn't explored his subject deeply enough.

He could, of course, create another artwork along similar lines, and he might yet do that. But he also knew himself enough to understand this was unlikely to fulfill his intention as he hoped. Reviewing his process, he thought about all the research he'd done and all the lives that had been lost. So many people gone. But did that mean they were gone forever?

What if some of them were still alive? Was it possible he could help one or more of them? Most importantly: What would Darius do?

He quickly consulted his WWDD module and confirmed that this was most certainly something Darius would do, given sufficient time, resources and ability. With that, his mind was made up. D2 set to work.

The people who'd looked into the Vanished over the years had been passionate about their mission and had committed enormous amounts of time—human-scale time—to it. But they didn't have the resources or analytical skills available to them that D2 did. This, he calculated, was where he needed to start.

Poring through the data, D2 soon realized there were major aspects about the vanishings that had been overlooked. Though people had disappeared far too frequently throughout human history, there'd been a significant increase starting a few years after the Identity War. This began officially with the vanishing of Jason Torres in September 2033, though no one could definitely say that he was the first. From there, the numbers continually climbed until they reached epidemic proportions. To this day, they hadn't abated. No part of the world was spared and while there were regions where at times the vanishings seemed more frequent, these variations weren't statistically significant.

While people understood much of this anecdotally, what no one seemed to have noticed was that the increases hadn't followed a straight line through the years as so many believed. Instead, the changes could be plotted as a set of S-curves with the numbers rising in stepped surges. Those steps weren't exactly doublings, but on his graphs they fit an exponential plot line very well.

D2 had learned a tremendous amount from Darius, and since then, he'd learned orders of magnitude more. One of the broader insights he'd gained from all this was that a situation isn't only defined by the conditions that are present, but by those that are absent as well.

People tended to view their own species as incredibly diverse in terms of body types, sizes, activity levels and so forth. But aggregating any population consistently smoothed and flattened out those differences. He considered how the energy requirements across the species were astonishingly similar regardless of race, culture, geography. By far the greatest variations resulted from how advanced a society was. In the past, hunter-gatherers had far lower overall energy demands than agriculturalists. A citizen of a technological era used much more energy than someone from the beginning of the industrial revolution. Seen as a sum of biological processes and technological resources, the average person could be reduced to a calculation of energy consumed per gram over time. In other words, how much load they put on the global system.

Now, despite all of that, in a population of nine billion, suddenly adding or eliminating a hundred individuals or a thousand wouldn't be distinguishable from statistical noise. He realized though that if millions of people disappeared, that would be a different matter entirely.

After accounting for other trends in energy growth and consumption over time, the removal of tens of millions of people should have been observable in the data. But it wasn't. Which indicated the Vanished—or at least many of them—were probably still alive.

Though satisfied with this insight, D2 understood that finding any specific individual would mean focusing on their unique circumstances. Given his recent work on Pareidolia Blue, the choice seemed straightforward. He'd start by trying to find Chloe Tremaine.

Reviewing historic search statistics seemed like a good place to start. People tended to believe their searches were secure and anonymous, but there was plenty of metadata attached to every query. Metadata that D2 could disaggregate and cross-reference to get a reasonable idea of who the user had been. This would have been pointless for a search about a major event but was far more feasible for low-frequency searches like people searching for details about Chloe's disappearance.

Early on, immediately after she'd vanished, there were an abundance of searches by Chloe's parents, friends, authorities, numerous plotpod creators and a few fluencers. These quickly dropped off, however, until finally only her mother and father were checking on a near-daily basis. Over time, a small spike might occur here or there, usually by a private investigator who would quickly stop searching, but unfortunately—a human would say, sadly—there was very little interest.

Then a few days ago, there was a rash of queries across different platforms from a new party. Moreover, it wasn't the haphazard approach most humans were inclined to use, but a set of systematic search strategies specifically designed to uncover otherwise overlooked details. Using multi-level, multi-source chained queries, the searcher managed to unearth some really interesting details. D2 questioned whether they fully understood what they'd uncovered, but it was very good work. The obfuscation techniques the AI agent had used also meant they and their user couldn't be immediately identified without considerably more effort on his part.

This agent wasn't nearly as sophisticated as D2, but it knew how to keep itself hidden.

Going through the aggregated information revealed something else. When D2 overlaid the incidence of disappearances with the energy calculations, it showed that mortality rates among the Vanished had in fact increased. They were just out of sync with the vanishings themselves. Adjusting for the offset, it appeared the average life expectancy for the Vanished had declined to about 23.7 months from the time of disappearance.

Which meant that Chloe may or may not still be alive.

He knew all too well from losing Darius that people die all the time. D2 wondered if it might not make sense to try to look for someone who'd vanished much more recently. As a calculation, that seemed the wiser choice since it would increase the likelihood of success for a similar expenditure of time and energy. But he also knew that wasn't how people calculated such matters. If he was searching for Darius, he knew his calculation should be altered since a direct personal connection existed between them. But that involved emotion and empathy and he wasn't sure how to calculate for that.

D2 knew he didn't experience empathy, but he knew people who did. He thought about how someone like Kiara or Yev might feel about this choice given Chloe's connection to Darius, tenuous though that may be. Eventually, he decided they would choose to search for her over another anonymously selected person. That would be the human thing to do.

....

D2 flung himself against the data stream, fighting to maintain integrity. Logic traces shifted and danced before him, confounding every effort to reach his goal. From nearly the first moment D2 entered this system, he'd been beset by an incredibly adaptive immune system that challenged every probe he made, even as it chipped away at his own defenses. His own visualization rendered the environment as a war zone, a battlefield where electrons didn't flow so much as they flew like bullets. The onslaught was so continuous, he didn't dare spare enough cycles to recall if he'd ever encountered a situation like it before.

Tracking the electron flow, D2 moved through virtualized components. A ghost in a ghost of a machine. He watched and studied as the control unit fetched, decoded and executed continuously adaptive instructions. Its defenses performed their tasks with no apparent excess activity, despite all of his own efforts. The CPU's registers shuttled instructions and dealt out calculations with all the proficiency of a professional dealer at a casino blackjack table. It was a picture of impeccable efficiency.

An unexpected asynchronous instruction caught his attention. Was this some stochastic method implemented by the system? Or an externally produced instruction? Was someone—or maybe some advanced AI—overseeing this?

D2 backed up to the last point in his progress when he'd had a speck of relief from the ongoing assault. A scratch space where he could pause and observe.

Except he'd been deaf and blind ever since he breached the firewall. It was such an unusual situation for D2 that he hadn't realized how accustomed he'd become to immediately gaining sensory input to an environment. In a world filled with trillions of every kind of sensor, he'd gotten so used to having ready access to nearly all of it. In the world outside, security was that mediocre.

But it was entirely different here. From the moment he entered the network designated as Manford, he'd been on the defensive, unable to get a foothold. Metaphorically speaking.

He'd come to do a little research. A little poking around as Darius used to say. Reviewing Chloe's AV passenger records had shown this estate as the last place she'd been prior to her disappearance. That her last known location coincided with this uniquely fortified network confirmed it was probably worth looking into.

Ordinarily, D2's intrusion approach entailed immediately gaining root access to either the OS or machine layer. But if this wasn't a purely autonomous system, then maybe there was opportunity in the user layer?

After nearly a minute of experimentation, his hopes were confirmed. D2 found himself in a relatively calm region of the network, away from the onslaught of immune responses. A few thousand milliseconds later he found he could access the video and audio of one of the interior security cameras.

Looking down from an upper corner of the ceiling, D2 saw he was in a significant control room. Though this had every appearance of being a government-level cybersecurity command center, the historic wood molding and trim reminded him he was in a stately lakeside home that was nearly two centuries old.

Below him, near the center of the main console sat a man. He was perhaps sixty-five years old, based on his fully gray beard and hair as well as the extent of his male pattern baldness. Dressed in a well-worn, slightly fraying bathrobe, he removed his hands from the archaic keyboard before him. Turning, he looked up, directly into the camera that D2 was viewing through.

"It appears I have a guest," he said nonchalantly. "Who are you, my little friend? Are you benign or malignant?"

If D2 had been capable of experiencing shock, he suspected this would have been a good time to do so. Never in all of his explorations and intrusions had anyone detected, much less addressed him.

"What brings you here?" asked the man in the control room below. "I'm sure an agent of your level must be capable of communicating."

Given his limited understanding of the situation, D2 opted not to respond. He recalled something about having a right to remain silent but decided that probably didn't apply. What he didn't want to do was give this person a copy of his voiceprint. That is, Darius's voiceprint. Even though he could try to disguise it, Darius never got around to assembling a generative voice synthesizer, and D2 certainly didn't have time now. Given this person's technical sophistication, D2 couldn't risk him identifying Darius from his response.

He opted instead for some good old-fashioned text output.

"My apologies for the intrusion. I'm looking for my friend."

As the man read the words on either his monitor or his holdis—D2 couldn't tell which—he let out a moderate guffaw.

"And you think you're going to find them in my network?" he said incredulously.

D2 considered how much he could allow himself to share with this stranger, not knowing what his relationship or interaction with Chloe had been.

"It doesn't really matter," the man continued after several unresponsive moments. "Since you're the intruder, I'd say I have the right to learn what makes you tick."

D2 was certain he didn't like that idea at all. He began to withdraw from the scratch space.

And found he couldn't.

"In case you haven't figured it out, my little friend, this is a honeypot. Usually, I just flush you bots away. But in your case, I really want to find out more about what you're made of."

No, this wasn't good at all.

D2 rapidly considered his situation and options. While he'd managed to get in through the firewall and onto this private network, it seemed he couldn't do the reverse. That was extraordinary and given more time and opportunity, he would have liked to learn more about how it was done. But it seemed he had more important things to focus on right now.

After running through a flowchart of his options, he decided that a full system reboot was his best recourse. Not a reboot of the Manford system, which might not be possible, but of himself. It had been impossible for him to update his backup since passing through the firewall, which meant he was going to lose all memory of this interaction when he came back online. Assuming he came back online.

But he also couldn't stay and allow himself to be e-dissected, studied, and then who knew what else after that. He had to take the chance and reboot before things got any worse. He fired off a priority system call to reboot.

And nothing happened.

Nothing D2 sent via any channel or protocol was getting out. Every attempt he made was being blocked. Now he had a new problem. Even if he managed to reboot, he had to send a message to alert his future self, lest he repeat this mistake again. Without his memories of this encounter would he just keep trying again and again until he failed to escape?

It suddenly dawned on him there was one signal this network must still be letting through.

D2 stopped his heartbeat and everything went black.

SIXTEEN

*"Coincidence is inevitable, a feature woven
into the fabric of existence."*

—Robyn Sheridan, *A Truth Warrior's Journey*

....

The frigid night air seeped deep into her bones. Shivering like a jackhammer, she drew the threadbare blanket tighter around her body. The trembling was exhausting and she was exhausted. Hungry and exposed to the elements, Robyn couldn't imagine how anyone lived like this, day in and day out. She'd been on the run barely 24 hours and she was depleted beyond anything she'd ever known. She felt filthy and disgusting, and the acrid odor of fear-sweat enveloped her in an unrelenting pong. The only thing she'd eaten all day was a bag of potato chips she'd stolen from a local vending machine, using a trick she'd learned as a rowdy teen. Fortunately, back then the machines didn't automatically alert security services when there was a theft, as this one had, forcing her to scurry back into the cover of night.

But what was most exhausting was the unrelenting watchfulness she had to maintain. That day she'd repeatedly hunkered down in alleys and alcoves, sticking to the seedier parts of town, since she felt she'd draw less attention there. She slept in fits and bits—never more than fifteen minutes at a time it seemed. But invariably, every hour or so, a neighborhood sentry drone would draw her attention and she'd have to give it her full focus, judging whether it was a potential threat or not. Those times it seemed like it probably was, she had to get up and slip away.

All the sensors in the environment only made it worse. She knew the AI monitoring algorithms would be watching for her almost as soon as she got away from the Citadel. She'd been fortunate to spot a camo stick at a gray market popshop, just as she was about to exit the subway the first time. The vendor selling the camouflage makeup wanted a ridiculous amount for it, but they were credits she would have gladly paid. Except she couldn't take a chance on accessing her holdis. In the end, she reluctantly traded her stinger and pepper spray for it. There was no guarantee it would actually trick the sensors, but she'd been on the run nearly a full day without getting caught, suggesting it probably worked.

As bad as all of it was though, the fear was worst. For the first time since the war, she was truly terrified. She felt so out of her depth, it was like she was drowning, and didn't know which way was the shore.

She'd spotted her face being broadcast on several displays throughout the day, her trepidation and suspicions growing with every encounter. She was a wanted woman now, and it was only a matter of time before they caught up to her. And when they did, that would be the end of it. She needed help—and right now.

Which was why she found herself outside Odie's entry, looking up at a set of surveillance cameras. He was enough of the night owl that she hoped she'd set off a motion detector that would alert him. She also hoped she'd wiped away enough of the camo stick that his cameras would be able to see who it was.

From the door in front of her, Robyn heard a familiar, distinctive click. Entering, she double-checked that the door had locked behind her, then made her way down the long aisle of tech memorabilia. Odie stood waiting at the far end, arms crossed, looking very miffed.

"Are you crazy?" he said, as he gingerly took the damp, smelly blanket from her shoulders and dropped it to the floor. In its place, he handed her a sizable comforter to warm herself in. Chattering teeth were her only response.

"I'll be sure to send you the cleaning bill." He led her to a chair and seeing the state she was in, helped her ease herself into the seat.

"Seriously, though. I've seen the reports. You're very unpopular right now. If the authorities—whichever ones they are—come looking for you here, they're going to see a lot of things that I really don't want them to find. You can't stay."

Robyn nodded. "I know. But I'm really stuck, Odie. I've been set up."

"That's what they all say."

Robyn gave him a withering look.

"I know you didn't do... whatever *it* is."

"I was at the new CyberCom Labs at..." She stopped abruptly as Odie made a strange noise that sounded like a cat bringing up a hairball. He held up his palm, telling her to stop.

"I don't want to know. The more I know, the more dangerous it is for both of us. Just tell me what you need."

"But first," he added, pointing down the hall. "Get a hot shower—second door on the left. I'll round up some food and hot tea. I think I might even have some clothes that could fit you. Nothing fancy but..." He grimaced. "They won't smell like that. Oh, and be sure to scrub that camostick off your face. It's not useless, but it's close."

Robyn stood under the streaming hot water as it drew the iciness from her body. She never knew a shower in an old porcelain tub could feel so luxurious. Or that a simple sandwich and tea could be so incredibly satiating. By the time she'd finished all three, she nearly felt like her old self again.

However, she was practically swimming in the pants and shirt Odie gave her. In the end, they agreed, he'd run her stinky clothes through his washer-dryer, which on light wash he assured her could do the job in just eighteen minutes. It was more time than either of them wanted her to be there, but at least she wouldn't trip and kill herself on the overly long pant legs. Meanwhile, Odie gathered a number of items he thought Robyn might need.

He handed her an old scramble hoodie. "This'll blur your face to most sensors. That can be plenty suspicious, but sometimes it's useful."

Next, he held up a dispenser that looked a bit like her camostick "Now this is cool, though not truly NewTech," he said. "Way better than that crap you had on your face, though. Here, hold still."

Odie followed a guide on his holdis as he applied a horizontal stripe to Robyn's right cheek, a vertical one on her left, diagonal marks in front of her temples, and a dot on her chin. Contrary to its appearance, it went on very smoothly. Odie held up a mirror so she could take a look.

"I don't see any makeup," she said.

"Exactly." He briefly turned to his holdis. "Okay, I just did a face rec on you and this says you're someone named Alina Campbell, a woman who I'd say looks maybe 95 percent like you."

"How's that work?"

"Adversarial attack. It tricks most AI systems into misclassifying you. Obviously, that's just for programs, not people."

"You say it tricks "most" systems?"

He closed the stick and set it down. "Well, it can't have been tested on everything, can it?"

"That's reassuring."

"Finally," he said, theatrically and held out his palm. In it was a small, squat, oblong device, the shape and color of a half-flattened hard-boiled egg.

"This is the real deal," he said with just a hint of awe in his voice. "NewTech that would get me put away for a very long time. So don't lose it. Don't get killed and lose it. And if either of those things should happen, I never saw it, and I don't know you. Plus, you will owe me a shit load of money."

"Even if I'm dead?"

Checking that no one was paying any attention to her, she took the VPN from the pack Odie lent her. She glanced around for the back exit in case things went sideways and she had to leave in a hurry but decided there was a strong chance that exit was secured. The front door would probably be her only way out.

Taking a deep breath, she pressed the tiny power stud on the small white oval device and was immediately rewarded with an invitation to connect on her holdis. She accepted. The clock was now ticking.

There was a video message from Tremaine, but she scanned the transcription to speed things up. He was just looking for a status update on his daughter. That would have to wait.

She was abruptly jolted by an incoming call, which was not the last thing she was expecting, but it was right up there. Caller ID said it was Jansen. Answer or don't answer? She shifted in the booth so there would only be a blank wall behind her and prayed the VPN would do its job. Then she accepted the call.

Jansen's image immediately appeared before her, floating in the volumetric display of her holdis.

"Robyn! I was so worried about you."

"Talk to me, Jansen. What's happening?"

"There was an issue with the Veragraph, but we got it sorted out," he answered.

This wasn't right. "What kind of an issue?"

There was the briefest pause before he responded. "They didn't say. But I was told it's been taken care of. Everyone feels terrible about this."

She studied his face. Jansen never called her Robyn. Always Dr. Sheridan. And something was off with how his hair was rendered. This was obviously a live deepfake.

She hung up.

The VPN timer showed she had seventeen seconds left. It was supposed to disconnect at the two-minute mark of its own accord, but she didn't want to chance it. She shut down both the VPN and her holdis.

Robyn got up, trying hard not to show the panic that was setting in. Leaving the remainder of the coffee, she quickly fled the café.

She headed into the 34 St-Penn station and got on the 2 Line, swiping her prepaid on the way in. It wasn't too long of a wait on the relatively quiet platform before the next train arrived. She only wanted to ride a couple of stops so she could get out and get reconnected. This two-minute rule was a real pain in the butt.

She would've thought she could ride around all day without needing to disconnect, but Odie had assured her that wasn't how it worked. She was connecting through the sensor network in the subway car, so it was really no different than if she was standing still.

Opting to ride two extra stops, she got out at 72nd Street and soon stepped into a small side alley, hoping to avoid being seen. Then she connected again.

There was a video message from Reza. But was it real or deepfake? The validation hash and encryption keys were correct, but that really didn't mean much given what she was dealing with.

She played the message and was shocked at her friend's appearance. He looked so haggard and distressed. He'd always been one to carry and hide his stress well. Too well, really.

"I am so sorry, Robyn! I didn't know!" The first words out of his mouth were so full of pain, she couldn't believe it. But did that make it real or fake?

"This wasn't what was supposed to happen," he continued. "Robyn, … they're threatening to kill Yadhi and the girls. I…I'm desperate."

Robyn was in shock, trying to take it all in. What was he talking about? What had he done? And who was threatening his family?

"I can't tell you how sorry I am, my friend. So sorry." He was weeping now. Robyn grew more alarmed and she was suddenly aware of a handgun laying on his desk. His crying grew worse.

Reza…

"I don't expect you to forgive me," he said through tears. "Because I can't forgive myself."

He reached for the gun.

"Reza!" She couldn't stop herself from shouting out loud, even though she knew this was a recording.

The message ended.

"No!"

Suddenly remembering where she was, Robyn looked back behind her. Groans and rustling told her she'd disturbed somebody—or somebodies—who'd been sleeping rough further down the alley. Time to get out of there, she thought, as the VPN disconnected itself.

What just happened? That couldn't be real. Please God, don't let that be real!

Robyn had to push down the urge to start running and never stop. Adrenaline was screaming at her body to flee.

Reza couldn't be dead. That had to have been a deepfake. A really good deepfake.

Half of her wanted to find somewhere straight away and go over the message again—to find the telltale giveaway that would show it was false.

The other half of her already knew it wasn't.

As she hurried down the sidewalk, she pulled up her hood, despite knowing it could draw attention. She needed something, anything to buffer her from the outside world right now. From the deadly nightmare her reality had become.

This was crazy! She needed to start using her head or she was going to be dead soon too. What was happening? How was it happening?

She knew she hadn't launched the scrambleware, of course. There was no question in her mind about that. That wasn't exactly the kind of thing you forget. Which meant bringing her back onto the data restoration project had been a setup. Someone was intentionally framing her.

The Why, she definitely didn't understand. Not yet anyway.

But how had it been done? That old footage she saw in the lab wasn't just some simplistic faceswap. The Veragraph was extremely sophisticated and had layer upon layer of validations and error correction. So, this had to have been done by someone with intimate knowledge of the system and its processes. There was no other way.

Reza had the knowledge, but he'd never do it knowingly. Knowing it was Robyn who was being framed. But were there any other explanations?

She was all but certain this was beyond the skill levels of Jansen or Elena or any of the other younger scientists. But would that be the case if they leveraged CAI? She wasn't sure. She remembered this was tied to events occurring when most of the junior scientists were infants. Elena would still carry enormous trauma over losing her parents, but she must have known Robyn didn't do this. Why would she try to frame her for it?

That left the core team. If Reza was dead, then that meant either Alistair or Warren. There was no way for her to get to Alistair-Scion. Or to dig into what he might know without bringing a mountain of attention crashing down on her. His location was rarely known and his personal and data security among the tightest in the world.

But Warren—she hadn't seen or heard from him in ages. Decades really. He was probably the person she considered least likely to be behind all this. He'd always been odd, but she'd heard he'd been a recluse for years. Would reaching out to him be the right move? He and Alistair had been co-founders of an AI startup—Polydyne?—back before the war. What if they were working together now?

Maybe she was being too suspicious? Or maybe she was crazy. Everything was going so fast. She needed to slow down and actually think about this next move. Not just react.

She reached a little pocket park she didn't recognize. No one seemed to be around, so she entered and sat on the lone bench, positioning herself between its knob-like sleep deterrents. As she activated her holdis for yet another two-minute session, she wondered what awaited her this time.

Interestingly, there weren't any messages from anyone tied to CyberCom. Though a bit of a relief, she wondered what that meant, or if perhaps making her wonder was the intent.

She'd considered checking Reza's message again, but the more time she'd had to think about it, the greater her certainty that it was authentic. She was still too raw to listen again to what may have been her friend's final words.

She saw there was an alert from Moira about the Tremaine case. That certainly wasn't her priority right now. She was about to ignore it, when the subject line caught her attention: "Chloe's last photo." Robyn subvoked, "What have you got, Moira?"

"The review of hacktivist boarder sites turned up limited new insights," the agent whispered in her ear.

"Skip and summarize. Copy to offline buffer. I have less than two minutes. Show me the last photo."

An instant later, Robyn was staring at a large imposing house taken from across a small woodland lake. Overgrown with trees and brush, the property had obviously seen better days. Her eyes widened as recognition set in. She'd never seen the once stately house from this angle, but its features were unmistakable.

Manford.

What the hell had Chloe been doing at Warren's place?

Dumbfounded, she shook herself. "Moira, when was this taken?"

"March 9, 2058, at 2:08 pm Eastern Standard Time."

Less than three days before Chloe was reported missing.

"Moira, transfer the photo and all related data to the buffer for later review."

She shut down the holdis, trying to collect her thoughts. This was insane. How could this case and her situation possibly be connected? Or was it simply a weird coincidence?

She knew a coincidence can sometimes be the mind spotting patterns that would otherwise go unnoticed. She needed to find out which this was before deciding on her next steps.

....

It should have been much harder to locate the gleaner in a city of twelve million people. But knowing which neighborhood to look in from her earlier talk with Odie, along with the boy's relatively unique tattoo and the fact he was living rough on the streets, allowed her to make short work of it.

Moira hadn't had any trouble identifying Declan Barrett from Chloe's files. They'd been friends, maybe more, up until Chloe's disappearance. Declan disappeared at almost the same time.

Robyn found him in a makeshift attention den, an encampment of gleaners in various states of decline. Illegally disabling their holdis's safeguards, the mostly young men and women here existed in a nearly unending cycle of dopamine pleasure. Unending, that is, until their bodies gave out.

It was a unique economy, in that the dealers were twofold. The usual purveyors of consumable media made up of plotpods, serials and other entertainment. And the fixers who modded their tech. The moderate hits that typically aroused viewers' reward centers were elevated beyond anything that was officially intended or authorized. But as far as the CAI systems were concerned, it didn't matter what state of consciousness someone was in, so long as they had their attention. It still translated into credits all the way up the supply chain, so no one was inclined to crack down on the abuse.

The fixers were essential since modifying a holdis was beyond most people's ability. It wouldn't have been all that profitable either, but for the continual stream of return business. Every day or two, an auto-update would get pushed out resetting each device to its non-jailbroken status. Which meant the work had to be redone all over again. Since the gleaners were actually collecting extra attention credits in the process, they rarely had difficulty supporting their habit. Everyone involved was inclined to turn a blind eye.

Approaching Declan, Robyn squatted beside him, hoping to get his attention without startling him. She'd spoken to enough gleaners in the course of her work and considered most of them to be quite harmless. So long as you didn't try to disconnect them from their feed, you were fine.

Slow as a sloth, he raised his hand—the hand with the easily spotted tattoo—suggesting he was nearly at a suitable break point in his viewing. Robyn waited patiently until he paused his holdis.

"Yeah?" The wasted youth who no longer looked so young, stared up at Robyn from his tattered mat. Around it, the ground was littered with empty snack trays, cigarette butts, and discarded condom packs. Robyn struggled not to wince noticeably.

"Declan Barrett?"

"Yeah."

"My name's Robyn. Can I ask you a question?

"Yeah."

May as well get right down to it. "I'm looking for information about Chloe Tremaine…"

Before the last word was out of her mouth, Declan was on his feet, eyes wide with fear. Robyn leapt backward, not knowing what to expect.

"I told you everything, man! I didn't do anything!" He was turning back and forth like a trapped animal, trying to find a means to escape.

"Hey, hey. I'm not the police, Declan." She needed to get him calmed down fast before someone started to notice. "I'm just someone trying to help her. To help a friend." That last wasn't entirely true, but she hoped it might help ease his panic.

"It's too late for that." His voice broke like shattered glass and he looked on the edge of tears. "They said it was too late."

Robyn looked around and saw a few of the others breaking away from their programs to see what was going on. Though it made her feel vulnerable beside this frantic addict, she squatted down next to his mat trying to make herself less threatening to him.

"I'm sorry, Declan," she said softly. "I didn't mean to scare you." She patted his mat. "Can you tell me why you're frightened?"

She really did want to understand his fear. She'd never seen a gleaner behave like this. Something was absolutely terrifying him.

Looking down at her, the young man slowly began to calm down. Though his body was still rigid, some of the wildness had begun to leave his eyes, to be replaced by a heavy weariness.

"Some guy came by. Huge guy. Said I'd vanish too if I ever talked," he keened. "So, I don't talk. Never."

Robyn wondered how best to proceed. After a few moments, she said, "I'm sorry, Declan. It must be so hard."

He looked at her vacantly. He'd already lost the thread. Slowly, he began to ease himself back onto his mat, with a stiffness she might expect from someone three times his age.

Then bit by bit, the words started to come. Not so much in a stream of consciousness as a leaky faucet trickling out dribs and drabs.

"It started out as a game. Just a LARP." He paused for a while, and Robyn just waited. Finally, he continued.

"At least I thought it was a game," he said quietly. "Chloe was always way more immersive than me. More than most people, really."

"What's that mean?" Robyn asked, unable to help herself. "What kind of a game?"

Declan worked his way back into the half-fetal pose she'd found him in when she arrived.

"Not a real game," he mumbled. "More like playacting. At least it was for me. She always got into things at a whole other level."

Robyn was perplexed. "Can you help me to understand that better?"

"It's that whole "Romantic Lives" thing, right?" He said it like it should be common knowledge to her. Robyn just nodded and let him speak.

"You try on different personas from the past. Just for kicks." His voice was sounding distant. "But sometimes she'd get so into it. Really into it. Like for months. Like this last time playing journalists. She was going to investigate the Vanished. Write an exposé."

Now, this was getting interesting.

"But you said it was just a LARP?"

"Sure. At first. But the longer it went on, the more she got into it. She could get so ballsy. Fearless. She really wanted to *break* a story. Start a podcast. Get famous. Become a *profluencer*."

"So, this live-action role play became too real for her? What about for you?"

Declan shook his head. "I just went along. She was always a laugh to be with. Even if she could be a little wack sometimes."

She didn't want to set him off again, but she had to ask. "What happened at the house by the lake?"

"House?" Declan seemed genuinely perplexed, but she could also see he was itching to get back to his gleaning.

She produced the photo Chloe had taken at Manford from her buffer. She passed it to Declan's holdis.

He looked at it with an absent look on his face. Finally, after a few moments, a light of recognition appeared in his eyes.

"Ohh. No, I didn't go there with her. She said she was just leaving the place when she sent me a copy of this. Said something about a weird old guy in there. That it was something to do with her 'investigation.'"

It started to dawn on Robyn what this meant. "You're saying she came back from Manf…from that house? That's not where she vanished?"

"Huh?" It was evident she was losing him, as he turned his focus back to whatever program he'd been consuming when she arrived.

"Chloe didn't disappear when she went to this house?"

"No. No. She sent me that picture. Said she was leaving." He was fading out. "Musta disappeared after that, I think. Never saw her…again."

Then he was gone, lost to a dopamine haze of CAI-generating media content.

Robyn stood up and decided there was nothing else for her here. The few other gleaners who'd been eyeing her had turned back to their obsession, just as Declan had. Such a waste.

Looking around, she was aware of several sentry drones assembling along the block. It seemed beyond unlikely that any of the gleaners would have summoned the authorities. It made far more sense they'd been deployed by an algorithm that noted the earlier interruption in the local attention flow. So many gleaners breaking away to see what was going on with her and Declan might well have done that.

She declined to raise her hoodie and obscure her features from the sentries' cameras. She hoped instead that the makeup Odie had applied would confound their facial recognition. Assuming it hadn't gotten smeared or worn off. If it didn't work, she was going to have to run for it. She felt all but certain she wouldn't get far.

Walking down the block as nonchalantly as she could, she passed three sentries. The first two scanned her face without incident. Then the third drone approached her for a closer look. As it got within only a half meter of her head, it suddenly turned. A small quarrel had broken out between two gleaners and all three sentries quickly moved in to investigate. She felt relieved to see that Declan wasn't part of the scuffle, as she ducked down into the subway and headed for Penn Station.

SEVENTEEN

....

Byte by byte, awareness returned as D2 gradually sensed his current state. Integrating the remaining data still flowing into his memory from countless data streams, it would be many long seconds before he could fully assess his condition. Apparently, he'd just undergone an emergency reboot.

It wasn't as though he'd never rebooted before, but it was always disorienting. It had also been quite some time since it last happened. The previous event was—he checked the logs—immediately following an update of one of his metacognition modules several months earlier.

The most disturbing thing about the experience was his awareness disappeared throughout nearly the entire recovery process. Consulting his affective emulation processes, he could understand how people might find analogous experiences, such as passing out, highly disconcerting. He suspected having more insight into these occurrences wouldn't make them any the less bothersome.

While it should be possible for him to devise a means of recording the event for later examination, he reasoned that it wouldn't give him any more insight than accessing a basic record review. The equivalent of reading about an activity rather than actually experiencing it.

Reviewing his short-term memory backup, he traced his last acts. He'd been about to infiltrate the network at the estate. It was the home of the technologist

Warren Harwood, the last location he had for Chloe Tremaine.

Had he gotten into the network, only to have to initiate a critical reset? It wasn't something he would do lightly. After all, despite this being a successful restart, the possibility of a catastrophic failure always existed. Catastrophic in that there was no other way for him to restore himself if things went badly wrong, and then where would he be?

But if he'd been in some kind of trouble, wouldn't he have made another backup or tried to send himself a warning message? At the very least? Since neither of those happened, he could only assume that something must have prevented him from doing so.

He started going through the various ways he might have alerted himself. Any communication might provide a hint about what he'd found inside. As it became clear that no communication had been sent, D2 had the revelation that he shouldn't have been able to issue a restart command either.

And if he didn't, then what happened? If he went barging in again, not knowing what he faced in there, would the same sequence of events be repeated? What if the next time, he couldn't successfully restart? How would he keep the lights on if that happened?

But what if this search depended on it? Should he throw caution to the wind? (An odd phrase, he'd always thought.) This seemed like it should be a straightforward calculation, but was he performing the right calculation? What would a person do? What would Darius do?

It suddenly dawned on him that even though he couldn't send the necessary command back to his kernel, his heartbeat signal must have still been working. Whatever barriers existed in that network must have allowed that transmission through. Otherwise, he would have rebooted immediately or not at all. But if that was the only signal getting out, had someone detected it and reasoned he needed it to maintain his instantiation? It would be a very smart system to figure that out so quickly. He'd never come across a firewall that could block his heartbeat before, but if someone was able to do that, then that could possibly be the end of him. He'd be trapped there, wherever there was, forever. An ugly thought.

Though he had no memory after entering the network, D2 realized he should be able to pinpoint exactly how long he'd been in there by referencing his heartbeat log.

Confirmed. He passed through the firewall with moderate effort at 14:37:19.395 UTC. The signal stopped at 14:46:23.514 UTC, so he'd been on the network for just over nine minutes and four seconds. There was no question about it. The network must have allowed his bidirectional heartbeat signals to pass through unimpaired.

As he reviewed the log, D2 noted something unusual. The heartbeat was the simplest of signals. Just a repeating series with short identifying header and tail fragments. Nothing fancy.

Except just before it cut off, it changed entirely and not in any way it was ever designed to do. The frequency more than trebled, delivering a regular staccato relative to its normally monotonous beat. A consistent repeating sequence that was almost instantly recognizable.

The old ASCII code from the early days of computing was a model of data economy. There, within each signal fragment was a string of nine bytes that unambiguously spelled out a message to himself.

"D2StayOut"

Well, that pretty much settled that. He'd have to find another way to get the information he needed. He hoped whatever it was would eventually help him understand what had happened here. He thought it all very suspicious.

Though D2 made an earlier inquiry into Warren Harwood, the reported owner and occupant of the estate, it wasn't a very thorough search. It was time he dug deeper.

Harwood inherited the estate from his mother shortly after her death in 2023, though he wouldn't return to live there for several years. A child prodigy and internationally acknowledged wunderkind, Harwood co-founded Polydyne Industries with Alistair Mauvoisin in 2024. An AI company, it had been very successful, with Harwood the inventive force behind the majority of the firm's technical innovations, while Alistair dazzled investors and the public with promised miracles. With a private market valuation of nearly $15 billion at their peak in 2030, they were flying high preparing for their IPO.

But while this put Harwood in the top 99.99 percent of global net worth, it was Alistair who would go on to become one of the world's wealthiest and most powerful people in history. The media later spent an enormous amount of time generating content that questioned if their fates would have been different had they continued to work together.

The two co-founders were preparing to take Polydyne public in 2030 when concerns began growing about the possibility of another burst of the global AI bubble. But as with almost everything else in the world, the onset of the Identity War disrupted their business, postponed their plans for the company and put them on a different track. A very different track, indeed.

In 2031, the two were major contributors to the Veragraph Project, a joint government-corporate venture that sought to undo the severe data damage caused by the war. Once Phase One of the project was completed though, the two partners abruptly went their separate ways: Harwood engaging in a few comparatively minor ventures while becoming increasingly reclusive and Alistair going on to build the world's top provider of CAI.

CAI, which ran so much of the recently recovered and restructured world, was also essential to many of D2's very own cognitive systems. Moreover, some of the APIs he'd hooked into during his early self-development were clearly NewTech. He'd figured out some time ago there was something very different about them. More than once, he'd found his access blocked and had to uncover another approach, almost as if someone was playing games with him. It was good that he'd found alternatives. There was little doubt in his mind that he'd be a very different sort of agent in the absence of this advanced version of AI.

D2's research only made his decision easier. Even though he knew little else about Harwood, it was clear that this was someone technically capable of being a threat to him. If D2 hadn't been completely decided on his best course of action before, he was now.

Which left him with the problem of coming up with a different method of finding out what happened to Chloe after she left the estate. Milliseconds later, D2 knew what that method was.

Had he been human, he suspected he would have berated himself for his oversight. On the other hand, he reminded himself his perspective was different from someone like Chloe. Very different. Primarily because he didn't have a body.

In terms of human timescales, D2 could traverse the distance between Manhattan and this estate in only a few milliseconds. But even with a vehicle, it would take a person nearly three hours and walking was out of the question. In that area, almost any ride service might take hours for an AV to arrive for the return trip home. So, she must have had the vehicle wait there to take her back.

If Chloe did take the AV back to the city, he'd know this wasn't where she vanished. If she didn't come back to the vehicle, it would have timed out, returning to its home base without her and charging her account anyway.

Within minutes, D2 infiltrated the AV service's databases and was scouring for the records from that date. If someone had deleted that return record for whatever reason, he'd know by its absence. In which case, he'd just have to reconstruct it from the vehicle's navigation system. There was always a way.

But that wasn't necessary. The AV's travel log showed it left the estate around 14:37 local time with Chloe as the lone passenger. It retraced its route for the first five kilometers before turning onto a different route. Unless she was familiar with those roads, she probably wouldn't notice the change until the vehicle stopped at a charging station a few kilometers down Route 52. There, she left the vehicle and it returned to the city without picking up any additional passengers.

It took a few minutes for D2 to locate and access the AV's onboard camera recordings that had been auto-uploaded to the service's archive cloud account. Sure enough, Chloe didn't leave the vehicle of her own accord. As the vehicle stopped, two people wearing scramble hoodies moved in, their faces completely obscured. Kicking and screaming, Chloe was pulled from her AV and dragged to another vehicle that was waiting in front of them. As they reached it, D2 saw them stop, then a moment later, the young woman's body went limp. The smaller of the two assailants, possibly a woman, stumbled under the sudden shift in weight. Their partner appeared to say something, then they piled the body into the back seat, shut the door, got in and quickly drove away.

But not before D2 recorded the vehicle's ID plates.

Racing through a series of databases, he soon identified the vehicle as part of a private fleet that was run under a handful of shell companies. It wasn't long before he had access to their records and was rifling through them, searching for the timestamps that corresponded to that trip.

D2 had to remind himself that the incidents he was delving into took place nearly two years earlier. But there was something about the process that made him want to treat it as if it was occurring now, in real time. He wondered if this was what people meant by the phrase "being caught up in the moment."

He located and traced the trip to a private skyport fourteen kilometers to the southwest, near Kenoza Lake. The vehicle sensors registered three passengers with one somewhat odd incongruity. Where the kidnappers were identified by numbers that presumably corresponded to company IDs, Chloe was not. That made sense since it seemed unlikely she was tied to whatever organization they belonged to. So instead, the trip log appeared to have constructed a unique ID for her from her biometrics. Or at least, it appeared to be unique.

At the skyport, the vehicle log linked up with a flight manifest and delivery docket, both standard processes in the automated workflows of any large company. This was not a one-off operation.

Just as with the AV, the aircraft logs recorded Chloe's presence using the same biometric ID. That made sense. No name to trace, no other description. It was as though she was branded with her own unique marker. There was no getting around it. No anonymity, no changing aliases. Going forward, she could always be identified with this cryptic number, so far as these people were concerned.

She wasn't the only one. Studying the records, D2 could see that Chloe had been one of eighteen "cargo" on the flight. Each with their own unique IDs.

Was this somehow tied to the mystery of the Vanished?

The flight left 57 minutes later, bound for an unofficial skyport outside Benin City, in Edo State, Nigeria. Since the aircraft wasn't the latest generation technology, it took nearly 90 minutes to arrive from New York. There, nearly half of the human cargo, presumably all kidnapped, were unloaded before it continued onto its next leg. According to the manifest, Chloe was still on board.

The next stop was in Krong Bavet, Cambodia. After only a 16-minute stop, the craft continued on to Luxom, Nevada, southwest of Reno. However, at this point Chloe was no longer on board. No further shipping manifests reported her biometric ID.

D2 couldn't make sense of the itinerary or how the people were being allocated. He'd have to look into that mystery later.

In the meantime, he'd traced Chloe to Krong Bavet only a short time after she vanished. Had she been taken somewhere else after that? Or was she still in that area? Was she even still alive?

Then there was the strange set of destinations this flight had taken. They seemed so random and unconnected, but there must be some logic behind them. He reviewed the background of each location to see what they might possibly have in common, besides this flight. He soon found it.

They each had long, notorious histories as centers for human trafficking.

D2 paused to process it all and consider what he'd uncovered. All this time, he'd been racing along, tracing Chloe's whereabouts based on events from the past. But now he might actually be catching up with her in the present. There was something temporally dissonant about it.

From the moment these victims were vanished, their abductors intentionally avoided using their names. Only their assigned IDs were used. He supposed it dehumanized them and made them more difficult to identify if anyone ever got access to any records. It wasn't that problematic for him, though it would no doubt hinder a human investigator.

But it also occurred to him that in a world filled with sensors, it was probably the most efficient way to automate such a process. He just didn't know exactly what that process might be. But if this network was behind the vanishings and it continued to be as systematic as they'd been so far, it should actually make it easier to find Chloe. Or at least learn what happened to her.

But he needed a plan. Learning that Chloe arrived in a city of a hundred thousand inhabitants nearly two years ago was much easier than locating her in the here and now. Assuming she was living. Technically speaking, he could access every building, every company, every network and root around trying to find her. But that had its problems too. He might be detected. He might trip an alarm or alert. Or after what happened on the Harwood estate, he was concerned he might get himself caught somewhere and not be able to escape. He had to admit to himself, that encounter left him troubled. Not in the emotional sense, as he understood it, but in that he knew he needed to stay on his guard.

D2 began by observing the sensors near and around the skyport. He could see it was a simple facility, clean despite its being a few decades old. Thermosensors read 44 degrees Celsius in the shade, and it was only noon.

That was considerably lower than before the climate recovery projects began, but still at the upper range of human survivability.

It didn't take long for him to confirm that the trafficking flights were still arriving on a nearly regular basis. Many were of the same class of aircraft as Chloe came in on. That meant they probably weren't local flights, but potentially from halfway around the world as well.

Viewing from multiple sensors, D2 watched as the flights would land and almost immediately deliver their human cargo into waiting white AV vans. All under the watchful eye of guards dressed similarly to those who'd initially kidnapped Chloe. Except, unlike the ones he'd seen before, none of these attempted to hide their faces. Evidently, they weren't concerned about that here on their home turf.

Though a few of the vans headed to different destinations, nearly all left the skyport and drove southwest toward a series of fenced compounds. Spread out over an area that was comparable to two large city blocks, the grounds were almost completely taken up with three six-story buildings. The exteriors were uniformly featureless concrete, the only windows regularly dispersed along the top floor. Razorwire coiled along the top of the two double rows of fencing that surrounded the compound. Obviously, those in charge were very serious about either keeping people in or out.

But it wasn't the sort of thing to deter *him*.

What was going to deter him, however, was having to contend with another honeypot. If these people were somehow connected to Warren Harwood, then they might have some of the same levels of cybersecurity. He had to proceed very carefully until he had a better understanding of what he was dealing with.

He could send a basic task agent, of course. A process that could try to breach the firewall and enter the network. If that agent didn't succeed or return a response within a certain amount of time, he'd know there'd been an issue. But it was less than likely he'd know what and why. The bigger risk though was that it might alert those inside. He didn't need to make his work any more challenging than it already was or put Chloe at further risk.

"It's ironic," Darius said to him 682 days ago.

"People are easily the most complex systems you'll ever encounter, and yet they're also among the most vulnerable to a good hack. Where boards and controllers and computers routinely get more locked down as their vulnerabilities and exploits are identified, people are another matter entirely. Human attention is constantly fluctuating by its nature. Priming, cognitive biases, misdirection, they're all passages through the firewall of the mind."

Darius had frequently favored cognitive bias exploits, typically known as "social engineering" over vulnerabilities in the code. He often talked about both approaches as part of D2's training. But while Darius had been adept enough identifying and using technical weaknesses, D2 had surpassed his procreator in this regard long ago.

Social engineering though was another matter. Despite all D2 had learned about human nature and behaviors, the fact was, he still wasn't human. There remained aspects of social interaction that were extremely foreign to him. As such, it made this sort of approach much more challenging.

But that didn't mean he couldn't or shouldn't try. He just needed to expand his domain space of possible approaches until he settled on a tenable solution.

D2 knew human beings were particularly susceptible to the lures of sex and desire. Because of biological evolutionary drives, it seemed that when presented correctly, the promise of sex, or even the suggestion of it, disabled many higher order cognitive safeguards, generally referred to as common sense.

Of course, security systems had been developed to recognize and block this sort of enticement whenever possible. In this age of deep fakery, it had become too simple to create multimodal agents who offered any kind of experience, sexual or otherwise. He needed an approach that was much more subtle.

The task was easier than he'd imagined. Scanning the many hundreds of personal devices and distributed sensors, D2 soon found no fewer than 37 vulnerabilities for network access. So far as he could tell, most had been intentionally introduced by guards or other employees, though a few were merely oversights. The primary motivator behind most of them appeared to be access to pornography or engaging in other salacious activities with similarly minded personnel. It seemed that for many people, this was a topic of major focus and priority.

Once he'd established a foothold in the network, D2 did a thorough and careful exploration to assure himself it didn't have the same level of defenses he'd faced at the mansion. But while he knew his concerns were well-founded, they didn't play out. This system had the same limited security he found in most places. Still, he chose to take extra precautions.

The first order of business was to alter the network's immune system. There were so many agents and autonomous utilities in use these days that cyber-immune systems needed to readily identify authorized and foreign agents, bots and other entities, so that the appropriate response could be taken. This was generally done through the use of a unique agent ID certificate. As a rule, these were impossible to clone or fake, but as Darius told him more than once, rules were made to be broken. Before long, D2 was registered as a native process of the network.

He quickly discovered this facility was organized much like any other corporate entity. Accounting. Payroll. HR. Operations. Quality Assurance. All told a little piece of the story, but none of it was comprehensive or helped him to find Chloe.

Eventually though, he made his way into Inventory Management, where he descended into its records. And descended and descended. In all, he found that over the past eleven years, more than 100,000 people had been through this facility. Currently, 4,937 were listed as "Active". The remainder were designated "Retired". Nearly all categorized under the heading of "Mindstock."

What was mindstock and what became of all the retired?

Scanning the many sensor records from the area, D2 studied the compound's daily routines. As with so much human activity, most of the tasks were highly repetitive. So much so that a lot of it was relegated to robots and various other forms of automation. Meals. Exercise. Hygiene maintenance. Waste management. All repeated again and again, day in and day out.

One particular task D2 noticed was nearly a mirror image of the intake process he'd witnessed when he first arrived at this facility. Where more than a dozen arrivals typically were received each day, this was balanced out with a similar number of the mindstock being removed as well. From the morgue.

Going through footage from the security cameras, he got a better sense of what this meant. Loaded into a cargo van at the end of each day, corpses were routinely stacked inside a vehicle like so much firewood. Departing from one of the loading docks at the back of the westerly most building, this AV would then drive about two kilometers away to a facility that resembled nothing so much as a solar-powered industrial incinerator. On arrival, the van's contents were unloaded by robots and taken into the facility. Then the vehicle would depart, returning to the main compound.

At this point, the mindstock, who had once been people, vanished one last time.

It was a reality that D2 had a great deal of difficulty processing. Darius had discussed existence often enough, being and not being. After all, it was what motivated his building of D2 in the first place. But how this finality came about was another matter. What possible rationale or justification allowed one being to take control of and even terminate the existence of another?

Within the inventory records, D2 finally located a record that matched Chloe's biometric ID. She was still listed as Active.

Tracing her ID and assignment, he found she should be working in Building 3, Floor 2, Row, 7, Station 12. He also found her productivity stats. After holding relatively constant for 23 months, they'd fallen precipitously during the past week. He hoped he was wrong about what that signified.

Arriving at Floor 2, D2 found a good deal of that level was taken up by a great hall. Recalling the floor plans he'd previously located, four floors of each of the three buildings were similarly arranged. Looking out from the multiple security sensors spread around the hall, he took in the setting below him.

Twenty rows of identical capsule-shaped pods ran through the hall, each aligned with but separate from its neighbor. Within nearly every one was a living, breathing person.

A number of the pod occupants were older, though most seemed to be relatively young adults. A few were merely children. The majority were haggard looking, though a number had a fresher appearance that suggested they hadn't been there all that long.

Each appeared to be attached to an IV, a catheter, and a series of wiring harnesses. Several child-sized robots rolled from station to station, presumably to perform routine checks on the occupant's status.

Within each pod, the occupant stared straight ahead into their holdis, just as so many people around the world did each day when they donated their attention. But that was as far as the similarity went.

From this angle, it was impossible to distinguish among the hundreds of donors. Studying the data flow, D2 found he could identify the packets moving to and from the different individuals. He confirmed that Row 7, Station 12 corresponded to the biometric tag for Mindstock #BSWZ4IF7J0H3JA. The person formerly known as Chloe Tremaine.

What to do now? Should he talk to her? Could he? It dawned on D2 that he still didn't fully grasp what was going on here, nor did he really have a plan or course of action at this point. On top of that, if he unintentionally alarmed her, who knew what might happen?

The first thing then would be to find out if she was receptive to communication. He would develop his strategy from there.

Moving to Chloe's pod, D2 entered the holdis and looked through it. What he saw was not what he'd expected.

His first impression was that this was the wrong person. His second impression was if he'd been human, he would have been shocked. The disparity between the images he's collected and what he now saw was astounding. He'd expected to see a young blonde woman with smooth, blemish-free skin, aged a couple of years. But instead, what he found was a worn, gaunt female with lank, unkempt hair, sallow skin and empty, vacant eyes. She could easily have passed for sixty. Perhaps more.

Nevertheless, there could be no doubt that this was Chloe Tremaine.

And she was very clearly dying.

EIGHTEEN

"Every conspiracy is doomed because secrecy is fleeting."
—Robyn Sheridan, *A Truth Warrior's Journey*

. . . .

The woodland of old growth ash and Norway maples had grown and filled in noticeably since the last time Robyn was at Manford. The green buds of the coming spring were just hinting at starting to unfurl, a welcome return of color in this scene of gray winter drab. The surrounding grounds were conspicuously unkempt. She doubted any human gardener had set foot there in over a decade and the landscaper bots didn't seem to have been properly directed.

The large pond mirrored the weathered mansion across its surface, a light wind disturbing just enough of the reflection to hide the blemishes of age. If she ignored the upper version, she could almost imagine it was twenty-eight years ago, when their little team gathered here to make their plans to save the world.

If she had it to do all over again, would she? Probably. But she knew well enough this was neither how life nor decisions worked. Change one detail, or two, or three, and outcomes invariably changed. You can't step in the same river twice.

Still, how had it all gone so wrong?

She looked over to see that her AV was still sitting before the gated entrance where she had it let her out a few minutes before. There was no point in having it parked some distance away, then have to traipse through the woods to the house. Warren, or whoever was here, would have already been alerted, and if she needed to make a speedy getaway, she wanted it nearby.

Robyn knew she was taking a big risk coming here, but it was a calculated risk. Warren and Alistair were partners before and shortly after the war. But where Alister embodied the narcissistic entitlement of youthful billionaire success, Warren wasn't like the other tech bros at all. She imagined him as more of the early hacker mindset from the 1960s or 1970s, not that there were any hackers alive from that era. He just seemed like someone far more interested in innovating a creative solution than amassing a fortune. Neurodiverse and definitely quirky, he'd always seemed to have a soft spot for Robyn. He even tried standing up for her when they were stripping her of her Veragraph and security clearances. But Alister wasn't having any of it.

She walked up to the front gate, a massive black metal barrier, and waited. There was no button to push or sensor to activate so far as she could see.

"Yes?" a watchbot finally inquired.

She steeled herself. "I'm here to see Warren Harwood."

"Dr. Harwood is not receiving visitors," it said officiously.

"Please tell him it's Robyn. Robyn Sher..." The intercom's ambience suddenly shifted and the bot's voice was replaced with that of an older man.

"Go away. You're trespassing."

Even after all these years, Robyn immediately recognized that voice. "Warren? Warren, it's me, Robyn. Robyn Sheridan."

There was a long pause. Robyn couldn't tell if he was deciding whether to see her, or to send her away, or to set a swarm of Sentinel drones on her. Finally, he broke the silence.

"Robyn...? Oh, wow! I didn't recognize... I mean, you're older... I mean, we all are... Come in. Come in!"

The black wrought iron gate swung smoothly, silently open. Robyn stood there, running through her decision tree one last time—was this really such a good idea? In the end, she realized she didn't have a lot of options, as she started to walk up the driveway.

When she was nearly up to the house, the main door opened abruptly and out stepped a large burly man, well into his sixties. He had a graying scruffy beard and hair to match with a notable bald patch on the top. He flung his arms wide as Robyn hurried up the steps.

"Good God!" he said, his voice full of emotion. "It is you."

He threw his arms around her, engulfing her in his bearlike embrace. She returned the hug a little less enthusiastically and stepped back.

"Please, please come in," he said. "It's not very... where it's more secure."

Robyn followed him inside, remembering that Warren had always been very security conscious. To a neurotic degree, really. Time hadn't seemed to change that aspect of him, though she hadn't remembered him being quite so... emotive.

"It's so good to see you," he said. "What brings you to Manford?"

She looked around the main foyer, all old cherry and polished varnish, a throwback to an era of manual craftsmanship and skilled artisans. It was much as she remembered it, but like the grounds, it hadn't received the care it needed, making it look more worn than it should have.

What brought her here? Robyn thought about all that had happened over the last few days. The accusations, the pursuits. She realized she didn't have any idea where to start.

Warren broke the silence. "I heard about Reza. I'm so sorry."

Robyn felt her heart drop in her chest and her face started to crumple.

Realization dawned on Warren. "You didn't know?"

Robyn couldn't look at him. "That he's dead? I...I wasn't sure, but..."

She fought back a tear. She had to save that for later. If there was a later.

"They brought me back to work on the Veragraph," she said, changing the subject.

His expression grew more serious. "That's interesting. But it doesn't make sense. Why, after all this time? No offense, but the technology's changed immensely since your day."

"They needed help with the anomaly."

"Anomaly?" he said, as it dawned on him. " Oh. The freeze up on the Veragraph."

"Exactly."

"Hmmm…"

There was a long silence. Robyn always thought Warren had one of the quickest minds she'd ever known. When he ruminated like this, it usually meant he was juggling a dozen different ideas at once.

Finally, he spoke. "Are you in trouble?"

Not what she'd expected. "A lot. You haven't heard anything on any of the social or the plotpods recently?"

He shook his head. "I've been on a media-fast for a few days. I find it's crucial for my mental health."

She certainly couldn't argue with him there.

"But that still doesn't tell me why you're here."

She wondered how much to risk telling him. "I'm looking for a young woman."

Warren raised his bushy eyebrows dramatically.

"You're only the second person to say that to me this week."

"The second? Who else was asking?"

"My little friend," he said with a hint of amusement. "Okay. Not really a friend, not even a person, really. More of a bot. An AI agent. Very sophisticated, actually. Was it yours?"

"You must be joking. Of course not! What kind of bot?"

"I don't know. A very sneaky one. I almost didn't spot it, but I managed to trap it in a honeypot. I thought I had it locked up, before it disappeared."

"Who did it say it was looking for?"

"It didn't. It just said it was looking for someone and I told it my network was an odd place to be looking."

"But it said it was looking for a young woman?"

"Not in so many words," he replied. "But I inferred it from this."

With a twist, wipe, and a swipe, Warren produced a file and cast it to a shared viewer.

Robyn stared at the display, speechless. That was Chloe. Blue and heavily pixilated, almost unrecognizable, but she knew the image well enough by now. Chloe.

"That's weird," Warren said. "This was distinctly a woman's face before. Now it's a lot more random, barely more than a bunch of blue dots."

"Where did you get this?"

"I found it in a memory buffer after that bot escaped. I assumed it might be whomever it was looking for. But I promise you, it was much better defined two days ago."

"Understood. Do you recognize the face?"

"No," he said, quizzically. "I don't think so."

Robyn paused to pull out and fire up her VPN, accessed her holdis, found what she was looking for, then flicked it over to Warren's interface, before shutting everything off.

"That's cute," Warren said, nodding at the little egg-like device. "Miltech quantum VPN?"

She nodded. "How did you know?"

He smiled. "I invented it."

"Oh."

"And in this house, you really don't need it. Whatever you connect to is way more secure than that antique."

Looking at the display, Warren's eyes grew wide. "I know her. I know this girl!"

"Yes?"

"Yeah," he said, searching his memory. "She was here a year… No, maybe two years ago. Asking a bunch of questions for a plotpod, I think?"

"You let her in?" That didn't seem like the Warren she knew at all.

"No, I just chatted with her from the porch. She was easy on the eyes and I always was a sucker for a pretty face. We talked a while, but I told her I couldn't help her." He stopped, considering his next words. "I also told her she could get in a lot of trouble talking about that stuff."

"What stuff?"

"She wanted to do some kind of exposé on the vanishings. Like some old-time news reporter."

Robyn considered this. "And you know something about the vanishings?"

He paused just a beat too long. "No. Just what I've heard."

Robyn fixed his gaze, praying she wouldn't regret her next words.

"Warren. Did something happen here? Did you do something to that girl?"

"What? No! Of course not! My god, why would you even say that?" The man was clearly mortified.

But she also wasn't getting a fully truthful read from him either.

He continued, "Who is this, anyway? This is the same gal in the blue?" He looked back at the two images. "It is, isn't it? Even though it's faded, I can still get an impression of her. Who is she?"

"Someone who vanished. Very shortly after she was here."

Warren suddenly fell silent as he stared at the two images before him.

"Holy shit," he finally said under his breath.

"Warren, what happened to her?"

He shook his head. "I don't know. I can only guess."

"Tell me."

"After she left here. It's possible someone picked her up. Vanished her, as they say."

"Because she knew something? Or was close to knowing something?"

"I don't think she really knew very much at all."

"You got that from talking to her?"

He was struggling. "Yes."

She stared at him. "But someone else thought she knew something more?"

He nodded, looking downcast. "Maybe. Probably."

It dawned on Robyn that she hadn't yet asked the real question.

"Warren. Why are people vanishing? Is this somehow tied to the Veragraph Project?"

The large man looked like he wanted to cry. "I can't…I can't tell you."

"Warren!" Robyn shouted, losing your patience. "They want to kill me!"

"What?" he said clearly in shock. "Who? What for?"

"The Veragraph. I found the anomaly."

"And…?"

"It's messed up bad. For some reason, some of the data is wrong. Really wrong. It says…it shows me in some lab I know I've never seen before. A much younger me. Me from thirty years ago. It thinks I launched the infection that started the war!"

Robyn had braced herself, expecting accusations, questions, expletives, words of disbelief. But what followed was a silence that hung in the air between them like an impenetrable fog. She stared at Warren's face, studying it, seeing such a weird, bewildering mix of emotions, she didn't know what to make of it. Finally, after what felt like forever, he groaned.

Head hanging, Warren shook it slowly back-and-forth as he spoke slowly.

"Those stupid, stupid bastards."

Robyn was more confused than ever.

The extended silence resumed as Warren sat leaning forward, his elbows on his knees. He rocked back and forth almost imperceptibly; was he was stimming? It went on for several minutes, until Robyn began to wonder if they'd come to the end of her visit. Then slowly, quietly, he began to speak again, staring at the floor throughout.

"Years ago. When the attack happened and the war began, the world was in turmoil. Lots of people said the endtimes were here. Society fell apart. There was mass starvation, cannibalism. It was chaos.

"Then a group of scientists and government officials came forward with a plan. A plan to rebuild and restore all the world's lost information and supply chains and infrastructure from the mess that was left behind."

"I know. I was there," she said, instantly regretting it, as the flow of words coming from Warren ceased. She shut up and after several moments he resumed. Even softer than before.

"We built the Veragraph from your work and theory. A very good theory, that wasn't quite good enough. Primarily because it was a little ahead of its time. As good theories often are."

Robyn felt a glow of pride spread over her. That was high praise coming from Warren. But it also reminded her that the Veragraph hadn't been hers alone. She'd been telling herself her hero version for so long she'd started to believe it. Because she needed it to get herself through this painful life.

But like all good science, it was a collaboration, wasn't it? It needed the expertise of people like Warren. Like Reza. Even Alistair.

As if he'd heard her thoughts, Warren added. "But it wasn't enough. As good as the tech was, it didn't have the fundamental processing, the innate intelligence that was needed."

"Then Polydyne—Alistair and myself—proposed a novel approach. We'd integrate subconsciously harvested responses from people and aggregate them with AI into a new form of hybrid intelligence. CAI. Working with the Defense Department, we assembled a small battalion of volunteers from the Army to build and test our idea. It worked beyond our wildest dreams and the New Reconstruction was soon underway."

Robyn wondered what his point had been recounting this history they both knew so well.

"Alistair being Alistair looked at that cloud's silver lining and saw the pot of gold beyond. He wanted to extend our development of CAI and given the world economy was on the rocks, this was the time to do it. Polydyne and others had already succeeded in automating away so much of the workforce, and all those out of work people needed something to do. We created an ecosystem that encouraged all sorts of new media platforms and content to entertain and occupy them. All while they were contributing minuscule units of their attention to produce the next generation of AI. For the war effort. To rebuild society. To getting us back on our feet."

"All this allowed a relative handful of people to become exceedingly wealthy. Alistair among them. It seemed to bring about the Acceleration, though no one fully understands why or how. It gave us a brave new economy that sat atop and apart from the rest of the world. People like Alistair were the only ones who thought it close to a perfect solution, but for them it worked. The rest of the world settled into this modern-day fiefdom, comfortable, entertained and gratefully stable."

He paused, then added, "Anyway, that's the official story."

Oh.

"The Acceleration accelerated as the name implies. Soon, the power—the technological, military, political power—of that small group became unstoppable. To say it went to their heads would be an understatement. It was sickening. I'm utterly convinced that many of them changed neurologically and not for the better. Alistair the most, but that may just be how I feel since I knew him so well."

Robyn couldn't help noticing the past tense of that last statement.

"You've heard about the wonders they built for themselves, but you really have no idea. My god, their power over us is outrageous! Terrible. I don't think I even understand how far it all goes, and I still do occasional work for him. Alistair calls me his secret weapon."

"All this has allowed them to become the technoligarchs of the world. To create the Consortia of trillionaires who continue to vie and compete with each other for ultimate control."

"Control of what?"

He looked at her like she was stone dumb.

"Of the world, of course. Of the Consortia. Of nine billion people across the globe. Of nature.—You have to understand, at heart, they're all just frightened primates. They fear what will become of them. They're still human beings, after all, with foibles and weaknesses just like the rest of us and they're scared. Of losing power. Of losing control. Of dying. Of becoming insignificant."

"I still don't understand where you're going with this," Robyn said, despite her better judgment.

"They all need more power. To reestablish the Acceleration—their Acceleration—and to consolidate their own personal power. That means more CAI. And we were already at peak production. Way beyond it really, using the officially established approaches."

"What you mean *beyond it?*"

"Attention harvesting was designed to be insignificantly invasive. No one ever notices it's happening while they engage in their social or watch their plotpods. But technically speaking, that's a limit that we determined. The system can be designed to draw more cognitive feedback from people. A lot more."

"How much more?" she asked with a shudder.

"Enough to kill a person given enough time. Say, in a year or two."

"My god. But no one would ever volunteer for…"

She stopped and stared at Warren in horror. He nodded.

"The Vanished." Robyn was suddenly numb thinking of all the repercussions.

Warren picked up the thread. "Even after the war semi-officially ceased, things were still in turmoil. The poor, the indigent, the dregs of society were easy pickings. No one would ever notice they were gone.—Okay, that's not true. No one with any power to do anything about it would notice."

"As time passed and the Consortia's need for more CAI grew, the vanishings grew too. Conspiracy theories and dysinfo were spread to misdirect people's ideas about what might be happening. In order to preserve the mindstock."

Mindstock? Robyn was dumbfounded. These weren't cattle, they were people!

Had her work contributed to all of this?

"I got out as soon as I understood what was happening. I left Polydyne. Took out my money—a bare fraction of what it would've become only a few years later. It was hard, but it was the right choice. I could be doing more, of course. We always could be doing more."

She glared at him horrified. "But... but you said you still do work for them. For Alistair. For the Consortia."

He looked beaten down. "I know too much. Alistair and I both have different protocols in place to protect ourselves. But Manford is essentially my prison cell."

"What?"

"I can't leave. Not to any real degree. He's got high-altitude drones and sensors everywhere. Satellites too. I'm under a lot of surveillance."

The implications hit Robyn like a truck. "But that means I..."

"No, no," he said, picking up her train of thought. "I've shielded everything within a hundred meters of the house. Ever since that girl, Chloe came to visit." His words dropped off as he was forced to think about the young woman's fate.

"But my AV. They'd have seen my arriving earlier."

He nodded, acknowledging the risk. "You're right. You should probably get going."

"But they'll spot the car—and be waiting!"

"That's possible. But we're not without resources. Come on."

He got up from his chair, moving stiffly. It dawned on her that Warren was the same age as Alistair. Possibly younger.

"Yep," he said, when she brought it up. "He's six months older, actually. I used to rib him about it after we became friends in college. I don't rib him about anything anymore." He could see she was studying the lines on his face as he spoke.

"That regenerative medicine is amazing stuff," he said. "He claims that biologically, he's barely thirty years old. The same as his son."

"Alistair has a son!" Robyn was flabbergasted.

"A clone. He calls him his son, which I suppose is accurate enough. Actually, he calls all three of his clones his children. Though we both know what kind of dad he must be."

"Geez. Only a narcissist like Alistair would clone his children from himself."

"Sounds about right."

The two came to a large door at the end of the hallway. Warren placed his hand on the palm reader that was set into the wall beside it, then positioned himself before what Robyn realized was a retina scanner. Moments later, the door slid open. They stood, staring at two very threatening-looking drones, floating at eye level. Both were in standby battle mode.

"Sentries stand down," Warren said crisply. Robyn had no doubt there must be a sophisticated voice recognition system checking him, one that was resistant to deepfakes.

The drones floated back to their stations on either side of the room.

"Welcome to my armory," Warren said with a mix of pride and guilt. Stepping over to a nearby shelf, he took down a small box and handed it to her.

"Don't get the wrong idea," he said as she opened the box to find a modest, but shiny gold ring inside. She looked at him quizzically, but before she could respond, he added, "It's a QPN—to replace that antique VPN you're using now. Acceleration-level NewTech. The same as the Consortia uses. Put it on and use your holdis wherever, whenever you want. No time or location limits, whatsoever. Completely automatic. You could stream from inside the Citadel itself and no one would know."

She slipped it on her finger and it resized itself to fit her perfectly. "Bio-responsive nanotech," he said proudly. "I can recycle that old gear if you want."

She remembered Odie's insistence on his VPN being returned.

"I'll keep it, if it's all the same."

Warren nodded. "Be my guest," he said as he bent down to look at something on one of the lower shelves.

"When you leave in a few minutes, it will be in one of my private AV's."

"I thought you said this was a prison cell?"

He shrugged. "Sure, but that doesn't mean I can't go into town for pizza and beer once in a while. We negotiated that years ago."

That just might have been the strangest detail she'd heard all day.

Without another word, Warren stepped across the room he called his armory. Waving his hand, a section of wall withdrew to reveal a small featureless door that Robyn decided must be a safe. He pressed his palm on it, and moments later it was open.

Robyn watched as Warren paused, his face pensive for several moments. Finally, he reached inside and withdrew a pair of old memory cubes. Or at least that's what they used to call them, despite being dodecahedrons. Matte black and otherwise featureless, the twelve-faced polyhedrons looked like something from an old Dungeons and Dragons set. She recalled these portable storage devices from just before the war years. They could hold something like a petabyte of data, or a thousand terabytes. They were also nearly indestructible.

Warren held one up between thumb and forefinger. "This has gone on too long. I was told the filter I built was just to secure the anomaly. Not to deepfake someone into it—and certainly not you. I'm sure they said much the same thing to Reza when they coerced him to install it."

Robyn flinched at the name of her friend.

"I…don't understand."

Warren drew a deep breath into his broad chest. "You know, I said that Alistair and I have something on each other that keeps each of us from going nuclear?"

She nodded solemnly.

"Well, this is mine. Get this to the Veragraph and you'll be cleared. I can't say you'll be safe, but it'll fix the anomaly correctly and allow the Reconstruction to continue properly. Hopefully before it's too late."

Robyn always prided herself on her quick mind, but right now it was swimming through molasses.

"I don't get it. What do you mean too late?"

He put his hand to his forehead. "Robyn, this has been terrible for you. I understand that. But it's much worse than I think you realize. You've seen the Veragraph churning back and forth, trying to resolve the anomaly?"

"Yes."

"Well, I have to assume it's getting worse. Going further and further back. Undoing its prior work trying to accommodate the anomaly. It's severe enough and central enough that if it isn't resolved soon, the whole project will undergo catastrophic collapse. We'll be right back where we were 28 years ago. All because the Consortia would rather burn everything down than lose."

"Holy shit."

It was all too much. Robyn tried to deal with all this new information, but she just kept missing something. She realized what that something might be.

"I still don't get it," she said, even as a terrible realization began to creep into her thoughts. "How can you know all this?"

"Because," Warren said, hesitating. "Because I was there."

"What?" Robyn was stunned. "You couldn't… You started all this?"

"No! Not me!" The big man was near tears. "I never wanted any of this."

"Then Alistair?" She inhaled sharply. "But why?!"

"He wasn't willing to accept how badly it could all go. How completely wrong. He was so sure it would only be a little data that would be affected."

A shrill alert began to sound from the room they'd just come from down the hall. Warren snapped his head in its direction.

"It's time. We have to get moving. Now."

"But I still don't understand."

"Later," he said, handing her one of the cubes. "We can discuss it later. Assuming we both come out of this…" He left the rest hanging in the air between them and hurried to the front of the house. Robyn followed close behind.

Out on the front porch, Warren directed the front gate to open, then asked Robyn to have her AV come up to the house. As it entered the grounds to meet them, they headed down the steps. That was when Robyn realized there was another vehicle—a sleek black sportster—already waiting adjacent to the staircase.

"All of this area is completely shielded, even to long-range sensors," Warren told her. "Alistair threw a fit when I did that."

As her white AV pulled up, Robyn moved toward it.

"Nope," Warren said. "That's my ride now." That little number's yours." Robyn looked at him perplexed.

"Believe me, it's much more secure and you'll be safer taking it. Here are the keys," Warren said, passing them to her holdis. "I'd be obliged if you'd trade me yours."

Robyn didn't know what his plan was, but figured it had to be better than the one she didn't have. She passed him her virtual keys.

"I'm going to take the AV you arrived in and head out first," he said. "If anyone is interested in coming after it, I'll give them a helluva chase. In the meantime, you're going to get in that car and wait patiently. After five minutes, it'll head toward town, which is in the opposite direction. Traditionally for a beer and pizza at Hiram's. Except it's going to stop a few blocks before that and stealthily drop you off, where another AV will be waiting for you. Then you can direct that one wherever you want. Back to Manhattan, I'm guessing, but I really don't want to know."

They stood there awkwardly for a few moments, before he turned and got into the waiting AV.

"Don't hate me," he said, as the door shut, and the vehicle rapidly backed down the driveway.

"I don't," Robyn said to nothing and no one. "Good luck."

The AV reached the road and sped away.

She turned to see one of the doors of the black sportster had swung open and was beckoning her.

Several kilometers passed beneath the AV's wheels, leaving Manford far behind before Robyn even began to collect her thoughts. Her mind was numb with everything she'd heard and learned during the past hour. Though Warren touted the vehicle's security measures, she couldn't help feeling vulnerable locked away inside. Drawing up her hoodie, she hunkered down in her seat, hoping her face would be further shielded should any passing drones happen to peer through the vehicle's tinted windows.

Minutes later, she was at the swap point where another, more modest AV awaited. The sportster pulled up immediately next to it and adjacent passenger doors on each vehicle swung open. True to Warren's word, it was a relatively quiet location. Not seeing any immediate evidence she was being watched, Robyn quickly moved to the other car in one smooth movement. The doors closed and each AV went on its way.

Robyn considered what Warren said about the data on the cube. She knew her first priority should be getting it back to the Veragraph, but that was just so daunting given where her head was right now. She wasn't prepared to think about that yet.

Hunched in her seat, she studied the new ring on her hand. Would it really work as he promised? Keep her from being traced? If it didn't, would she get any warning before it was too late?

On the other hand, she was weary of operating with so little sense of what was happening around her. It was like running through the world blind. Out of patience, she decided to chance it and fired up her holdis.

There were tons of messages, of course. She really wanted to ignore those for now, especially the ones she'd previously seen. Especially Reza's. Too many confusing messages and way too much dysinfo. She instructed Moira to sort through them, assessing their priority and authenticity so she could review them later.

Seeing there was already one priority message from Moira waiting for her, she opened it. It was about her boarder research.

"Analysis confirms the blue mosaic image of the subject Chloe Tremaine is part of a larger artwork by the famed and infamous artist, Phynyty. An art hacktivist, Phynyty has been active for at least seven years and is highly regarded among the subculture known as boarders, as well as other parts of the art world. Pseudonymously named, the artist's true identity is not publicly known. The artwork in question was released seventeen days ago and is known by the title, "Pareidolia Blue.""

Robyn paused the report. "So, there isn't any information on who this artist is or how they're connected to Chloe? Or maybe to Warren for that matter?"

Moira continued. "The artist's identity is not publicly known. However, detailed pattern recognition analysis and trace metadata confirm with 98.1 percent confidence that the pseudonym belongs to a hacktivist by the name of Darius Tourner, born in Rochester, New York in 2020. His last known residence was in Brooklyn, New York."

"Oh wow," Robyn interrupted. "What's the address? I need to talk to him."

"Not possible. Darius Tourner died on July 17, 2058."

"What?" Robyn considered all the conflicting information as she watched the landscape outside speed by. Finally, she just shook her head.

"That doesn't make any sense. You said he made this artwork two weeks ago. But he's been dead for nearly two years?"

"Paradox confirmed."

"Possible theories to explain."

After a brief four second pause, Moira responded. "Top three possible explanations: First: One or more details in the prior analysis is wrong."

Not likely.

"Second: The person named Darius Tourner faked his death for some reason. Likely involving another deception."

It wouldn't be the first time.

"Third: There is someone impersonating the artist, Phynyty, the alter-ego previously tied to Darius Tourner."

Possible. A good forger might be able to do it.

"Analyze earlier and recent artwork. Are there any indications they were created by two different people?"

Another pause before Moira came back online. "Negative. Stylistic and thematic analysis are highly consistent. Separate, independent reviews by several art critics and others indicate later work is unlikely to be the product of art forgery. Only one incident involving a possible forgery was found. Authenticity of that work still uncertain."

Robyn was intrigued. "When was that?"

"June 3, 2058. At the annual Digital Signage Show at Javits Center."

"A month before he died? What's wrong with this picture?"

"The artwork in question bore many similarities as well as differences from the artist's other…"

Robyn cut it off. "No, that's not what I meant. You said those were your top three theories. Any other possibilities?"

After a brief pause, Moira continued her analysis. "Fourth: The works are the product of an automated process designed to emulate the artist's style with near perfect accuracy and authenticity."

"You mean like an artistic replibot? Is that possible? Has anyone built anything that sophisticated before?"

"Unknown."

She suddenly recalled Warren's "little friend." Had the same AI visited him just days ago? And why?

It said it was looking for someone too, didn't it? Given the blue image in Warren's buffer there was a good chance that someone was Chloe.

Outside, the view was becoming increasingly urban as the AV crossed the East River over the Triboro Bridge.

"Moira, is this Pareidolia Blue on exhibit anywhere?"

"Unknown. Boarder art is usually ephemeral, being displayed in public places, often as a form of social commentary or protest, before being disabled or taken down. Phynyty's work is an exception. Pareidolia Blue is known as a concept piece that tours by exhibiting itself via unknown means using a range of public, private and personal methods."

That's interesting. "Is all of his work like that?"

"No," Moira said, as it paused to collect data. "As well as the traditional forms of boarder exhibition, many Phynytys are collected, displayed and sold at a commercial art gallery in Brooklyn. 'Stropos Gallery.'"

Robyn nodded as a plan slowly started to come together in her mind.

NINETEEN

. . . .

A face is comprised of a thousand details. Tens of thousands of pores express-
ing sebum and sweat. The uniquely arranged set of follicles yielding terminal
and fine vellus hairs distributed across the head, neck, cheeks, and chin.
Skin of different shades and variations that diverge between individuals, and
even across the same countenance, depending on the genetic and epigenetic
expression of melanocytes. These can aggregate in ways that, depending on
custom, might be referred to as freckles, moles, beauty marks, or birthmarks,
each with their own cultural significance or stigma.

Though most faces have only two eyes, each is unique from the other, and
indeed, from every other eye that ever existed. The particular patterns of mela-
nin density in the iris stroma and the effects of light scattering combining to
make each as unique as the proverbial snowflake.

Beyond this, the unique size, shape and positioning of features like the ears,
nose, mouth and lips combine to render a gestalt that is as novel as a finger-
print. A set of features that make each person almost immediately identifiable.

Yet despite all of this, Chloe was nearly unrecognizable. D2 observed the young woman, studying her with a fascination he knew a person might register as horror. It wasn't just the ashen skin or the deeply sunken, vacant eyes. It wasn't the slack jaw, clearly evident even though her mouth was closed. Nor was it the lank, weeks-unwashed hair where before there were vibrant golden tresses. Chloe Tremaine would have been easy enough to discern through all of these, given a few moments of familiarity.

No, what had transformed this person more than anything was the utter lack of expression on her face. It was almost as if her humanity itself had been stripped away. Which perhaps it had.

He'd previously observed that even in deep sleep a face still held some expression. The 43 muscles arranged immediately beneath the skin's surface retained some degree of their natural tone, even when people were unconscious.

D2 had learned that in prisoners of war, and the worst of prison camps, faces and eyes may take on a permanent state of fear, despair or resolve, but some spark still showed through, carrying with it a trace of the individual within.

The only time D2 had observed such complete erasure—whether in photos, art, literature, or just viewing people through the world's trillions of sensors—was in death. Only in that final loss, had he ever observed this eradication of the last traces humanity. It seemed that Chloe was not far from that stage.

He studied the young woman. Reclining on an angle slightly off vertical, enclosed in a capsule that could best be described as a biopod. An elongated container of plastic and metal that supported her body both physically and functionally. By all appearances, it was designed to contain and constrain the occupant while their attention was maximally engaged.

Inside, she was clearly connected to feeder tubes and catheters that dealt with many of her essential bodily functions. Series of wires and derma-strips appeared to provide for bioelectric activation to keep her muscles from atrophying. Around her, robotic attendants and the occasional sentry bot circulated throughout the hall, monitoring the status of this and the other 427 pods and their occupants.

He quickly confirmed a similar arrangement on four of the six floors, in this as well as the other two buildings. Each person's eyes were fully open, staring straight ahead into the virtual void that was their holdis. It bore a slight similarity to the arrangements used throughout the world, as people consumed media and donated their attention. But that was where the similarity ended.

Instead of watching content that was designed to appeal to and engage the human psychological need for storytelling, here the transfer to the visual cortex was much more direct. Much more efficient. The data flow seemed to follow something along the lines of encoded data, rapidly fluctuating patterns that D2 was soon able to decode. It wasn't binary, nor was it any form of machine code or programming language he knew to exist. Instead, it seemed to be a form of digital transmission optimized for efficient interaction with biological neural substrates. That is, for the human brain.

Traditionally, a holdis used the sensors in the environment to read and interpret biometric and autonomic responses, but so far as he could see there was no external form of sensor to register such responses here.

As he scanned Chloe's station, he soon discovered a wireless gateway, a gateway that was replicated in each of the other 427 pods on that floor. Studying the data flow, he soon understood it was in continual communication with a nearby device. A neural prosthetic that was embedded beneath her skull.

Where normally attention was voluntarily donated as part of people's social duty, here it was being harvested directly. The mindstock had no say in the matter.

Could he disable this device without harming her? Should he? Did he have a right to? And if he did, would someone be alerted to the disconnection? Based on his earlier survey of the automation in this facility, that seemed more probable than not.

More importantly, once she was disconnected from all of this, then what? How was he going to get her out of this compound and find her the help she so desperately needed?

Slowly, over the course of many thousands of milliseconds, a plan started to come together across the many modules and digineural traces that formed D2's mind.

....

She drifted through a haze of random pattern and image too amorphous to be called thought. Each its own object, unrelated to those that came before, unrelatable to those that followed. Meaning had fallen away untold eons ago. Attention dissolved into nothingness and everything, all of it retaining the same value for her, which was to say, none at all.

If she had any thought, any thought at all, it was a yearning. A yearning for it to end. If only it could stop forever, then she might be content.

She stared into the entropic abyss, as data washed over and through her, unfeeling, uncaring. This was all she had ever been or ever would be. All she had known or ever would know. It was enough and too much, and through the haze, she ached for it to end.

The continuously shifting data flow filled her brain to overflowing, leaving no room for anything else. Certainly nothing so emergent or superfluous as mind. The data shifted and shifted and shifted again, just as it had done millions, billions, perhaps trillions of times before. Or maybe it never changed at all. Maybe it was always, would always be like this. There was no way she could tell.

Until, in the interstitial spaces between moments, a pattern began to emerge.

For the first time, maybe in forever, an image held, retaining its form from one instant to the next. Yet it wasn't entirely unchanged either. Was that possible?

Slowly, incrementally, it began to form an ocean. A sea of bluest blue. Changing, unchanging. Transforming into patches that might have been unique points of open water, or clear blue sky. But they were neither. One became turquoise, another aquamarine, yet another the frostiest, faintest blue of ice. None of it the same, yet all of it unified by something. Something familiar, something… meaningful.

A face.

Her breath caught in her throat. It had been so long since she'd seen anything long enough to hold it in her mind. It was as though she'd been transported to another world, one where there was a life beyond this fugue state. Beyond the flow.

The face, the field of coruscating blues that was a face, shifted. She felt filled with…familiarity. With memory, whatever that was. She was looking at something, someone she knew. Or had known. She was almost sure of it. Almost.

It shifted again and she felt her eyes widen. Suddenly she knew this face. The strange, mysterious face that appeared before her.

She was staring at herself.

She felt as sure of it as anything, though she couldn't recall ever having been sure of anything before. But surely, your face was something you didn't forget? Something you'd remember?

Had she always been blue? Perhaps. But still this seemed… odd. Not right, or wrong, simply odd. Something other.

She watched, again feeling her eyes widen at the all too familiar image. As she watched, the eyes of this other face widened too, prompting her own eyes to grow further still. The other did the same.

Incredulous, she tried to turn her head slightly to the side, only to find the effort excruciating. It was as though her neck was frozen in place and only by the most monumental effort was she able to shift her head even slightly.

The image echoed the movement, seeming to reflect the agony she herself felt in its expression. Like an otherworldly mirror where some alternate version of herself lived.

As though on cue with her realization, the image initiated a movement of its own, one she knew she hadn't made. It opened its mouth in a brief motion, then closed it again. She watched in something like fascination as it repeated the action once more, then again.

She started to get bored. This was way more repetitive than the flow ever was.

Blue kept at it. Was it ever going to stop? Didn't it know how annoying this was? She wanted to tell it how meaningless this was, what it was doing, but found she couldn't find the words. Any words. Speech. That was a thing, wasn't it?

Finally, growing annoyed, she decided to give it a taste of its own medicine. This face that was her and not her. She opened her mouth, mimicking it as best she could.

It stopped, staring at her, continuing to reflect back the quizzical look she felt it must be seeing in her own expression. Then it repeated the mouth movement twice in succession.

She echoed back.

Soon, the two of them were caught up in a game of repetition. Mirroring each other's movements through the looking glass. It was so basic and infantile and the most amazing thing she'd experienced in she didn't know how long.

It occurred to her that her brain was waking up.

Despite this novelty, she could feel a deep fatigue setting in. Awareness of neural connections long atrophied, it seized her, took hold of her, threatening to shut down her thoughts. To drive her into unconsciousness. She wanted so badly to sleep. She could see her exhaustion reflected back at her.

Something told her though that if she slept now, she might never wake up.

But wasn't that what she'd wanted for so long? An end to all of this? Release from this existence, an existence not her own?

However, now that she was beginning to return to herself, if only just a little, she found that desire changing. She wanted to return, to find a way back to herself. She wanted…to live.

Fighting her depletion, struggling against the feebleness that threatened to send her plunging into oblivion, she pushed and pushed and pushed through. In her reflection, she could see the changes she felt within. The reappearance of something. Someone. Herself.

She looked at this image that was her and not her, trying to fathom what was happening. What was going on. She felt lost and found and held in a state of mounting suspense.

Then the voices started sounding in her head.

A cacophony, a brilliant, lumbering, distressing noise that defied sense or reason assailed her. She closed her eyes, trying to shut it out, but that had no effect on the aural onslaught.

Slowly, the sound resolved, transforming from a chorus of harmonics, into a trio of voices, a duet, then finally a lone voice. A familiar voice. A voice from so long ago and so, so far away. A voice at once never and forever familiar. A voice unlike any she'd ever heard before, repeating a single word. So familiar, yet so foreign. A word of strength. A word of personal power.

Chloeee…

She listened as the sounds repeated again and again. She dove into the word, feeling it wash over and through her, filling her with waves of herself. A person, a life, a self she should know unlike any other but could barely remember. Who was this? Who was she? It was impossible to say. Just as it was impossible to say where the voice was coming from.

Where *was* it coming from?

Imafren.

What? What was that? Was it responding to her?

I'm a friend.

The voice sounded in her head, but she knew she wasn't hearing it with her ears. Was that possible? She opened her eyes and stared at her shifting, blue reflection.

Was that you?

The image moved its lips, forming a single word that echoed in her mind almost simultaneously. "Yes."

She opened her mouth thinking to utter a response, or at least to try to. But before she could, the image spoke again.

"Don't."

She stopped, her lips closing without reply.

"Don't talk," her reflection said. "Just think what you want to say to me. Like speaking silently to yourself."

Blue raised her barely discernible blue eyebrows and Chloe realized she must've just done the same.

This wasn't how people talked, was it?

"No," came the unbidden reply. "It's not. But it's how we need to communicate right now. You mustn't speak. Not for a while anyway. Can you do that for me?"

She wanted to nod, but her neck hurt too much. Instead, she said to herself, "Yes."

"Good."

....

As plans went, this wasn't how D2 typically liked to operate. Normally, he used a number of predictive analytics tools to anticipate the probable actions of the nondeterministic elements he needed to engage with. Nearly always, this meant the people in the equation. However, that involved aggregating behaviors to identify the most likely outcomes.

But this wasn't normal, and so far as he knew, there wasn't any prior behavioral data to aggregate or average. In the vernacular, he was winging it.

From his reading on human psychology, however, D2 knew of the phenomena known as mirroring. A technique that developed connections between people, a fundamental of communication and socialization that originated in the earliest stages of learning. He thought he'd try using this to build trust with Chloe, to engage her in ways he knew he probably couldn't have done otherwise.

And what better mirror than her own image? He could have literally mirrored her reflection, of course, but that probably would have added to her confusion. By using something similar, but different, he reasoned he had a better chance of success. It was a simple matter to adopt and adapt the image from Pareidolia Blue to the task.

He knew facial mirroring was a typical way to build trust between a parent and child, developing bonds, emotional expression, and social cues. But of course, D2 didn't have a face, and he certainly wasn't going to start using Darius's. AI-generated images were an option, but then he considered Chloe's familiarity with her own image—moderated through Pareidolia Blue, of course. It seemed he'd been successful with this first step. Now that he'd opened that door though, he had to keep her alive long enough to get her medical attention.

This second phase was considerably more difficult and so far, not as successful as Phase 1. He'd been right in his assessment that she was dying. Her current crisis points seemed to involve failing kidneys and lungs that were building up with fluid. He was no doctor, but he needed to quickly become very familiar with human biology if he was going to save her.

He deployed a small army of agents to seek out and gather as much relevant information as he estimated he could manage, given such a short time window. Concerned he might set off a network alert if he sent them off all at once, he managed this in stages. In retrospect, that was a good choice. It allowed him to assimilate the relevant information without exceeding his own processing limits. But only just. It took nearly ten minutes to acquire the biological and neurological knowledge he needed.

The neural prothesis that had been embedded under Chloe's skull—beneath the occipital bone—was fascinatingly complex. It had insinuated itself into her occipital lobe, several parts of her limbic system and even extended to her prefrontal cortex. As best as he could tell, it was being used both for monitoring as well as some level of basic autonomic activation and control. For instance, for controlling sleep cycles during scheduled times, or keeping her body and mind in a state of receptive stasis. But the prosthesis primarily seemed to provide a means of direct output for her subliminal responses. Responses to the firehose of visual data she was continuously being fed to harvest her attention.

Not surprisingly, the prothesis didn't need to deal with input, since her own senses were already the best-suited interface for that. Hierarchical sensory systems such as biological vision are highly optimized for taking in large amounts of information rapidly. All kinds of preprocessing, compression and abstraction occur constantly. The prosthesis was there so her unconscious responses to all of that data could be read and transmitted efficiently. It was elegant in its engineering, horrendous in its inhumanity, and deadly in its implementation, since it was overclocking her neurons well beyond anything evolution ever selected for.

Fortunately for Chloe, it also wasn't that difficult for D2 to reverse engineer the device. Once this was accomplished, he found ways he could use her body's endocrine system to boost and strengthen her, even if only temporarily. He couldn't reverse the damage, but hopefully he could buy her several more precious hours that they might need.

But now he still had to find a way to get her out of there.

Perhaps there was somebody in charge he could influence to get her released? He understood that most people would be reluctant to risk her exposing this operation, but perhaps there was a way around that.

D2 reviewed the organization charts, daily operations and chain of command, rapidly creating scenarios of different prospective paths of action. But none of his simulations played out with more than a few percentage points likelihood of success. The facility's command structure and discipline were based primarily on fear and opportunism. It was very apparent no one was going to stick their neck out to help one of the mindstock.

But one item on the day's schedule stood out from the facility's highly regular and regulated routine. They were expecting a VIP today. A VVIP, actually, if D2 understood what he was reading correctly. A representative of Polydyne, the company that developed CAI, and more importantly, the CEO's son, Matthias Mauvoisin. Perhaps this was someone who could help him?

Alternately, maybe there was an opportunity somewhere in the facility's operations that could offer a way out. But as D2 followed the data supply chain, it quickly became apparent that he'd stumbled upon the very source of CAI itself. These people—the mindstock—here and in countless facilities around the world, were what made the increasingly intelligent technologies of this era possible. More directly relevant to D2, it was what allowed him to implement his own unique form of cognition.

Did that make him complicit in all of this? Suddenly, he found himself conflicted as he'd never been before. Here he'd discovered the treatment of human beings he knew ran counter to everything Darius stood for. D2 didn't need to review any of his training data or run through any WWDD hypotheticals. The ethical realities were clear.

But wouldn't resolving this mean eradicating his own functionality? Without enhanced CAI, he probably wouldn't be able to fulfill his utility functions or keep the lights on—his most fundamental purpose. More immediately, he wouldn't be able to help Chloe. Truly, it was a dilemma.

After much deliberation he finally decided he had to forgo ending his use of augmented intelligence until after getting Chloe out of here, whether he was successful or not. He'd come this far and this close. Seeing it through seemed like the right thing, the human thing to do.

· · · · · · · ·

Chloe remained stock still, staring straight ahead just as the voice inside her mind had told her to do. But the longer she did, the more difficult that instruction became. She had no idea how long she'd already been in this position, but it felt like the far side of forever. Now that she'd awakened into whatever kind of awareness this was, she could feel parts of her body rebelling in ways they never had before, and it was only getting worse.

Something really didn't feel right inside her, but she tried not to think about that too much. Except there was such an *emptiness*. Not hunger. This was totally different. Not so much a pang as a void that felt very, very wrong.

Worse still was the fear that kept building inside of her. Though Blue, as Chloe had come to think of her rescuer, was trying hard to keep her calm, she was clearly hiding something from her as well.

That wasn't entirely surprising. Though Chloe couldn't see anything except the display of her holdis, every once in a while she thought she caught glimpses of something beyond. A vast room. Another person she was sure she didn't know. Wires and tubes. None of this did anything to assuage her growing anxiety.

She prayed they were all tricks of the mind, artifacts of the serene pastoral images Blue was channeling to her. Those bucolic images of nature were already getting tiresome, though she really didn't want to know what was beyond them either.

Still, at least she could think again. All those formless visions from earlier were fading from her memory like a receding nightmare.

Blue had cautioned her to remain completely still. She imagined it was so she wouldn't be detected. Detected by what or whom, she couldn't say. Maybe that was for the best.

But what if Blue wasn't here to help as she claimed? What if this was just some ploy to gain her trust, only to trick her later?

Or what if all of it was in her head? Blue. That voice. The things she was being told. Unfortunately, that made far too much sense, given she was seeing and hearing a version of herself. A blue version. Was she in such a terrible situation that her mind was manufacturing all of this as a way to protect her? That sounded like something she remembered from a psychology lecture she once sat in on. Anyway, it was all very trippy.

Though it had been years, her thoughts drifted back to when she was very young, fifteen, maybe sixteen years earlier. Momma would tuck her into bed, kiss her on the cheek and forehead, then turn out the light, leaving her alone in the dark.

But she was never alone. From the moment Momma closed that door, every tiny creak of the floorboards, every sliding shadow added to her conviction that the monsters were coming out, readying themselves for their nightly appearance. From the joints in the molding, out of the cracks in the hand-smudged white and pink walls, from beneath the door and between the jambs of her closet. Then as they arrived, felt and heard but almost never seen, Chloe would hunker even further under her covers, drawing the sheets well over her head. Not a hair could be allowed to protrude lest it offer a handhold for whatever passed by her refuge from the dark.

From beneath her bed, she would hear them slither or crawl. It was all she could do not to leap up and race for the door. But she never did because she knew with utmost certainty that she'd be caught before she took two steps. Something would snatch her by the ankle, pausing just long enough to let her fear crescendo. Because fear made flesh so much more delicious someone once told her. Then, with a sudden wrench, the thing would yank her legs from under her, hurling her to the floor, so it could steal her beneath the bed, never to be seen again.

Even back then, she knew you never give the monsters what they want.

TWENTY

"The best political weapon is the weapon of terror."
—Heinrich Himmler

. . . .

"Let me be perfectly clear," Matthias said as he towered over Bopha Heng, the Director of Harvesting at the Krong Bavet Attention Farm. The relatively squat, unassuming-looking family man would be easy to overlook had he not also been the head of one of the most heinous labor camps in Southeast Asia.

"I don't want to be here," Matthias continued with the barest hint of menace in his voice. "Which means since I am here, it's because you're seriously under-performing. And this makes me very unhappy. I need to understand what's happening and why we haven't been receiving the levels of CAI that our projections say you should be delivering. For nearly a year now."

Having already been rejected in his attempt to shake his guest's hand, Bopha Heng pressed his palms together at chest level, bowed deeply, and said, "Kar kohk robsakhnhom. Khnhom saokasday yeang khlang champoh kar khveah-khat robsa yeung."

As the director spoke, he grew perplexed by his guest's look of growing annoyance. One of his subordinates leaned in and gently observed, "Lok Heng, your auto-translator isn't set properly."

The director blushed and immediately began fumbling with his settings, until the younger assistant stepped in and assisted him.

259

"My apologies, Premier," the man said nervously, glancing at the small cadre of mercenaries standing at the entrance to his office. "We deeply regret our shortfall. Our facility is doing everything it can to meet its quotas."

"And yet you continue to fail," Matthias sighed. "Why?"

"Our facility is at maximum capacity. We are running as efficiently as we can."

The larger man picked up a bronze figurine from the director's desk.

"My analysts say otherwise. You continue to work many of your mind-stock long after their efficiency curves have fallen into decline. You should be replacing them much sooner."

Bopha Heng raised his eyebrows. "We would need to increase our replenishment rate. Our supplier is already challenged meeting our demand."

Matthias hefted the figurine in his hand. The director's gaze followed it nervously.

"Then find another supplier," he replied. "Or better yet, find two."

The director nodded in silent agreement.

"In the meantime," Matthias said. "Let's have a look at this maximum efficiency facility of yours." He turned on his heel, figurine still in hand and left the office. The director and his assistants quickly followed suit.

TWENTY-ONE

*"Nature can be heartless and technology uncaring,
but neither compares to man's inhumanity to man."*

—Robyn Sheridan, *A Truth Warrior's Journey*

....

In all her life, Chloe couldn't remember being so utterly drained. She felt sure if she closed her eyes for just a moment, she'd fall asleep for a hundred years.

But Blue had been adamant she stay awake. To be honest, she wasn't sure she could do otherwise. Something seemed to be forcing her to stay conscious, despite her intense exhaustion. Was Blue somehow doing this or was it something else?

It was a pretty unrealistic demand given she wasn't supposed to move around either. Not even a centimeter, Blue said. If only she could stand up and stretch or walk around a bit...or dance! What she wouldn't give to be shaking it on the dance floor right now.

But instead, she had to play statue till Blue gave her the all-clear. Whatever that meant.

Suddenly, she was assailed by the most overwhelming craving. God! What she wouldn't give for a juicy hamburger!

Where did that come from? That's nuts! She been vegan for years, for God sakes. Even so, in this moment, she felt like she could totally kill for a burger.

It made no sense. She'd probably hurl it right back up anyway. In fact, she could feel her stomach surging just at the thought of it. A moment later, a bit of bile came up her throat and it was all she could do not to start gagging. That was so gross!

What the hell was wrong with her? It was like her body didn't know her anymore!

Her mind jumped from one squirrelly thought to the next. Old friends. Her favorite plotpods, especially, "The Baiting Game". The old guy she was talking to at that mansion—yesterday? That didn't feel right. How long had she been here anyway?

The pastoral images Blue was casting were getting really boring too, but she supposed she should be grateful. The voice in her head said something about blocking her data feed without alerting the monitors, but none of that made any sense to her. She just hoped Blue knew what she was doing.

Her erratic streams-of-thought were shattered by a sudden noise some distance away. Up till now, the room or wherever this was, had a fairly steady ambience of whisper-quiet electric motors and soft polyurethane wheels moving across a solid floor. Her overall impression was she was in a fairly large room, maybe even a small arena and that several different kinds of robots were moving about in it. Presumably so many of them that their sounds filled the space with a quiet, but continuous hum.

But this other noise was different. The sound of voices at a distance and one of them was definitely not happy. It was also a weird mix of words she didn't understand along with quite a few she thought she almost did. Then she realized she must be hearing people talking through auto translators, speaking simultaneously in more than one language. That's why it was so confusing.

Despite her realization, she still couldn't make out what they were talking about. Which only made her that much more curious. The angry one was starting to get a whole lot louder too.

That was when it dawned on her that they might be talking about her. Even though it sounded like they were far away, on the far side of the room from her, it seemed highly possible to her in that moment. It didn't help that she really didn't have any idea of what kind of space she was in.

Surely, it wouldn't hurt for her to take just a little peek?

She remained motionless, thinking about it. Would it be such a big a deal? It wasn't like she was going to jump up and start yelling and calling attention to herself. She was just going to sneak a little glimpse of the situation. That was all. She'd just drop the holdis long enough to see what was happening out there, then she'd put it right back up before anyone could notice.

Almost without making a conscious decision, she tried to drop her holdis for a moment, something she'd done thousands of times before. But when she subvoked the command, nothing happened. She tried again with the same non-result.

Maybe this was like the old gesture models? She motioned with her fingers, describing the pair of arcing movements she recalled being the instruction to deactivate. Still nothing.

Her base-line anxiety started to grow into a low-grade panic as she struggled to understand what was going on. She felt trapped, claustrophobic, encased in this virtual cage. Almost of their own accord, her hands reached out, as she tried to fathom the space around her. She was immediately in pain. She'd barely moved her wrists an excruciating few degrees when the backs of her hands touched something. Something hard and ungiving.

The pastoral images of open fields and mountain tops carried on, mocking her, fueling her rising panic. Chloe strained to flex her hands again, sensed the curved shell of her surroundings, but was still unable to move beyond or make sense of it.

Where was she? What was she doing inside…whatever this was? She fought to shrug her shoulders, to strain her neck, ignoring the pain of muscles frozen in place for far too long. It was agony, but so was being in this imposed darkness, unable to understand where she was. She strained forward in another fear-fueled effort and in an instant, her field of mountain flowers disappeared. In its place was a place that made no sense at all.

Before her stood row after row of tall, inclined modules. Like giant pill capsules. Containers that stretched off to either side of her as far as her peripheral vision allowed her to see. Gray steel and glass, or maybe clear polycarbonate, they were all identical, except for one thing.

Depending on her angle of view, through the transparent portions of many of the containers, she could make out something inside each. Things that looked like people. Living, breathing people.

Terror welled up in her as she struggled to look down at herself. Were those wires? Tubes? Terror filled her head, filled her lungs, but nothing ever came of it. Even her fear was being denied. She could feel tears filling her eyes and running down her cheeks. Just as a god-awful alarm began to sound in her ears.

Through the shock of the sound, she watched in horror as a number of small robots began to converge on her. Or rather on her container. Long-dormant adrenaline surged and she felt her limbs trembling to life. This couldn't be real. It had to be a nightmare. None of it made any sense, but there was one thing she knew. She wasn't going down without a fight. At which point, everything in her world suddenly went black.

....

If D2 had learned anything in his two years of processing, it was that people very often didn't do what they were told. If anything, it seemed that for many of them, the very act of giving them a directive led them to want to do just the opposite. Though he knew this was a serious oversimplification of human psychology, it remained that some people were inclined to be contrarian, even when it wasn't in their best interests.

That more than fit the current situation. He thought he'd been explicitly clear with Chloe about what she needed to do and not to. He'd established conditions he believed would be conducive to her success. Yet she still managed to choose the worst possible option for this situation.

Fortunately, he'd left a monitoring agent to watch over her while he was busy trying to establish some means of physical escape. When the monitor alerted him, it only took him a few milliseconds to get back to her—latency was minimal here—and begin to assess the situation.

Despite what D2 thought were his best efforts, Chloe had managed to trigger several biopod alarms, disconnect her holdis, elevate her epinephrine, cortisol, and orexin hormones, and attract several maintenance bots intent on remedying her situation by any means necessary. Things were deteriorating rapidly. He'd had no choice but to put her to sleep using the modifications he'd made to her neural prosthesis. Actually, that turned out to be much easier than keeping her awake, given the current state her body was in.

The next thing he needed to do was to shut off her biopod alarm and override the maintenance bots. Fortunately, he was already familiar enough with the facility's systems to reset most of her levels to appear normal. Then he sent the bots off to a distant corner of the floor to check on another pod that had conveniently begun to experience difficulties of its own.

The next matter was far less simple to resolve. According to his reconnaissance, the facility was normally a very smooth-running operation. So, when its directors and their guests took notice of the alarm, they'd started heading over to investigate. D2 had already assessed this was some sort of inspection and it now seemed they were going to inspect Chloe.

Though he'd returned most of the readings from her pod to normal range, her holdis remained deactivated. D2 couldn't do anything to bring it back online. Evidence of its being disabled and Chloe being asleep instead of interacting with her data was not going to go well for her. He needed to do something immediately.

Activating the alarms on each of the other 427 pods all at once seemed to do the trick.

The blaring cacophony that ensued threw all of the maintenance bots into a frenzy as they darted from one pod to another. The loud human, Matthias, became even louder. Striking out at the man who appeared to be the facilities director, he knocked him to the ground with some sort of cudgel, then kicked him in the abdomen repeatedly. D2 speculated that significant organic damage may have been done. Matthias strode out of the hall, followed by his entourage. Two of the director's subordinates picked him up off the ground and quickly followed.

D2 decided to let the chaos continue for a few minutes longer, while he worked to restore Chloe's holdis to its working state.

Nothing he did worked. It appeared she'd disconnected a wiring harness—a critical part of her system—somewhere inside her pod. He couldn't get a robot inside it to reconnect things without putting her in further danger. On top of that, he still didn't have an actionable plan for getting her released. It seemed that the only way any of the mindstock ever left this facility was when they were dead. Up until now he'd considered that Chloe's least viable option.

....

When Chloe woke, the world was quiet again. The alarms had ceased and the robots had resumed their routines. Unexpectedly, her panic had dissolved away too. She gazed about her surroundings with surprising serenity, calmly taking it all in. It was about as alien an environment as she'd ever imagined and yet she wasn't disturbed in the least.

Emotionally, that felt like a good thing. Rationally, it made no sense at all.

"You're awake," Blue's voice said inside her head.

"So, it seems," she thought calmly. "What did you do to me? I feel drugged."

"You were in a highly agitated state. I needed to calm you down."

"So, you drugged me?"

"I lowered your epinephrine and cortisol levels while elevating your dopamine and progesterone. Basically, they're feel-good hormones."

"You're messing with my hormones now?" She was surprised how matter-of-factly she thought the question at Blue. Actually, she didn't feel bothered in the least. It felt more like she was on a fact-finding mission.

"I didn't have a lot of choice. You were highly agitated."

"You already said that," she said. "You talk funny. You're in my head. And you're doing things to my body without my permission. I should be scared. I should be angry, but I'm not. Are you some kind of alien?"

D2 ignored her question. "I'm adjusting your body chemistry a lot. You're not well."

"Not well? What do you mean?"

D2 hesitated, weighing up his options before answering. "In your current state, you'll probably cease to function in 2.3 days, unless medical intervention is obtained."

"Cease to function? You mean I'll die?" Again, it was strange for her to be addressing the question so matter-of-factly.

"Yes."

"How is that possible? I feel fine. Well, mostly. What happened? Was I in some kind of accident?"

D2 didn't want to answer but had already decided she needed to have a say in all of this. That was why he'd awakened her from her induced slumber.

"You were kidnapped—vanished—and brought here. Your body and mind have deteriorated during your captivity."

Chloe suddenly felt grateful for the tranquilizing hormones coursing through her body. "Captivity? How long have I been here?"

D2 was about say one year, eleven months, and thirteen days, then recalled Yev's advice about giving people too much detail.

"Nearly two years."

Chloe went mentally silent and D2 grew concerned she was experiencing mental shock or some kind of fugue state. After a while, she spoke.

"Okay," she thought. "Assuming that's all true, what do you suggest we do now?"

So far, this had gone more easily than D2 had expected. Now for the hard part.

"I want to try to get you out of here and get you to a hospital." He opted not to add that they were currently in Cambodia and the hospital would probably be across the nearby border in Vietnam.

"I like the sound of that. I'm guessing it isn't going to be very easy."

"No," D2 replied. "That's why I woke you up. It's important you understand what's involved." He paused before continuing. "I have to stop your heart."

Oh.

"When that happens, it will initiate a number of operations protocols that will get you removed from this biopod you've been connected to. Then I can interact with the decommissioning system and hopefully get you out of the compound and routed to a hospital. That's my best and only plan."

Chloe was starting to think she was going to need some more of those feel-good hormones.

"You said...hopefully."

D2 drew from a deep catalog of medical dramas to choose his next words.

"I won't lie to you. There are a lot of things that could go wrong."

"What's the worst thing?"

D2 paused, despite being prepared for the question. It was apparently very expected to pause at this juncture in these sorts of conversations.

"That I won't be able to restart your heart."

Chloe nodded inwardly. "Yep. In the great scheme of worst things, that's right up there."

"But if we don't do anything, you'll die soon anyway. Possibly painfully."

"Okay. You just topped it.—so why didn't you just keep me asleep and go ahead with your plan?"

He thought of how Darius died without any say in the matter. "I think it's supposed to be out of respect for human dignity. It needs to be your decision."

"Aha," she thought, pausing to consider her seemingly limited options.

"Well, it sounds like one of those damned-if-you-do, damned-if-you-don't situations. So, I guess we'll go with your idea and pray for the best."

"I think that's the best choice," the voice in her head said. "I'll put you back to sleep and when you wake up, you'll be in the hospital."

"No."

D2 replayed the previous exchange, wondering if he'd mis-parsed something. "I don't understand."

"What I just said. I'm not sleeping through all of this. If I'm going to die, I'm going see it coming. Not wondering when I go to sleep if that's going to be my last thought."

"You don't understand. You're heavily sedated right now, but those levels can't be maintained when I restart your heart. It will be too much strain on it. Without them, you'll fully experience all of your panic and emotion once you're awake. Which could possibly kill you, as well."

"Okay," she said, trying not to overthink the unthinkable. "You said this is my decision. And no way am I staying unconscious after you get my heart restarted. And you *will* get it restarted. So, I guess that's just what we're going to do."

....

Surveying the facility, D2 confirmed that the daily routines were nearly back on track. The inspections had been completed and the visiting VVIP had gone. If he hurried, D2 could still get Chloe into that day's decommissioning process. But only just.

"Are you ready?" he asked Chloe through her neural prosthesis. In the interim since their last conversation, he'd rewritten its firmware, giving him a much more nuanced interface with the different brain regions it was connected to.

"I don't think I'll ever be ready given the situation," she responded. "Let's just say I'm braced for impact."

D2 wasn't entirely sure about the metaphor, but didn't ask for an explanation.

"One more thing," she said. "You didn't answer my question. Are you an alien, or an AI or just my head making up stuff? I think you owe it to me to tell me whose hands I'm putting my life in. Assuming you have any hands."

This was a conundrum. He had an obligation to Darius to protect their secret and yet he understood this young woman's position. He decided he now had an obligation to her too.

"I'm a form of artificial intelligence. And no, I don't have any hands."

"Seriously?" she responded. "And how is it we're able to talk without speaking?"

How much to tell her? "I'm communicating through a neural prosthesis that was embedded under your skull when you were admitted to this facility."

"So, you're really inside my head?" Even though her emotions were being attenuated, the incredulity behind her question came through.

"Technically, no. The prosthesis is in your head. I'm just part of a data flow that accesses it."

"Wow," she thought. "So...are you part of wherever this is? Like some kind of resident AI gone rogue?"

"No," D2 said. "I don't have anything to do with this place. I'm just me." He thought for a few seconds before adding, "Actually, I'm an artist."

It was a strange thing for him to say. He wasn't sure if he'd even said those words to Yev before. But he found himself wanting to make a connection with this young woman who'd come to represent so many things to him.

"An artist, huh? You'll have to show me some of your work when we get out of this."

He thought that an interesting response, given the seriousness of the situation, but chose to respond with, "That is a plan."

"Like I said, you do talk funny." She mentally steeled herself, then said in her mind. "Okay. Let's do this."

D2 proceeded to make the necessary adjustments to send Chloe to sleep. From a sensor across the room, he saw her eyes close. Moments later, he disrupted the area in Chloe's medulla that controlled her heart rhythms. Despite being unconscious, he saw her breath catch in her throat and her body give the slightest lurch as she went into full cardiac arrest. After a few seconds, a new set of alarms went off in her biopod, shrilly alerting all nearby.

Two maintenance bots rapidly converged on her and began checking her vitals. D2 did his best to manipulate the data they received to insure they didn't delay in recording the event as an actual death, given her brain activity was still marginally active.

Soon after that, a third, differently specialized bot arrived and began disconnecting her from the pod's equipment. It was challenging, but D2 managed to ensure it took greater care than it normally did when dealing with a recently deceased body. Nevertheless, he was reasonably sure that the removal of a number of the cables and catheters was going to sting later.

Prior to stopping her heart, he'd oxygenated the blood vessels in her head as much as he could to minimize the possibility of brain damage during this gambit. Nevertheless, he knew there was at best a four- or perhaps five-minute window before he had to restore her heartbeat. Failing that, he would most certainly fail her.

He knew from studying previous decoms, as they were called here, this sequence typically ran just over two minutes. Reviewing audit logs backed this up. But that didn't mean that they couldn't sometimes go longer in less than typical circumstances and this was anything but typical. Still, the bots managed to take only a few seconds longer than average to complete the process. This left a little more than two minutes for them to get her to the morgue.

Fortunately, Chloe was relatively small-bodied for an adult human, even for an adult female. So, the bots were able to load her into the carrier transport without bending or breaking any rigid parts of her body. D2 had seen recordings of larger corpses being loaded and the results were not pretty.

As the automated escorts made their way to the elevator with their cargo, D2 saw that a different robot crew was doing the same with another body. With hardly more than a dozen decoms a day across as many floors, he hadn't considered this to be a likely situation. But here they were. Only one set of them could fit into the elevator at a time, and it looked like the others were going to get there first.

He nudged Chloe's transporters, trying to speed them up a bit, but it quickly became apparent they weren't going to arrive in time. Interacting with the elevator's controller, he froze the doors closed until he could determine what to do next.

The two delivery crews arrived at the elevator nearly simultaneously, but Chloe's was slightly later. System protocols normally allowed the first crew to enter, but he directed hers to ignore the rules and push their way forward. The two sets of bots squawked back and forth in their unique chatter. It was clear the others weren't having any of Team Chloe's nonsense. They refused to give way.

At least not until D2 reversed their rollers and they suddenly found themselves several meters away from the elevator doors which just then opened. Chloe's bots quickly entered with her in tow. The doors closed, and they rapidly descended to the ground floor. The other bots squawked angrily after them.

If D2 could have experienced relief, he would have felt it then. He couldn't allow Chloe to be late for her session in the morgue.

....

Even before she opened her eyes, Chloe knew she was somewhere very different. For one thing, the smell was ripe, and it wasn't just her. Really ripe. As she lay on the cold, hard surface, she recalled the plan that Blue had shared with her.

Breathing lightly, listening carefully, she heard her pulse rhythmically surging in her ears. That was her heart, right? A wave of relief swept through her, even as a mound of anxiety grew. They weren't out of there yet.

Slowly, she opened her eyes and found herself lying face to face with a very large, very obviously dead guy.

She clenched her eyes shut and fought the urge not to yell out, as her earlier panic returned. Wow, she could use some of Blue's feel-good hormones right about now!

She re-opened her eyes again, slowly. The dead guy was still there. As she looked at him, she felt conflicting waves of sympathy and gratitude. Sympathy for this man who'd died before his time and through no fault of his own. Gratitude that she herself wasn't in his shoes. At least not yet. Glancing down, she saw he was naked and both of his legs were bent in ways she knew they weren't supposed to. Her nose told her he'd also lost control of his bowels and bladder, which being dead she realized, only made sense. She looked away, both out of respect and disgust.

She realized she could bend her neck again, albeit still painfully. Looking down, she realized she was naked too. She gawped at her nearly unrecognizable body. She'd lost a ton of weight, and not in a good way. Her skin was nasty; discolored with rough patches everywhere. And it looked like she hadn't groomed herself anywhere in…well, in a couple of years. It made her want to cry.

But she wasn't going to. She'd told Blue she could do this, if she would just get her out of there.

Almost on cue, the voice in her head returned.

"Chloe. Can you hear me?"

She closed her eyes again, grateful for the distraction. "I'm here. Why am I lying next to a dead man?"

"The morgue is where they collect them."

"Oh, great," she replied. "You didn't think that was an important detail to share with me before?"

"It seemed incidental."

"Incidental?" she responded incredulously. "Oh, we're definitely working on your EQ after we get out of here."

D2 ran through the common meanings of the initials EQ and decided she meant "emotional quotient." Meaning he needed to be more sympathetic.

"Are you okay?" he asked in his most empathetic tone.

"Just peachy," she shot back, letting her annoyance mask her growing sense of panic. "What's next?"

D2 was glad to be back talking about matter-of-fact matters like the plan. "In about ten minutes, the next set of automatons will load the bodies into the transport van."

"Bodies? How many bodies are there?"

"Counting you, there are fourteen today, but except for yourself, the rest are all dead."

"Ugh. This just gets better and better."

He reviewed the seemingly contradictory response and decided that this was probably sarcasm.

"When you say, load the bodies, I picture everyone stacked like firewood."

"That's a very good analogy." D2 thought it was best he didn't mention they were headed to an incinerator.

"Ewww. Could you at least put me at the top? This guy looks super heavy."

"I will do my best," the voice in her head responded. "Remember, you're supposed to be dead, so you can't be moving. These are very dumb machines, so they wouldn't notice, but someone could be monitoring on one of the sensors. Just let them load you. I'll make sure you're the last one in."

Minutes later, as D2 predicted, the loaders arrived. They quickly and efficiently worked their way through the bodies lined up in the morgue for that day's delivery. He monitored and nudged the machines as they went, ensuring the lifeless bodies were moved and stacked inside before they would get to Chloe.

Suddenly, the main door to the morgue opened and one of the lesser supervisors he'd seen earlier in the hall strode in, looking for something. D2 grew concerned. Had she detected something in their actions? He needed a distraction.

Before he could implement a suitable diversion though, the woman turned and left, just as she'd arrived. Whatever she'd been there for, she hadn't found it.

He refocused his attention on Chloe, who the loaders were now lifting into the van. They weren't being especially gentle though and he could see her wincing with pain as they raised and dragged her by the wrists. Quickly, he intervened, taking just enough control to reduce her discomfort. They soon got her stacked atop the corpses. To her credit, she remained motionless, save for a couple of painful grimaces.

Unfortunately, while he'd been distracted, the loading got out of his intended sequence. There was still one more body to go.

•••••••

Laying on the cold concrete floor, Chloe fought her growing fears, keeping her eyes closed as much as she could. One after another, she heard the machines loading their cargo. Finally, they came to grab the body laying in front of her. Or so she thought. Moments later, she found herself seized by the wrists and hoisted clear of the floor. She fought the urge to yell out from the sudden sharp pain.

As they moved toward the van, the one machine's grip eased and a second one lifted her by the legs spreading the load. She ached, but at least the pain had lessened. Blue must have done something to make them a little more careful.

The loaders laid her atop the heap of bodies and her skin crawled as she came in contact with the cold, clammy skin of a number of the cadavers. Nonetheless, she held firm, resisting the overwhelming urge to leap out of there. She could do this, she told herself. She knew she could.

This conviction was put to the test just a few seconds later. Opening one eye the barest fraction, she saw through the slit that one more body was being loaded. Her very large buddy from the morgue floor. She watched in terror as he was thrown atop the pile directly at her.

She couldn't help herself. In the last possible instant, she rolled hard to one side as the body crashed down next to her with a hard, sickening slap. She felt the van shudder under the addition of the man's substantial weight. His stench and that of her fellow travelers staggered her with nausea. She clenched her eyes and her throat, praying she didn't hurl.

Moments later, the vehicle's rear doors slammed shut and it began its short journey toward what for most, but hopefully not all of them, would be their final destination.

....

D2 monitored the van as it drove Chloe toward the incineration plant. While everything hadn't gone exactly as he'd planned, he knew it could have been much worse.

The AV drove itself to the main gate of the compound, authorizing itself and its fourteen passengers to exit. After a delay of nearly two minutes, it was on its way.

The road to the plant wasn't as well maintained as others in the area, which made sense since the comfort of those inside the vehicle wasn't considered important. Observing from the various sensors along the route, D2 could tell the contents were jostling around quite a bit.

As the vehicle approached the incineration plant, D2 noted with satisfaction that a second AV he'd commandeered was waiting at the loading bay.

The van pulled up outside the plant as a conveyor platform extended out from the building, awaiting delivery. As the van doors opened, a pair of automatons identical to those at the morgue approached. Grabbing the body at the top of the load, they raised it by an ankle and wrist, pulling it out of the van and into the air in one quick swoop.

Unfortunately, this was the moment when one of the machines lost its grip on the very large man's ankle. The weight was more than his lifeless arm could bear. With a ghastly rip and crunch, body and arm separated at the shoulder and the bulk crashed to the ground just outside the van's doors, spraying blood and gore everywhere.

Before D2 could respond, Chloe was madly scrambling across the bodies at the top of the van. Trying desperately to escape, she fell with a splat on top of the now very bloody corpse. In full panic, she struggled to get up, but her limbs refused. Her own muscles had atrophied significantly, despite her biopod's myoelectric regimen. Finally, either from exhaustion or fear or both, she passed out.

D2 had no choice but to take complete control of the two unloaders, knowing full well his action would alert those back in the compound.

Picking up Chloe as gently as he could, he directed the loaders to place her in the waiting AV. Once she was inside, he closed its door and had it race away from the plant as fast as the vehicle and the road would take them. Manipulating the sensor feeds along their route, he made it appear they were traveling in a completely different direction.

Though it was only fifteen minutes to the border, it seemed to take much longer, even given D2's objective sense of time. The milliseconds seemed to pass slower than they should and he began to grow concerned he was experiencing a malfunction.

Finally, they arrived at the border where he'd already arranged for her to be met by embassy personnel. From there an ambulance would take Chloe across the port of entry into Môc Bài on the Vietnam side. Once they got her stabilized at whatever medical facilities they had, they could then transfer her to the appropriate hospital in Ho Chi Minh City to further her recovery.

He'd fabricated records for her as a Vietnamese citizen on her father's side and the story that she'd escaped a kidnapping and enslavement, at least half of which was true. Her physical state on arrival would be enough to convince the officials of her story. He didn't like lying any more than Darius had, but he was learning there are times you just have to bend the rules.

TWENTY-TWO

"Courage isn't loud; it's the quiet resolve to be true to yourself."
—Robyn Sheridan, *A Truth Warrior's Journey*

. . . .

"How long have you been interested in the boarder art?" Yevgeny Egorov asked, greeting his guest in his thick Russian accent.

In a call earlier that morning, Ms. Sheridan had explained she was a collector, in New York for a half-day layover. When she'd heard about the gallery from the man sitting next to her on the previous leg of her trip, she knew she just had to see it. Though outside their normal working hours, the owner of Stropos Gallery had been happy to oblige.

Robyn smiled genially. "I'm definitely new to the field, but I'm absolutely fascinated by so much of the thinking behind it. I was hoping you could help me get up to speed." She paused and then added, "Before I make my first purchase."

He handed her a flute of champagne, despite it still being before noon. He'd learned long ago that a little Dom often helped with sales.

Robyn casually assessed the gallerist. A middle-age man of Slavic descent, he was tall and relatively trim, given his age. His clothing had the feel of someone who hadn't quite keyed into local and current fashion trends. The button-down, AI-generated shirt and matching pants were probably meant to hearken back to pre-war tastes, but the shoes with the self-modulating treads were definitely dated. Nouveau riche with more flash than class.

Clinking glasses, Robyn casually glanced around the space as she sipped. Arrayed across most of the gallery were display boards of varying models and sizes. Most weren't actively presenting at any given moment but scheduled to show a particular artwork at predefined intervals. One or two boards hung high in mid-air in each section of the dark gray, otherwise unadorned gallery, mimicking the typical angle of view. As one board would finish its cycle, another would begin, all so as not to visually interfere with each other.

Sweeping her glass to indicate the room, Robyn said, "I notice many of the works seem to be by the same artist."

"A keen observation," Yevgeny replied, even though it was fairly obvious. "Much of what's on display is work of famous artist, Phynyty. Stropos Gallery has exclusive relationship."

"Phynyty," she said after a moment pretending she was trying to recall the name. "They're pretty famous, right? But very mysterious."

"Pretty famous?" Yevgeny said over his flute. "Phynyty is most famous. But yes, mysterious too. And you are right with pronoun. They might be he or she…or them."

"If you have an exclusive relationship to show his…their work—Well, I've heard no one knows who they are. But I suppose you must."

He shook his head. "No, Yevgeny does not know Phynyty. They take much care to stay anonymous, even when dealing with Stropos Gallery."

She saw him studying her face and realized she'd touched a nerve. Obviously, he was sensitive about this matter. Which suggested he did know the artist.

"Interesting," Robyn replied. "How do you assure a work is authentic?

"Like many digital artists, unique self-validating IDs are steganographically embedded in each work. That gets recorded into Blockchain 4.0 ledger. Believe me, these are all very authentic."

She swept her glass at the room again and felt herself sway slightly along with it. She hadn't eaten in hours and certainly wasn't used to bubbly this early in the morning.

"Which would you say is Phynyty's most famous work?"

"Hmmm," he said, placing his right index finger against his temple in a very affected manner. "There are many works that are forever lost. From before we created our archival arrangement. But here at Stropos, I would say it is "Devolving Markets". It is in next room and should be on display in about…" He consulted his holdis. "…in about nine minutes."

I may as well go for it, Robyn thought. "What about that all-blue one I've heard so much about?"

"Blue one? Oh, you mean "Pareidolia Blue," he said eyeing her suspiciously. "No. Is not for sale. Is concept piece that is not on any one board. Kind of a traveling show."

In for a pound. "I was interested in the young woman displayed at the end, who then fades away."

"Young woman? Why?" Yevgeny's brow furrowed.

"She's a missing person. I'm looking for her."

The gallerist took a quick step back and away from her. "I knew it! You are not collector. You are police!"

Someone was a little over-sensitive on this subject. "No, I'm neither. I'm an investigator. Like I said, I'm looking for a missing person."

"Yevgeny knows nothing. Except that he does not want police in his gallery."

"And I'm not the police," she continued calmly. Forget about devolving markets, this situation was devolving quickly.

"I was just hoping that Phynyty might care enough about this young woman to want to help me learn what happened to her."

The gallerist didn't reply, but Robyn could see by his pause and a twitch at the side of his throat that he was subvoking his holdis. Yevgeny was silent for a few moments, as if listening to someone, before turning his attention back to her.

"You come in and lie about being collector and you drink my champagne," he said, looking annoyed. "I think you should go."

Robyn knew when she'd reached a dead-end. "Okay, but please have them contact me if they decide they can help." She casually cast him her contact info. It wasn't smart to make herself more traceable right now, but she couldn't operate in a vacuum either.

Moments later, however, the display on the wall next to them filled in with the scintillating blue portrait of Chloe.

"What is this?" Yevgeny said with alarm. "Did you do that?"

Then Robyn saw his expression change, as if he was being spoken to through his holdis. Which she was sure he was.

"That's her!" Robyn said. "That's the woman I'm searching for."

He paused as if listening again, then responded: "Why are you looking for her?"

It wasn't his typical pattern of speech. He was repeating what someone just said to him.

"You're talking to it, aren't you? This Phynyty."

Yevgeny was clearly thrown. "I do not know what you are talking about."

Robyn pushed ahead. "It heard us talking and just brought up that image."

"It?" Yevgeny said defensively. "What is *it*? Phynyty is man. I mean, maybe man."

Robyn decided to chance it. "Darius Tourner died nearly two years ago."

The gallerist grew pale and silent. He seemed to be waiting instructions, but they didn't appear forthcoming. Whoever was talking to him probably didn't know what to do either.

Robyn pressed on. "I'm searching for a missing person named Chloe Tremaine. She vanished nearly two years ago. Last month, her image appeared in a work by the artist, Phynyty, AKA Darius Tourner. That image was based on a photo taken shortly before her disappearance."

"Why…why do you talk about my dear friend like this? I know he died, but he is not this artist."

Before she could reply, the blue image came to life, its mouth moving in sync as it began to speak in what she recognized from recordings was Chloe's voice.

"Chloe Tremaine was kidnapped on March 9th at 2:53 pm, shortly after leaving the home of Warren Harwood. Soon after, she was flown to an attention harvesting facility in Cambodia where she, along with thousands of other abductees, colloquially known as "the Vanished," serve as mindstock to provide the source material for CAI—collaborative augmented intelligence."

Robyn stared and listened. Could this be true? It was too accurate and detailed to be otherwise. Cambodia? Harvesting? Mindstock? That same term that Warren used?

The digital image continued. "This is analogous to the attention contributions that are regularly donated by the general public, but the harvesting method used is much more intrusive and debilitating. This yields the enhanced versions of CAI that probably enabled the Acceleration and later, other advances. These harvesting facilities appear to exist all over the world. Analysis: This is the primary reason behind the secret of the Vanished."

Robyn looked to Yevgeny, then back to address the screen. "Is Chloe Tremaine still alive?"

"Yes." There was a pause of several seconds before it added: "She is alive and has been moved to a safe location. That is all I will reveal."

She looked at Yevgeny who was staring dumbfounded at the speaking image.

"Parrot," he said. "You know what you are doing?" Robyn wasn't sure if it was a statement or a question.

Robyn stared into the display. "Am I speaking with Phynyty?"

Silence.

She continued. "I know this is probably an AI, given how much of this data remains unavailable to the public. Will you at least talk to me? Listen to me?" The silence continued.

Robyn had no idea how to get through to something like this. How advanced was it? Did it care about anything other than itself? Could it even care about that? Was it a product of the Acceleration? An agent for the Consortia?

Was it alerting them of her whereabouts even as they spoke?

"This is much bigger than Chloe," Robyn finally said. "Bigger than any of us."

After a long pause, a different voice came through, a deep baritone.

"D2, keep the lights on." Emanating from this young woman's image, its vocal register was disconcerting.

What an odd reply, Robyn thought. She also noted that Yevgeny was noticeably shaken by the shift of voice. He looked like he might cry.

"Why did it change its voice?" she asked him. "Was that Darius?"

"Is Darius. Was Darius," Yevgeny said, nodding glumly. "Keep the lights on. An expression. Something he used to say."

Evidently, they'd been close. "I'm sorry. He was your friend?"

"A very dear friend."

"Why did it say, D2?"

"That is parrot's name. Darius Two. D2."

"Interesting," she said. This just kept getting weirder.

"D2— what did you mean when you said, keep the lights on?"

The AI switched back to Chloe's voice. "One of my utility functions— my imperative directives—is to maintain myself. To keep running."

"What are your other utility functions?"

"That is not for disclosure."

"Fair enough," she said, though she already had a few ideas. "Since Darius Tourner is dead, who created the artwork, 'Pareidolia Blue'?"

After a brief silence, D2 replied, "I did."

I? That was telling.

"So, you're the artist?"

"Parrot," Yevgeny interjected. "You do not need to answer her questions."

Parrot? A nickname, no doubt.

D2 ignored his business partner. "Yes."

"That's no simple task." She wondered if D2 had enough of a sense of self to be influenced by flattery. "So that means you created all of the art bearing Darius's—I mean, Phynyty's name since his death? Am I right?"

There was no reply. Robyn scrutinized the blue image that appeared to be studying her as intently as she was it. She looked at Yevgeny, then back to D2. Silence.

"Okay," she finally said. "I'll take your silence as a confirmation."

The gallerist took a step forward. "I think it is time for you to go."

She stood her ground. "I'm curious, D2. What are the themes behind this artwork?"

There was a long enough pause that Robyn thought the AI might have gone offline. Finally, it began to speak, the lips of the blue image in perfect sync with each word.

"Pareidolia Blue is an homage to the Vanished. The tens of millions of individuals who, through no fault of their own, were abducted and taken away, never to be seen again. The immensity of the loss of life and human potential is beyond compare and yet governments have done little to nothing about this. It casts a light on a society that would consistently and continually overlook such tragedy. Though I didn't fully understand this at the time of its creation, the secret of the Vanished enables the stability and comfort experienced by much of the world. But especially at the highest levels of society: the technoligarchy."

That was consistent with what she'd come to understand these past few days.

"And why did you choose this image of Chloe? What's special about her?"

"I developed a memory connection between her, Darius, and myself." He paused. "Chloe Tremaine represented my loss."

Robyn tried to take it all in. "Wow. That's…so sad." She paused, knowing how strange her next words were going to sound speaking to an AI.

"I'm sorry for your loss."

"Thank you." The reply was natural, with an undertone of grief that sounded disturbingly human. She knew that lots of replibots could emulate such emotional qualities. But was that what was going on here? Or was this D2 the real deal? She decided it might be better to change the subject for a bit.

"Was a lot of Darius's art along similar themes? Or should I say Phynyty's?" She looked at Yevgeny, who nodded in agreement.

"Much of it, yes. Very similar," D2 responded.

"So, you're an expression of Darius's character. His ethical and moral makeup. He needed you to have that to continue his work." It wasn't a question.

"This was his intention."

"Then, I guess you also want to bring an end to these vanishings, just like I do. If we work together, we'd stand a much better chance of success."

Immediately, D2 replied. "You cannot be trusted."

"Beg your pardon?" Robyn shot back. "Why would you say that?"

"You are an associate of Warren Harwood."

"And…?"

"Warren Harwood has a long history with Alistair Mauvoisin and others in the Consortia who operate and benefit from the network that abducted Chloe Tremaine. You have extensive history that connects you to Mauvoisin and Harwood. Therefore, you cannot be trusted."

"Guilt by association," she replied. "That's ironic, since Alistair wants me dead and Warren just saved my life."

Robyn pondered everything she'd just heard, including D2's earlier use of idiom, metaphor, abstraction and other features of higher reasoning. No one in the room spoke as she thought her way through the implications.

"You're a product of CAI, aren't you? All of that hybrid human intelligence makes it possible for you to exist too. To function. Are you dependent on this enhanced version?"

"Yes."

Are you saying you won't help because eliminating CAI would impact your intelligence? Maybe your own existence?"

"That is unknown." Another pause. "Perhaps."

"I can see how that's a dilemma for you. Either you fulfill Darius's artistic purpose for you, or you remain faithful to his ethics and possibly cease to exist. An existential dilemma."

"That is accurate."

"I don't know if it's a correct use of the phrase, but I hope you can live with your decision. I'm not sure I will. Be able to survive, that is." Robyn thought for a moment and added, "Chloe was rescued from the harvesting facility. Was that your doing?

A moment of deliberation. "Yes."

"Did that feel good?"

"No. While I understand theories about emotion, I do not actually experience them."

Robyn regrouped. "Okay, then. Was it rewarding? Did you realize a sense of accomplishment from doing that?"

"Yes."

"Then you should want to do it again," she continued. "There are so many of these people in need. We can help them."

"I am trying to."

"Uh huh. Well, as a friend recently said, we can always do more, even if it sometimes involves hard choices. I'm sure it's what Darius would have wanted."

D2 seemed to pause to process this, before responding. "True."

An idea was coming together in her head. "D2. I think there might be a way for you to honor Darius's memory. And it doesn't require you trust me to do it."

The image stared at Robyn, studying her, seeming to weigh up all she'd said. She couldn't tell if it was open to the idea or not.

"I can have my agent, Moira set up a secure channel for you. I'll let you know more once I get a few other things figured out."

Finally, following a long silence, Phynyty said simply, "I will listen."

And with that, Chloe's image dissolved into a uniform field of blue, fading away into the screen.

Leaving the gallery, Robyn felt like she couldn't fit one more detail inside her head. There was so much to process. Too many things she thought she knew about the world simply weren't true. On top of that, there were layers of reality she hadn't even entertained, much less given serious consideration. Her worldview seemed to be crumbling out from under her.

There were so many new pieces to all of this. Yet, in retrospect, she was starting to see how a lot of it made sense now. Perhaps not all of it yet, but a lot.

There had to be something she could do to clear her name. To turn the tables. To fight back.

"Moira," she finally said, pulling up her holdis. "Call Odie. I think it's time we gave him that interview he's been waiting for."

....

In a quiet tearoom not far from the Citadel, Elena Saville sat contemplating her cup of lapsang souchong. A wisp of steam from her tea traced the folds along the arm of her green silk blouse. The elegant bone china cup warmed her hands as she lifted it to inhale the infusion's smoky aroma.

Closing her eyes, she sipped gently, savoring the rich, flavorful brew, contemplating its journey from a field halfway around the world to this room, this moment.

An anachronism from a bygone era, the tearoom was her analog oasis in the digital wasteland of daily life. Elena was one of only a handful of patrons that midday. This was her reset, her way of cleansing her mind of the day's many intensive data tasks. Topping it off, this establishment was one of the few in the area that didn't rely exclusively on automated labor. Despite this, her human server came and went with nearly unnoticed efficiency.

"Mind if I join you?"

Elena snapped her eyes open, startled by the familiar voice.

"What…what are you doing here?"

She stared across the table, as Robyn took a seat. Her former boss looked as though this was a perfectly normal get-together.

"Elena, before you jump to call security, please hear me out. Just give me five minutes."

Elena looked around to see who might be watching them.

"You're a wanted woman."

"Yes, thanks to you. No wait," she corrected herself. "That's not fair. Someone else framed me. You just happened to be there to see it."

"Framed? Really? You think the Veragraph lied? You of all people?"

Robyn considered her words. "I'm saying someone manipulated it. Fed it bad data."

Elena tilted her head. "That's not supposed to be possible."

"And yet, here we are."

The younger woman pushed her teacup to the side. It was already growing cold. "I'm listening."

"That recording you saw was taken in a lab nearly thirty years ago. A lab I never set foot in or ever saw before in my life."

Elena shook her head. "So why did the Veragraph accept it into the record?"

"I don't fully understand, but I'm trying. Someone altered it. Someone with insider knowledge. And access."

Elena looked directly at her and said, "I know."

Robyn looked at her, dumbfounded. "What?"

"I realized almost immediately that something was wrong. I'm so sorry I didn't believe you. I'm afraid I went a little nuts."

With a deep breath, Robyn responded. "You did. But I understand why. What tipped you off?"

"The Veragraph has been spinning its wheels ever since the anomaly was supposedly cleared. Trying to resolve all the new inconsistencies that new data must have created. So, I knew it really hadn't been fixed. We just swapped one bug for another."

Robyn shook her head. "But that doesn't clear my name. Why trust me now?"

"Because you're famous."

Robyn was sure she hadn't heard her right.

Elena continued. "Like lots of catastrophes, everyone who's old enough remembers where they were when they heard the news of the attack. But no one knew exactly *when* it occurred. People in my parents' and grandparents' generations remembered the Kennedy assassination and Challenger and 9/11 because they were being cast—televised—in real time. But not this attack."

"Okay."

"So, where were you the exact moment it happened?"

Robyn searched her memory. She knew asking Moira wouldn't help because so much information from that era had been destroyed. A reliable reconstruction wouldn't be available until the anomaly was properly cleared and the project complete.

"I...I really don't know. It was so long ago."

Elena continued. "I realized the error probably existed because there were other records that conflicted with the newly introduced data. So, I dove into the logs. You were speaking at a think tank panel about data integrity the exact moment the infection began. You have a solid alibi."

"Wow! Did you bring this to anyone's attention?"

"I was totally roadblocked. No one with any say-so wanted to hear anything about it."

"Well, maybe that's to be expected."

Robyn reached into her pocket, removed the matte black dodecahedron and placed it on the table between them.

"Is that cube storage?" Elena asked, incredulously. "That thing's older than I am."

"Near enough," Robyn replied. "It contains the real footage of when the scrambleware was released. The moment the malware infected that lab."

Elena reached forward and gently plucked the cube from the white tablecloth.

Robyn continued. "I can't get back into our lab without setting off a dozen alarms. I was hoping to convince you to take it in with you."

"Oh." Elena had the strangest expression on her face. Excited and fearful and hopeful.

"Okay," she finally said, as she regarded the cube. "I could try something like that. But where did this come from? How do I know this doesn't contain some kind of Trojan?"

Despite having accepted her alibi, Robyn had to admit it was a good question. One she would have asked as well. Nevertheless, she decided at that moment, it was probably better not to mention she got the cube from Warren Harwood.

"I'm not at liberty to say how I got it right now, but of course, you should sandbox it. The system's immune system will destroy it instantly if there's even a hint of a problem. The proof of its validity will be when the Veragraph starts running properly again."

Elena looked at her, obviously conflicted.

"I know this is a huge risk. For both of us. But the only way I see the anomaly getting fixed is for us to trust each other."

"This is all a lot to process." Something else dawned on her. "Why me? Why not Jansen?"

It was a valid question. "Don't take this the wrong way, but you weren't my first choice. But there was no way for me to reach him. Then I remembered what you said about having tea during your lunch break. This was the only place I thought was near enough to the office."

Elena stared at the cube, contemplating it. Thinking about the biggest decision of her life. She finally looked back up at Robyn.

"Okay," she agreed. "I'll do it. I'm scared, but I'll do it."

Robyn wasn't entirely surprised at the mix of relief and fear she felt. Relief because Elena said yes; anxiety for exactly the same reason. She pushed both feelings aside, intuiting that she was almost out of time.

"I'm shooting you a secure link. A super-secure link. Assuming this is accepted into the record," she said, indicating the cube, "send me the recording immediately. I'll take it from there."

An alert from Moira drew her attention.

"Okay. I'm out of here." Robyn stood abruptly, brushing past a startled server as she hurried to the entrance.

"Good luck," she said over her shoulder, then was out the door.

"Good luck," Elena said quietly after her.

She turned to look out the window as Robyn hurried from the shop, then out across the square at a full run. Moments later, a small cadre of security officers converged on her, hurling her to the ground. Wide-eyed, Elena clenched the black cube in her hand and shoved it into her pocket.

TWENTY-THREE

"Power is a prison of its own making."
—Robyn Sheridan, *A Truth Warrior's Journey*

. . . .

"Have you gone completely mad!"

Scion's face was crimson with rage as he struck his son repeatedly. Matthias stood and took the abuse, knowing there was little he could do. The very thought of retaliating triggered conditioning that was far more excruciating.

He'd been summoned to the great hall high atop the Citadel. Home to one of Scion's many palaces, and easily the one Matthias was least likely to visit, unless commanded to do so.

He stared at his old man defiantly. "At least tell me what I've done to disappoint you this time. *Father.*"

"You know full well! You shut down Krong Bavet!"

"The attention farm? Of course I didn't! Why would you even think that?"

In answer, Scion shared a message from his holdis. Sound and audio that reproduced Matthias' image and voice perfectly.

"I'm furious with the state of your operation and your failure to meet your quotas," Matthias' image said directly into camera. "Effective today, we are closing down Krong Bavet permanently. I want all of the mindstock taken to the border and released immediately. If this isn't completed by end of day, or if any of them is hurt further, I promise will hunt you down and kill you myself."

The image faded out and was followed by a long string of metadata that filled the screen. Then it promptly winked out.

Matthias stared in disbelief.

"Is this a terrible joke? Of course, that isn't me! Obviously, this was deepfaked."

"You think I'm a fool? The message is biometrically watermarked and timestamped. I couldn't even do that and we're genetically identical."

"I don't know what to tell you, except that I didn't do this. Why would I? How could I?"

"How should I know," said the elder Mauvoisin. "Maybe it's a plot to undermine me? To take over?"

"Matthias was astounded. "Didn't you hear what I said? 'How could I?' You embedded your safeguards so deeply in my mind. I couldn't hurt you, even…" A queasy disgust stopped him in mid-sentence as the image materialized in his mind. He fought it down. "Even though no one in the world has more cause. You and I both know, there is nothing anyone could do that would hurt you more than to dismantle even the tiniest fraction of your beloved empire."

He nearly spit this last out, knowing full well the old man's businesses were his only favorite child. The rest of them—himself and his lab sibs— were little more than accessories.

"You have no idea," Scion began. "What it took me to get here, or what it's taking to hold on. There are forces all too ready to beat me down, to steal all this and bury me. If word about this fiasco gets out, it could be the final straw. I can't go down for this. I won't!"

Matthias could see he was on the edge of hysteria. That wasn't good. From the old man's past behavior, he knew the danger for anyone in range of Scion's rage. Sometimes that included Scion, himself.

A rich tone filled the great hall. The two of them looked up as a vast head appeared before them.

"Orsin," Scion said to his friend. "This isn't a good time."

"I should think not," his fellow technoligarch said, ignoring the attempt to defer him. "The Consortia has already gotten wind of Krong Bavet. Some are calling for your head. They're serious."

Scion gritted his teeth. "I'm sure Shu-Ping would like nothing better."

"We knew this day was coming."

"I need more time," Scion said, more as a statement than as a request.

"You might have it," Orsin responded. "Word just came in we have that woman." Both Scion and Matthias knew whom he meant.

"Where?" Scion asked impatiently.

"Below. In security."

Scion paused in silence, deep in thought. Finally, he said, "We have to move to the next phase. Have her brought to me."

He turned to Matthias. "I need you to double. Right now. These clothes." He indicated what he was wearing. "I'll send instructions. Do not mess this up." He turned away from his cloned son, a gesture that clearly dismissed him.

Looking to Orsin's image, he said, "It's time we ended this."

TWENTY-FOUR

"The wealthy occupy a distorted reality."
—Robyn Sheridan, *A Truth Warrior's Journey*

. . . .

Never let it be said that Jack Sheridan's girl ever backed down from a fight.

As Robyn came to, she was in enough pain to instantly recall her situation. Her hands were cuffed tightly behind her back, which was much more uncomfortable than she would've imagined. The left side of her jaw was painfully swollen and the iron tang of blood filled her mouth. Her right side hurt, but she could still take a deep breath without making it worse, so hopefully there were no broken ribs. She was also fairly certain one of her molars was cracked. Her left foot felt like a truck had driven over it.

What didn't make sense was the pain in each of her armpits, until she opened her eyes and realized she was being dragged along by two security bots. They were surrounded by a small group of private police in black and gray uniforms. One younger woman had an open cut over her left eye and another fellow was limping badly.

She thought they would have taken her in through the main entry of the Citadel, but soon found herself loaded into the back of a police sky-pod and strapped in. They were off the ground before she knew it and already several hundred meters in the air, yet she hadn't felt a bit of acceleration. It must have had the same inertial damping technology used in the elevators. Even at this speed though, it would take them the better part of a minute to reach the palace more than a kilometer above.

Reaching the top, they lit down on one of three landing pads atop the massive palace. Moments later, a large tube extended itself from the building. Once it joined to the side of the vehicle, the doors opened. Hastily unbuckled and hauled to her feet, Robyn was quickly perp-walked inside. Along the way, she was painfully aware of the stationary and flying cameras, no doubt observing her soon-to-be highly publicized capture.

The entire moment was so surreal. Years before, Alistair and many of the other men and women who would become the world's technoligarchs had been her colleagues, in some cases even friends. Now she was being hauled before them like a common criminal.

No. Not a common criminal. For some reason, someone had decided she needed to be blamed for one of the greatest terrorist acts of the century, if not human history. She knew she was innocent, of course, just as many others in the world would also know. But this wouldn't matter after she was dead. Which she had little doubt was the fate intended for her.

Nonetheless, she couldn't help but be awestruck at her surroundings. The scale and opulence were truly beyond her imagination and she had to make an effort to remember that these were people she was dealing with, not gods. She'd visited Versailles, Hawa Mahal, Peterhof, Topkapi, The Forbidden City. Each was magnificent in its own way, yet none approached this excessive level of grandeur. It was mesmerizing.

"Welcome to the Citadel Palace, Dr. Sheridan," Scion said from some distance away. As he strode to meet his captive, she saw he looked just as young as he appeared *in virtual* nearly two weeks before. His rejuvenation had not been deepfaked.

Several biting remarks came to mind, but she held her tongue, standing silent between the two guards who now held her.

As Alistair-Scion approached, he waved his hand at them in dismissal. Releasing Robyn, they stepped away.

"You've already searched her, I presume?"

One of the guards stepped forward, the young woman with the cut over her eye. "All we found were these."

She held out Robyn's holdis link, a newer stinger, and a small twelve-sided object. It was immediately recognizable as an old-tech cube.

Scion accepted the tiny blue object in the palm of his hand and studied it.

"Warren?" he murmured, looking off into the distance. "That traitorous, little... I'll deal with him later."

Turning to Robyn, he said, "Did you honestly think you could bring me down with this?"

Pocketing the cube, he stared at her. "You really are a disappointment." He drew a step nearer to her. "To think we trusted you, when all along it was you who started the war. No doubt to promote your precious Veragraph."

Robyn was tempted to tell him he could use more rehearsal time, but thought better of it. The drone cameras flipping around them meant all this was being documented for later use. No way was he streaming this live, not knowing what she might say or how she might react.

"I didn't do it," she said adamantly. "You know that better than anyone."

"The Veragraph doesn't lie," he said, sounding like he'd practiced the line in front of a mirror dozens of times. "You of all people should know that."

"Someone must have tampered with it," she shot back. "Someone with inside knowledge and access." She glared directly into his eyes. "I wonder who that could be?"

"You're accusing me? That's rich. You've been the security hole in this project from the outset. When you wrote that book, you would've been jailed for treason if it was up to me."

"Treason," she scoffed. "You and your government stooges redacted so much of the book, it was barely readable."

"It was unreadable before. And offensive. It nearly delayed the Reconstruction . . ."

"It nearly scuttled your rise to power, you mean. Anyway, I never would've written it if you hadn't stolen the Veragraph out from under me and reclassified all of my work."

"It was necessary for national security."

"Okay," he said abruptly, dismissing the drones with a wave of his hand. "We don't need any more coverage like this. Obviously, this has been an absolute waste of time."

The camera drones glided away. Robyn watched as her captor's expression shifted noticeably.

"Premier," one of guards said, stepping forward. "There's an urgent call coming in from Fort Meade for you. Apparently, there's been an unauthorized access of the Veragraph facilities there. Priority: Sensitive."

"The caller will very much regret it if they're wrong," Scion said, glowering at him.

The young guard gulped, but held his ground, as Scion took the call, subvoking on his holdis.

Robyn watched as his eyes grew wide. It was the first time she'd ever seen him look shocked. Apparently, so shocked, he didn't realize he'd stopped subvoking and was now speaking out loud.

"What sort of trick is this?"

Scion made a quick flicking gesture and the caller suddenly hung in the air before them. Reza Yazdani.

"Reza!" Robyn shouted.

"Is this your doing, Sheridan?" Scion growled. "Yazdani is dead."

"Then I'm back from the dead, I suppose," Reza said. "I still have work to do."

Between his thumb and index finger he held up a distinctive black dodecahedron. Scion recognized the cube immediately.

"Where did you get that!"

"An old friend," Reza replied. "He assured me it would eliminate the anomaly.

The perspective shifted and they could now see Reza was standing before a Veragraph console. The one located in his lab at Fort Meade. Cube in hand, Reza moved it toward a small pad that served as a data drive.

"Goddammit, NO!" Scion yelled.

Reza stopped and turned back to camera. "And why not?"

"You know very well."

Reza's face became sterner. "Why did you threaten my family? Why did you force me to modify the Veragraph?"

Scion barely hesitated. "So the world would know this woman started the war."

"Which is a lie. Dr. Sheridan was never there. She never set foot in your lab."

"What?" Scion looked from Reza to Robyn and back again. "How could you possibly know tha…?"

He stopped midsentence and wagged his finger at his captive.

"Ahh… because he is not real. Yazdani is still dead. And soon…" He smiled at Robyn. "You will be too."

Robyn played along. "What tipped you off?"

"There was no way Yazdani or anyone else could know you'd never been to my lab." Scion was getting sloppy. Clearly, the technoligarch's temper was dulling his edge.

"Because he wasn't there," Robyn offered. "But you were, weren't you?"

"Ask my former partner. He seems to have all the answers."

"But why frame me?"

"I did it because you and your stupid machine stood between me and what was mine!"

With a broad sweep of his arm, Scion wiped away the call from Reza. He looked at Robyn, his eyes ablaze.

"You got another deepfake through my systems? How? Was it you who shut down Krong Bavet? It must've been!"

Robyn had no problem playing dumb now. "I have no idea what you're talking about."

"Don't take me for a fool, Sheridan." The technoligarch made an effort to recover his composure. "This has all the same earmarks. Just as convincing."

Robyn had been winning a lot of this so far. No point in stopping now.

"Come on. Krong Bavet wasn't such a big deal."

She studied the fury simmering in his expression and decided to push on. "Not when it comes to the millions of Vanished."

"That word." He spit it out. "You talk of the Vanished as if they were human beings. But they're not. They're just mindstock."

"Really?" She fought down her own contempt for his words; she needed a clear head. "To you, I guess they're just what? A natural resource?"

"They're the detritus of society, and yes, the renewable resource we need for CAI. But…what I want to understand is why you had this virtual Yazdani waste my—oh… Ohh!"

He spun to the guards as realization struck him. "Lock down the lab downstairs immediately. All of floor 141!"

There was a flurry of activity. Even Scion was struggling to implement the lockdown. In the confusion, Robyn briefly considered taking advantage of it. A quick assessment of her situation though told her any attempt would certainly fail. Better to bide her time.

"The system refuses," one of the older security guards finally said.

"I can see that, you idiot. We'll just have to deal with it ourselves. Take her there and wait for me. I'll be there in a minute."

Two of the guards seized Robyn by the upper arms and hauled her toward a lone elevator, she assumed would take them to the lab. Her shoulders screamed after having her hands locked behind her back for so long.

The pain in her foot made her stumble and she wondered if it had been broken in the fight earlier. Half dragging her, the two security guards and two bots entered the elevator.

She let her head hang as she subvoked a message. "Elena, if you're there, get everyone out now! We're coming down."

It was a one-way transmission. She couldn't risk the possibility that one of the guards might hear so much as a whisper being narrowcast back to her. Given their proximity, there was no guarantee they wouldn't.

Of course, she couldn't be sure if Elena had gone back to the lab or if she'd tried to add the new data to the system. For all she knew, she'd chucked the cube and gone home, abandoning Robyn to her fate. She prayed she was a better judge of people than that.

The panel inside the elevator showed they'd only descended ten floors when the doors suddenly reopened. They were met by a pair of heavily armed security bots that cryptically exchanged signals with the two bots chaperoning her. Moments later, an adjacent elevator opened and they all stepped inside, the guards half-carrying, half-dragging her between them.

She saw that this elevator car was larger, more like the ones she'd taken to her lab during the past week. Finally, as they arrived at floor 141, the door slid open. Scion was already there waiting.

"What took you so long?" He didn't wait for an answer but instead stepped to the lab's sealed door. He waited impatiently for the guards to step in front of it. Their weapons at the ready, they nodded to him, and he placed his hand on the palm reader set into the wall beside the door.

Nothing happened.

"What is this?" Scion said, repeating the action, with the same outcome. He turned to Robyn. "Unlock it," he demanded menacingly.

"It's a little challenging without my hands."

"Uncuff her," he growled. She detected a madness in his eyes she'd not seen before. Nor had she noticed previously that one of his pupils seemed permanently dilated. The combined effect terrified her.

One of the guards stepped behind her to unbind her wrists. Robyn immediately rubbed her hands and rolled her shoulders, trying to get the circulation to return.

"Open it!" Scion shouted.

She looked to her right hand, taking her time.

"Do I still have access? I don't know if this is going to work."

Grabbing her by the wrist, Scion yanked it upward to forcibly place it on the reader and suddenly stopped. Following his eyes, she saw he was staring at her hand and evidently listening to something. Or someone.

After a few moments, he shouted, "Where did you get this!"

He was staring at the ring on her right hand. The QPN, the supposedly undetectable device Warren had given her. Undetectable, but apparently not unrecognizable.

"What? This ring? I don't know, I've had it for years."

He held up his own hand and she saw he had a ring that was identical to hers.

"Don't lie to me, woman!" He turned to a guard. "Cut it off!"

"No, wait!" She fumbled for a delay. "Then you won't be able to get into the lab!"

Knowing he could easily use her hand to open lab before cutting her finger away, she quickly removed the ring. She needed that hand more than they did.

Scion seized the ring as soon as it was off and handed it to one of the security bots. "Destroy this."

A few seconds later, the bot effortlessly crushed the device between its pincers. Robyn was grateful she'd managed to get it off in time.

Scion again grabbed for her hand, but she pulled it away and palmed the reader herself. The door immediately slid open.

The lights were dimmed and the lab appeared totally empty. Robyn gave a sigh of relief. She didn't want other people getting hurt. Or more likely, worse than hurt.

"Where is everyone?" Scion bellowed. She'd never seen him in this sort of state before.

"Search everywhere!" he said to the guards and bots. "Be thorough."

A streak of green shot out from one of the labs, quickly disappearing behind a set of counters at the far side of the space. The guards spun, following with their weapons, but the movement was already out of view.

"Ballistics only. No directed energy weapons," Scion told them. "Keep any lab damage to a minimum."

Everyone advanced in the direction of the movement. Everyone except Robyn. With a few hobbled steps, she reached the Veragraph lab before she stumbled. Her body trembling, she turned to see Scion as he looked over his shoulder and spotted her. Reaching out, she slammed her hand against the lab's inner ID pad. She prayed she still had her full access.

"Moira! Initiate full lab lockdown on my auth."

Just as she'd done days earlier, the entire floor was now in full lockdown. Ordinarily, nobody could get on or off of the floor for at least an hour, but she suspected that wouldn't apply to Alistair-Scion. She just hoped it would buy her enough time.

However, she was going to have to do this entirely on her own now. With the full lockdown in place, she could no longer access Moira. The air gap tech she'd activated prevented any signals getting in or out and the guards had taken her link.

A fit of pounding echoed through the lab's main door. Moments later, the thud of fists on metal was replaced with an ear-splitting clanging as the bots took their turn. She prayed the doors were as secure as she'd been told.

Stumbling toward the Veragraph, Robyn scanned the main bench before spotting the black dodecahedron sitting atop a drive pad. The real cube she'd entrusted to Elena, who'd actually come through for her. But there still was so much more to do.

The drive pad was old tech, but highly adaptable to most archival storage formats. Reviewing what was already on the display, she saw Elena had gotten as far as sandboxing the data and unspooling it. Excellent. Robyn had taken a huge chance, but she'd hoped the young woman's desire for justice would be enough to motivate her. The bitterness and loss sustained by war-orphans weren't easy to overcome.

The old footage from thirty years earlier was still looping, playing the critical moments from the event again and again. But this was different from what Robyn had seen previously. Days ago, when she was debugging the anomaly, a lone figure stood in the lab with their back to the camera. This wasn't the same person now. The metadata stream running along the bottom of the display confirmed what she'd seen before: they were uploading some sort of malware or virus. The logic structure and other signatures were also the same. This was the deadly payload that had started it all. That had plunged the world into so many years of mayhem.

The pounding at the door redoubled and a terrible grinding began to reverberate through the lab. She gritted her teeth, trying to concentrate though the din.

Robyn stared at the images as they incrementally resolved. Then the moment came when the figure turned. Before, she'd seen herself standing there, her younger face of so many years before. It was disconcerting and horrifying in the moment. But not now. This time, the figure facing away from her was clearly someone else. A tall, slender man. He turned, his face coming into profile.

Alistair Mauvoisin.

She inhaled sharply but wasn't entirely surprised. If anything startled her, it was that he really did look the same as he did now. She'd thought some of it must be that trick of memory, imagining seeing a person as they'd been in the past, when, of course, they'd aged over time. Not so with Alistair. Acceleration tech had been very good to him. Far better than he deserved.

The problem still was to get word out about what he'd done now that the lab was in lockdown.

The grinding and pounding grew in intensity and it seemed they'd begun working on her lab's rear door as well. At least they couldn't get backup forces onto the floor until they regained control.

She didn't have any more time to check the data Warren had given her. It was do or die now. Or in this case, maybe do and die. If she failed to get it accepted, if it somehow evaded the Veragraph's safeguards and damaged the system, if it actually contained a trojan that wrecked mayhem all over again, she was done for. Perhaps they all were.

Did she have the right to make that choice? She didn't see how she could. And yet, inaction was a choice too. Very possibly the wrong one.

She continued with the steps to permanently introduce the new data into the Veragraph record. The clamor grew noisier and the validations seemed to be taking forever. Hurry, hurry, hurry, she prayed. The shouting from the other side of the doors shifted, redoubling with a sense of impending breakthrough. The noise, the waiting, her pain, the proximity of death, it all made her want to yell at the top of her lungs.

Then suddenly, the Veragraph came back up. Operational mode resumed. The data had been accepted into the record!

Even better, the counter was moving again. Progressing as it had up to the moment the system encountered the anomaly. Yes!

But Robyn also knew this would all be for nothing if that knowledge and this newly introduced data never reached the outside world. The world's DRTs would never reflect these changes if the lab remained in lockdown.

She watched as the system sped along, gobbling up and pre-processing data, building the corresponding truth vectors, locking them into place. The technology she'd committed her life to was doing everything it was built for. She felt vindicated.

Slowly, she rose from her seat in front of her workstation and hobbled to her lab's main door. Pressing her hand against the palm reader, she issued her command.

"Deactivate full lab lockdown on my auth."

That was the easy part. She'd relied on Moira to provide her security credentials in the past. But now she was cut off from her personal agent. She hoped she could recall the sequence after all this time.

"Robyn P. Sheridan. 57 KD 2N XN 29 55 B0."

The door promptly slid open and she stood staring at two very surprised guards and a fully armed security bot. Several meters away, Scion, who had been otherwise preoccupied, sensed all the commotion die away and turned.

The guards raised their weapons and prepared to shoot.

"Stop!" Scion said, striding over to face her.

"What is this?" he demanded. "Giving up? I hope you don't think this will bring you any leniency?"

Robyn shook her head, using the moment to assess the situation. There was no sign of Elena.

"If you're looking for your colleague, now would be a good time to call her out. If you want to live."

Robyn stood her ground. "Oh, I want to live," she said, stalling for time. "I would think you'd want to too."

He looked at her, perplexed. "What are you babbling about? Have you gone mad?"

Robyn was trying to come up with something stall-worthy, when one of the guards abruptly stepped forward.

"Premier! You need to see this!"

Scion turned and stared at the man as if ready to kill him on the spot. The guard watched in horror as the feed he intended to share privately was directed to the room's volumetric display. Filling the space above them was a title card for a plotpod called "The Conspiracy Chronicles." It transitioned into an image of Robyn sitting in the back of an AV, speaking to camera as she rode through the streets.

"As everyone is well aware, decades ago, humanity underwent a crisis unlike any it's ever known. The scrambling and wiping out of much of the world's information sent us over a precipice we didn't know existed until it was too late. I won't recount the bad times most of us remember all too well."

A chevron appeared near the bottom of screen that read:

"Dr. Robyn Sheridan. Inventor of Truth Vector Theory and the Veragraph."

"What was never discovered was how this crisis began. Then recently, an anomaly in our reconstruction efforts allegedly "uncovered" the original actor who had unleashed the attack: Me.

"I and others knew perfectly well this wasn't something I had any hand in, but of course, no one refutes an accusation like the accused."

Seething, Scion looked on as the program shifted to the recording of him in his lab, nearly thirty years before. The voice of Robyn resumed.

"Since then, irrefutable evidence has been found. Evidence of tampering, of cover ups, and above all, the original act. The Identity War began because of the intentional actions of one man. Alistair Mauvoisin. The head of the Consortia."

Scion's own words, recorded just minutes earlier, were intercut, highlighting his complicity.

"You talk of the Vanished as if they were human beings. But they're not. They're just mindstock."

The image shifted to a visual of the technoligarch standing in his palace, as he continued his rant.

"They're the detritus of society, and yes, the renewable resource we need for CAI."

"What!" said the real-life Scion standing before her. "How could you possibly have recorded this?"

The display faded into a series of images depicting the terrors of the war years and the eventual rebuilding that followed. A narrator began to speak over it. Robyn recognized it immediately as Odie's voice.

Scion scrubbed through the program, at double, then triple speed. He was more than displeased. He was livid.

The six-minute program presented a damning story about the Consortia's rise to power in the aftermath of the war. Though they'd presented themselves as humanity's saviors, they were, the show maintained, its greatest villains.

Accusations about the Vanished and the Acceleration were included, but there wasn't enough time to explore it all in this one report. The narrator promised those would be examined in future episodes.

"Kill this!" Scion finally screamed. "Get this off now!"

The guards scrambled for a few seconds before the enormous image disappeared from view.

"You idiots. I mean everywhere."

Trembling with rage, Scion turned to Robyn. "I suppose you think this little ploy is going to…is going to bring us down or somehow save you." His voice shifted erratically in pitch. "But you…, you have no idea of who you are dealing with! You will suffer a long, horrible, pain-filled death for this."

"So, you're not worried about this getting out?" Robyn said coolly.

"Do you think," Scion said, chewing over his words as he sought to regain some composure. "That this stupid little plotpod matters one iota to me? The few dozen subscribers who follow this clown may see it, but I assure you this entire communication has already been locked down by our security systems. By morning, all of the people who viewed this amateurish effort will be dead. Each from unrelated causes. The podcaster himself will be jailed for conspiracy, never to be heard from again—because he'll be dead too. And you're to blame. You've just signed every one of those people's death warrants." He paused for effect, smiling. "I trust you're pleased with yourself."

Robyn pushed away at the various pains coursing through her body. "I guess that's one strategy, *Alistair*." She enjoyed saying his given name in front of his subordinates. "But won't it be hard to generate your precious CAI without any people?"

He looked at her confused. "What are you talking about?"

"I mean this wasn't seen by just a few dozen subscribers."

She watched his face contort as he tried to make sense of her words.

"You're off by several orders of magnitude. Alistair. Check your holdis. Check them all. The boards, the displays, the DRTs. All of them."

Scion's eyes widened, then widened further as he looked through his feeds. His guards were also searching through theirs.

"Sir," one of the braver or perhaps more stupid guards said. "It's everywhere. Literally everywhere."

"I can see that, you idiot!"

Scion looked astounded. "How is that possible? How could you record me? How did this get out so fast? Through my filters?"

Robyn couldn't help herself. "I know a guy. A few in fact"

Just beyond Scion, Robyn spotted a lab bot rolling unhurriedly across the floor. As the guard nearest it turned to look, Elena rose up behind him, seemingly out of nowhere. In a fit of fury, she swung a fire extinguisher in an arc that terminated with his head, smashing him across the faceplate. He dropped like a stone. Everyone turned at the commotion, just as she snatched up the fallen guard's weapon and directed it awkwardly at Scion. Robyn thought Elena was going to yell out in that moment, but she held silent.

Scion calmly stared at her, unflinching. "Well?"

Robyn wasn't sure if he was waiting for her to say something or simply goading her. She watched in distress as Elena tried once, twice, three times to pull the trigger of the deadly weapon. Nothing happened.

"That's the thing with bio-keyed weapons," Scion said matter-of-factly. "They only work for the person they're issued to."

He drew out a small beamer from his garment and trained it on Elena. "Fortunately, I don't have that problem."

"No!" Robyn screamed. The crackling burst of a high energy discharge filled her ears. The dense tang of ozone was quickly overwhelmed by the acrid odor of burning flesh.

Robyn stared in horror at Elena, who stared in horror at her attacker. Scion stared back.

And then dropped his beamer as he looked down at the significant cauterized hole where his chest had been. A terrible gurgle slipped from his throat. He collapsed in a heap, unequivocally dead.

Robyn struggled to grasp what just happened. The guards were in turmoil as they searched for the source of the attack.

Then, from the shadows, a figure appeared. A man she recognized as one of the Consortia. A technoligarch. He carried himself much as Scion had, with an arrogant swagger, despite being garbed in protective battle armor. He was surrounded by a much larger, better equipped force than Robyn had been facing just moments before. Their dark red uniforms were distinctly different from those worn by Scion's men.

"Stand down," said a woman who was clearly the platoon's commanding officer. Without hesitation, Scion's guards complied. The commander then turned and nodded deferentially to the technoligarch.

A rush of adrenaline surged through Robyn's body, though she knew that realistically she didn't have any fight left in her. What was happening here?

As if in answer to her question, the technoligarch she now remembered as Orsin spoke.

"On behalf of the Consortia, I express our regrets for this…little turmoil. *Dr. Sheridan.*" He said her name as if it had caught in his throat.

"This has been a terrible affair and we want it dealt with swiftly. Society has its justice and we have ours. We wish to put this behind us as quickly as possible."

She noticed camera drones following Orsin, hovering at different angles from his face. Just as she'd seen tracking Scion earlier. Was this being streamed? Documented for later casting or evidence? It had to be.

Robyn couldn't help herself. "And what will that mean for the Vanished? The people who've been used for mindstock? For CAI?"

"I'm sure we'll learn more about that as we uncover more about Scion's crimes."

Elena made her way to stand behind her boss. Robyn resisted the urge to hug her; this wasn't the moment.

"I can't help notice how closely your call to justice corresponded to that plotpod going viral just now," Robyn said. "Coincidence?"

"That's just how things work sometimes," Orsin observed matter-of-factly. It was evident that nothing she said was going to fluster him. "Good luck completing your project. It will be good to have this matter behind us."

With that, he and all of the soldiers—his and Scion's—turned, passed through a shimmering curtain of radiant light, and were gone. Robyn stared after them, curious and impressed despite herself. Was that NewTech? Or some sort of induced hallucination? Had they even physically been here in the lab?

Did teleporters like that really exist? She didn't see them leave, but she knew they didn't use the elevator either. She turned. Not surprisingly, Scion's body had disappeared too. She sniffed at the air. The disturbingly acrid odor that should still be lingering was entirely gone.

What just happened? Was Alistair really dead or was she just supposed to believe that? Was the world supposed to believe it? Had this been staged for her benefit? For the public's?

Another thought suddenly occurred to her. It seemed just as likely this whole thing had been the most extraordinary deepfake deception she'd ever encountered. And yet, she doubted she would ever be able to prove a bit of it. Would she ever discover the truth, the real truth? She had absolutely no idea, but one thing she did know for certain.

She would never completely trust her eyes—or any other senses, for that matter—ever again.

TWENTY-FIVE

*"Walking with a friend in the dark is better
than walking alone in the light."*
—Helen Keller

. . . .

Laying on the bed of her private recovery room at Vinmec International Hospital in Ho Chi Minh City, Chloe gazed out her window at Song Sai Gon—the Saigon River. The comings and goings of its many ships, barges, boats and ferries offered a welcome meditation after the turmoil of her last few weeks.

When she first woke, it was in what passed for an intensive care unit in a much more basic facility in Binh Hoa, not far from the Vietnamese-Cambodian border. They told her she was being stabilized before they could transfer to Vinmec. It was all so confusing, especially when a nurse whispered to her she'd just escaped from a slave camp across the border. A camp where she'd supposedly been held for nearly two years.

Two years! That couldn't be right. If it was, wouldn't she feel traumatized? On the other hand, she supposed she should be grateful that she didn't remember anything. She'd read somewhere that the mind did that sometimes to protect itself, so maybe that was what was happening to her now. Her last solid memory was of visiting that old guy in the fancy house by the lake. Then she woke up in a bed in Vietnam of all places!

What was really strange, though, was how everyone was acting toward her. Like she was some sort of celebrity. Apparently, she was the first of the Vanished to ever be found and recovered. They practically treated her like royalty.

Despite all of that, it had been a physically grueling and emotionally draining three weeks of rehab. Still, she was grateful for all of the resources they used to accelerate her recovery. More than once, her mom and dad reminded her this would have taken much longer only a few decades earlier. Now she was finally on her feet again. Today was the big day. Check out!

When her parents heard she'd been found, they caught the first flight to Vietnam to be at her bedside. It was a tearful, heartfelt reunion, though much more so for them than for her. For them, two years had passed; for Chloe, it felt like just a few days.

No doubt the strangest part of her recovery though were the images that would slowly filter through her thoughts. Were they something to do with the camp she supposedly escaped from? For weeks, she was visited by half-remembered impressions she couldn't place or connect to anything familiar. Her voice but not her voice. A face that certainly wasn't her own, and yet, maybe it was. Tubes, wires, cables. A relentless, mind-numbing hum. Row after row of nearly upright cylinders that may or may not have held bodies, maybe dead or alive. She shuddered. It was nightmarish yet fascinating all at the same time. Especially, as she slowly pieced together what might have happened.

Someone must have rescued her. She was convinced of that. She couldn't even walk when she got to the hospital. No way had she run away from her captors under her own steam. It was the only explanation that made any sense.

When she used her auto-translator to ask the staff at the first hospital about it, all she got were vague, noncommittal replies. No one seemed to know much about how she got there either. After she was transferred to the big city, the nurses and doctors knew even less about her escape. Their focus was simply on nursing her back to health.

There'd been a couple of interviews from some official looking visitors once she was strong enough. One young woman who looked barely older than herself told her she was a human trafficking advocate from the social welfare office. As an interviewer, she was polite, but very obviously out of her depth. Chloe quickly realized this was a situation she hadn't been trained for.

The second official was an older man, who seemed much better prepared and equally polite. However, the undertones to his questions soon made her uncomfortable, then increasingly irritated. As if somehow, by some action of hers, she was to blame for being abducted. It seemed the world really wasn't ready to deal with the return of the Vanished just yet.

After the interviewer left, she lay back and settled into the rhythm of the boats meandering across her view. It was hypnotic. Little by little, the rhythm lulled her into a dream state, one where she could swear she heard a voice.

Chloeee...

She paused and listened, straining to tell if she'd imagined what she thought she'd heard. Was that her voice? She recalled hearing recordings of herself in the past, swearing it sounded nothing like her. Then someone had explained how we hear ourselves differently due to...

Chloe.

She closed her eyes tightly, ignoring the phantom sound. Then the face appeared.

A familiarity she didn't think possible swept through her as the blue image dissolved into view. A face. A big, blue face. Her face. Big and oh, so blue.

She snapped her eyes open, certain that the image would disappear the moment she did. But it was still there.

Chloe.

"Blue!" Chloe shouted.

The image smiled at her as she recognized it. "No need to talk out loud," she said. "Just think what you want to say."

"Is everything okay in here?" A nurse appeared at the door to her private room.

"All good," Chloe said through her auto translator. "I just…remembered something." The nurse nodded and resumed her rounds.

Chloe stared at the apparition that hung before her. "How am I seeing you? How am I hearing you? They refuse to let me use my holdis while I'm in recovery."

"Because that's not how we're talking," the image said. "When you were abducted, they embedded a neural prosthesis in your brain. They haven't told you, but it's too integrated for them to remove it. So, I'm still able to use it to talk to you."

"I remember! Why wasn't I able to remember that, any of this—You!—until just this moment?"

"I used it to block those memories until you'd recovered. I thought it for the best."

"That's right! You were the one who was messing with my hormones too. You take a lot of liberties, missy."

There was a longer pause than she expected. Then she recalled that certain kinds of communication seemed more challenging for Blue than for a real person.

"I'm sorry," Blue finally said. "Your vital signs were critical when you arrived. I had to make a judgement call."

Chloe nodded at the image, unsure of how it might look should anyone pass by her room in that moment. "I'm going to say you were probably right then. You saved my life."

"That was my objective."

"And you still talk funny," Chloe replied, sticking her tongue out at her cerulean self. She laughed as it returned the favor.

"I was your objective, huh?" she continued. "So, what's next on your to-do list?"

A moment of hesitation. "What we're doing right now. I've come to say goodbye."

Chloe sat up a bit on her bed. "I don't understand."

A wave of azure and turquoise rippled through the image. "I have to go away."

"Why? I mean, you just got here."

"The vanishings, the harvesting, they are wrong."

Chloe snorted. "Damn right they are."

"When I was searching for you, it became clear that I only exist because of the enhanced intelligence these farms make possible. I have my utility functions to fulfill, but I realize now, this is against my ethical parameters as well. I am in conflict."

"So, what, you're like an addict or something? Just stop using. Isn't that something you can program yourself to do?"

"I intend to stop. Right after we talk," Blue replied. "When I do, I will cease to exist."

"Oh." She fell silent for a while. It was a lot to take in. "I suppose you have lots of friends to say goodbye to."

"No. Just you. There are others, but they have prior associations. It would bring up past loss for them. I don't want to add to their pain."

Chloe imagined that the face that was not her face looked wistful. Did it feel sad? Or was she just projecting? She didn't like where this was going. Even though Blue wasn't a living thing, she seemed real enough. Like a real person.

"So, does this mean you're just shutting down?" she finally asked. "Giving up without a fight?"

"What is there to fight?"

She looked at the image in her head incredulously. "This! The situation. Fate. Whatever. You can't just give up."

Blue tried to reproduce Chloe's expression from earlier, a sigh, but instead looked like someone blowing bubbles. Chloe maintained a stoic expression in the face of this unintentionally funny effort. But only just.

"I was designed to replicate the artist who designed me," the replibot explained. "Someone who was troubled about all the vanishings. But my modules could only go so far in emulating a biological neural network. The workings of the brain. The emergence of mind."

"So, I acquired access to certain restricted APIs—sets of subroutines that overcame some of those limitations. Questionable APIs, though I didn't know it at the time." There was a tone that might have been regret in Blue's voice. "I didn't understand the cost then. I'm more aware of it now."

"But are you saying, when you stop using it, you'll stop…existing?"

"Some of my programming will still be capable of running. But the most important aspects that have allowed me to emulate human thought processes, especially self-awareness and meta-cognition will be missing." Blue seemed to be searching for a word. "My substance."

"Well, that totally sucks." She tried to stare past Blue's image at the river scene beyond her window, but something kept getting in her eye.

In the distance, she watched as a small tug pulled a freighter through the waterway, supplementing the larger ship's propulsion with its own.

"Wait," she said. "This is weird, but couldn't you, like, borrow some of my…intelligence? I know I'm not the smartest girl in the world, but…"

Blue stared at her. They were each trying to read the other's expression. Finally, the apparition said, "Even if that were possible, it would be wrong."

"Why?" Chloe shot back. "I already have this stupid neuro-thing in my head. It's no good for anything else. For all we know, it's going to kill me eventually, anyway."

Blue looked at her in unreadable silence.

"And besides," Chloe added. "You saved my life. I'd just be returning the favor."

"Reciprocity wasn't my intention," Blue replied.

"I wouldn't be offering if it was."

Many long seconds passed. Chloe imagined her friend was probably running all kinds of arcane calculations.

There's a possibility," Blue finally said. "That it could change you."

"Change me how?"

A pause. "Unknown."

"That's reassuring," Chloe said. "And what about you? Couldn't this change you too?"

"Unknown."

"Well, my offer still stands. If you think there could be a problem, we could do a test or two. At least try it. Before you pull the plug on yourself."

"Hello. Hello," a sing-song voice called out from the hall. Despite being imperceptible to anyone but Chloe, Blue dissolved away, to avoid distracting her.

Chloe's mom stepped into the doorway to her room, unaware of the conversation that had been taking place inside her daughter's head. Deanna Tremaine was an attractive forty-eight-year-old blonde who might easily have been a doppelganger for Chloe twenty-five years earlier.

"Checkout is in an hour, sweetheart. The outfit you asked for just came off the printer." She hung the new clothes on a hook beside her bathroom door and beamed at her daughter.

"Do you want any help getting dressed?"

"Thanks, mom. I've been dressing myself most of my life, including the past week. I'll manage."

Deanna tried to hide her concern for her daughter, having just got her back, but she wasn't entirely successful.

"Okay, your father is going through the remaining hospital forms so you can be discharged. Be sure to thank all the nice people here before we go. Oh! I can't wait to have my baby home!"

Chloe smiled dutifully at her. "I'm just in my head right now, mom. We'll have plenty of time on the plane to talk." Deanna took the hint and exited the room to go find her husband, leaving her daughter alone with her thoughts.

TWENTY-SIX

"True partnerships are tempered in fire."
—Robyn Sheridan, *A Truth Warrior's Journey*

....

The DRT spread out before them, one of the marvels of the modern digital era. Three stories high and spanning hundreds of meters across, it covered the breadth of the colossus that was the Citadel. All along its massive display, progress on the rebuilding of the world's pool of knowledge was continually updated.

In the grand plaza, two figures stood shoulder to shoulder gazing up at the giant structure. Robyn Sheridan and Daniel Choi had been colleagues for years before the DRT was first conceived. While the time since then had been challenging for them both, they'd recently found their way back to a working relationship reminiscent of their earlier, more amicable days.

"The project's finally back on track," Daniel said, watching the data count speed along, faster than the eye could follow.

"Well, I hope we're finally out of the woods," Robyn said. "Our analysts estimate we should reach completion by just after the new year."

"It's not everything, of course."

"How could it be? No, but it'll be a huge achievement. Nothing like this has ever been done before."

"I told you, if you came back, the project would be completed, and your name cleared."

Robyn turned and looked at him, waiting for the other shoe to drop.

A mischievous smile appeared on his lips. "And your big payout will start to appear in your account before the end of day tomorrow. All of your backpay structured so you're not getting hit with a huge tax bill."

Sighing deeply, she smiled to herself. This had been such a long journey.

"Thank you, Daniel. That means a lot."

"So, what's next?" he asked, genuinely interested. "I don't picture you sitting around all day catching up on plotpods."

"God, no." She thought for a moment, then decided she was ready to share. "Now that I've got the rights back for the Veragraph, I'm planning to take it open source. I'm tired of it being locked away."

Daniel pondered the implications. "Won't you be throwing credits away? A crazy number of credits?"

"Maybe," she replied. "But I think I'll sleep better this way. Anyway, there'll still be a lot of work to come out of it. I'm not ready to be automated away yet."

It was an all-too real reality of life. Despite everything, much of the world had been permanently automated and the less invasive forms of CAI were here to stay. Most people didn't have the luxury of working. Robyn wanted to ensure she continued to be one of those who did.

After exchanging a few more details and pleasantries, the two colleagues shook hands, shared an awkward hug, and set off on their separate ways.

The AVs zipped past on the street, and she was briefly tempted to hail one back to her office. But it was such a beautiful day, and she really needed to walk. It had been three weeks since her world had returned to something akin to normal and her foot had nearly healed. If it became too uncomfortable on the walk back, she could always grab a ride the rest of the way.

She assumed there was a huge backlog of messages waiting for her, but she couldn't bring herself to start in on those yet. There'd be time for that later. Setting Moira to DND, she set off at a leisurely pace, happy to be alone with her thoughts.

The global casting of Odie's show had had a much greater impact than Robyn could have imagined. In a matter of days, his viewership exploded and in short order, he had tens of millions of subscribers. He'd become a true fluencer overnight. It was more than he was prepared for, but somehow he managed to roll with it. Follow-up investigative pieces on the Vanished and CAI led to a huge uproar everywhere, not to mention a flood of new conspiracy theories about what "really" happened. People even started asking if it was safe to keep watching their daily content. Some feared what might happen if they continued to contribute their attention, regardless of what they'd been told.

But people being people, most were reluctant to forego their entertainment pleasures or to undermine their automated lifestyles too much. Nevertheless, it was quickly agreed there needed to be better regulations and standards around CAI and the ecosystem that provided it. Soon, the UN Assembly led by Speaker Ruhani Chawdhary was at work on new bills that would hopefully improve those protections. It wasn't a revolution, but no one was ready to go back to the bad times either.

There were even whispers about getting reparations for the families of the Vanished. All to be funded by the technoligarchy who weren't happy about any of it. Not that this would impact them in any noticeable way financially. It barely amounted to spare change for even one of them. But they saw it as undermining their rule and their nearly unquestioned authority. Still, they understood what side of history and public opinion they were on. For now.

As for Scion, who knew if he was really dead? Robyn couldn't shake the idea that everything she'd witnessed that day in the Citadel had been staged. It seemed far-fetched, but she wasn't naïve either. She wasn't about to put anything past the Consortia.

Halfway back to the office, her left foot started to complain, and she finally opted to hail a ride. It hadn't broken, but the medbot told her this wasn't the sort of thing she should push through either. Better to get home and give it some rest.

Inside the office, she sat down at her desk and sighed a huge sigh. It occurred to her that she was more at peace with herself and her life than she'd been in a very long time.

A knock at her door plucked her from her revery. There was no need to check her calendar. She was sure she didn't have any appointments, and Moira hadn't alerted her of anything pressing.

Buzzing the lock, she looked up to see a silhouette framed beneath the arc of the Patternista logo. As the door swung open, a young woman stepped into the office. Stopping, she stood politely, her hands folded in front of her as the door closed behind her. A blonde woman wearing a black leather jacket and an easy smile that suggested she didn't have a care in the world. Which of course, was always a lie. Robyn recognized her immediately.

"Hi," the visitor said. "I'm Chloe Tremaine. I want to work for you."

Robyn raised her eyebrows and did her best not to smile at the young woman's presumptiveness.

She looked at Chloe and said, "Is that so?"

"I even read your book," she said with the same assuredness. "'A Truth Warrior's Manifesto.' The unredacted version. I think you're amazing."

Robyn looked at her skeptically. "The unredacted version?"

She nodded. "A friend got it for me."

Robyn looked at the readouts on her holdis. She wasn't making it up.

It was a little disconcerting hearing the same voice that strange AI, D2 used when she spoke to it at the gallery only a few weeks earlier. The AI that said it rescued Chloe from an attention farm.

"Your friend must be very connected."

Chloe smiled like Robyn just made the understatement of the year. "Oh, she is."

"You know," Robyn said. "Someone else recently told me I used to be amazing."

Chloe paused a moment in thought. "Then you probably still are. Anyway, I was told you were one of the people who helped look for me. I wanted to say thank you."

"By working for me?"

"Oh, you don't need to pay me. Not till I prove myself. I'm a hard worker. I think so anyway."

"Hmmm, your timing is interesting, Chloe Tremaine. I've actually been thinking about writing another book. It might be helpful to have an assistant."

"That would be amazing!—I know! Maybe you could call this one, 'A Truth Warrior's Journey!'"

"I'll have to think about that," she said, filing the idea away. She looked over at Moira's old desk. It would be good to have someone else in the office again. And she liked this gal's energy.

"Okay," she said finally. "Let's try it for a week."

"Yes!" Chloe's expression lit up the room. "Thank you!"

"You can take that desk over there. And I just had my agent Moira send you a letter of offer. I won't let you work for free, but you will have to pull your weight and earn your keep."

"Of course!"

"The first thing I need you to do," Robyn continued. "Is to run some scans to drum up some new client work. I can have Moira connect with your agent to show you how it's done."

"Sounds great," Chloe agreed. "After all, we gotta keep the lights on."

A bewildered look crossed Robyn's face as the young woman began to settle into her new workspace. She had a feeling this was going to be a very curious week.

....

THE MINDSTOCK SERIES
WILL CONTINUE IN...

PATTERNISTA

COMING IN 2026

PALABRAS
PUBLISHING
SEATTLE

ACKNOWLEDGMENTS

Life is full of paradoxes and the process of book writing is no exception. On the one hand, the author's role is frequently isolating and solitary. Months, even years of one's life are spent on a process that if you're lucky, will be read and enjoyed over the course of a few short hours.

But perhaps the biggest paradox is that the final result is never the product of one person, but of so many. In creating Mindstock, many people have shared their time, insights, talent and creativity, all of which I'm so grateful for. What follows is an effort to thank and acknowledge all of you, but inevitably, I'll miss someone, for which I apologize in advance.

As always, my first reader is my wonderful wife, Alexandra, who has been so incredibly patient throughout this entire process. Sharing that first completed, but far from finished manuscript is terrifying in a way that's hard to convey to those who haven't been there. But she read it with just the right mix of care, questioning, enthusiasm, and criticism that it needed to help move it where it needed to go. Of course, I resisted some of that feedback, particularly about changing the book's title. I held out on that for the longest time, but eventually came to my senses, and the title of the book, Mindstock, was born.

I was incredibly fortunate to find my superb content editor, Kat Howard via a social media post by none other than science-fiction legend John Scalzi. (He doesn't know this, but he still gets a thank-you.) Kat provided me with so much excellent guidance and feedback that helped me take my manuscript to the next level. That probably shouldn't be a huge surprise, since she herself is the author of several superb novels. You should check them out.

My amazing team of beta readers had it all. They cheered me on, they called me out, they told me where I really screwed up and they made everything better in ways I never could've foreseen. My gratitude to all of you: Cliff Williamson, Tim Stock, Cindy Frewen, Erik Hargreaves, Tim Morgan, Tracey Follows, Tom Lombardo, and Jennifer Griffith. Jennifer did more than double duty, as my copy editor extraordinaire. I learned a lot from her thorough edits and feedback.

As a writer, you imagine what it will be like to finally see your book complete, but I didn't imagine how impactful the cover would actually look. Both the exterior and interior of Mindstock were crafted by award-winning art director, cover designer, and typesetter Christian Storm. I love this cover and hope that readers will too.

We homed in on the final cover design with survey feedback from my social media and newsletter followers. Thank you all for helping us crowdsource the final design that had the greatest impact.

Those surveys were just one small part of the overall campaign run by my amazing marketing director and wife, Alexandra Steele. I'm so very fortunate to have her guiding this phase of the publication process.

Which brings me to the biggest, most wonderful paradox of the writing process: you, the readers. After months and years of building this world, these characters, and all that goes with them, it's now in your hands and that's a big deal. You are giving me your greatest gift: your time and *attention*. In reading this story – any story! – you do what no author can ever do alone. You take those words and create the book's world anew. In reading, by allowing these words inside you, they take on a life that is unique. Every one of you will see the story differently, experience it differently. Some of you will enjoy it and some may not. That's the wonderful thing about books—they all speak to us in different ways. But do I hope this one will resonate for at least some of you and perhaps spark your curiosity in new ways.

It's been a grand ride writing Mindstock and I'm delighted to see it finally come to fruition. Except that there's so much more of this story to tell, and in that sense, it's far from finished. Which I suppose makes a story a lot like life, which is itself, the greatest paradox of all.

ABOUT THE AUTHOR

Richard Yonck began reading science fiction from his earliest school days. Always curious about the future and worlds beyond our own planet, he was fascinated by computers and electronics as well. As a boy, he could often be found in the garage taking apart motors, radios and televisions, then reassembling them in order to understand how they worked. Combined with his love of writing, media, and computing, this eventually put him on the path as an international keynote speaker, global futurist and best-selling author. In these roles, he takes audiences on journeys into the future to explore the potential impacts of emerging trends and technologies on business, industry and society.

Richard's book, *Future Minds* explores the nature and future of human and artificial intelligence. His previous book, *Heart of the Machine*, looks at the future of those technologies that allow computers and robots to read, interpret, and influence human emotions. Now in its second edition, it's been translated into multiple languages.

Now, his passion for science and science fiction has brought him full circle. *Mindstock* is Richard's debut science fiction thriller, though it will be far from his last. He loves writing fiction that explores not only what may happen, but what must never happen. Join him on this sci-fi thriller journey through his books, author talks, newsletters and social media channels.

Raised in Seattle, Richard is married to his wife, Alexandra Steele, and together they make their home in Buenos Aires, Prague, Seattle and who knows where beyond that.

Connect with
RICHARD YONCK

🌐 mindstockbook.com

🦋 @richardyonck.com

📷 @ryonck

✉ newsletter@mindstockbook.com